BLUE FIRE

An Alex Graham Novel

Katherine Prairie

Stonedrift Press Ltd
Kingston, Canada

Published by Stonedrift Press Ltd.

First Canadian edition 2018

Front cover image: Bespoke covers
Illustrated maps: Margaret Kernaghan

Stonedrift Press Ltd.
Box 22031, RPO Cataraqui
Kingston, ON K7M 8S5

www.stonedriftpress.com

ISBN 978-0-9949377-5-9 (paperback)
ISBN 978-0-9949377-7-3 (epub)

Printed and bound in Canada

10   9   8   7   6   5   4   3   2

For Bill

*Discovery consists of seeing what everybody has seen,
and thinking what nobody has thought.*

— ALBERT SZENT-GYORGYI

Brazilian State of
Minas Gerais

N

Brazil

Brasília

Salinas

Coronel Murta

Rio Jequitinhonha

Araçuaí

Diamantina

Teófilo
Otonio

Belo
Horizonte

Atlantic
Ocean

São
Paulo

Rio de
Janerio

1

Teófilo Otoni, Brazil

ALEX GRAHAM HURRIED across the cobblestone to meet a man from her past, the one person who might help her.

She skirted a throng of men who thrust folded white packets toward a middle-aged couple in their midst. Their excited voices spurred others to leave their shaded spots and scurry across Teófilo Otoni's centre square. Elbow to elbow, they pushed for a spot closest to the woman, vying for her attention. Soon other visitors would arrive in this Minas Gerais town, the Brazilian hub of the coloured gem trade, but for now this couple, European from the chic look of their clothing, was the prize attraction.

Alex brushed close enough to a balding man shouting to be heard to catch a glimpse of polished green gemstones nestled in the folds of white paper held open in his palm. Emeralds. Or perhaps less-valuable tourmalines, those chameleons of the gem trade that could pass for the rubies and emeralds these men purported to sell. Even if these were real emeralds, this couple would be no match for the dealers here. These Brazilians knew the precise carat value of each gemstone in their carefully folded paper packet, and they had already decided what the black-haired woman and her attentive husband might pay.

There were no deals to be had here in the square. It was more likely that this woman in her crisp linen tunic would pay hundreds of dollars over the true value of a stone — worse, she might take home a fake or flawed stone. A single chip or the slip of the cutting blade would drop the value of an emerald dramatically, but neither could be seen with the naked eye. The woman would learn the truth only later when she took her emeralds to a jeweller to be made into a necklace or earrings.

The voices faded when Alex turned the corner to a leafy street that was barely awake. Steel doors rolled open on cement-floored spaces that looked more like garages than the shops they were. She smiled at a woman straddling baskets of glassware using a tall pole to hook a T-shirt hanger on wire hung across the doorway. On another day, Alex might have stopped to browse, but not today. Instead, she hurried down the sidewalk toward an open-air cafe, its half-empty chairs mercifully shaded from the scorching heat.

Scott Miller stood as she drew near, and as always, her heart fluttered at his smile. Each time they met, she felt as though they might pick up where they'd left off five years ago, when they'd bonded over their shared obsession with precious metals and gemstones at a Houston mining conference. They'd managed to meet a few times since that conference, but the timing never seemed right for her and the Denver-born geologist. It was no different this time, not with Eric Keenan in her life.

"Always a pleasure Alex," he said as he folded her hands into his.

"How long has it been? A year?" He slipped into his chair, watching her do the same. "Maybe that restaurant in Rio last fall?"

She remembered that evening in Rio de Janeiro well — too well — and quickly changed the subject. "Have you been home since then, Scott?"

"Not often. These days Brazil feels more like home than Denver. I'm working almost exclusively down here now ... enough that it made sense to buy an apartment in Buenos Aires."

"Really?"

For him to settle in one place surprised her. Mining geologists like them went where the mineral trail led, and that was often a lonely valley far from civilization. If they were lucky, they'd find a bad motel along the highway with a shower that worked. Usually a nylon tent served as home, slim protection from the heat of the Amazon jungle and African grasslands or the frigid cold of the Canadian north and Siberia. Only their discoveries — gold, silver, diamonds, and more — made it all worthwhile.

"Loft with a great kitchen, terrace … the works." Scott's wistful smile said almost as much as his next words. "Not that I spend much time there. You know how it is."

"No kidding. Hell, sometimes I wonder why I even bother to unpack." It had been five weeks since she'd set foot in her Vancouver condo, but she wasn't about to tell Scott that she'd been working here in Brazil.

"So—"

The arrival of coffee, dark and fragrant, and icy glasses of water broke their conversation. Alex reached for her wallet, but Scott had already handed rainbow-coloured Brazilian reals to their server, a young woman dressed in a skimpy tank top and body-hugging shorts.

"I took the liberty … double-shot espresso, if I remember correctly," Scott said. "But I thought in this heat you might want something cold too."

An intimate gesture, one that brought a smile to her lips.

Alex wrapped her hand around the ice-cold glass, resisting the urge to press its coolness to her chest. "I don't ever get used to the heat when I'm in South America."

"You just have to spend more time here." Scott smiled. "Or better yet, in Buenos Aires."

With me. She finished his thought, one made clear by the way he looked at her. She shifted in her chair, unsure of how to respond, grateful when he jumped in as though realizing his mistake.

"Although I'm sure you've been spending all your time up near Nelson working the Donnovan claims … or should I say *your* claims? Quite the coup you pulled off."

"I'm still a little in shock over it myself." She cocked her head. "And a little surprised that you know about it."

He spread his hands wide. "What can I say? Baxter Donnovan's collection of silver claims in the Slocan Valley is legendary. Lots of people were keeping an eye on them, waiting for his widow to put them on the market."

Her finger traced the rim of her water glass. She wasn't about to elaborate and fill in the gaps about how Sylvia Donnovan had quietly come to her seven months ago to offer the claims to Alex first. That small act to honour Baxter's wish that Alex be the one to take over the claims had nearly cost Alex her life. But it also led her to Eric, a gift she still didn't quite believe.

Realizing that she wasn't about to say anything more, Scott changed the subject. "Your message said you were looking for tourmalines. Anything in particular?"

She sipped at her drink, trying to shut out her dad's warning, his insistence she not share a single detail about this project.

Drop everything. Mosi will meet you in São Paulo day after tomorrow with details. Critical that you keep this to yourself.

From that cryptic message alone, she suspected her dad had made a new discovery, and for him to dispatch Mosi Ongeti from Tanzania meant it was something big. Alex had booked the first flight out of Vancouver and quickly handed off her projects to another of the geologists at Graham and Company without explanation, not that they needed one.

Every one of the men had worked alongside her dad long enough to expect almost anything. From maps scribbled on the back of paper napkins to intricate computer-generated models, last-minute business class flights to Moscow to harrowing prop-jet journeys to obscure landing strips in the Gobi Desert — they'd experienced it all. Brian Graham was a crackerjack mining geologist with a talent for finding what others missed, so they embraced his unorthodox style and forgave his idiosyncrasies. As did she.

But the news Mosi delivered put her in a tailspin and sent them chasing down one dead-end path to another. She'd known Scott was in Brazil and that this gem hunter might help, but she'd fought the urge to involve him, afraid of the trouble it might bring his way. Until he was their only option.

"Pinks."

"Specimen or facet grade?"

"Specimen," she said, referring to the gemstones displayed on countless museum and collectors' shelves rather than a jewellery-quality stone. "My client is looking for a piece for his new office reception area … you know the sort of thing."

"Eye-stopping…" Scott stretched a hand above his head. "And as big as possible."

"You got it." She tried to laugh, but it came out forced, like a cough on a dusty road.

Breathe, Alex. You're halfway there.

She dropped her gaze to the table and watched the trail left by her finger in the sheen of water that coated her glass. Last night, she and Mosi had spent hours working out an angle, a way of getting the information they needed without revealing too much to Scott. Now her story sounded flimsy, too rehearsed, but it was all she had.

"Anyway, he wants something deep pink," she continued. "He likes the look of tourmaline, especially the raspberry rubellite variety, which as you know isn't that easy to find. My dad found a few pieces in Tanzania, but they weren't quite what my client is looking for. I'm hoping for better luck here."

Her words tumbled out, but if Scott thought her behaviour strange, he gave no indication. Instead he leaned forward, his eyes bright with excitement.

"The dealers here have a few nice pieces, but I have to take you to the Cruzerio mine. I can get us in there this afternoon." He was already pulling out his phone. "Alex, you're not going to want to leave once you've seen their super pockets of tourmaline crystals. It's a little like they're digging into a room full of glistening rainbow-coloured rock." He grinned like a child who first realizes the vastness of starry sky and dreams of adventure. "You're not going to leave without buying one — although you're more likely to fill your suitcase with these babies."

She had to smile. She'd dangled an irresistible temptation in front of a man obsessed with gems, and he could focus on nothing else.

Now or never.

"What about the mines up near Coronel Murta?" Her hand tightened around her glass. "I heard that the Novoteras mine might be worth a visit."

Scott shook his head. "Off-limits to visitors."

"But surely you've been in the mine?"

"No, and I don't know anyone who has, not even the GIA."

Every company knew the benefit of opening their mine to organizations like the Gemology Institute of America. With so much interest in ethically sourced gemstones, the stamp of approval from the GIA was only good business. But a privately held mine didn't have to open its door to anyone except regulators.

"I can get you into a Paraíba tourmaline mine, and that's definitely worth a visit. Have you seen the stone?"

"Paraíba?" She pictured the tourmaline gemstones she'd seen, trying to place this particular variation in the colour spectrum. Scott saved her the trouble.

"Blue tourmaline. Brilliant blue, almost neon. Spectacular. Just spectacular." Coffee cup raised, he gave her a sly smile. "Anywhere from sixteen thousand to one hundred thousand dollars per carat."

Her jaw dropped. "Are you kidding? What's the price of a quality diamond right now ... five or six thousand a carat?"

"A bargain, right?"

"No kidding." Safely tucked inside a rosewood box in her Vancouver condo were a pair of diamond earrings and some pearls that had become hers when her mom died. Otherwise, Alex owned little valuable jewellery and nothing nearly as expensive as the Paraíba tourmaline Scott described.

"We can stop by the Cruzerio mine this afternoon, and then pick up a flight north ... we enjoy a nice dinner and visit a Paraíba tourmaline mine tomorrow morning." He picked up his phone. "A couple of quick calls and I can set it up."

"Yes to the Cruzerio mine, but I'll have to take a rain check on the Paraíba mine ... I'm tight on time."

She'd known that visits to other mines would be necessary, if only to cover her interest in Novoteras, but she couldn't afford two days — not now. And she needed Scott to make a different phone call.

"Do you know anyone connected with the Novoteras mine?" she asked. "My client seemed convinced there were deep red tourmalines being pulled from that mine, some unique pieces."

"Not from that mine, not from what I've heard." He touched his phone, lighting its dark surface with a vibrant photo of an emerald. "I'm sure they find a few nice specimens, a few facet-quality stones, but that's not what's keeping the mine profitable. They have a thick vein of average-grade tourmaline, the stuff the Chinese snap up for their carving and bead market."

It doesn't add up. The money poured into security alone suggested the Novoteras mine produced something far more valuable.

"Could they be going offshore for their mineral-specimen buyers too?" She fingered her coffee cup. "My client has ties to Asia, so maybe someone overseas mentioned this particular mine to him?"

"Maybe, but I'm skeptical." He shrugged. "You know how it is ... people who work at these mines talk. If they found a pocket of large tourmaline gems at the Novoteras mine, the news would spread like wildfire, but I haven't heard anything. Not even a rumour."

Damn. She'd hit a dead end. One that left her with a single option — a move that squeezed her heart with fear.

2

Araçuaí, Brazil

ALEX SLIPPED INTO a wicker chair across from Mosi Ongeti. He'd chosen a table in a quiet spot near the edge of the courtyard of this *pousada,* a twenty-room Araçuaí inn that had served as their home for the past two weeks. The location, two hours away from the Novoteras mine, made for plenty of driving, but the steady trickle of overseas tourists shielded them from interest.

"Did you sleep?" she asked.

"No." His brown eyes met hers. "I had hoped for better news when you returned from Teófilo Otoni."

She sighed. "So did I. I—"

A couple strolling arm-in-arm along the pathway that wove through the courtyard garden approached, shutting down their conversation. The grey-haired woman smiled at Alex, but thankfully she offered nothing more than a simple hello in accented English. It was only after the couple disappeared through the glass doors of the lobby that Mosi spoke.

"I worry." He turned to her, his eyes soft. "This friend of yours, this Scott, are you sure he does not suspect?"

The same question had stolen her sleep. Again and again, she replayed their conversations at the cafe and later in the two tourmaline mines they visited. She thought about Scott's words, pictured his expressions. His excitement at sharing these Brazilian mines with her had been as obvious as his disappointment when she turned down his dinner invitation.

"He can't ... he doesn't. We spent hours together, and he didn't ask a single question about the Novoteras mine."

"He never asked why you were here?"

She smiled. "He knew better than to ask." They might be friends, but she and Scott were still competitors in a cutthroat business. "Even if he didn't buy my story about the client, he probably thinks I have a lead on a tourmaline deposit that would make a good mine." She shook her head. "Nothing he'd be interested in. Emeralds are his focus right now — at least that's what he said."

Whether she believed Scott or not didn't matter. As long he ignored the Novoteras mine, he'd stay out of their way. Out of danger.

Mosi turned his dark-skinned face up to the morning sun, the way he always did when deep in thought, as though he sought answers there. The creases that etched his forehead, the ones that gently reminded her that he was ten years her senior, all but disappeared in the bright sun. In this moment she instead saw the young man she had met when she was a child, someone as close to a brother as she ever had.

"I talked to my dad. He managed to get into one of the Colombian mines yesterday, and he doesn't think the geology is right for tanzanite."

Tanzanite. The rarest gemstone on earth, found in just one location: the Merelani Hills of Tanzania. If her dad was right, there was another deposit here in South America in one of the mines owned by Tabitha Metals. A mine worth killing for.

"And the other two?"

"No progress." She shook her head. "But he said that he might have a lead on a consulting engineer who works at one of them. I wish we could say the same."

Of the fifteen mines owned by Tabitha Metals, four in Colombia and one in Brazil seemed most likely. Brian Graham started in

Colombia, and she and Mosi planned to join him there once they finished with this mine. But it wouldn't be necessary.

Novoteras. A mine they were convinced held the tanzanite they sought.

"It is time." Mosi's words broke her thoughts. "Tonight there is no moon."

She sighed. "I hate this plan." Her hand tightened against the worn leather strap of her watch, but the graduation gift from her dad nine years ago offered no comfort. "I know I've done some things barely this side of legal, but this — we're planning to break into a mine, Mosi. There has to be another way."

"I can think of nothing. Security is too tight for the men to smuggle anything out of the mine."

They'd been through this a dozen times since she'd returned from seeing Scott. Each time, they came to the same conclusion.

"I still think I should be the one who goes into the mine," she said. "I can see the mineral seam for myself and—"

"That is not possible, Alex."

A flash of irritation hit at the foolish superstition that would force her to stay behind, the fear that a woman in the mine would bring bad luck. Women geologists twice her age had no doubt heard this same foolishness countless times, but attitudes had changed over the past thirty years. More women than ever worked underground, while others took over operations. Yesterday, she'd seen that for herself when Scott introduced her to one of the owners of the Cruzeiro tourmaline mine — a woman. But despite Alex's best arguments the two Brazilian miners refused to budge.

"Then we should wait for my dad. He said he could be here in two days."

"By then we will have lost the advantage of darkness. We would have to wait another month to get into the mine. The miners grow anxious even now ... they may change their minds long before then."

The high fence and the guard station at the mine entrance served notice to visitors that only those who belonged could enter. They'd been forced to dig deeper, to find miners willing to do the unthinkable. Mosi had practically grown up inside the mines of Tanzania, and he knew how to find such men and how to convince them.

"These miners, Paulo and Benjamin. How do we know we can trust them?"

"We cannot know." He smiled. "But the money we pay them will give their children a future. I understand such men — they will do as we ask."

Mosi's limited Portuguese, learned years ago in Mozambique, had been enough for him to forge a bond with these miners before she finally met them. Still, they were entrusting their lives to men they barely knew, a thought that pierced her heart.

"For eight nights, Alex, we have watched the guards. You have seen how they patrol only the mine tunnel entrance. Only once have we seen the guards walk the fence line of the mine property, and even then they stayed within sight of the entrance."

No fewer than two guards paced past the well-lit metal gates that barred entry to the ramp down to the main gallery of the mine and to the tunnels beneath it. Beyond those gates, spotlights cast only shadows on the few buildings clustered nearby. The rest of the mine property, more than a hundred acres of trees and grass that to the uninitiated looked no different than so much of Minas Gerais, lay bathed in darkness — including the many air shafts that punched into the network of tunnels below.

"And the snipers? There are *three* sniper towers, Mosi." She shifted in her chair, unable to still herself. "We just don't know how much of the mine's property those snipers can see … whether they can see the air shaft. And it doesn't matter if there isn't much light — not if they're using infrared gun sights."

"We will be far from the tower at the front gate near the highway. The other two…" He trailed off. "Only the one on the hilltop keeps me awake at night, but it is more than a mile from the air shaft." He smiled. "That is a very difficult shot, even for the most experienced African hunter. And I do not believe those snipers watch anything but the mine entrance."

"But if—"

He covered her hand with his. "I have outrun more dangerous predators."

Whether he spoke of man or beast, she wasn't sure. "This is *different*. If just one of those snipers spot you, they'll raise the alarm. You'll be trapped." Her voice dropped to barely a whisper. "Kanoni would never forgive me for being part of something that took you away from her and your children."

Eric. If she too were caught, she might never see him again.

"Kanoni will understand." He smiled. "And you underestimate me."

In his eyes she saw his calm confidence and his determination. There was too much at stake to turn back. Everything from the ultra-tight security to the gems described by the miners pointed to this mine being something other than it was portrayed. If this mine secretly produced tanzanite, it was the reason four people were already dead — and it could mean the deaths of thousands more.

I have to know.

"We go tonight."

3

Novoteras Mine

MOSI BLINKED BACK salty beads of sweat before he dropped his foot into the emptiness beneath him. Hands slippery with sweat, he gripped the thick rope and felt for the next rung of the ladder, praying his aching arms would keep him from plunging to his death. And when the toe of his boot caught the thin wood slat, he breathed deep.

He slid his foot forward onto the slat, testing its strength, testing his balance, before he eased his two-hundred-and-ten-pound frame onto it. He longed to lean back and rest against the timber-lined shaft, but he dared not. Not without knowing how far above him Benjamin Costa climbed. An impossible task in darkness so complete that he could not see his own hand.

He reached his foot downward once again, like he had done dozens of times already, dropping deeper into the mine. But this time, instead of the thick rope, his boot clipped solid rock.

Finally.

"Reach out your hand."

A quiet voice in the darkness, closer than he'd imagined. Mosi stretched his hand out in the dim light toward Paulo Alvarez.

The young Brazilian man's calloused hand closed against Mosi's wrist, and he stepped off the ladder, half expecting the move would pitch him into the depths of darkness. But the sole of his hiking boot gripped the rock.

Paulo held him steady, guiding him over the rock floor to stand clear of the ladder. Mosi had only just turned on his headlamp when Benjamin jumped from the last rung and shimmied cat-like toward them.

Almost an hour had passed since they sprinted from the fence to lift the grate his young guides unlocked from inside the mine. Since then, they had climbed down what was more of a rat hole than a true air shaft.

With Paulo in the lead, the three men finally pushed into a tunnel wide enough for a team of men and equipment. And as they put the vertical shaft behind them, the air grew warm and stale.

They had climbed three ladders to what he guessed was the one-hundred-and-fifty-metre level, the deepest working part of the mine. He now stood more than three hundred feet underground, beneath two levels of galleries that tunnelled through miles of rock, like this one did. Mine security was no longer a threat — this deep, the danger came from toxic gases that killed without warning.

He knew of many men suffocated by carbon dioxide in the Merelani mineshafts of Tanzania, a merciful death compared with that suffered by men torn apart in methane explosions. He knew nothing of this mine, of its temperament — its ability to kill.

His hand touched emptiness as they passed stopes, ragged holes dug out of the rock walls. Some, likely excavated with dynamite, were as wide and tall as a room and followed thick mineral veins, while others slanted upward, raises that let miners scramble up to rich gem deposits between levels.

Paulo pivoted into an opening hardly big enough for a man to squeeze through. Mosi twisted back. Reassured that Benjamin was tight behind him, he scrambled ahead, determined to keep Paulo in his sights.

The jagged rock that protruded from the low ceiling flashed into view too late for Mosi to call out a warning. But the spry Brazilian miner passed beneath it without difficulty — a reminder that this mineshaft was meant for nimble young men, not someone his age.

He gave silent thanks for the helmet, a luxury not often given to men who mined the depths in Tanzania. In his younger years, he had often worn nothing but a small flashlight attached to a cotton hat with the flimsiest of brims, little protection from the rocks that gave way in mine shafts dug for speed rather than safety.

With his left hand braced against the rough wall, he crouched and slipped beneath the hazard. Pain flared as his wrist caught against a sharp rock, and he jerked his hand up into the light. Blood streaked down the back of his hand, vivid against the grey dust that coated his skin, dust that quickened his pulse.

Graphite.

His face pressed close to the wall, he peered at the marled rock and smiled. The geology was similar to what he had seen before. He wiped his bloody hand against his pant leg and turned.

In the darkness he could find no sign of light, no sign of Paulo.

He jerked his head back. Benjamin should be right behind him. But his light revealed only empty blackness.

I am alone!

He pressed his palm against the rock wall. Rooted in place, afraid to lose his sense of direction, he twisted his body around, searching for a pinpoint of light from another's helmet.

Did these men bring me here to die?

He heard only the echo of his ragged breath. He shifted his weight from one foot to the other, hand tight to the wall as though held by glue.

Can I find the ladder?

They had walked fifteen, maybe twenty minutes to this point. Two turns, maybe three. Mosi jerked his head left, then right, his hand never leaving the wall.

There! The faint glow of light. And a single breath later, he saw Benjamin's dust-covered face.

"Are you hurt?" Benjamin asked.

Mosi pulled his hand from the wall. "It's nothing. A cut."

"Then we go."

With Benjamin tight behind him, Mosi plunged ahead into the

darkness. Each step took him farther into a tunnel that grew increasingly tight, forcing him to stoop low to avoid the rock ceiling. Then he broke free into a wide, rock-carved tunnel, where Paulo stood waiting.

Mosi swept his headlamp across a rock wall marred by picks. Glittering crystals shone in the dim light of his headlamp, translucent quartz held tight in a gnarled mix of minerals. He was not a geologist, but he recognized pegmatite, as did every miner who worked in the African Great Rift Valley. Here lay the prize, a rich vein that would bring wealth from gems like emerald and topaz.

Paulo rested his finger against the rock. "This is what we take from the mine."

He drove the tapered steel of his pick into the wall, digging out this fragile prize. After several strikes, he dropped his pick and used his fingers to pry free a rock the size of a golf ball. He brought it up close to his face for a brief moment before he handed it to Mosi.

"This is a good piece. It has much purple and blue in it."

Mosi took the fragment and cradled it in the palm of his hand. When his light struck the lustrous rock, revealing a flash of purple, he stopped breathing.

Tanzanite.

He shone his light over the wall and saw more of the same purple-hued mineral thought to exist only in Tanzania.

"How long have you been mining this stone?"

"Here, in this place, not for very long. But for seven years I have worked places like this in the mine. It is a good mine."

Seven years? He could not believe it. Did not want to believe it.

Mosi closed his hand over the gem. "This is what I came for. We can go."

Paulo clapped Benjamin on the shoulder. They spoke in rapid words he did not understand, but their smiles told the story. He could not blame the men for their excitement. They had been promised ten thousand dollars, a small fortune in this part of the world, if Mosi found the rock he sought. Just as important, they did not need to risk any more time in the mine.

Benjamin took the lead at a pace that was almost a run, and he was soon down the rabbit hole that snaked back to the level from which they had entered. Mosi struggled to keep up, his head low and his ankles rocking with each step on the uneven ground.

His boot clipped a large rock, dropping him hard onto his knees. Pain shot through his left kneecap, and he dared not move. He forced air deep into his lungs, willing the pain away.

Paulo crouched beside him. "Can you walk?"

"I must." Mosi grabbed Paulo's extended hand and pushed himself to his feet, relieved that the pain did not worsen. "It is bruised, not broken."

But with his first step he faltered, saved only by Paulo's strong arms against his back. Supported this way, he limped to the ventilation shaft, where Benjamin stood waiting.

When they were within reach of the ladder, Benjamin climbed the first few rungs and then turned, waiting for Mosi to do the same.

How? And yet he must.

He swung himself onto the ladder and pulled up his injured leg. When the knee bent, pain surged through his leg. Through clenched teeth he pushed himself forward, up an endless set of rungs to the surface.

I will not be caught underground. He forced his thoughts to his children, to his wife, and to Alex, who waited for him above.

His headlamp faltered before they reached the third ladder, but the air grew sweet. And then his hand touched Benjamin's boot.

"Wait," Benjamin whispered down to him. "I must be sure no guard is here."

Mosi had barely caught his breath before he felt Paulo's hand against his own boot. He whispered Benjamin's warning back to Paulo, and together the three men, their head lamps off, stood in the darkness.

"Come!"

Benjamin's command spurred Mosi upward in one final push, and he landed hard on the ground.

"Quickly!" Benjamin sprinted for the path beyond the fence.

Mosi pressed his balled fists into the ground and climbed to his feet, but he could only limp on a knee made worse by the climb. From behind, Paulo wrapped his arm around him, giving him strength.

Crack!

A bullet hit his leg. He thudded to the ground, taking Paulo with him. The young miner scrambled to his feet and threw a hand out to him.

A second rifle shot. Shouts. The pound of boots.

"Quickly!"

Paulo yanked him to his feet, and together they plunged into the darkness.

4

Novoteras Mine

A gunshot!

Hands tightly curled around the steering wheel, Alex stared down at the sprawling mine with its prison-like security. The darkness, punctuated by spotlights and a blaze of fluorescence from the main building windows, revealed no movement. Not inside the buildings or near the narrow path through the trees, where she expected Mosi to emerge.

A second shot cracked the silence.

She watched the darkness, willing the men to appear. They had to be down there — had to be coming her way.

Finally, a dot of light near the fence. *A flashlight.*

She blew out a breath she didn't know she held. Mosi, Benjamin, and Paulo were climbing toward her — fast.

Her finger hovered over the ignition button. She'd wait another few seconds until the men were closer to the highway before she risked the noise.

The ink-black shadow of a man appeared near the top of the path. She punched the ignition button and jammed the 4x4 into gear.

She froze.

In the headlights she saw the unmistakable barrel of a rifle.

A shout, angry, demanding, pushed her into action. Heart pounding, she stomped on the accelerator. But the guards were closing on her.

A bullet slammed into the side of the 4x4. She swerved without thinking, sending the nose of the truck toward the hillside just as another bullet hit. Her foot pounded on the brake for the barest instant. She yanked the steering wheel around hard — too hard. The vehicle careened across the centre line before she managed to gain control.

A shot crashed through the back windshield. She ducked, head barely above her white-knuckled grip, just as another bullet hit.

Five seconds. Then she'd be out of range. Or around a curve. She pressed harder on the accelerator.

Silence.

Eyes fixed on the rear-view mirror, she watched the empty highway through the shattered back window. She leaned into the curves of the highway, foot barely lifting off the gas.

But each mile took her farther from Mosi.

Two shots. She'd heard them before the guards appeared on the road. The men had been gone more than two hours before the first gunshot. Whatever had gone wrong happened when they surfaced or when they tried to slip through the mine fence.

If she were lucky, the guards had caught only the barest glimpse of the 4x4. Even that, though, was enough for them to find her on this deserted highway.

Her boot tapped the brake, and she scanned both sides of the highway for one of the many side roads that snaked through the countryside. Despite driving this road for weeks, nothing looked familiar.

She glanced up at the rear-view mirror, expecting headlights. If the guards pursued her, they were far behind. It gave her time. Still, she yanked the steering wheel toward the first strip of gravel that crossed the highway edge, not caring where it led.

The rumble of rock beneath her wheels sounded too loud to her ears. Afraid someone would hear her, she slowed to a crawl past fields where cattle grazed and farmers slept in homes just out of view. Only when she found a dark patch of road bordered by trees did she finally ease the 4x4 over to the side.

She reached across the seat for her cell phone. No service. Her satellite phone lay buried in her backpack, but it was of no help. Mosi carried only a prepaid cell phone like the phone in her hand, both purchased in São Paulo six weeks ago. Even if Mosi did escape the mine, he was on his own.

Paulo and Benjamin would know how to escape, where to hide. But would these men take Mosi with them or cast him aside like dead weight?

They'd planned to meet in Coronel Murta if anything went wrong, a plan that now seemed ill conceived. That town lay half an hour south of the Novoteras mine — an impossible distance with guards in pursuit or if one of the men were injured.

I have to go back.

In a few hours, she might slip into the line of traffic headed toward the morning shift at the mine. The guards could hardly expect her to return that way, and all she needed was enough cell service to reach Mosi to arrange to pick him up. But this rental, new and expensive, would stand out, especially with its shattered window. If the guards patrolled the highway, she might be arrested before she could find Mosi.

She ground the heels of her palms against her thighs. Every geologist at Graham and Associates knew their first call should be to Tracey Caminski, their unflappable manager with a reputation for working miracles in tight situations. She'd do no less for Alex if she were arrested, but Tracey could do nothing for Mosi until he surfaced.

Coronel Murta — it was her best choice. That's where Mosi would head. And there were enough back alleys in the town of nine thousand for her to hide until she heard from him. First she had to get rid of that back window.

Stretched across the seat, she dug a flashlight out of the glove box and scrambled out of the 4x4. At the back window she pulled her sleeve down over her hand before she pushed at the spider-webbed fracture, but the glass held firm.

She grasped the angled edge of a glass shard and tried to wriggle it free, only to yelp as the razor-sharp edge sliced into her finger. Blood ran over the palm she held up to the light.

She yanked the back door open and dropped the flashlight onto the seat. Digging into her backpack, she found a tissue and wound it tightly around the stinging cut. As she twisted back to the door, she saw it.

A hole in the leather seat back, just inches below the driver's side headrest.

She dug her finger into the hole and touched the cold steel of a bullet aimed at her. The guards had appeared on the highway with guns blazing, as though they'd known she waited there. Paulo, Benjamin — one of them had betrayed her.

No. The timing wasn't right. Those two gunshots came just minutes before the first guard showed up. They must have fired on Mosi and chased him up toward the highway. The guards had found her by accident. They *must* have.

But I didn't see Mosi.

Whatever the answer, she needed to find a safe place to hide. She scrambled from the vehicle and searched the roadside until she found a grapefruit-sized rock. At the back fender, she heaved the rock into the window, showering the cargo area with glass.

Dogs barked in alarm. She whipped her head around, searching for lights, but if there were a house nearby, she couldn't see it.

Heart pounding, she jumped into the 4x4 and hit the starter. She pulled into a tight U-turn and headed back to the highway. For the briefest second she hesitated, wanting to turn left up the highway, back to the mine, knowing she couldn't.

A glance at the rear-view mirror revealed only black pavement, but still she floored the gas pedal. Only when the first of the tiled roofs of Coronel Murta came into view fifteen minutes later did she ease off.

Slowly now, she drove past darkened windows until she neared the centre of town. She squeezed into a row of parked vehicles and shut off the engine.

Her phone showed just one bar of signal strength, but it was enough. She redialed Mosi's number, and hand tight on the phone, listened to each ring. Fingers tapping the steering wheel, she waited for his smooth voice to replace the static that crackled in her ear. But the phone rang until his voicemail picked up.

"I'm in—" She cut herself short. There was no way to know who might listen to Mosi's messages, who might come looking for her. Mosi would see the missed call and hear her voice. It had to be enough.

She dropped the phone into her lap and closed her eyes.

He has to be okay.

Mosi, the gentle bear of a man who'd taken her by the hand to explore life beyond the Tanzanian mine sites that stole all of her father's attention, had to come back to her.

5

Novoteras Mine

ONE MORE STEP. It was the mantra Mosi repeated each time he dropped his weight onto his injured leg. He clutched Paulo's shoulder for support and felt Paulo's grip against his waist tighten as they manoeuvred through the narrowest of gaps between the trees.

His foot caught in a tangle of branches, and he pitched forward, saved from crashing to the ground by Paulo's strong hands. Teeth gritted, he froze, waiting for the worst of the pain to pass.

How far they had travelled since they had slipped through the mine fence, he did not know. But he could go no farther.

"I must rest."

Paulo jerked his head back, scanning the shadows, before he answered. "For a few minutes only. We cannot stay here. We must keep moving."

Leaning heavily on Paulo, Mosi eased himself down to sit next to a slender tree trunk. Eyes closed, he rested his head against the rough bark, forcing breath slowly into his lungs in rhythm with the pain that pulsed through his leg.

Paulo crouched beside him. "Where is the bullet?"

Mosi stared down at his left leg and ran his hand gently over his thigh. When he felt the wetness of blood near his hip, he stopped. "Here, I think."

Paulo yanked off his cotton jacket and pulled the belt from the loops of his cargo pants. Down on his knees, he forced the leather belt beneath Mosi's leg.

"How far are we from the highway?" Mosi asked this man close enough that he could feel his breath.

"Not far. But we cannot go in that direction." Paulo did not look up from the belt in his hands. "The guards will be there. Your friend will be captured."

Fear stabbed at his gut. He prayed Paulo was wrong and that Alex had heard the shots and fled. He would never forgive himself if anything happened to her.

"And Benjamin?"

Paulo reached for the jacket and wadded it into a tight square before he replied. "If he escaped, he will find his own way to safety. We can do nothing more."

Mosi swallowed hard. *Survival.* He too had done things no man should have to do just to survive, to claw his way out of one of the poorest Tanzanian villages. Brazil was no different.

"It is best if they do not find you or the woman. If they learn foreigners broke into the mine, there will be very much trouble."

He is right. Theft could be accepted, but the mine owners could not risk news of their find reaching the outside world.

"There is a man I know who lives not far … maybe half hour from here. He will help us."

Mosi winced and clenched at the grass when Paulo pressed the jacket against the wound.

"I will only slow you down. Go."

Mosi stared into the face of the man who had saved his life. But in the dim moonlight he could not see the man's eyes, could not see into his soul.

"Go. Find help and come back for me."

What does he fear most? Staying or leaving?

Paulo dropped his head. "You will need to hide, keep low in the bushes."

Mosi clenched his jaw against the explosion of pain that hit when Paulo cinched the belt against the makeshift bandage. And then the bronze-skinned Brazilian slipped through the trees.

He watched the spot where Paulo disappeared, his leg held steady against the pain. There was no way to know if this miner with a quick smile would return. He knew little about this man he now depended on for his life — their meetings, furtive and brief, had not allowed for it. Only when they had first met had the thirty-something miner talked about his family, a wife and eight-year-old son. They were the reason Paulo had agreed to the offered money, and now they would be the reason Paulo walked away.

He closed his eyes and summoned his own wife's beautiful smile. How he missed Kanoni, the woman who had been by his side for almost ten years. She had pulled him from the pit of despair when his first wife, Chania, died of malaria and left him a widower with two children to care for. Kanoni became the only mama his son Abasi and his younger sister knew — even he had long forgotten the delicate curves of Chania's face.

His hand rested on the gold buckle of the leather belt that tortured him. He desperately wanted to pull it free, to loosen it, but he knew it might be the only thing that would keep him alive. The only thing that would deliver him to his beloved family.

I will not die here.

He shifted his weight onto his left hip, a move rewarded with a jolt of pain. Hands tightened into fists, he sucked air through his teeth. One breath, then another, until the pain eased.

He zipped his fleece jacket tight to his chin, shivering now that the cold dampness of the ground seeped into his muscles. His eyes darted skyward to the clouds that hung in the starry sky. If he were lucky, the rains that had dogged them these past few weeks would hold off until morning. By then, he and Alex would be far from the mine.

Unless she has been caught.

He refused to believe it. The gunshots would have warned her, and she had a head start on the guards. She must have escaped and gone on to Coronel Murta, as planned.

Unless she had waited there on the highway for him to return too long, and she had been captured.

No! She knows better.

From his pocket he dug out his cell phone. He touched the screen, sending a too-bright light into the dark night, a beacon that would betray his location in an instant. He hunched over the screen just long enough to see that no signal travelled this far from the mine and the main roads.

There would be no call to Alex. *Not from here.*

His head snapped up at the crack of wood. Quickly, he stuffed the phone back in his pocket, dousing the light.

The thud of boots, quick steps taken without care on the uneven ground, closed in.

One man? Two? Uninjured he would easily survive, but now? How foolish to sit, to make himself weak to his prey.

He whispered a prayer, one that had comforted him many times before. Face pressed against the tree, he searched the tangle of branches and leaves for his hunters. The dim beam of a flashlight approached.

He dropped his face to his chest. He knew enough to hide his eyes from these men. He would not give their flashlights anything to fix on.

The crunch of leaves.

One man. Close now.

He clenched his hand into a fist, his only defence. It would do nothing to stop a bullet.

But he would not let this man take him alive. He would not lead them to Alex.

The footsteps stopped. The sweep of a beam cast a shadow beyond his feet. It passed left and right and then just as quickly delivered him again to darkness.

The hunter moved on, pounding a path through the dense jungle.

He closed his eyes, willing his heart to slow. He could do nothing to help Paulo. The young miner would meet his fate in the hands of this hunter or safely return to this spot.

If he returns. The young father could easily leave him here and turn his back on this dangerous situation.

None of them had expected the guards to shoot at them. Maybe they should have — he should have. More than the others, he knew that mine security had hairpin triggers when it came to theft. Each guard bore the responsibility of stolen gemstones under his watch. It made them as desperate as the men who sought to steal the precious stones.

He had seen men shot dead without question just for being inside the fenced area of a mine. *Too many men.* Yet it did nothing to deter them, because a single piece of gold or a small diamond could feed a family for a year. For many uneducated men struggling to support their families, it was the only way.

If not for his father, Mosi might have been forced to do the same. His father, who had worked long weeks away from his family at a menial job at a safari lodge, wanted something more for his son. He saw the guides and drivers, the ones who boasted of big tips from foreigners, and knew Mosi was smart enough to join their ranks.

Every penny was saved so that Mosi could go to Catholic school. But when his father died in a car crash, his life changed. As the eldest, he had to support his two mamas and his nine brothers and sisters, all but three of them half-siblings.

Mosi had dropped out of high school to work the underground tanzanite and gold mines, spending his days deep beneath the surface in foul, dangerous tunnels. His nights were spent combing the tailing piles, the leftovers, in search of the smallest piece of gold or tanzanite cast aside in the rubble. *Theft.*

He pushed back the memories of things done that were best forgotten, actions necessary for his family to survive. Only when he met Brian Graham at one of those mines did his life take another turn.

The faint rustle of leaves.

The hunter has returned.

Mosi stared at the sparse brush that sheltered him. The jumble of leaves that might be the last thing he ever saw.

6

Novoteras Mine

JORGE SILVA HAD barely passed through his office doorway before a guard of no more than twenty set a steaming cup of milky tea on his desk. He expected the man to say something, but he scurried from the office.

From outside the building came shouts, but Jorge could see only the chain-link fence with its barbed-wire cap through the window. He would have to wait to learn what had happened, what had forced him back here in the dead of night, a first in his seven years as manager of the Novoteras mine.

He draped his navy jacket over the back of the chair and reached for the single sheet of paper centred on his desk. Under the harsh fluorescent light, he scanned the tight-lined report detailing the previous day's mine production. Nothing in the report explained the call from the security head, Carlos Pinto, a mere half hour ago.

The shrill ring of the cell phone had set his heart pounding, a reaction to too many late-night calls during his years as a police officer. He'd snatched it to his chest to muffle the ring, afraid it would wake Zahra or one of the children, answering it only when he had stepped on the cold bathroom floor and eased the door shut. But he need not have worried. His pregnant wife never moved, not even when he quickly dressed in a uniform pressed and ready in their dark bedroom.

A guard had quickly waved Jorge through the front gates, but he had seen nothing out of the ordinary as he wove down the red-dirt road. The dynamite storage shed, the processing area, and the main building all stood dark and silent. In the blaze of light that framed the metal doors at the entrance to the mine tunnels, two men stood guard, as expected. Only the small administration building that housed his office showed signs of life, and even then just three windows were lit.

Knuckles rapped against the door frame, and he glanced up to see Carlos. In the shadowed light cast by the door, the jagged scar beneath the captain's left eye looked like a black ink trail made by a shaky hand. He had heard varied stories about the scar, from a drunken bar fight to an argument with a young mistress's husband, but none matched the character of this intelligent, thoughtful man who oversaw security.

Jorge beckoned the balding man into the room. Carlos stopped in front of the desk and thrust his chest forward, a sign of his military training. The nervous captain did not wait for an invitation to launch into a rapid-fire account of the night's events. Words that set Jorge's heart racing.

"*Dois homen?* Only two men. You are sure?" Jorge ran a hand over his stubbled chin, wishing now that he had taken more time to properly present himself before returning to the mine. There would be no quick return to his bed. His day had started, and it would not end until the thieves were caught.

"Yes."

"None of them could have escaped?" Jorge asked.

"It is possible. It was only after the first shot was fired that we knew the men were there."

"But there was just one vehicle?" Jorge reached for a pen and pulled a pad of paper from the top drawer of his desk.

Carlos nodded. "A truck parked on the highway."

A single vehicle would not hold many men. It suggested that the men seen by his guards were the only thieves.

"The man who was shot. Did he say anything before he died?"

Jorge saw the sadness in his eyes. This deeply religious Catholic would not have left their thief. He would have held the thief's hand, offering comfort and prayer to the man who died at his feet.

Carlos shifted his weight from one foot to the other. "He called out a woman's name, Eva. Nothing more."

Jorge scribbled the name on the thick pad. "You have searched the man?"

A nod. "A flashlight, water, bread and cheese were found in his pockets. He carried no ID."

"Nothing else? Not a single piece of rock?"

The thieves could have been in the mine for hours, enough time to hammer out more than a few pieces of rock from the rich vein that was currently mined. Although even he had to admit that the rock they worked so hard to free from the earth did not look valuable.

None of the rock they mined, neither the thick vein of pink and green tourmaline in the upper tunnels nor the brown rock in Tunnel Five, seemed of similar quality to the fine gems sold in Teófilo Otoni. From time to time they found other gemstones, like emeralds, rubies, and sapphires, but only in small quantities. Their main product was tourmaline of such quality that only bead-makers in China were interested. It was a lucrative market that made this mine earn an estimated thirty million U.S. dollars a year, but that was a fraction of the revenue of the local emerald and ruby mines.

The elaborate security he had been directed to put in place at Novoteras hardly seemed necessary. But he knew better than to question an order.

"The man you chased. The one who was shot. Why was he allowed to escape?"

"By the time guards ran to where he had fallen, he was gone. The guards assumed he fled to the highway." Carlos dropped his gaze. "A mistake."

"How could you miss the man?" He swung his hands wide. "The guard house is directly in front of the main entrance to the mine. How could you not see him leave the mine?"

Carlos shook his head. "The man fell near the *sete* air shaft, number seven, the one that is more than a kilometre back from the guard house. It was only pure luck that one of the snipers saw him at all."

"The air shaft?"

"*Sim*. Yes. The metal cover had been removed, and we believe the men entered the mine through that shaft."

A well-planned intrusion. Their thieves knew the routine of the guards, and they had unlocked the grated cover over the air shaft beforehand. They also knew that this specific shaft, narrow and barely visible in the grass, dropped through three of the mine tunnels that stretched like stacked logs below the surface.

"My men are searching the area beyond the fence. An injured man on foot cannot go too far, but there are many places to hide." Carlos spat out the rambling assurance. "As soon as the sun—"

Jorge raised his hand. "What about the truck? Do you have men searching the highway?"

"Two vehicles search the highway, but the driver was at least ten minutes ahead of us, maybe more."

With a head start, the driver could easily reach the villages that dotted these rolling hills before his guards did. No, the man who fled on foot was more likely.

"Pull those men back. I want every security guard on the other side of that fence. Call the day shift and get them here now."

Carlos spun on his heel and hurried from the office, slamming the wooden door shut behind him.

Jorge stood and pulled his jacket from the chair back, walking it over to the coat rack and carefully slipping a metal hanger into the sleeves.

Hands clasped behind his back, he stared out the window. In the past seven years, not a single major security problem.

Until now.

He had implemented a strict security regime to control theft. X-ray scanners, closed-circuit cameras, more guards, specially trained snipers — everything he had asked for, the mine owner agreed to readily.

Yet thieves had slithered through a hole cut in the fence and slipped into the mine through an almost forgotten shaft on this moonless night.

How?

7

Coronel Murta, Brazil

ALEX SHIFTED HER WEIGHT, trying to ease the stiffness that had taken hold after too many hours in the driver's seat of the truck. Her eyes darted to the rear-view mirror and then up at the dark windows of houses that lined this quiet alley in Coronel Murta. None showed signs of life, not yet, not with dawn still two hours away.

He'll be okay. He has to be okay.

She stared at the bright screen of her phone, willing it to ring or announce a text from Mosi. But its icon-crowded surface remained unchanged. She considered a message to her dad before rejecting it in favour of waiting until dawn. By then she would either have heard from Mosi or she and her dad would be forced to come up with a plan to find him.

Instead, she scrolled through emails she'd seen dozens of times in the three hours since she'd fled the mine. Her finger stopped at the last message from Eric, one she'd read often enough to know by heart. Twice she'd typed out a reply, only to delete what she'd written. She couldn't answer his questions about how her project was going or when she would be home. How to explain any of this when Eric didn't even know she was out of the country?

Their long-distance relationship, and the wonders of international cell service, had made it easy for her to say nothing about this hastily planned trip to Brazil. She'd expected to be back in Vancouver in a week, maybe two, and Eric had learned long ago that she rarely talked about work in anything but the vaguest terms. He did the same when it came to the patients he treated in the Kootenay Regional Hospital emergency room, and so they'd more or less come to a mutually agreed upon decision to keep work out of their precious conversation time.

The crash of metal jerked her upright. Heart pounding, she searched the darkness for movement, relieved to see an orange tabby jump from a garbage can. But just as quickly, a light appeared in a second-floor window.

Breath held tight, she watched for the shadow of movement in the window, the sweep of a curtain. None came, and a moment later the light was doused.

She was safe here until the sun came up. After that, a Caucasian woman seated in a truck too long would draw stares in this part of the world. Without knowing if she'd been seen by the mine's guards and whether they searched the nearby towns, she wasn't keen to spend time in a café or restaurant either. Safety lay farther south, in Araçuaí or another of the large towns, but she wasn't ready to put another two hours of distance between herself and Mosi.

Her eyes darted to the back seat, to Mosi's over-stuffed duffel and his backpack. He had nothing with him, no survival gear but a flashlight, unless he'd tucked a knife or box of matches into his pockets. All of their gear had been loaded into the truck when they checked out of their hotel and headed for the mine. As soon as the men had surfaced, they'd intended to hightail it south to the Belo Horizonte airport with just the barest of detours to the villages where Benjamin and Paulo lived.

What the hell were we thinking?

She'd been shocked by the story her dad had told. A gemstone courier, just twenty-two, shot and left for dead in an Amsterdam alleyway. Three days later, her boyfriend and her parents found murdered as well. Their client received a perfect tanzanite gemstone with a note from the courier — a note that mentioned the name Tabitha Metals and little else. Police shrugged at what seemed a meaningless message, and when private detectives could offer little help, she went to Brian Graham. He'd recognized the importance of the gemstone immediately — and so had Alex.

She clenched her hands around the steering wheel, itching to start the truck and drive back to the mine. In the rear-view mirror, she stared at the jagged shards of glass that stubbornly clung to the rim of the empty back window frame. The bullet-cracked glass might be gone, but if police had a description of her truck she'd be stopped, especially if she were anywhere near the mine.

Her hands fell from the wheel. She could do nothing but wait.

The shrill ring of the phone cracked the silence, and she grabbed for it. Tears sprang to her eyes when she heard the deep voice of her friend.

"Mosi, thank god. Where are you?"

"Near Salinas."

North. Her hand clenched. He'd gone in the opposite direction from her, and the mine now stood between them.

"How—"

"Alex, are you hurt?" he gently asked before she could finish.

"No, no. I'm okay." Her chest tightened. "I'm sorry, Mosi. I had to leave. Guards were shooting at me." Her voice cracked. "I couldn't wait."

"Good. We—"

"Paulo and Benjamin are with you?" She felt foolish now for doubting the miners. "I was afraid you were alone."

"I would not have made it this far without Paulo." His voice quiet, he continued. "But Benjamin did not make it out of the mine. The guards shot him."

She dug her fingernails deep into the palm of her hand. "How bad?"

"I do not know. We saw him fall, but he was too far away for us to help him."

Her gut clenched at the news.

I have to do something! The soft-spoken miner had risked everything to help them, and she couldn't abandon him. But right now, the best she could offer would be a lawyer drummed up by Tracey. Even that would have to wait until Benjamin was officially charged. To do otherwise jeopardized them all.

"Where are you exactly? I'm coming to get you."

"No. Paulo will find a way to get me to Belo Horizonte. We will meet there."

She heard the sharp intake of breath. Something was wrong.

"What aren't you telling me?" But he didn't answer. "Mosi, tell me."

In the long silence that followed, her mind swirled with possibilities, none of them good.

"I was shot in the leg. It is nothing, but if we are stopped on the highway—"

He didn't need to finish the sentence. It would take a miracle for him to explain away a bullet wound if police stopped them. She leaned her forehead against the steering wheel, fighting back the nausea that tore at her gut.

"I'm coming to get you," she said quietly.

"No. Go to Belo and wait for me. It is too dangerous for you to come here … we cannot know what Benjamin has said."

He's right. By now, mine security could be all over the highways looking for them — for her. But she'd be damned if she'd let Mosi try to get to safety on his own.

"Give me your exact location," she demanded. "I'm coming to get you."

She stared out into the dark alleyway, one breath, then two, waiting for his reply. But none came.

"My friend, we have to do this together," she softly pleaded.

She heard him sigh, and then he rattled off details to a small village too near the mine.

"Got it. I should be there in an hour. And if I'm not…" She bit her lip. "If I don't show up in the next two hours, it means I've been arrested. Call Tracey for help."

"They will not call police. That will bring too many questions about the mine."

Her breath quickened. "So you found it?"

"Yes."

They had to get out of Brazil. *Fast.*

"Mosi, sit tight, I'm on my way."

She dropped the phone on the seat beside her and hit the starter. The cat scuttled behind a garbage can at the roar of the engine. She resisted the urge to stomp on the gas pedal, to send the truck flying down the alley. Instead, she tapped the gas and slowly rolled past the dark windows. She needed a quiet exit from this town and a careful drive down the highway.

Back toward the mine.

8

São Paulo, Brazil

SHEN LI WOKE with the first shrill ring of the phone. The glowing 4:13 a.m. display warned of bad news even before he snatched up the handset.

"This is Jorge Silva at the Novoteras mine. I am sorry to wake you so early Mr. Li, but there has been a break-in at the mine. One man is dead. The other was shot but he escaped."

Jorge Silva. Direct and to the point, as always. One of the many things about working with Brazilians Shen would never get used to.

"What are you doing about it?" He pulled back the duvet and swung his legs over the edge of the bed.

"The guards have searched the area around the mine, but they cannot find the man. There was a driver in a truck waiting on the road. The guards tried, but they could not stop the truck."

A waiting driver meant this was not a simple break-in.

The nearby emerald and gold mines made far more appealing targets to would-be thieves. This mine wasn't worth the risk. Unless someone had discovered the truth about the mine.

Or Tabitha Metals. All of his South American mines could be under investigation.

"Only three men? Are you sure?" Shen asked as he slipped into a silk robe.

"It is impossible to know. The police may—"

"No police. You must handle this yourself," he demanded. "I will make private resources available."

"Yes, sir," came the quick reply.

"Did you find gems on the dead man?"

"No. Either the men did not take anything from the mine or the missing man has them."

Shen went cold at the thought of even a single piece of rock from this mine out of his control. "How did they get into the mine?"

"They came out of air shaft number seven, and I believe they entered the mine the same way. It is the only way they could have avoided the sniper towers. We will have to wait until the supervisors show up in the morning to confirm the dead man works here, but their use of the air shaft suggests he is one of our miners."

The air shaft.

A collapse in a shallow tunnel of the Novoteras mine five years ago had entombed fourteen men behind a thick wall of rock.

The mine's engineer sank a narrow shaft near where the men were believed trapped, while workers clawed through the boulders that sealed off Tunnel Two. The shaft punched through the rock into the tunnel the second day, keeping the men alive while rescue efforts continued. But Shen ordered the shaft widened enough for a man to slip through while work to clear the tunnel continued. It was an expensive decision, but he would do whatever it took to avoid a lengthy entrapment.

This mine would not — could not — be subjected to the worldwide publicity seen after the 2010 Chilean mine collapse that left miners trapped for sixty-nine days underground. As it was, too many people had come through the mine gates for Shen's liking. The families of miners were quickly joined by outsiders, reporters, and government officials, all asking too many questions.

Workers broke through the blocked tunnel entrance long before the shaft was completed. Six days after the collapse, all but four men were rescued from the mine, and the gates slammed shut to outsiders.

But the engineer convinced Shen to widen the shaft as planned and extend it to give access to the deeper tunnels if needed again. It seemed a wise precaution and served to reassure miners reluctant to go back underground. Now one of those men had betrayed him. The entrance, a boarded-up sliver cut into the ground, wasn't obvious. So an insider was stealing from them through a shaft meant to save their lives. It was an insult.

"Why wasn't the air shaft entrance guarded?"

"To post a guard at that entrance announces its existence. Instead, the snipers sweep the grounds and check the fence line. One of them saw the men come out of the air shaft, and his gunshot brought the other guards running."

Jorge's voice betrayed his fear, but there was no hint of deception. Shen had personally recruited the ex-policeman, had met his family and talked to him weekly. In China, he'd expect more to develop a true *cheng* relationship, to fully trust this man who managed the mine, but Shen knew the Brazilian to be loyal. He couldn't say the same for the men under Jorge's command.

"I want every guard on duty questioned. I want to know if they were part of this break-in."

"But they shot at the men who were in the mine. They would not have done that if they were partners in this —"

"Or they did it to deflect suspicion."

He listened to Jorge argue that his men could be trusted, that every one of them was loyal.

"Prove it. Until then, you will treat every guard as a suspect ... or I will send someone there who will."

"Yes, sir," came Jorge's crisp response.

Good. It was the response of a disciplined police officer, one who understood the chain of command, one who would do his bidding.

"The man who got away ... you said he was shot. He'll have to go somewhere for treatment."

"I will call the nearby clinics in the morning and warn them to look for such a man." Jorge paused. "I cannot control whether they will call police."

"Find a way." He understood even as he barked the order that it would be necessary to call in a favour to keep police away from this matter. Jorge's network of police contacts, stale and based mostly in Belo Horizonte, would be of no value.

"I expect you to tell me you have found him when you call again."

Shen typed out a terse email to the remaining South American mine managers. If anyone had been asking questions, he would know by morning.

There would be no more sleep. He tied the belt of his robe tight around his firm waist and pushed the thick brocade curtains aside.

Pinpoints of light from thousands of windows in the city of São Paulo stretched before him. The sounds of this city of twelve million, the fetid sewage-filled Pinheiros River, the thick air clogged by too many cars, the forty floors beneath this penthouse barely kept it all at bay.

Nine years he'd been in this cesspool, and although he longed to be back in London, this was where he would stay. Here, he controlled Chairman Jianyu Wei's most important source of funds, a coveted role within the Long Bridge Merchant Group's innermost circle.

Only those men closest to the Chairman were privy to the illegal arms deals, transactions they financed through manipulation of the legitimate Long Bridge Merchant Group holdings under their care. The Novoteras mine profits outperformed them all and made Shen the most powerful of the Chairman's advisers, his dragons.

Uncle, the man who'd opened his Kensington home to a nephew he didn't know, had predicted great things for Shen. He had pushed him to pursue a business degree from Cambridge University and taught him the strength of his Chinese heritage. When the time was right, Uncle had introduced Shen to the most influential men in China, including Jianyu Wei.

Shen owed it all to Uncle — and to Mother, who had insisted he leave China. He would not dishonour them now.

He glanced at the clock. It was only late afternoon in Shenzhen, China — the Chairman would still be at his desk. But Shen made no move to pick up the phone.

He ran a hand through his hair, his fingers betraying an emerging bald spot in what was once a full head of thick black hair. Much better to deliver good news instead of bad, to wait long enough for Jorge Silva to find the second thief in the trees outside the mine fence.

And if he doesn't?

9

Near Salinas, Brazil

ALEX KNOCKED LIGHTLY, her focus on the dark windows of the neighbouring house. She watched for signs of life, ready to bolt at the slightest movement.

For the past hour, she'd jumped at every headlight that appeared in her rear-view mirror. And when she passed the side road that lead to the mine, she held her breath, fearing guards would be clustered there. Only when she finally turned down the dirt road that led to this small farmhouse did her heart finally slow. But they weren't safe yet.

The door inched open, and Paulo's brown eyes were on her. He opened the door just enough for her to squeeze past and then quickly shut it behind her.

The Brazilian's grim face and his urgent stride down the narrow hallway made her heart pound. When she finally stood at the doorway to the small bedroom, she understood.

Everything, from the way Mosi sat rigid on the bed with his hands tight against his leg, to his sunken eyes and sweat-laced forehead, broadcast an injury far more serious than she'd been told. He smiled at her, but even that appeared forced and unnatural.

She swept into the room and crouched next to the narrow bed, dropping her pack at her feet. "You'll be okay." Her hand reached out to him, and she forced a smile as artificial as his. "I'm going to get you home."

"We must leave." Hands pressed against the mattress, he started to lift himself, but she stopped him.

"Not until I know you're okay." Years of first aid training fuelled by adrenalin took over. "Where are you hurt exactly?"

"Here." He pointed to the inside of his left thigh. "The bullet caught me as I ran. I would have fallen if Paulo had not been next to me."

She swung around to look at the miner and for the first time saw his torn shirt and bloodied hands. "Are you bleeding? Were you shot?"

"No." Paulo scrubbed his hands against his shirt. "It is from when I tried to stop the bleeding."

It was a stark reminder that these men had been in a race for their lives, something she couldn't imagine Mosi doing alone with a bullet in his leg.

"Thank you for helping my friend," she managed before her voice cracked.

She turned back to Mosi. "Are you hurt anywhere else?"

When he shook his head, she twisted back to Paulo. "Can you get a glass of water? And if you can round up some old towels and a pail of warm water, it would help."

The dark-haired miner slipped through the doorway, leaving her alone with Mosi. It gave her just a few minutes to freely talk to her friend. She leaned in close and gently ran her hand across his cheek, wiping away grey dirt and mud.

"The police … Alex, they did not see you on the highway? You had no trouble?"

"No. But I'll feel better once we've put some distance between us and the mine." She dropped her voice to a whisper before she added, "We'll go to Belo and find some place to wait for our flight … maybe a motel by the airport."

Twelve hours. Somehow they had to stay out of sight until their flight out of Belo Horizonte this evening.

"I have to see how bad the wound is." Her hand rested on his leg. "It's going to hurt."

His eyes soft, he whispered, "You do what you have to do, *Nafisa*."

Nafisa. Swahili for precious gem. She swallowed hard at this childhood nickname he'd given her back in their carefree youth under the African sun.

Paulo appeared beside her, his step so light that she hadn't heard his approach. He placed a glass of water on a small dresser near the bed and quickly departed.

She reached into her backpack and pulled out a first aid kit that she flipped open on the bed. This tightly organized kit held more than just the basics, but not enough — not for this.

"These will help." She ripped open a small packet of ibuprofen and dropped two pills into Mosi's palm. It was the best she could offer. Long ago, she'd stopped carrying even codeine, a drug on too many controlled substance lists in the countries she frequented.

Paulo said nothing when he returned; he simply set a basin of water and some towels within her reach. By the time she turned to thank him, the slender Brazilian had already retreated to the doorway, his hand tight against the doorknob.

She tugged at the buckle of the belt cinched around Mosi's thigh, a move answered by his sharp intake of breath through clenched teeth.

"I'm sorry. I'll be quick."

Her eyes firmly avoiding Mosi's face, she slipped the belt free and lifted the cloth, grateful to see that not too much blood had soaked the fabric.

"I need you to take off your pants … or at least lower them as far as your knees if you can."

She stood and extended her hand to help him, but Mosi swung around to put his feet on the floor on his own. Only when he eased himself to stand and then shifted his weight carefully onto his injured leg did his tight smile betray his pain. Yet he said nothing as he stepped free of his bloodied jeans and swivelled back onto the bed.

In the dim light, she gently washed the blood away, searching the wet skin of Mosi's thigh for a bullet hole. Finally, a swollen patch pointed the way to what seemed an impossibly small bullet wound.

"Mosi, I need to see if the bullet went right through. Can you roll over?"

She gently placed her hand on his shoulder and helped him roll onto his side. Her slender fingers gliding against his black skin, she felt for a tear on the side or back of his leg but found none. *Shit.*

"The bullet is still in there. Maybe it ricocheted." She sat down on the edge of the bed next to him. "We have to find a doctor."

By now, police would have alerted every hospital and clinic within driving distance of the mine. *How far do we go?*

In less than five hours they could be in Diamantina, another four and they'd reach Belo Horizonte. Both cities, though, still lay within the boundaries of the state of Minas Gerais, part of the same police district as the mine.

They'd have to go farther, south to São Paulo or Rio de Janeiro, or west to the Paraguay border. Each meant at least a day's drive with a bullet in Mosi's leg and still might mean arrest if a suspicious doctor called police.

And then there's Paulo.

She turned toward the Brazilian who'd put himself in such danger for them. "Paulo, were the guards close enough to see your face? Could they recognize you?"

"No," came his quick reply. "We saw no guards … not until we were close to the fence."

"But how—" Her chest tightened. "The shot came from the sniper tower. How the hell did they see you?"

"I do not know." Paulo dropped his head. "It should not have been possible."

Had they been set up?

"And you're sure Benjamin was shot?"

"I heard the shot … and his scream." Paulo raised his face to her. "He was not far in front of me, and I saw him fall. I could do nothing."

Paulo's quiet words and his grief-filled eyes tore at her heart. She couldn't imagine what it had taken for this young man to leave his friend behind.

"I'm sorry, Paulo." She swallowed hard. "I'll do everything I can to help him … I promise."

There was little she could do except provide a lawyer. As long as Benjamin had not taken any of the gemstone from the mine, a judge might be lenient. His capture, though, put them all in danger.

"We have to keep you safe, too." She dug into the first aid kit, avoiding eye contact when she asked, "Do you think Benjamin will tell police about you?"

Paulo straightened. "Never," came the strong retort. "We have been friends our whole lives. He would never do that."

"Good … that's good." She looked up at him and smiled. "But the people you work with … they will know that you and Benjamin are friends. It may be a problem."

"Many men know Benjamin," Paulo argued. "We are all friends."

"Alex, all of these men who work in the mine … they all know each other," Mosi said. "It is not a problem."

She rested her elbow on the bed and turned to face Paulo. "Then you have to go to work today. You have to go back and act as though nothing has—"

An insistent voice interrupted from the hallway, and Paulo quickly left the bedroom.

Alex's Spanish was good, but it differed just enough from Portuguese for her to lack understanding of the rapidly whispered conversation in the hall. But the tone of the conversation told her that the men argued.

"I think we've overstayed our welcome," she whispered to Mosi. "We've got to get you ready to move."

She grabbed a roll of sterile gauze and tape from the first aid kit. The voices outside the room went quiet, replaced by the scuff of boots against the wood floor.

"My cousin wanted to know if you need food," Paulo said when he stepped into the room.

"Nothing else? It sounded like the two of you were arguing."

"A little." Paulo shrugged. "I promised him money, but he refuses to take it."

She sucked in a deep breath. They were safe.

For now.

"Paulo, your shift starts…" She checked her watch. "In one hour. You should leave now."

"But—"

Mosi's deep voice interrupted him. "It is safer for all of us if you go back to the mine. Safer for your family."

She quickly added, "And it's the only way we'll know what's happened to Benjamin. I'll call you tonight, and we will work out a plan to help your friend."

Paulo dropped his eyes to stare at his muddy boots. She said nothing more, not knowing how to convince him. What she did know was that Paulo was running out of time if he hoped to reach the mine before his shift started.

Paulo shifted ever so slightly and then met her gaze. "I will go. But you must call me."

"I promise." She nodded. "I will call you tonight."

Without another word, Paulo left the small bedroom, and she heard his voice in quiet conversation. Finally she heard the front door close.

They couldn't stay here much longer. The bloodstained sheets and towels were already more evidence of their untimely arrival in the middle of the night than their host could possibly explain.

We have to move!

But where the hell are we going?

10

Novoteras Mine

JORGE STOOD OUTSIDE the doors of the mine building, his fingers pressed deep against a neck muscle that pulsed with pain. For the past six hours, under the buzz of fluorescent lights he had directed an aggressive search beyond the mine property. Two teams drove the nearby roads, and every other available guard scoured the underbrush beyond the fence, yet none reported a single sighting.

Their state-of-the-art closed-circuit camera system, with its focus on the main mine entrance, the processing room, and the worker's change room, was of no help. The cameras recorded only worker theft or a direct incursion, not a furtive entry through a locked air shaft a mile back from the mine entrance.

He stared past the chain-link fence topped with razor-sharp wire, a fence meant to deny entry, a fence that had failed. Guards had found the cut links, the narrow opening carefully closed to avoid detection from casual view, only after sunrise. Since then, his men had walked a grid search that fanned out from the breach, a search that grew more futile with each passing hour. Like a jaguar, their thief had silently slipped through the tall grass to disappear into the vast savannah, the *cerrado*.

How many times?

He closed his eyes. He had not yet dared to share this particular fear: that last night's break-in was not the first, and he had failed to keep the mine secure for weeks, or months. The guard in the hilltop sniper tower had only by chance caught sight of the marauders more than a mile away from his perch. That perfect shot gave them their only clue, a dead man lying in the infirmary.

He zipped up his navy jacket, all too aware that the white shirt beneath it bore the dark stains of sweat. He longed to return home, to change and shower, but that would have to wait.

Quick steps delivered him to the building that housed the workers' change room, their cafeteria and lounge. Inside, men in various states of undress crowded near the lockers that would hold their civilian clothes and belongings until the end of the shift. Nothing from the outside went into the mine and nothing came out, a rule enforced by a scanner through which every man, wearing only a mine-supplied apron, must pass.

Few watched him, fully clothed, enter the scanner and stand with his hands held high waiting for the camera lens to complete a full rotation before he could step free of the glass-walled machine. His shoes echoed against the smooth tile floor more accustomed to cotton booties. He hated this windowless hallway, thankful when the cubbies and hooks of the change room came into view.

Here among the early arrivals, men turned his way but just as quickly went back to outfitting themselves for the mine depths. Their curiosity over why Jorge would be in the mine was trumped by the need to report to their shift on time — not one of them would dare jeopardize their job.

Jorge tried to ignore the rich aroma of coffee and frying meats, smells that reminded him of home. By now Zahra would be awake, preparing breakfast for the children and reading the note left lying on the kitchen table. As soon as he was done here, he would call to reassure her that everything was fine.

Is it?

He'd been luckier than most, born to an engineer father who scraped together enough savings to send both of his boys to university. If his father was disappointed when, unlike his brother Antonio, Jorge had decided on law instead of engineering, he never let on. His father had proudly celebrated Jorge's first job with the Policía Civil and bragged to everyone about his son's quick rise through the ranks to land a coveted spot on the major crimes squad.

His father was less enthusiastic about the move that put Jorge in charge of this mine, because he understood all too well that Jorge would shoulder the blame for anything that went wrong. But this job meant more money than Jorge ever believed possible, ensuring that his family would want for nothing. Almost as important, it meant that he would never again face a bullet. The deaths of two fellow officers during a bank robbery investigation and his own gunshot wound still left him in a cold sweat too many nights.

Jorge pushed open the door to the infirmary to find the three shift managers he asked to see waiting there. They stood in a tight line, well back of the narrow bed with its sheet-covered body, their fear filling the room. He watched their unsmiling faces as he slowly crossed in front of them to stand near the head of the bed.

These men, in their khakis and knee-high rubber boots, supervised only the thirty or so miners who worked the main tunnels, a fraction of the ninety-four workers at the mine. His instincts told him that their thief was most likely a miner, not an electrician or geologist, and not likely someone who worked in the processing plant or the kitchen. One of these men must know him.

Without warning, he threw back the sheet covering the body, his eyes never leaving the men's sombre faces.

The room hissed with loud breath and murmured prayer. Fernando, the oldest of the men, crossed himself and touched a gold crucifix to his lips. The other two, Sabion and Ernesto, leaned tight together with shoulders almost touching, as though to keep themselves from falling to the floor.

"Do you know this man?"

None of the men replied. They dropped their eyes to their boots, refusing now to even look at the body.

Am I wrong?

His shoulders sagged. Of all people, he had expected Fernando, a friendly sixty-year-old who had been with the mine since the beginning, to recognize the dead man. But there was no proof their thief worked here.

Except for the air shaft.

"Come closer. Look at his hair." Jorge stared down at the face of the dead man. "The shape of his nose. The scar on his chin."

Jorge looked up at the men. "He is as tall as you, Sabion, maybe five-foot-seven. And to me, he looks thirty, maybe thirty-five … your age."

Sabion shook his head and shoved both hands deep into his pockets. If the father of six recognized the dead man, he hid it well.

Jorge's eyes travelled down to the dead man's chest ripped open by the sniper's high-velocity bullet. He tried not to think about this skinny man's last moments, the frantic efforts of guards to staunch the bleeding and keep his heart beating.

"He spoke a woman's name before he died. Eva."

Other than the shuffle of boots, the rub of cotton from arms folded against tight chests, the room was quiet as a crypt. He pulled the corner of the sheet up over the body, but even then, the men did not relax.

"This man did not work alone." He turned slowly from one man to another, gauging their reaction, finding only frozen stares.

They know nothing.

"Go back to work. I want to know immediately if one of your miners does not show up today. If any of them are acting strangely."

The men were quick to obey, leaving him alone in the white-walled infirmary. He walked over to the stainless steel counter on which the dead man's possessions lay. His hand wrapped around the handle of a long pickaxe, and he tested its weight. To carry such a heavy tool into the mine and return empty-handed made no sense. Yet in the hours since the break-in, he had examined every pocket, every seam of the man's clothing, and found not a single gemstone. They had X-rayed the body, searching for swallowed gems, a common ploy, but the scans had revealed nothing.

The muddy rubber boots, the dirt-smeared khaki pants and T-shirt — all pointed to time spent in Tunnel Three, where flooding had left the rock floor slick with water. But if that were the case, then the man would not have carried a pickaxe to steal tourmaline that could almost be pulled from the surrounding rock with your fingers.

Unless this man went deeper.

Tunnel Five.

11

Diamantina, Brazil

ALEX'S GRIP ON the cell phone tightened with each unanswered ring. *Come on. Come on.* But her plea delivered only Eric's canned voicemail greeting.

"Eric, call me as soon as you get this. It's urgent."

She gave Mosi a weak smile and dropped the phone on the desk beneath the dim lamp. "He'll call. It's only 5:00 a.m. in Nelson ... if he's not at the hospital, he's at home." She leaned against the desk, arms folded across her chest. "Even if he's sleeping, he'd hear the phone ... his cell is always within reach. He'll call." Whether she tried to reassure herself or Mosi of this fact, she wasn't sure.

They'd sped down the highway for more than four hours, finally stopping at a *pousada* just outside of Diamantina. Direct access to rooms kept Mosi out of the lobby, protected from view as he hobbled through the parking lot in his bloodstained clothes. Still, it was risky — even though she'd paid cash for the single room, her passport had been photocopied by the front desk clerk — but to leave Mosi's wound untended for any longer was even riskier.

In the tiny bathroom, she soaped her hands and scrubbed under water hot enough to sting, staring into the mirror. Thirty-six sleepless hours had left her eyes as dry as the Sahara and her skin as pale as desert sand. Only the angry road map of scars on her forearm blazed with colour.

Eric.

If not for an intentionally set tent fire in the remote British Columbian mountains near Nelson, she would never have met Dr. Eric Keenan. She'd never forget the kindness he'd shown her in the ER that night when he treated her burns — that and the fact that he saved her life just days later. They'd been in a relationship ever since, a relationship she was counting on now.

"Alex, I am sorry," Mosi said quietly when she returned to his bedside.

"For what?" She set antiseptic wipes, gauze, tape, and scissors out onto the bed.

"For all of this." He fixed his brown eyes on her. "I never should have agreed to involve you."

"My dad is a very persuasive man." She shook her head. "You and I never really had a say in this."

She lifted the edges of tape from his bare leg and eased the gauze pad from his thigh. "It doesn't look like it bled any more … that's good." The ragged tear in his skin looked like nothing more than a tiny cut. She ripped open an antiseptic wipe and gently ran it over the wound, watching Mosi's face for any hint of pain.

Control the bleeding. Clean the wound. Treat the pain. The fundamentals of wilderness first aid. But she'd been trained to treat broken bones and cuts, not bullet wounds.

Her head jerked up at the sound of a man's voice too near to ignore. Each breath shallow, she stared at the wooden door and the heavily curtained windows, waiting for a knock that never came. Instead, the voice faded as the man moved farther from their door.

She crossed the threadbare carpet to the window and eased the floral curtain aside. A dusty sedan now sat parked a few doors down.

Hand tight on the curtain, she shifted from one foot to the other, nervous energy propelling her exhausted body. She'd backed the truck into a spot near the fence, its broken rear window hidden from view, but there was no way to know if this was enough. *No way to know if mine security had her licence plate number.*

We're running out of time.

She hid her fear beneath a smile when she turned back to Mosi. "It's nothing. People checking in or going to the cafe."

A familiar ring sent her racing to the desk for her cell. She barely glanced at the caller ID before she hit the answer button.

"Eric! Thank god." Her fingers pressed deep against the furrows of her forehead.

"What's wrong? Alex, are you okay?"

"I'm okay. It's just…" She struggled to keep her voice steady but failed. "Eric, I need help. My friend's been shot."

"What do you mean he's been shot? Are you—"

She knew the question that was coming. "I wasn't with him, Eric. He's the only one who's hurt. I just—"

"Where are you? Which hospital? Vancouver General? I can be there in a few hours. I can call their ER and see who's on duty … maybe someone I know is on. Either way, I'm coming."

If only it were that simple.

"We're not at a hospital. I—"

"What the hell are you thinking? You *have* to go to the hospital. There's no way you can take care of this on your own, Alex. Get your friend to the ER now."

She'd expected him to be the calm ER doctor — not this. Eric seemed almost as panicked as her.

"I can't." She turned to look at Mosi to shore up her courage before she plunged ahead. "We're in trouble, Eric. We can't go to a hospital … I have to do this."

She held her breath, listening to the silence, waiting for his voice. Eric was a compassionate doctor, but she was asking him to put aside his ethics.

"I need to see the injury," he finally said. "Are you able to video chat?"

Her deep exhale, like that of a drowning woman pulled from the deep, met his words. She checked the reception on her cell, frowning when she saw just a single bar.

"I don't think my signal is strong enough for that."

"But you can send a picture? Text me?"

"Yes. I'm doing it now." The phone held close to Mosi's thigh, she snapped two photos and sent them off. "It's a small wound, so there's not much to see."

"You said he was shot. How? What happened?"

She clutched the phone hard, her knuckles turning white. *What do I say?*

"He was running and took a bullet in his leg. The bullet's still in there ... I can't find an exit wound."

"Rifle or handgun?"

"Rifle. Probably a long-range, high-velocity sniper rifle. But the shooter was at least a mile away."

She held her breath, waiting for Eric's demand for more of an explanation, but it didn't come.

"I have the photo now," he said. "Where exactly is this wound?"

"Inner thigh ... maybe eight or nine inches above his knee."

"The medial thigh? Shit! Alex, this isn't something you want to mess with. There are major arteries running through there. If the femoral was nicked—"

"It isn't bleeding, and it hasn't been for at least five hours."

"Okay. That's good. That's really good. Now, can you put me on speakerphone so I can talk to him. What's your friend's name?"

"His name is Mosi." She set the phone on the bed and eased herself to sit on the mattress edge. "And he can hear you now, Eric."

"Mosi, we're going to run through some questions, but first I want to know if you're hurt anywhere else."

"No. Only my leg."

"Did you hit your head or lose consciousness at any point?

"No."

"Can you—"

"Wait..." Alex interjected. "Mosi, you were alone for an hour, maybe longer. How do you know that you didn't black out?"

Over the past four hours, Mosi had detailed everything he had seen in the mine and his escape from the guards. But he said little about the time he spent hidden in the trees, waiting for Paulo's return.

"I was awake the whole time," Mosi said. "I am sure of it."

Eric rattled off more questions, whether Mosi could put weight on his leg and walk, whether he had any numbness or tingling, and if he could wiggle his toes and feel some sensation there. This was the Eric she knew: a calm, steady force in the face of a storm.

"Alex, do you know how to check peripheral pulses?"

"I think so. It's been a while…" She rubbed her hands together. "There's one near the inside of the ankle, right?"

"That's right. Don't press too hard … you need a light touch."

She leaned over and rested her fingers near Mosi's ankle, shifting them a little at a time. "Nothing … no wait." She went quiet. "I can feel a pulse beneath my fingers. It's steady."

"Good. That's really good, Alex. I want you to cover the wound with—"

"What do you mean cover it?" She stared at Mosi to see his eyebrows raised in disbelief. "Doesn't the bullet have to come out?"

"There's no real reason to remove it, Alex. I'd guess that the bullet is embedded deep in the thigh muscle — it's going to hurt like hell for a while, but it'll heal. What have you got for pain meds?"

"Not much, Eric … just ibuprofen and acetaminophen."

"Dose him with ibuprofen every six hours and acetaminophen every four. It probably won't be enough, but it'll help."

"But can he walk—"

"Mosi's already done that, and putting weight on it isn't going to make things worse. What you don't need is infection. Clean the wound and change the dressing every twelve hours and smear whatever antibiotic ointment you have onto the wound."

"But how do we get through airport security with a bullet in his leg?" She blurted out the question without thought.

"Airport? Alex, where are you?"

He deserves the truth. Her eyes on Mosi, willing him to understand, she finally said, "Brazil."

"*Brazil?* What the hell's going on, Alex?"

"It's a long story." Mosi's tightly pressed lips kept her from saying any more. "We've got a flight booked out of here tonight, and I want to be on it."

Her statement was met with silence. She bit her lip, waiting for him to say something, anything.

"You should be okay at the airport, Alex. I mean, even if you were naked you might not get through a checkpoint without setting off one of those damn wands. They'll check his pockets, but then they'll let him through."

"And if they're using those new full-body scans?"

"That I'm less sure of … but he can object to one. Say he's afraid it will cause cancer or something. They'll do a manual search in that case."

That might work. Still, it might be safest to push on, to drive another eleven hours to São Paulo to pick up their African flight there. Belo Horizonte might be only four hours away, but if they left from that airport, they'd have to run the security gauntlet twice before they were safely out of the country.

She closed her eyes and took a slow, deliberate breath. Whether she could make it that far without sleep was the problem.

"Alex, your friend will be fine," Eric gently said. "Just get on that flight and come home."

If only it were that easy.

12

Novoteras Mine

JORGE STARED AT the unsmiling face of Benjamin Costa in a photo taken seven years ago. The round face, the contours of the nose, the lips — all resembled their corpse, but this was the face of a mere boy, not a man, and it lacked the distinctive chin scar.

The black ink fingerprints Carlos delivered were crude and smudged, not unexpected from a man untrained for such a task. But Jorge was not about to release the body to police without also providing the dead man's identity. He would give the police no reason to do anything more than record this thief's death.

Jorge painstakingly compared the whorls and ridges against the fingerprint cards on file for each of the fifteen miners who had failed to report for work this morning, searching for sufficient similarities to declare a match. Of three likely sets of prints, this man, Benjamin Costa, looked most like the man lying dead in the infirmary.

He set the photo aside and studied the opening page of Costa's personnel file. The twenty-four-year-old miner listed a wife, Eva, a match to the name whispered in the moments before death. Two children had been added as dependents in the past five years, but otherwise Costa's file read like that of so many of the miners — little education and a lifetime spent within fifty kilometres of this mine.

Costa had started with the mine when it opened and joined the Tunnel Five crew just a year later. Each year since, Sabion Lacerda's scrawled handwriting had recorded the young miner's exemplary performance and near-perfect attendance.

So why did Sabion not recognize him?

He looked up at the rap of knuckles against the door. "Come."

Carlos, hand gripped on the doorknob, leaned into the office. "The first of the men is here. Miguel Alegre." He swung the door open just enough for his charge to enter before he pulled it shut and retreated to the safety of the outer office.

Miguel, dressed in his civilian clothes, cut-off jeans and a yellow football jersey sporting Neymar's number, took just two steps into the office. His thumb dug a trail down his thigh, the only movement from a man firmly rooted in place.

The nerves were to be expected. Security guards had gone to Miguel's home to deliver him to the mine without explanation.

With a smile, Jorge waved the man forward. "Please, sit."

The thirty-year-old shuffled into the room and folded his stocky five-foot-seven body into the chair. If the man had been injured, he hid it well.

Jorge waited until the man's brown eyes were fixed on him before he asked his first question. "Why are you not at work today, Miguel?" He slipped a folder from the top of a stack of files on the corner of his desk and left it unopened in front of him.

"My children are sick." The words were softly spoken.

The gentle tone surprised him. Whether it was the miner's square jaw or his deep-set eyes, Jorge had expected a gruff answer.

"And your wife? Is she not able to care for them?"

"She is sick as well." He dropped his gaze.

Jorge opened the folder and flipped through its pages until he found what he needed. "You have worked at the mine for six years ... almost as long as Benjamin Costa." He tapped his pen against the desktop. "Do you know where he is?"

He was not about to let this man know that Benjamin Costa was dead.

Miguel simply shook his head before he quickly dropped his eyes to study his hands.

"But you have worked with him many times, you know him, you are probably friends."

"No," came the too-quick response. "We live far from each other. We do not see each other except at work."

But you know where he lives. A small piece of information readily given to defend himself but enough to contradict the denial of friendship.

"Six years is long enough to know a man. Who are his friends?"

"I do not know."

"Your family..." he paused. "Were you with them last night?"

The cocked head, the rapid blinking, both announced confusion over the question. "Yes. Of course."

If asked, this man's wife would lie to protect him. But Miguel now understood that he was a suspect.

"Does your wife know Eva Costa?"

"No." Miguel's hands clenched into white-knuckled fists.

Jorge caught the subtle move, a telling sign that this question had hit a nerve.

He ran his finger down the front page of Miguel's file until he found the information he sought. "You live in Rubelita?" he asked, naming a neighbouring town of under ten thousand.

"No," he countered. "Outside of Rubelita, near my father's farm."

"But you go to town, to the cafés, or maybe play football in Rubelita with Benjamin Costa?"

"No." He dropped his eyes to his lap and fingered the edge of his jersey. "I go straight home from the mine. My wife is sick. She has cancer."

His chest tightened as understanding over Miguel's discomfort at the mention of his wife's name dawned. Jorge had seen too many fellow officers bully suspects, take advantage of their weakness, but it was something he resisted. A cornered man gave you only what he thought you wanted, not the truth you needed.

"Go." He waved his hand. "Take care of your family."

Miguel scrambled out the chair and out the door without a word. With the door open, Jorge could hear the nervous voices, the swift footsteps. Every man in this building was on edge, each watching the steady parade of guards and miners to enter Jorge's office, each worried that they would be the next to be interrogated.

Jorge picked up the list of miners who had failed to show up for their morning shift, Benjamin Costa among them. Their injured thief was likely on this list, a man home nursing his wounds or already on the run. He would know that he could not pass naked through mine security without revealing his injuries.

But the driver — he was a different matter. The man had nothing to hide, and his safest choice was to return to work as though nothing had happened.

Sabion?

The man had shown revulsion at the sight of the dead body, but Jorge saw no fear in his face. Still, there was some reason why Sabion refused to identify Benjamin Costa, and the question of just how many men were involved still remained.

He snatched up the phone and dialled Carlos. "Bring me the personnel file of every man who works in Tunnel Five, and when they are done with their shift I want them brought here."

Jorge did not dare shut down work in Tunnel Five, not with their current production so far below the quota of rock demanded at week's end. Shen Li had little tolerance for failure, and the mine's head engineer, Tim Wong, would use a shutdown to firmly shift blame Jorge's way.

He stared down at the list of names, convinced his thief hid there.

I will find him.

13

Belo Horizonte, Brazil

MOSI OPENED HIS EYES to a room he did not recognize. He glanced over at the twin bed next to him, expecting to find Alex, but found only covers cast aside. In the dusty beam of light that spilled through the closed curtains he saw the worn desk with the bright red first aid kit open beside an old-style TV, and in the corner his backpack, but not hers.

She is gone. She had lain down as he had, exhausted by their four-hour drive from Diamantina to this Belo Horizonte motel, and he had not heard her leave.

Beside him, the glowing numbers on the clock radio read 5:17 p.m. He fumbled for the switch beneath the plastic lampshade and stretched for his cell phone, a move rewarded by swift, sharp pain.

Head slumped back against the pillow, he watched the slow spin of the ceiling fan waiting for the throbbing pain to subside. Soon they would be on a plane. Soon he would be home.

He slid his legs over the edge of the bed and pushed his fists against the mattress to propel himself onto both feet. For a moment he stood there, easing weight slowly onto his injured leg before he took his first step. And when the pain grew no worse, he slowly crossed the tile floor toward the bathroom.

At the sink, he wetted a towel, pressing its coolness against his face. He did not hear the click of the door lock, only Alex's brief greeting.

She rushed in like a cheetah, fast and sure, slamming the door behind her too quickly for anyone to catch a glimpse of the room — or him. In her hands was a large bag that she set down on the desk.

Back turned to him, busy with the bag, she said, "I was able to reach my dad. He's going to book a flight out of Bogotá tomorrow … he'll meet us in Arusha."

He stood in the bathroom doorway, braced against its frame. He could hear the excitement in her voice, the happiness. Alex had spoken to Brian only a handful of times in the last six weeks, and he knew it disturbed her. He had heard them argue about Brian's decision not to bring his satellite phone, his communication lifeline in remote locations. But he also understood Brian's reluctance to carry anything that might link him to Alex, especially given the danger he faced in Colombia.

"I checked, and both our flights are on time. We have another three hours before we have to be at the Belo airport." The rustle of paper and the squeak of Styrofoam accompanied her words. "I brought some soup and those *empanadas* you like." She twisted back to face him. "Which—" She stopped midsentence. "Mosi, you're bleeding!"

He stared down at the blood that trailed down his naked leg. *How?*

And then Alex was there, next to him.

"We have to get you back to bed." She grabbed a towel and balled it against his thigh. "Hang on to me."

He wrapped his arm around her shoulder, and with Alex's hand clamped over the towel they hobbled to the bed.

"Easy…" Alex cradled his leg in her hands and helped him lie down on the bed before she sat on the edge of the mattress. "How long has it been bleeding?"

"I do not know. I did not see any blood when I got up." He clenched his teeth when she ground her palm against the towel. "It is painful. Much worse than before."

"Keep whatever pressure on it that you can." She bumped the edge of the bed in her hurry to stand. "I'm going to call Eric."

Cell in hand, she paced the floor at the foot of the bed. She shook her head. "No answer." After a quick message, she pushed the phone back in her pocket.

"Alex," he said. "Leave me here and get on the plane. I will go to a clinic and take my chances."

"No way. We're getting on that flight together." She jammed her hands on her hips. "Would you have left me to the lions when I sprained my ankle? Or walked away that time I got the truck stuck crossing the muddy river?"

He wanted to argue that she had been just a child then, that he had been responsible for her in the Serengeti. But she had grown into a woman as stubborn as her father, and he would not win this argument.

"We just have to keep pressure on that wound and stop the bleeding." She turned to the first aid kit. "I have lots of gauze and—"

He heard but a single note of her ring tone before she leapt up to answer. *Eric.*

She kept her voice low, but he could hear her fear.

"Okay." She came to stand next to his bed and lifted the towel with her free hand. "I'm looking at the wound. There's lots of blood, but it doesn't look arterial … it's not bright red." She dabbed the wound with the edge of the towel and watched the crimson streak that reappeared on his skin. "And it's sort of seeping out of the wound."

"Right. Peripheral pulses." She pressed three fingers near his anklebone. "I can't feel it." She slid her fingers over the skin. "I can't feel it, Eric. It's there, it *has* to be."

Her fingers continued their fumbled search, but her attention was on Eric's voice.

"We can't go to the hospital," she argued. "I just—"

Mosi rested his hand over hers. "You found this pulse before, and you will find it again. Put the phone down, and come … sit on the bed, so you are closer."

"You're right. You're right." She dropped the phone on the bed and perched on the side of the bed. "I need less pressure."

Mosi barely felt her fingers this time. And the smile she flashed announced her success even before she grabbed her phone.

"Eric, I found it! That means there's good blood flow to the leg. I just need to keep pressure on it for a while, and he'll be fine, right?"

Her head bobbed in unison with each "yes" she answered to questions he could not hear.

"*What?*" She dug her fingers into her thigh. "Eric, we can't—"

Head down, Alex paced the room, one arm tight across her chest. She and Eric argued, but about what he did not know. In time the conversation quieted, and from her words he knew that Eric comforted her.

Good. It had been a long time since such a man had been in Alex's life. In Tanzania a woman her age would have children by now, and he hoped soon Alex would find such joy. He closed his eyes at the thought of his sweet children and breathed deep.

I will see them soon.

He heard Alex sigh, and when he opened his eyes he saw her slumped in the wooden chair near the window. Her face, like that of a hunter who had lost his prey, spoke of her despair before she uttered a word.

"Eric doesn't think it's a good idea for us to get on that plane yet. He thinks the bullet must have shifted, and that's what started the bleeding. If the bullet is next to an artery or major vein, and it moves again..." She stood and pushed the curtain aside to stare out at the parking lot. Only when she dropped her hand and turned back toward him did she continue.

"There are just too many things that can go wrong while we're in the air. He wants to give the wound a chance to heal, to stabilize, so it won't open up again. At least twenty-four hours."

"Then we must move. It is safer to go to São Paulo than to stay here."

"Eight hours, Mosi ... it's another eight-hour drive to São Paulo." She walked over to the bed and sat down beside him before she spoke again.

"We should get rid of the truck and rent another one. That broken back window and the bullet holes are just too obvious in the daytime. If we leave the truck at the Belo airport, they might think we flew out of there … it buys us some time."

"It is a good decision." He folded his hand over hers. "But if they find the truck, they will learn my name. You must promise to leave the country without me if I am arrested at the São Paulo airport."

"*No!*" She jumped up as though bitten by a snake. "I'm not leaving you behind. Not like this."

Back turned to him, she stood at the desk, clutching its edge. "We don't know if the guards saw enough of the licence plate to track us down. Even if they did, it will take time for them to start searching this far from the mine." She swivelled to face him. "And that piece of rock you took could be nothing more than a worthless piece of tourmaline. I need to take another look at it."

The rock they had worked so hard to obtain was soon cradled in her hand beneath the bedside light.

"I can see a little blue and purple if the light hits it just right, but somehow I expected raw tanzanite to look less yellow-brown."

"In Tanzania we call this colour 'diesel' because it looks like the fuel. It will not be possible to see the true potential of this rock until it is heated and cut. Only then will you see the blue-violet gem you know."

She closed her hand around the rock. "What if we're wrong?"

"And if we are right?" He shifted without thinking, and with lips pressed tight, he waited for the pain to pass. "They will not risk calling police, Alex. But they will hunt us. "

She watched him, wordless, for a full minute before she strode back to the desk.

"Paulo has to know something by now." From the front zippered pouch of her backpack she pulled out one of the prepaid cell phones they had purchased when they first landed in Brazil. Untraceable.

Phone tight to her ear, she stood with one arm folded across her chest. She finally shook her head.

"Nothing. His shift ended two hours ago. He should be home." She rocked from side to side. "Something's wrong, Mosi."

14

São Paulo, Brazil

SHEN SKIMMED THE LATEST Long Bridge Merchant Group financial figures, the dip in profits as obvious as a flare in darkness. Last month's sinking of a heavily-loaded cargo ship in an Atlantic storm had been the start of a string of bad luck that ended with the arrest of two of their diamond couriers at the Amsterdam airport just weeks later. Several million dollars worth of weapons now sat at the bottom of the ocean, a loss almost equal to the bribes and expenses needed to erase all records of the incident in Amsterdam — and to eliminate the couriers foolish enough to be caught.

Chairman Jianyu Wei accepted that he held no power over nature, but he refused to accept mistakes made by men in his employ. Questions about how the couriers were caught smuggling two packets of flawless Russian diamonds dogged Cheung Zhou, the Beijing--educated lawyer responsible for their European operations. They'd sat together at the executive table for the past eight years, and Shen thought the man careful and clever, but whether Zhou would find a way to appease the Chairman, or a newcomer would rise to take his seat at the table, remained to be seen.

It also made this a dangerous time to deliver news of the Novoteras mine break-in — not without the thieves in his grasp.

In just ten days, Shen was expected to deliver the largest ever shipment of gemstones to a waiting ship in the São Paulo harbour. Only after the gems were cut into exquisite jewels worth more than ten million dollars would they finance the acquisition of the surface-to-air missiles, assault rifles, and other armaments the Chairman promised to deliver. And only when the military weapons were in the hands of the buyer prepared to pay triple their worth would Shen's obligation be met.

This theft jeopardizes everything.

He jerked at the ring of the phone, relieved to see a Brazilian area code and not a Chinese one.

"What have you learned?" he asked Jorge without preamble.

"I have identified the dead man as Benjamin Costa. He is one of the miners working Tunnel Five."

"*Tunnel Five?*" His pulse raced. "You believe that is where these men went?"

"I do not know. The air shaft they entered leads directly to Tunnels One, Two, and Five. But this man, Benjamin Costa, has worked in Tunnel Five for seven years."

Shen stared out at the blackness of the night. Just two men at Novoteras, the engineer and geologist, knew the truth about the mineral seam mined in Tunnel Five. Both had been hand-picked by the Chairman, and neither would dare cross their benefactor. No, this had to be a simple theft from the tourmaline-rich shallow levels.

Silva must be wrong.

"And you're sure that Benjamin Costa had not even a single gemstone on him?"

"Yes, sir. I have searched very carefully. Costa did not steal anything from the mine. I cannot say the same for the man who escaped."

"I want him found." Shen balled his hand into a fist. "He must work at the mine ... one of the guards or a miner. He would not dare show his face there today."

"I have personally met with every man who did not show up for work at the mine today, and none of them is injured. Either the man who escaped was not shot, or he does not work at the mine. As for the driver, it may yet turn out that he is one of our mine workers ... we are checking every vehicle."

Shen might not like the answer, but he couldn't fault Jorge's methodical approach. Still, he needed more — a name, a reason for this theft — and he needed it now.

"Sir, I believe it is necessary to involve the police," Jorge continued. "I would like to search the home of Benjamin Costa and interview his family, but I have no authority outside the mine gates."

Authority? A headache that would not be of concern in China. Jorge did not yet realize that he could do whatever was necessary — the judges, police, and government officials on Shen's payroll all but guaranteed it.

"The police will not concern themselves with anything you do. You will continue to handle this investigation yourself."

The sharp intake of breath revealed Jorge's surprise, but he simply said, "I will send my guards out immediately."

Good. Shen's lips curled into a smile. He'd chosen well in selecting this ambitious police officer from the three English-speaking men offered to him. Any of the men with their shiny reputations would have served as the shield of legitimacy, but in Jorge Silva he saw something else — more than ambition, he'd seen the man's fear. Fear that made Silva controllable.

"What of the other men who work in Tunnel Five?"

"I have only just sent them home. I will continue to investigate each of these men carefully, but the air shaft cover was unlocked from inside the mine, something every man who works here knows how to do. We cannot assume our thief is one of the men in Tunnel Five."

"And you've found no evidence? No fingerprints?"

"We have found no useful fingerprints on the metal handles of the air shaft cover. The two hundred feet of ladder inside the shaft will be covered in fingerprints, and it is very difficult to lift prints from its rough wood surface or to tell fresh from old prints. Our time is better spent looking for the truck."

Shen shifted in his chair. He'd seen rapid-fire changes in his own world, and the world of forensics had probably also changed in ways Jorge might not know of since he left policing. Shen would have to quietly find someone who could advise him in this matter. For now, he had no choice but to follow Jorge's lead.

"So…" He tapped his jade ring against the desk. "What do you need?"

"We have just two numbers of the licence plate of the truck that waited on the highway. It is described as new and expensive, so it is not likely owned by one of the miners, but I would like a list of every vehicle owned by anyone employed at this mine. And I would like a list of all current SUV rentals."

Shen's lips curled into a smile. Jorge would know that such information was not easily obtained, even by police. He had to know, too, that legal methods would not deliver these lists.

"Is it possible to send men to the airports and bus stations? Our injured man may try to leave the country — if he has not already left."

"Yes, of course." Shen reached for a gold pen. "Which airports?"

"Rio, São Paulo, Brasilia, and Belo Horizonte. The Belo airport should be the priority because it is closest and gives many connections to the others." Jorge paused. "We also need to consider border crossings into Argentina or Paraguay … but they are unlikely to try that without a different vehicle. There is at least one bullet hole in the truck, and my men are sure the back window is cracked. So we must also have a list of all vehicles rented today."

Jorge thought of things others might miss, but this manhunt would cost Shen more than one favour from his carefully cultivated network of contacts. And it would take time.

Shen fingered the edge of his silk tie. "What have you told the workers about the break-in?"

"Almost nothing. Only the supervisors know that Benjamin Costa is dead."

"Tomorrow you will announce that Costa was shot while trying to break into the mine. You will not mention the air shaft or that Costa was in the mine. Only an attempt. Is that clear?"

"Yes, sir."

"And you will offer a reward for anyone who comes forward with information."

Money. A powerful motivator.

"A reward? I fear it will bring every man in the mine to my office. We will spend days following up on information of little value. It is too early for—"

"Do it."

15

São Paulo, Brazil

SHEN CLICKED OPEN the photo sent by the manager of his Colombian emerald mine, a grainy black-and-white image of the man who had toured the mine just two weeks ago.

Unlike Novoteras, this emerald mine was not closed to visitors, and the mine manager had signed in the visitor, a geologist named John Michaels, without asking for even the simplest of identification. The manager had been quick to try to rectify the oversight, but his security team had found no record of such a man at the local hotels. It left this photo pulled from security cameras, their only clue to the man's identity.

Until he was found, Shen must assume that Tabitha Metals was under investigation — under attack.

Shen dialled a private number in Shenzhen, China.

"Yes." The single word was spoken in a hushed voice by Chairman Wei after just two rings.

He's in a meeting. As he almost always was when Shen called. But the Chairman of Long Bridge Merchant Group did not hesitate to interrupt even the most serious conversations to answer this particular phone.

"Chairman Wei, there has been a break-in at the Novoteras mine. One man is dead, and we are searching for his partners. We do not know if they are in possession of any gemstones, and we do know their purpose ... questions are also being asked at our Colombian mine."

The quick intake of breath warned of the Chairman's displeasure.

His words, when they came, were veiled and controlled. "That is most unfortunate."

Shen did not expect him to say more, not in the presence of others in the meeting room. The sixty-year-old Chairman had risen to the top of the business world through careful words and thought, a necessity for those under the watchful eye of the Communist Party.

Chairman Wei had quietly acquired businesses in more than thirty countries before the age of forty, amassing enough foreign dollars to build a much-rivalled portfolio of real estate and business in China, and one that guaranteed power and privilege. Few would suspect that the man who controlled Long Bridge Merchant Group was also one of the most powerful arms dealers in the world.

"I trust it will not affect your deadline?"

"It is a minor annoyance only," Shen said with more conviction than he felt. "The ship will leave São Paulo as planned. The gemstones will be in the Hong Kong cutting rooms by next week."

Three gem cutters, among the best in the world, waited in Hong Kong for the arrival of the shipment. They would remain locked in isolation, away from prying eyes, until every rough stone had been cut into a perfect gem.

"See to it. I expect resolution of the other matter before the shipment leaves port."

His chest tightened at these simple words that gave him just ten days to find his thieves. "I—"

But the Chairman had already clicked off.

Shen held the cell phone, considering one name after another, men who might be trusted to help find his thieves.

But unless this was a simple theft, a crack in his network had occurred.

Shen had built Tabitha Metals slowly, acquiring both profitable and speculative ventures in Argentina, Colombia, and Brazil. Unlike the gold, diamond and emerald mines, the Novoteras mine had promised only a small profit from its tourmaline operation, but it too served an important role: legitimacy.

Under Shen's control, every mine expanded its operation and its workforce, paying almost double the salaries men expected. Tabitha Metals quickly gained a reputation as a well-funded company, and local governments laid out the welcome mat.

And then an exploratory hole dug by a newly-arrived geologist from the China office to map out an expansion of the Novoteras mine instead discovered a mineral deposit like no other.

Tanzanite. A coveted blue-violet gem found only in Tanzania, Africa, and believed to exist in no other location on Earth.

A one in a million chance. According to the geologist, those were the odds of finding this unique gemstone anywhere but within a sixteen-kilometre area of the Merelani Hills of Tanzania. Even the gem's discovery in the 1960s seemed a once-in-a-lifetime event: in the aftermath of a lightning-sparked fire, stunning blue gemstones appeared as if by magic to a Maasai tribesman. Although this legend could never be substantiated, it was consistent with what Shen had learned about this gemstone: only under extreme heat would the blue-violet colour of tanzanite be revealed.

Shen had seen the potential immediately. Like its colour, sales of the tanzanite could be hidden from view — the Novoteras mine held buried treasure that carried none of the risk of their smuggling operations.

To the outside world, the Novoteras mine produced only tourmaline, and each shipment was fully reported and legally exported from Brazil. Even the miners assumed that the brownish tanzanite with its hints of blue and violet was tourmaline, a gem that appeared in so many colours, including blue. And the profits from the sale of the tanzanite, millions of dollars in excess of what tourmaline would generate, never need be reported. Not even the Tabitha Metals staff knew the truth.

Shen slipped every piece of tanzanite from the Novoteras mine into the gem trade as though it had been mined in Tanzania. He went further to introduce the Brazilian gems in such small amounts that the price per carat, which rose steadily as the supply of tanzanite in the Merelani Hills diminished, remained unaffected.

But even he never imagined that the Novoteras mine held billions of dollars of untraceable wealth — enough to spark his meteoric rise to the Chairman's inner circle.

I will not see it end now.

It had taken time to cultivate the relationships necessary to build the Novoteras mine with minimal interference, to keep it a quiet operation of no interest. Whether someone knew the truth about the mine or had quietly whispered their suspicion to another, he wasn't sure. What he did know was that a greed-fuelled theft was far preferable to an outside investigation.

Even a hint of the true nature of the mine would deliver government officials with their expert geologists to his doorstep. Once they descended into Tunnel Five, they would quickly discover the tanzanite, and Tabitha Metals would come under intense scrutiny.

He was confident that accountants would not find the money skimmed from the profits of their other South American mines, and the smuggled gemstones and gold used like cash in the black market would not be discovered. The Novoteras mine was enough, though, to send him to jail.

Only the thinnest silk strand tied Tabitha Metals to Long Bridge Merchant Group. Chairman Jianyu Wei would never feel the sting of an investigation — Shen alone would bear the burden.

A jail cell in Brazil might be the result, but the Chinese crackdown on corruption made it far more likely that he'd be thrown into a Chinese prison, a hole from which he would never emerge. His gentle mother, a poet, had barely avoided such a fate herself.

The memory drew his eye to the Ming vase with its cobalt blue lotus blossoms, Mother's favourite flower. He seldom saw his widowed mother more than once a year, the minimum obligation of the elder son. While he provided for her, he'd left her care in the hands of his younger brother and his dutiful wife.

Uncle, the man who had shaped his life, was the one he saw most often. In his pin-striped suit, Uncle had stood tall while Shen had received his degree at Cambridge, and when Shen joined Long Bridge Merchant Group, Uncle had bragged about his successful nephew to all who would listen. If Shen were arrested, disgraced, Uncle would not survive the shame.

I cannot fail.

16

Belo Horizonte, Brazil

ALEX MANOEUVRED her truck into an empty spot in a crowded aisle of the Belo Horizonte airport extended parking lot. The lot was busy, both a blessing and a curse.

There was nothing she could do about the truck's bullet-ridden frame, the broken glass in the cargo area, or the missing back window. Once the truck was found, police would be called and Mosi's name would become known. Whether authorities would link the truck to the mine break-in was less clear.

Mosi was right. If what they'd stolen really was tanzanite, then the Novoteras mine owners wouldn't risk involving police, at least not officially. But to hide a secret like this took massive power and money, enough to control an army of corrupt officers, never mind private security. Their fate rested on timing. They needed this truck to be ignored just long enough for them to escape Brazil.

Eyes on the rear-view mirror, she waited until a smartly dressed man parked one row over pulled his suitcase from the trunk and set off down the seemingly endless row of cars before she stepped out of the truck. Backpack slung over her shoulder, she took one last look at the back window of the truck. From a distance it might look intact, but not up close. She had to hope that the lot wasn't routinely patrolled.

She turned her back to the truck and headed for the terminal, comforted by the sight of a couple of cracked back windows and a crumpled fender as she passed by the row of parked vehicles.

Inside, she inhaled a deep breath of pizza and hot dogs as she wove past families and business travellers alike. She'd only been in this airport once before, nine years ago when she'd first graduated from the University of British Columbia, and she remembered nothing of its layout. Most of her work took her through the mega-airports of São Paulo, Buenos Aires, and Santiago, and even those she didn't know well. Like all airports, though, the car rental companies were crowded near the luggage carousels in the arrivals area, and that's where she headed.

Hand tight on her backpack strap, she wove between people lugging suitcases through the terminal until she spotted the bank of signs she sought.

She picked the shortest line and waited behind a man dressed in khakis and work boots, likely one of the many foreigners who arrived here to work the mines. At least in her hiking boots and yellow plaid work shirt, she blended in.

Except. She gave a quick downward glance at her clothes, reassured that her dark jeans hid the bloodstains she knew were there. She tucked her hair behind her ears, smoothing the shoulder-length strands, wishing for a comb.

The man ahead of her smiled as he turned away from the counter clerk, keys in hand. She quickly took his place at the counter and just a few minutes later held keys of her own.

In a quiet corner of the airport, she pulled out her cell phone and dialled Paulo again. They'd called him only twice before today, each time to arrange a meeting and nothing more, and each time they'd done it from this prepaid cell phone. It offered them anonymity, but each call showed up in Paulo's call history, something that put him in jeopardy.

I have to know that he's okay.

She paced a tight circle, listening to each ring, coming to an abrupt stop when she finally heard his voice.

"Paulo. Thank god! I tried calling earlier but there was no answer. I've been so worried. Are you okay?"

"I—" His voice cracked. "Benjamin is dead."

The news hit like a punch. Hand clamped against her mouth, she slid down the wall to a crouch.

"I have only just now come home from the mine. The mine manager had many questions for me."

She fought back panic. Even though they'd all known about the risk of arrest, none of them were truly prepared for it, least of all Paulo.

"I can get you out of the country. Now. Tonight. We—"

"I do not want to leave my home. And these men who run the mine know nothing. They questioned many people today, everyone who worked with Benjamin. They are searching."

"For what? What did they want?"

"They asked about my friendship with Benjamin and whether I owned a truck. I told them the truth."

She forced air deep into her lungs. Guards hadn't seen the licence plate, not if they were searching for the owner of the truck. It bought them a little time, but was it enough?

"And nothing else?"

"Only where I was last night. I told them I was at home with my family, asleep, and my wife will tell them this too. They do not know about you or Mosi."

They'd taken a risk using their own first names with Benjamin and Paulo, but neither miner knew anything more about them. Still, coupled with a description of them, it might be enough to lead police to them.

"Be careful … please. If the police—" She pressed her fingertips against her temple. "Hide the money we gave you. Make sure you can explain the calls from this phone number." She stared down at the tiled floor. "And Paulo, promise that you will call me if you are in trouble. I will do everything I can to help you."

Paulo had barely hung up before she scrambled to her feet and punched in Tracey's number. Her dad had warned her not to tell Tracey anything about this project in Brazil — a first since she'd joined him as a partner in his geological consulting company. But right now she didn't give a damn. She needed help, and Tracey could give it to her.

"Tracey, this is urgent." There was no time for their usual small talk, not now. "My friend needs a criminal lawyer, a good one. Someone who works in one of the bigger cities like Belo Horizonte."

"I'll have one for you in a few hours. Do you want the lawyer to contact your friend or—"

"Just email it to me. No, wait…" Her fingernails dug into her palm. "Don't put anything in writing. Call me when you have a name."

"I won't leave the name in a voice message either. If I can't reach you, I'll just tell you to call me."

She forced a breath. Tracey had bailed enough of the geologists at Graham and Associates out of trouble that she knew the ropes.

"We have to forget about the flight out of Belo Horizonte. I'm going to push on to São Paulo, but there's no way we'll make our 3:00 a.m. flight. I need you to rebook it … something after 4:00 p.m. tomorrow. Business class seats if you can find them — I don't care about the cost."

First class tickets might ease their way through airport security, their final hurdle out of the country. There'd be added attention from the flight attendants, but they'd also be left alone to sleep, and the flat beds would at least give Mosi some relief.

"I think there's a British Airways flight—"

"No connecting flights in Europe. I want to head straight to Africa. Nairobi or Johannesburg … something like that."

At least if Mosi were on the African continent, she could get him home more easily.

"And I'm going to need a hotel in São Paulo … something near the airport, with underground parking." Alex prowled the floor as she spoke. "Make it a prepaid room, and book it in your name, no, wait—" She couldn't link Tracey to them. "My dad. Put the room in his name and add mine as a guest."

Alex would still have to show her passport at the front desk to check-in, but Brian Graham's name would be first to show up in any enquiry, not hers.

"What's going on, Alex?"

The question stopped her in her tracks. The two women were as close as sisters, and she trusted Tracey with her life, but she couldn't tell her — not this. She didn't dare involve her friend any more than she already had.

"Later, okay…" She didn't give Tracey a chance to argue. "What time is my dad's flight?"

"Tomorrow, 11:55 p.m. out of Bogotá. He's routing through Paris and Nairobi … arrives in Arusha two days later at 8:35 a.m."

"You couldn't get him something that leaves earlier?"

"Absolutely, but he insisted on this one. He said there's someone he has to meet in the morning."

The engineer. Brian must have managed a meeting with the Tabitha Metals consulting engineer.

"If you hear from my dad before I do, tell him what happened. Tell him we've been delayed. And if you can't get us into Arusha, let him know where to meet us."

"You're okay, right? I know you're in trouble, and I need to know that you're okay … Mosi too."

Her eyes closed. *It's as if she knows.* Tracey's intuition was legendary, but no matter how much her friend might have guessed, she could never imagine the truth.

"We're okay," Alex said with as much conviction as she could muster. "We just need to get out of Brazil. First flight you can find tomorrow night, Tracey."

Alex only hoped it wouldn't come too late.

17

Novoteras Mine

JORGE POURED a glass of water and set it in front of Eva Costa.

Five hundred American dollars. Not what he had expected would be found in this morning's search of Benjamin Costa's home. But enough to bring Benjamin's widow into his office.

Eva Costa sat in front of him, her shoulders hunched in the worn black wool coat she had yet to remove.

"There is nothing I can tell you," she quietly said. "I do not know anything about this money."

"The smallest detail can help."

He poured water for himself, giving her time to consider his question, before he spoke again.

"Did your husband meet with anyone unusual? Or talk to someone on the phone that you do not know?"

Eva stared into her lap and ran her fingers around the crumpled tissue tightly gripped in one hand. Soon she would break down in tears, and Jorge would learn nothing more.

"These men who forced him to come to the mine killed him. Not the guards. If you know something, then we can arrest them and they will pay for their crime."

His argument did nothing — she refused to look at him or speak a word.

A knock at the door broke the quiet tension. He had warned his men that he was not to be disturbed. For Carlos to disobey meant there was news.

"Please excuse me." He pushed his chair back and stood. "I will be only a moment."

He stepped out into the hallway and eased the door shut behind him. "What is it?" he quietly asked.

"Sabion Lacerda asked to see you." Carlos pointed to his left. "I put him in the empty office down the hall."

Jorge raised his eyebrow at this unexpected turn.

He swivelled on his heel and hurried down the hall. Sabion did not turn when he entered the room and closed the door. Only when Jorge eased himself into the chair behind the desk did Sabion's eyes meet his.

"What is it you wish to tell me, Sabion?"

"The dead man, he is Benjamin Costa."

"Yes, I know. But what I do not understand is why you did not tell me this yesterday when you saw his body."

"I was unsure." Sabion shifted in his chair.

"Unsure? You have worked with him for six years, yet you did not recognize him."

Sabion slumped in his chair but said nothing.

He watched him for a full minute, waiting for the miner to fill the uncomfortable silence. But no words came.

"Why did you not mention this when you came to my office last night? Why wait until today? Do you come forward now only because of the reward?"

"No. No." Sabion jerked forward as though slammed from behind. "I was unsure. It was only when Benjamin did not show up for his shift that I believed it might be him. Only when I went to his house last night and found that he was missing did I know it was him."

And yet the widow had made no mention of a visit from her husband's supervisor. If the woman hid this simple truth from him, then she hid more … much more.

"Did you break into the mine with Benjamin?"

"I would never do such a thing!" The man's eyes bulged. "I was not at the mine with him. I knew *nothing* of his plan to do anything so foolish."

Jorge searched the man's face and saw the slick sheen of perspiration on his smooth forehead. "I do not believe you."

"But you *must.*"

"Why? You lied to me once already when you refused to identify the dead man. Why should I believe you?"

The man's eyes darted everywhere, as though searching for escape.

"Answer me."

"I was afraid." Sabion looked away.

"You will cooperate now or I will have you arrested." He let his words sink in. He had no such power, but Sabion wouldn't know that. "How well did you know Benjamin Costa?"

"He is — he was a good miner. Friendly with everyone." Sabion ran a hand over his chin. "But he was much younger than me. Just a boy."

"Yet you knew him well enough to go to his house."

"Yes." Sabion nodded. "I have worked with him for seven years … but we were not friends."

"But you know which of the men were Benjamin's friends."

"He was friends with all the men…" He dropped his eyes.

"I want specific names," Jorge pressed.

"He was friends with all the men I supervise," he insisted. "I heard them talk about football games and their children, but I do not know which of these men were his true friends. There are younger men who can give you better information."

Jorge pressed his pen point into the yellow pad. "Names."

"Paulo Alvarez, Lucas Santos, and Victor Rossi."

Jorge scribbled the three names he recognized from the Tunnel Five crew, all of these men seen in his office yesterday. "Would these men be foolish enough to break into the mine?"

"No. But…" He bit his lip. "There was a black man in Coronel Murta asking questions about the mine several weeks ago. He spoke to me."

Jorge leaned forward. "What did he want?"

"He wanted to know about the brown stones we mine here. He wanted to see one."

Jorge drew in a sharp breath. "He asked you to steal a stone?"

Sabion nodded. "I told him it was impossible. That he should forget this idea."

True or not? It was just as likely that Sabion was covering his tracks, afraid he had been seen talking to this stranger. Or that he wanted to collect the reward.

"How long ago did this happen?"

"Two weeks, maybe three."

Enough time to find a willing miner and enough time for more than one entry into the mine.

"Did he give you his name?" Sabion shook his head. "Where did this conversation take place?"

"In a cafe where many of the men go after a football game."

Miguel Alegre's football jersey flashed in his mind. Like so many of the young men who worked the deep, Miguel proudly wore the jersey of his favourite Brazilian player, and football consumed whatever leisure time he had. An empty field, a riverbank — it would be easy to track men from the mine to those spots where they played.

"You will stay here and record everything you remember about this man." Jorge slid the pad of paper across the desk and set his pen on top of it. "His height, his clothes, how he talked — no detail is insignificant."

Jorge rose from his chair and left the room without another word. In the hallway, more men were gathered, waiting to be ushered into his office.

As he neared Carlos's desk, the security officer looked up at him with bloodshot eyes.

"Have you found anything?"

"More than a dozen vehicles so far match the partial licence plate."

"Make any truck rented for at least two weeks your priority."

He turned to face the closed door to his office. Now he would find out exactly what Eva Costa knew about the men her husband played football with.

And the foreigner Benjamin had met.

18

São Paulo, Brazil

THREE HUNDRED MILES, six hundred kilometres of dark highways. Twice, Alex had been forced to pull over to close her eyes, if only for a few minutes, which had pushed this trip to ten hours.

They had remained at the Belo Horizonte motel for just four hours more, long enough to be certain that Mosi's leg had stopped bleeding and to give her a few hours of sleep. Then they were back on the highway with Mosi stretched out in the back seat, this time at least, without the worry that their vehicle would attract attention from police. Even if they found the truck she'd left at the Belo Horizonte airport, police would not easily link them to this new rental in her name alone.

Still, each time a set of headlights appeared in the rear-view mirror, Alex's hands tightened against the wheel. Only now that they neared the São Paulo airport, and she parked their car in an empty spot on the lowest level of the underground garage, did she relax.

"I'll be back as soon as I have a key to the room. And if I'm not—"

"You will be back." Mosi smiled. "No one knows your name, Alex. You will not have trouble."

"You're right. I know you're right." She grabbed her backpack from the front seat. "But I won't believe it until we're on that plane."

She left him to cross the cold cement of the dimly lit garage in search of the elevator she'd seen when they drove in. There were other cars parked there, but she couldn't keep herself from checking over her shoulder with each echoed step.

You're safe. But Brazil's high crime stats pushed back. Only when she rounded the corner and saw the elevator did she feel herself breathe.

She pressed the lobby button and reached for her wallet and passport as soon as the doors slid closed. And when she emerged into the spacious lobby, she hurried past plush seating and a cozy bar, focused on the front desk and its sole clerk.

"I have a room booked under Brian Graham." She slid her passport and a credit card across the reception desk toward the acne-scarred clerk. She forced herself to keep her gaze forward, watching the young man's slender fingers tap the keyboard in search of their stay details.

She had no idea what Benjamin might have said to police before he died. Paulo wasn't yet implicated in the break-in, but Benjamin could easily have given up their names to police. Just how much of a manhunt that would trigger, she didn't know.

The mine owners weren't going to draw attention to the Novoteras mine — not if the piece of rock in her bag was tanzanite. It might be the only reason they would make it out of the country.

The clerk handed her the receipt and waited for her signature before giving her a key and wishing her a good day. She smiled at him, but he had already turned away, indifferent.

Thank you, Tracey! The desk clerk, so used to business travellers arriving at all hours of the day, had thought nothing of Alex's 8:00 a.m. check-in. And this high-end hotel chain had everything they needed — food, an ATM and reliable internet service.

She moved quickly, following the now familiar route through the poorly lit garage toward their parked car. Still, she clutched her bag tight against her body and listened for the slightest noise. Only when she saw Mosi open the back door of the car did she slow.

"I've got a key," she said as he eased himself to stand. "I'll come back down for whatever we need. We just need to get you into the room. We'll have to switch elevators in the lobby, but the front desk is around the corner."

Even with her arm wrapped tightly around Mosi's waist, she

scanned the dark corners of the garage, watching for movement. And when they finally arrived at the elevator, she gratefully entered its mirrored embrace.

"Just a few minutes more, and we'll be in the room." She smiled and stepped through the doors that slid open to the lobby. "I'll be so glad to get some sleep and—"

The surprised faces of a couple loaded down with luggage stopped her short. They watched Alex and Mosi approach the bank of elevators that gave access to the upper floors.

The woman didn't miss a thing: Alex's arm around Mosi's waist, his around her shoulders; their lack of luggage. She gave Alex a knowing smile before she turned and whispered to her husband.

Alex kept her eyes on the lit floor numbers above each of the six elevators. She desperately wanted to check Mosi's clothing for bloodstains. She pressed her hand against her own white shirt, silently cursing her decision to change into it before they arrived.

As soon as the elevator doors opened, she stepped inside and hit the top floor button. Mosi followed right behind her, and the two of them stood tight to the back of the elevator while the couple wheeled their bags inside. Alex watched their backs, turning to face to Mosi when the elevator doors slid open on three, and the couple ambled out.

"Eight a.m.," she said when the gleaming doors finally closed. "There was no one at the desk when I checked in. Not a single person in the lobby. And we end up with these two waiting for the elevator." She pressed the sixteenth floor button, their true destination.

"How long is it before our flight?" Mosi asked.

"Ten hours, but we'll have to leave for the airport in eight."

When the doors opened, they walked soundlessly down the carpeted hallway. She grabbed a newspaper from a table as she passed and tucked it under her arm. They'd heard nothing about Benjamin's death or the break-in on the radio or internet. She expected the same from TV and newspaper reports. Benjamin Costa's death was just another statistic, and the mine owners would keep the break-in to themselves.

Seven doors down from the elevator, she slid her card key against
the lock. Mosi had barely entered the room before she put out the
"do not disturb" sign and bolted the door.

"I'm going to try my dad again." She pulled her phone from her
pocket as she spoke. "He has to be somewhere with cell service by
now."

Twice while they were on the road she'd called him, both times
reaching his voicemail on the first ring — a sure sign he was out of
cell service range. She had assumed that his meeting was near the
mine, but now she wondered if he hadn't driven through the night
to Bogotá.

The text flashing on the screen delivered an answer.

Tracey told me what happened. I'm rerouting to Nairobi to meet you.
No cell service until I reach Bogotá. I'll try you then. Stay safe, Alex.

"It's from Dad. The message must have come in while I was in the
parking garage or the elevator." She typed out a reply. "I missed it."

She stared down at the phone, waiting for the familiar ping, but
nothing came.

"Shit! He's not answering. I missed this call by maybe ten minutes
… he should answer."

"He will call when he can, Alex."

"I'll leave my phone here in case he calls while I'm getting our
bags from the car." She set the phone down on the nightstand next
to where Mosi now lay. "And if he does…"

"I will keep him on the phone until you return." Mosi grinned.
"I will not let him hang up."

"You can try." She smiled. "You know what he's like, though. He'll
tell you he'll call back in five minutes and disappear for five hours."

"Brian loses track of time. You of all people should know that.
Do you not remember when he took you to the Olduvai Gorge for
one day, and you stayed for a week?"

"Hard to forget that one." She shook her head. "I missed my flight
home … Mom was furious!"

"In two days Brian will be in Nairobi. This will be over then."

Two days.

After six long weeks, she could hardly believe that in two days she would finally see her dad. With luck, she'd be headed home to Vancouver before the week was out.

"Let me check your leg before I go down to the car." She walked over to the desk. "I want to order something from room service too."

By the time she found the menu and crossed back to the bed, Mosi lay on top of the white duvet, his legs bare.

"No blood on the bandage … that's a good sign." She eased the tape from his skin and lifted away the gauze. "And—"

The sheen of sweat on Mosi's face stopped her short.

Her hand touched his forehead.

And she felt its heat.

19

Nelson, Canada

DR. ERIC KEENAN WAITED until a pair of EMTs pushed a gurney past the nursing station before he tried to manoeuvre his way to the treatment bay of his young patient, Christopher Henson.

The thirteen-year-old's mother stood anxiously at the side of narrow bed, her hands clutching her son's scraped and bruised arm.

"I've just seen the X-ray, and the leg is definitely broken. It's a clean break, though." Eric touched the swollen skin about six inches above the ankle. "Right about here."

"So he'll have a cast?" the boy's mother asked.

"That's right." He smiled at Christopher. "No dirt-bike riding for a while."

"I can do it." The boy grinned. "Even with a cast on."

"Christopher, that bike will be locked up until your leg is one hundred percent," his mother warned. "And there will be no more flips, twirls…" her hands waved and twisted in the air "—or whatever other nonsense you and your friends were up to today."

The boy rolled his eyes at the lecture and smirked at Eric.

Eric forced back a smile — he knew better than to get in the middle of a family squabble. Instead, he turned to the boy's mother. "I've asked an orthopaedic surgeon to come down and take a look at your son. Christopher may need surgery to stabilize the broken bone, but we'll wait to see what Dr. Chernley says. It could be an hour or more." He put his hand on the boy's leg. "No food or drink while you're waiting Christopher, just in case Dr. Chernley decides to operate tonight."

He had barely closed the curtain to the treatment bay before mother and son were arguing once again.

"What's going on in there?" Susan English's chin motioned to the curtained room.

Eric chuckled. "The usual teenage boy stuff." He tapped the screen of his tablet, scanning the boy's medical history. "Suspected penicillin allergy?"

"Mother says he developed a rash within a few days of starting a course of penicillin for a throat infection last year." She tucked a pen into the pocket of her maroon scrubs. "The family doctor switched the antibiotic just to be on the safe side."

"Well, I'm not going to take any chances. Better put an allergy band on him."

"Already done." She smiled.

"That's what I love about—" The vibration of his cell stopped him midsentence.

One glance at the caller ID and he was on the move. He dashed out of earshot of the nursing station before he hit the answer button. Over the last three years, he'd come to trust Susan's ability to keep things quiet, but this was one conversation he didn't want his favourite ER nurse to hear. Not one word.

He'd barely said hello before Alex launched into a rapid report.

"Mosi has a fever, and it's going up. I've tried cold cloths, ice … nothing helps, Eric."

What the hell?

His runners squeaked with his abrupt stop. He stared up at the patient tracking board that hadn't eased since he'd started his day some five hours earlier. He needed this to be simple.

"Send me a picture of the wound."

The close-up, when it arrived, looked like a healing wound. A scab had already started to form, and swelling was minimal.

Susan pointed up to a flashing entry that indicated lab results were back on an eight-year-old girl with suspected pneumonia. He nodded and flashed his hand. *Five minutes.*

He leaned against the wall next to a wire-shelved cart stacked with sheets and blankets. "How bad is his fever?"

"Hovering around one hundred and one."

He could hear the fear in her voice and knew that she needed reassurance. He wanted to say that it was likely a minor infection and that her friend would be okay after a few days of antibiotics, but he wasn't sure.

Brazil. The Amazon. He ran his finger through his hair. If he'd learned anything from his stint with Doctors Without Borders, it was that yellow fever, Zika, malaria, dengue, typhoid, and dozens of other tropical diseases could complicate symptoms.

"Are Mosi's travel vaccinations up to date?"

"You think maybe something else is causing the fever? He hasn't had any vaccinations, except yellow fever. He's not taking antimalarial drugs. Mosi had malaria before, so maybe this is just a recurrence?"

What the hell? He knew Alex to be a careful traveller, and he'd expect the same from her colleague.

"Where was Mosi when he was shot?" Silence met his question. "I don't need specifics. I just want to know if he was inside or outside."

"Outside."

"Did he wade through water or get the wound wet in any way?"

He heard her ask the question of her friend and heard a mumbled response.

"He wasn't in any water. He was sitting on the damp ground for an hour, maybe two, but the wound was covered, and he's sure it didn't get wet."

At least it's not water-borne bacteria. Although without a culture and gram stain, he couldn't be certain. All he could do was try a broad spectrum antibiotic and wait. Alex and Mosi would be home soon.

"Do you have antibiotics with you?"

"Sure. Yes. My family doctor gave me ampicillin, Clavulin and—"

"Clavulin … that's what I want. Give Mosi five hundred milligrams every twelve hours. You should see some improvement in about twenty-four hours."

"Another twenty-four hours! We have a flight in eight hours, Eric. We *have* to be on it."

Just how much trouble is she in?

"There's no reason for you not to be on that flight. Even if Mosi's fever hasn't dropped, he's not going to get any worse. He'll be pretty uncomfortable, but he should be fine. I'll—"

He pressed a finger to his ear to shut out a torrent of curses screamed out by a woman in one of the ER bays.

"Mosi will be fine, Alex. Just get on that flight and come home." His voice softened. "I know you're scared, Alex. I'm off in four hours, so call me then, okay? You can give me an update, and we can talk a little more then."

He'd barely ended the call before a text message from Susan flashed on his screen. Dr. Chernley was at Christopher Hensen's bedside.

But his feet refused to move.

I need to be there. I need to go to Vancouver and meet that flight.

He pulled up his calendar and checked his jam-packed schedule. Dr. Lillian Sayer still owed him for the weekend he had freed up for her, and he intended to collect. He fired off a text to her and then sent an email to his chief of staff, Dr. James Callaway, asking to be removed from the following week's schedule.

Callaway would demand to see him so he could lecture Eric on responsibility, a lecture Eric had heard a dozen times in the past ten months. Even now that the military had left the Slocan Valley, and life here had returned to normal, the ambitious surgeon hadn't yet forgiven Eric's insubordinate actions, and he hadn't stopped blaming Eric for putting him in the hot seat.

Right now, Eric didn't give a damn.

20

Novoteras Mine

JORGE DROPPED his pen onto the desk and rubbed the back of his neck. He had been here too long, staring at these lists of names. He had expected fewer visitors in the nearby towns, especially at this time of year, not this list of more than a thousand people.

These records had arrived within hours of his call to Shen Li, records that would have taken him days, if not weeks, to acquire when he had worked with the police. To deliver so quickly took powerful connections.

He had known from his first meeting that Shen Li was a man used to getting what he wanted, and from all appearances, he succeeded. Thousand-dollar suits, expensive watches, fancy cars — Li had them all. He could only imagine the man's home, a penthouse in São Paulo's best neighbourhood, from what he'd heard.

Jorge had asked questions about Tabitha Metals, and the man who ran it, before he'd accepted the job. Little was know about Shen Li, except that he'd been born in China and educated in Britain before he started Tabitha Metals. The company itself had several profitable South American mines and a reputation for treating its workers fairly. It had been enough for Jorge to take the job of mine manager, a decision he did not regret. Tabitha Metals paid him far more than he could ever earn with the Policía Civil, and he was home with his family every night.

He had hired Carlos, a military captain, as his right hand and put him in charge of security. Neither of them knew anything about managing a mine, but the high wages Novoteras paid attracted experienced miners and other staff. The mine operation itself fell to engineer Tim Wong and geologist Qiang Ma, both supplied by Li.

Money had never been an issue, and during their weekly meetings, Li rarely disagreed with Jorge's requests for more staff to meet the growing production demand, extra comforts for the men, or additions to their state-of-the-art security. His boss encouraged Jorge to maintain his police connections, and not once had he even hinted at circumventing or ignoring Brazilian law.

So why did Shen Li refuse to involve police now? And why did this breach matter so much? No matter how long their thieves had been in the mine, they could only have chipped out a small amount of tourmaline and given what he knew of the value of the rock they mined, it represented a minor loss to the company.

Which brought him back to the question that nagged him. Why had no backpack, no knapsack, no carrying bag at all, been found on Benjamin Costa? If the thieves intended to steal as much of the gemstone as possible, why did not each of the men have the capacity to carry out a load? He would find an answer only when he found the man who had talked Costa into entering the mine.

Sabion Lacerda had described a tall, black man of about forty, with curly black hair, brown eyes and an accent the miner could not identify.

Eva Costa vehemently denied seeing any such man with her husband and had insisted that Benjamin had never even mentioned a foreigner in town.

It had been clever for this foreigner to look to the football fields, where most of the men who worked at the mine could be found several times a week, if not nightly. It meant, though, that the man had spent much time in the villages surrounding the mine.

Someone must have seen him.

Jorge reached for his coffee cup, refilled countless times over the past twelve hours. He'd left the mine early enough last night to spend a precious hour with his wife and children before bed, but he had left this morning before any of them awakened. Since then, he had barely moved from his chair, reading and rereading hundreds of pages, tracking visitors in Minas Gerais.

Their thief would have stayed locally, within driving distance of the mine, so he could easily follow the miners at the end of the day. Coronel Murta, where Sabion had met the black man, was a possibility. But there were many other cities that the man could have chosen, places where he would have been overlooked in a sea of foreign faces.

There were many people who had been here for two weeks or more, enough time to plan a break-in. Almost all of them had foreign-sounding names, and even though their home address and citizenship were often recorded, it was not enough. Without photos, there was no way of knowing which of these men might be black.

Carlos gave the barest rap at the door before he swept into the room. From the smile on his face, Jorge knew the news was good.

"I think we have found the foreigner," Carlos blurted out before Jorge could say a word. "A black man checked out of the Pousada do Centro in Araçuaí yesterday, and the manager said he had been there for several weeks. The licence plate of this man's rental vehicle — a black truck — contains two of the numbers that our guards saw."

Finally!

"What is his name?"

"Mosi Ongeti."

Jorge flipped through his hotel listings. "Here, here he is." His finger traced a line across the page. "The *pousada* staff recorded the man's passport number and an address in Tanzania."

An African. The man would have an accent, one not often heard here in Minas Gerais.

"You said they have his licence plate number too?"

"Yes." Carlos nodded. "I have found it in the rental car lists — it has not yet been returned."

"Then Ongeti is still in the country. There is time yet to find him."

Jorge leaned forward on his elbows with his hands tightly clasped. "Has the room been rented out yet?"

"No, but it has been cleaned. We will search it thoroughly for anything left behind. I have also asked the manager to keep the room vacant for now."

Carlos might be a military man, but his investigative instincts were good. This former captain's efforts, though, would yield little. Every scrap of paper would already be gone, and common surfaces that might have yielded a recent fingerprint would have been polished clean.

"Have your men interview the staff at the *pousada*. I want to know everything about him — who he saw, who he was with, whether they saw him with a bag from a local shop, when he came and went — everything." His mind whirled. "And I want the name of every person who checked out yesterday. This man was not alone."

"Yes. Yes, of course." Carlos started to turn.

"One more thing — get Sabion Lacerda back here. I will ask for a copy of this man's passport, and as soon as it arrives, I want Sabion to look at the photo."

Carlos had barely slipped through the doorway before Jorge picked up the phone and dialled Shen Li.

21

Nelson, Canada

INTENT ON THE X-RAY up on his computer screen, Eric almost jumped at the sound of Dr. Doug Chernley's voice behind him.

"Looks like an obstructed bowel," he said as he slid into the chair next to Eric.

Eric nodded. "Seventy-eight-year-old woman with cardiopulmonary disease and diabetes. I just paged Jamie." He only hoped that the general on-call surgeon arrived as quickly as Doug had.

"I think he's in the OR — could be a while." Doug reached into his pocket for his phone. "I'm going to set Christopher Hensen's leg as soon as an operating room opens up," he said, his finger scrolling through a busy schedule. "Could be another hour, maybe two." He dropped his phone back into his white coat. "Anything else you need before I head upstairs?"

The offer, one that signalled an understanding of the difficulties faced in the ER, was one of the many things Eric liked about this orthopaedic surgeon who'd joined the Kootenay Lake Hospital just a month ago. The forty-three-year-old was only six years older than Eric, but Eric didn't see them developing much of a friendship outside of the hospital. Like many of the doctors who relocated to Nelson, British Columbia, Doug spent every free hour skiing or hiking in the mountains, while Eric tried to squeeze in swimming, a game of tennis or a few hours playing his sax, none of which he'd managed in months.

Eric shook his head. "Maybe a broken arm in bed two, but I won't know until —" A quick glance at his cell phone was all it took. "I have to take this."

He was out of his chair before Doug could respond, phone to his ear.

"Mosi is worse. God, Eric, I don't know what to do," Alex blurted out in panic after he'd barely said hello.

"Alex, it'll be okay. Just tell me what's going on."

"His fever is worse, and he's in pain. Lots of pain."

His sneakers squeaked in protest when he skidded to avoid an incoming gurney that rounded the corner too fast. One of the uniformed paramedics yanked the metal frame away from him just in time, but her partner seemed oblivious to the near crash.

"Send me a picture."

Hand clenched on the phone, he sped down the hallway to the doctor's lounge and pushed the door open, relieved to find the room empty. At least for now.

The ping of a text message delivered a photo nothing like the one seen before. The wound looked puffy, with a bull's-eye of crusty scab edged in bulging, paler flesh.

Abscess. A cauldron of bacteria beneath the scab with nowhere to drain, and until it was treated Mosi's fever would continue, and so would his pain.

"I have the photo, Alex … I need you to get your first aid kit. I want to go through the contents with me."

"Right, right. Okay."

The rip of a zipper replaced her voice. A suitcase, or her backpack maybe. He heard muffled voices, hers and a man's. At least Mosi was conscious and talking.

What the hell happened? He'd been so sure that the antibiotic would be enough.

"I've got the basic equipment: gauze, scissors, tweezers, bandages, gloves." She rattled off the list to the crinkle of paper. "Antiseptic wash, antibiotic ointment—"

"What about a scalpel?"

"No. Wait, I do have one. Why—"

Lillian Sayer pushed the lounge door open and smiled at him.

Shit! He flashed a brief smile at Lillian and pointed at the phone held tight to his ear. She'd understand, or at least he hoped she would.

"Hold on," he said as he jumped up from the chair. But Lillian held up a hand and pulled the lounge door open, leaving him alone once again.

He heaved a sigh of relief. Privacy was almost impossible to find in this place, something his good friend understood all too well. Lillian would be curious about who he was talking to, of course, but he'd deal with that when the time came.

"Alex, your friend has an abscess, and you're going to have to open the wound to drain it. I'll talk you through it, don't worry. It'll be a quick cut."

"Okay … whatever I have to do. Just tell me what to do."

Eric wanted to see the wound, to guide Alex's every move. But a video call here in the doctor's lounge just wasn't a safe option.

"We're going to need to irrigate the wound, Alex. Do you have a kettle in your room so you can boil some water?"

"No kettle, but I have a water purification kit."

"What kind? What does it do?"

"I've got two with me … always carry them. A microfilter and a UV light."

He ran his hand through his hair. "I don't know anything about these things, Alex. Be specific."

"The microfilter gets rid of particles, dirt, and most bacteria. What it doesn't get the UV light will."

"Good. Good." It wasn't perfect, but she'd be home soon, and Mosi was already on antibiotics. "Get your water ready and find a clean towel. You're going to need a scalpel, gauze and a syringe — I want you to put all of those things on the towel. And I want you to wash your hands really well."

With a steaming pocket of bacteria in the bullet tract, a sterile field was the least of his concerns, but he'd be damned if he'd neglect the very basics of good medical treatment hygiene.

"It'll take a few minutes, and I'll have to put the phone down."

"That's okay, I'll wait."

I have to get back to my patients. But he couldn't move, couldn't hang up until he knew Alex's friend was safe. That Alex could get home.

He paced the scuffed tile floor end-to-end twice before forcing himself to stop at the tiny kitchen counter. Phone tucked under his chin, he reached for the coffee pot and then decided against the black sludge that had sustained him through the morning. The switch from nights to days was tough enough without the addition of caffeine this late in the day. He pulled the fridge door open but slammed it shut at the sound of Alex's voice.

"I've got the phone on speaker, and I'm ready. What do I do?"

"Pick up your scalpel." He dropped into a chair. "We don't need a deep cut, just a tiny poke. Make an incision right through the centre of that scab … you want your cut to extend just beyond the edge of the scab."

He heard a grunt of pain and Alex's quick intake of breath.

"I can't do this. Eric, I'm hurting him. I can't—"

"Alex, you can do this. You have to keep going if you want to help your friend."

A scream of pain told him that Alex had made the incision.

"You're almost there, Alex. Keep going." There was nothing more he could say, nothing he could do to make this easier.

"There's creamy yellow pus coming out now. It smells awful!"

Definitely an abscess. He closed his eyes and nodded. This he could deal with, even remotely.

"The smell is from bacteria, and we have to force it out. So I want you to put the scalpel down and use your fingers. Press the sides near the incision and push toward the opening." His own fingers pinched together, mimicking the action he described. "It's going to hurt him, but you have to do it. We have to clear that wound."

The man's screams drove him to his feet. His eyes on the lounge door, he pushed the volume on his phone down as low as he dared.

"Lots more—" Her voice faltered. "There's lots of pus coming out now."

"Good, Alex." He rubbed his cheek, the day-old growth like sandpaper against his hand. "That's really good. Now we want to keep pushing toward the incision until that creamy discharge, that pus, stops."

Eighteen minutes. He'd be missed in the ER soon. *I have to get back.*

"Okay, okay … there's nothing else coming out."

Finally.

"Good. Now we want to irrigate the wound to remove any remaining infection. Use your syringe to force water into the incision. And Alex, you'll have to really plunge down hard on the syringe … we're trying to flush the wound clean."

"Shit! This is harder than I'd expected. All I managed to do is get water on Mosi's thigh."

"Take a deep breath Alex. You've finished the hard part. Push the tip of the syringe into the wound before you press the plunger."

"Okay … it's working better now."

"Good. Do that a few times and then start pushing gauze into the wound. We want to fill up that space we just drained."

He heard the ping of an incoming text and glanced down at the message from Susan English. The on-call surgeon had arrived, and so too had two new urgent cases.

"It's not going in much. Shit!"

"It's okay, Alex. We're just using the gauze to keep the wound from closing up so it will keep draining. Just push as much as you can into the wound and leave a tail of gauze sticking out.

"It's not going in, Eric. It's just not going in."

"Just push in as much as you can, Alex. And then I want you to cover the wound with a gauze pad. Wind gauze around the whole thing … tight enough that pad doesn't shift. I want to keep as much of that gauze you worked so hard to push in, to stay there."

"Right. Good. I can do that." She sighed. "But then what ... we're supposed to be on a plane in four hours, Eric."

"He should start feeling better pretty quickly now that you've drained the wound. Keep giving him the ibuprofen and acetaminophen ... Mosi should be fine for the flight."

"I don't know what I would have—" Her voice dropped to a whisper. "I don't know how to thank you, Eric."

He folded his arms across his chest. "Just come home, Alex. Get on that plane and come home."

22

Nelson, Canada

ERIC KICKED OFF his running shoes and dropped his keys and the newspaper on the hall table. He eyed the stairs, deciding that a shower would have to wait. So too would his first real meal since yesterday.

He flicked on a light in the living room and turned on the stereo as he passed by on his way to the kitchen. This morning's coffee cup and cereal bowl still sat on the table, and the fridge door opened to wire shelves that looked bare even to him. With all of the extra shifts he'd picked up over the past few weeks, trips to the grocery store, laundry, and just about everything else in his life had been pushed aside. He'd slid into the bad habits of living on cafeteria food and wearing hospital scrubs, habits that had crept up more often since he'd started spending his off-time in Vancouver with Alex.

A glass of apple juice in hand, he scrolled through his phone contacts until he found Tracey Caminski's cell number. Alex had been quick to introduce him to Tracey the first time he drove to Vancouver for the weekend. The two women were tight as thieves, and he was convinced that if Tracey hadn't given him the green light, his relationship with Alex would have floundered. But he'd found it easy to like thirty-five-year-old brunette, and he didn't hesitate to call her now.

"Tracey. It's Eric." He skipped the niceties when she answered on the second ring. "I want to meet Alex in Vancouver when she lands. What time is her flight due?"

"Have you talked to her? She'd be the best one to give you the details."

He leaned back against the granite counter. Tracey was damn good at keeping secrets, something he'd learned was essential in the mining business. But all he wanted was a flight number, not some trade secret.

"I talked to her less than an hour ago, just before my shift ended. She told me she was flying out in a few hours, but I don't know which airline or flight number." He turned on the charm. "I would bet a month's salary that you booked that flight. And let's face it, she'd just tell me to call you anyway."

"Probably." Tracey laughed. "But are you sure she told you she was flying to Vancouver tonight?"

Did she? His free arm across his chest, he tucked his hand into his armpit. "What aren't you saying, Tracey?"

"Maybe you better call her back and—"

"Where's she going Tracey?"

His question was met with silence so complete that he thought the call had disconnected.

"Tracey? Are you there?"

"I'm still here." She sighed. "It's just ... Eric, you really need to talk to Alex."

What the hell? Tracey knew him, knew that Alex trusted him. It should be enough, but it wasn't. Tracey was acting like a mother bear protecting its cub. But from what?

"Look, Tracey. That bullet wound—"

"What bullet wound? Who's hurt?"

He swallowed hard. In the months that he'd shared with Alex, he'd heard enough to know that Alex trusted Tracey with her life. For Alex to keep her friend in the dark about the shooting didn't make sense.

"Alex is fine, Tracey." His voice took on the calm reassurance he used with families and patients alike. "It's her friend, he's—"

"Mosi? Mosi's hurt? Is he okay?"

"He'll be okay." He pushed off from the counter and turned to face the window. "I should have realized that he worked with you."

"He's ... he's like family, Eric. Are you sure he's okay?"

"He took a bullet in the leg, and the wound is probably infected. He'll be okay, but he's going to need a doctor. Which is why I'm heading to Vancouver to meet their flight. So if you can—"

"What the hell happened, Eric? How did Mosi get shot in the first place?"

"No idea. All I know is that they can't go to a doctor in Brazil. Alex is pretty scared, and she's desperate to get on that flight tonight." He forced himself to breathe, to quiet his voice. "What's going on in Brazil, Tracey?"

He waited, praying that this mother of two toddlers would take him into her confidence. And when she said nothing, he tried again.

"Please, Tracey."

Finally, he heard her sigh. "I don't know much about anything, including what she's doing in Brazil. All I know is that she asked me to find a good criminal lawyer for a friend down there. Did she mention this other friend to you, someone other than Mosi?"

"No. She didn't mention anyone but Mosi ... I'm sure of it."

He stared out the kitchen window at the darkening sky. A third person? A lawyer? It hammered home the fact that Alex had shared few details during their phone calls. But Alex shared everything with Tracey — so why not this?

"Tracey, she's in trouble. Serious trouble. And she's not telling either of us the whole story. Maybe she doesn't want us to worry, but right now I'm damn scared. For all we know, she's injured too, or she's about to be arrested. Tell me everything you know ... please, Tracey. What's going on in Brazil?"

She sighed. "I don't know what's going on, and that's the truth. I do know that Mosi is in Brazil with her, and there's some connection between what they're doing and whatever Brian is working on in Colombia ... or at least I think there is." She talked fast now, without reservation. "Whatever it is, they're keeping the project off the books, and I have no idea why. I can't even tell you if she's been in Brazil or Colombia for the past six weeks. I should know, but I don't."

Six weeks! He paced the kitchen floor, trying to absorb her words. "But you practically run Graham and Associates, and Alex says you're in constant contact with every geologist." He threw up his hands. "How can you not know where she's been for six weeks?"

"That's my point. Honestly Eric, I can't think of a time when I've known less about what's going on. Alex tells me everything — so does Brian. But this? This is different."

He dropped into the kitchen chair. Nothing about this made sense.

"I need to meet that plane, Tracey. I need to see Alex … see for myself that she's okay. When does her flight land … please, Tracey."

"She's not coming to Vancouver … she's flying to Nairobi."

"Nairobi!" He jumped to his feet. "What the hell! Why is she going there? She needs to come home."

"Mosi is Tanzanian, Eric. She's taking him home. I could only get her as close as Nairobi, and Alex plans to drive across the border from there. He'll be okay once—"

"No, he won't." His hand clenched into a fist. "I just talked Alex through a procedure to drain an abscess in that man's leg. If that abscess reforms while they're on that plane, or if that bullet moves even slightly…" He didn't finish the sentence. "If Alex has to take him to a doctor, he'll be arrested."

And so will she.

"How fast can I get to Nairobi?" He was already on the move. "Can you book me a flight?"

"Eric—"

"Whatever's going on Tracey, Alex needs help. I can't just sit here. *Please.*" He climbed the stairs two at a time. "I can be at the Nelson airport in half an hour."

"I'll call you back in ten."

In the bedroom, he threw open the closet door and yanked out a suitcase.

Whatever was going on, he'd find out soon enough.

23

São Paulo, Brazil

IN THE CROWDED São Paulo airport, Alex watched a young girl struggle with a rolling suitcase that was more than half her size. As the girl pulled, the bag with its Hello Kitty decal wobbled on its small wheels, threatening to fall over and take her tumbling to the floor with it. But even from this distance Alex could hear the girl's laughter, her excited chatter over the din of the crowd.

Alex had to smile. So too did everyone else who watched the girl … including Mosi.

He'd dressed carefully in a white shirt and khaki trousers, the best clothes he could find. Over one shoulder hung his tattered backpack, and he gripped his duffel in the other. A man who didn't stand out among the other travellers.

As agreed, he went ahead of her to check-in at the South African Airways counter while she stayed behind. Only when he was clear of the counter and headed to security would she approach the counter herself with two stacked suitcases, her own and another, newly purchased from the hotel, that held most of Mosi's things.

He tried hard to cover his limp, but the painkillers and ice could only do so much. His awkward movement betrayed a painful injury to anyone who saw Mosi walk more than a few steps.

Alex scanned the airport concourse again, searching for signs of watchers. If airport security had been alerted, she saw no evidence of it.

She heard the clang of metal against the tile floor and turned back toward the little girl. The suitcase now lay on the floor, and the girl's mother helped right it. Beside them stood Mosi.

The girl's mother seemed to be apologizing to Mosi, and he gave her a kind smile. This girl was probably about the same age as Mosi's daughter Adimu, the one he doted on most. *He must miss his family.* Mosi travelled with her dad from time to time, but not for as long as this. Even she was starting to miss home after six weeks away, and she missed Eric.

And then she saw her.

A woman dressed in sneakers, jeans and a T-shirt, with a pack on her back. She looked like just another of the ten thousand passengers who passed through the São Paulo–Guarulhos airport every day. Except there was something about the way she pushed through the crowd. She moved with intent, solely focused on Mosi.

A hunter.

The woman kept her eye on Mosi as he closed in on the South African Airlines check-in counter. And then she turned to the glass entrance doors to watch a woman who rushed through.

The hunter tracked this new arrival through the crowd, breaking off only when the woman joined a man dressed in shorts and a T-shirt at the far end of the concourse.

And then her attention went back to Mosi.

Alex went cold. Somehow this hunter knew about both her and Mosi. Their descriptions, their names — everything could be in the hands of airport security.

She wanted to shout, to warn Mosi. But she could only watch her friend hand his passport over to the airline agent at the first class check-in counter.

Alex held her breath, watching for any reaction from the agent. Mosi's demeanour was casual, friendly even. And when he laughed at something the agent said, Alex finally relaxed.

Until she saw the hunter closing on Mosi.

With a phone in her hand.

24

São Paulo, Brazil

ALEX YANKED HER WHEELED BAG sharply and darted toward the woman, who had Mosi in her sights.

She didn't hesitate. She threw herself against the woman's back with enough force to send both of them to the floor.

Heads turned and hands reached down to the pair of women sprawled on the floor. Other people pulled back, reluctant to get involved.

Alex grabbed the outstretched hand of a young man in an army fatigue jacket and worked her way to her feet. Her backpack had taken the brunt of the fall, but pain ripped through her hip as she stood.

The bearded man held firm, supporting her until Alex said, "I think I'm okay now." She smiled. "Thank you."

He reached down to retrieve a paperback book and handed it to her before scouting the floor for more lost items.

"Did you not see me?" challenged the woman, now on her feet and standing too close to Alex.

The woman's anger pushed like a wave against the crowd, and almost as one, the other travellers stepped away from the two women. Now Alex and the hunter stood alone.

The dark-haired woman tried to bend her leg, wincing at the movement. "My leg could have been broken. It is your fault."

"I'm sorry. I didn't see you." Alex reached her hand out. "Can I help you get to a chair so you can sit down?"

The woman ignored the question. "My phone." She scanned the floor. "Do you see it? It must be here."

"No, I'm sorry I—"

The woman swung her head toward the South African Airline check-in counter.

Alex did the same, breathing only when she saw no sign of Mosi. It wouldn't take this hunter long to find Mosi again. Already, the woman had turned toward the security gates.

I have to stall her.

"Do you know this airport well? I'm in a hurry to make my flight, but I can't find the check-in counter. Can you help me?"

"Ask at the desk over there." The woman pointed to her left and then turned her back to Alex.

"Azul Brazilian? It's got to be here somewhere. I can't miss my flight. I need help," Alex pleaded. "Please."

This time the woman didn't answer. Instead she made a tight circle, methodically searching through a sea of feet and luggage.

"Can I show you my ticket?" Alex reached into her pocket. "It's—"

Alex jumped at the touch of a hand on her arm. She swivelled to find a girl of no more than sixteen standing tight behind her. In her hand was a cell phone.

She thinks it's mine. Heart pounding, Alex dropped the offered phone into her pocket with a smile and quiet word of thanks. The girl quickly stepped away, back to her mother, a woman who smiled at Alex when their eyes met.

Alex wasted no time. She wove through people and luggage to the South African Airways counter. As she approached, she saw just one person, a grey-haired man, at the first class check-in. Mosi was gone, headed to security.

In place at the front of the line, she forced herself to keep her eyes on the man at the counter. She studied his navy slacks, white shirt and leather loafers, his ring-adorned left hand, and the way his head bobbed as he chatted with the airline agent on the other side of the counter — anything to keep from turning.

She felt the hunter's eyes on her, even knowing it was unlikely. By now, the woman would have given up on her phone and raced down the concourse toward gate security — and Mosi.

Alex willed the grey-haired man to stop talking to the airline agent, but the two of them seemed in no hurry. Then, with a final laugh, the man relinquished his spot at the counter and Alex hurried over.

"I have an e-ticket. Alex Graham." She handed her passport to the agent and dropped her bag on the weigh scale.

The agent, with her perfect makeup and a crisp uniform, magnified Alex's haggard look. But thankfully this woman so used to weary travellers made no comment about the deep lines and dark circles beneath Alex's eyes.

Alex held her breath as manicured fingers entered her name into the system. She told herself it was okay, that even if police had found the truck at the Belo Horizonte airport, they wouldn't have her name — only Mosi's. And he had checked in without issue.

It seemed forever before the young woman lifted her head. "You have just the two bags?"

Not trusting her voice, Alex only nodded.

Alex caught the faint scent of roses as the slender woman threaded a tag around the handle of each suitcase.

And then it was over.

The agent handed Alex a boarding card. "Enjoy your flight."

Alex smiled, and paper in hand, she quickly turned. Saddled only with a backpack, she wove through the crowd at a sprint. She only slowed as she neared the security gates.

The uniformed guard scanned her boarding pass and waved her inside after only the briefest look at her face. If these guards had been alerted, they weren't looking for a woman.

Shoes off and her tote and jacket in a basket, Alex whisked through security. She craned her neck, trying to see over the travellers ahead of her, searching for Mosi's tight, black curls. Nothing.

She checked her watch a dozen times as she shuffled into the customs hall. There she watched the uniformed men and women stationed in the glass booths, watching for anything that suggested they were on high alert. But they quietly processed travellers, stamping passports too quickly to be asking in-depth questions, too quickly to be looking for someone.

Finally, her turn. Lips forced into a tight smile, she presented her passport to a man who scrutinized her face before he turned to his computer screen. She couldn't breathe. She didn't breathe. Not until the metal stamp thudded against her passport and the man waved her through. She was in.

The brightly lit departure lounge with its crowd of storefronts and swarm of people was her last stop on the way to freedom. A quick check of the map directed her to the Star Alliance lounge, and in less than five minutes she pushed open the door to a sanctuary from the noise and crowd. Her feet sank into the plush carpeting as she crossed the dimly lit reception area toward a woman whose smile warmly welcomed her.

Alex handed over her boarding pass, thankful that the receptionist didn't engage in small talk. It was as though this woman knew that many who arrived in this lounge wanted nothing but a quiet refuge.

Once past the reception area, the lounge itself hummed with conversation and television dialogue. Quick steps propelled her past well-dressed businesspeople, the buffet table, and bar. Most of the men and women behind their newspapers and laptop screens ignored her, but a few bored souls, wine glasses in hand, openly stared. She needed to sit down, to blend in, but she couldn't. Not until she knew Mosi was here.

Her gut clenched in fear, she searched the corners and chair backs for any sign of Mosi. Until finally, in a leather chair in the back corner, she saw a familiar toothy grin.

She heaved a sigh and hurriedly dropped into the empty chair next to him.

"I was afraid you wouldn't be here," she whispered. "There was a woman watching you ... Mosi, they're looking for you."

"I did not see anyone. Where was this woman?"

"Back at the check-in counter. I'm afraid police may have found the truck, and if—"

"If they had found the truck, I would not have made it through security. But they barely looked at my passport." His voice, smooth and deep, reassured her. "We are safe."

Are we?

Alex counted down the minutes. Fifteen minutes before boarding, a half-hour longer on the tarmac — long enough for their hunter to track them to this flight and alert authorities.

Only when Brazil freed its grip on their plane would they truly be safe.

25

Salinas, Brazil

JORGE REACHED ACROSS the kitchen table and intertwined his fingers with his wife's. In the light thrown from a single lamp in the hallway, the two of them sat wordless, their breath the only sound.

For the first time in three days, silence surrounded him, as though protecting him from the maelstrom that had occupied every moment since the break-in. The crisis was far from over, but for a few hours at least he could be here with his family. He had arrived home too late to see his children, but even the glimpse of their innocent faces fast asleep brought him comfort.

"What will happen to the family of Benjamin Costa?" It was the first and only question Zahra had asked since he had told her what had happened.

In the shadowed light, he saw the sadness in her eyes. It came as no surprise that his wife, with her gentle soul, thought only of the dead man and his family.

Zahra had been in her first year of university, destined for medical school, when they first met. Just two years later, when they married and she quickly became pregnant with their son, she had been forced to drop out. His mother had offered to care for the baby while she went to class, but Zahra chose to take a job as a shop assistant instead. Only when Jorge became mine manager did she quit, but medical school was no longer an option. Their move from Belo Horizonte to the small village of Salinas, north of the mine, put them hundreds of kilometres from their families and the nearest university. With two children and a third on the way, her dream of becoming a doctor died.

"Benjamin's family must find a way to survive." He ran his hand across his cheek. "There is nothing I can do."

Zahra pulled her hand away. "You must."

"Even if it means jeopardizing our own lives? Zahra…" He shook his head. "I cannot be seen to help the family of a man who stole from the mine I manage."

Her eyes downcast, she brushed her hand against the bright blue tablecloth, sweeping unseen crumbs to the tile floor. "Why is a piece of rock coming from that mine more important than a man's life?"

"It is theft, no matter the value."

He steeled himself for the argument to come. When he worked for the Policía Civil, the crimes he investigated had been easier to understand. Bank fraud, money laundering — thefts, where criminals, many of them wealthy, were tried and jailed. Never before had he tried to justify the death of a criminal at the hands of police, never mind a private security guard shooting a man to protect property.

Zahra, though, simply rose and rested a hand on her pregnant belly. "You look tired. Let me fix you something to eat, and then you should go to bed."

He shook his head. "I must leave shortly. I will eat something at the mine."

She ignored him, reaching into the fridge for a clay pot of leftover stew that she set on the stovetop to warm. The flare of flame and the steady hiss of burning propane filled the silence, soon followed by the clank of a spoon against the pot and the scrape of china as she pulled dishes from the cupboard. She kept her back to him, a move he had seen her make often enough to know that it was best to sit quietly at the table and wait for her next words.

Zahra ladled *feijoada* into a bowl and set the black bean stew in front of him. He sunk his spoon into the thick broth and lifted a piece of pork to the surface. He breathed in its garlic, its smokiness, but could not bring himself to lift the spoon to his lips.

"You must eat something, Jorge." She pushed a basket of *pão de queijo* toward him. "At least a cheese roll. I baked them this morning."

His hand fell away from his spoon, but he made no effort to reach for the basket. Zahra was tempting him with his favourites, but he had no stomach for any of them.

She eased into the chair across from him. "Why does this investigation worry you so much?"

They kept no secrets from each other, and he would not make this the exception.

"Mr. Li sent me hundreds of records from rental car agencies, and hotels — information even police struggle to obtain. Every major airport is under surveillance, and every border crossing has been alerted. To do this ... it requires much money and many connections."

"Is that so unusual? This mine, it takes money to run. And for a foreign company to build it in the first place, connections are necessary."

"Yes, but this..." He dropped his eyes to the table. "Mr. Li ordered me to handle this investigation without the police. I reported the death of Benjamin Costa, of course, but I told police only that he was shot when he was found inside the mine fence after hours. They know nothing of the break-in or the other men we seek. I lied, Zahra."

"You told less than the full truth. Sometimes it is necessary, Jorge. Mr. Li must be worried that news of a break-in will affect the mine ... nothing more."

"Whatever the reason, it puts the investigation in my hands." He held his palms out to her. "I feel the weight of it, Zahra. I fear the consequences if I do not find the thieves."

"But you have managed the mine for seven years without a single problem! Surely that will count for something," she argued.

He shook his head. "Mr. Li has already ordered every security guard on duty last night fired — all but the sniper. Every one of these men have worked at the Novoteras mine as long as I have. Mr. Li did not look at their personnel files, he did not even ask their names."

"But you said that Mr. Li fears that one of the guards might be part of the theft. I can understand why—"

"It is more than that, Zahra." His eyes met hers. "I am the mine manager, and I will be made to pay for this theft." His father's words echoed back at him.

"Why you? Why not Carlos?" Her hands slapped the air with each question, and her voice rose. "Carlos is the head of security, and he should be the one to pay for this break-in. He should be the one who is fired."

"Zahra—"

"I gave up everything—" She jumped from her chair, as though scalded. Arms folded across her chest, she leaned against the counter. "You *must* make Mr. Li understand, Jorge."

She stood too far away for him to read her face in the dim light, but from her tense posture and the way she rocked side to side, he knew her fear. Even so, for her to serve up another, especially Carlos, a man who had brought his family to their home, seemed unlike her.

"Zahra, I am the one who put all of the security in place at the mine, not Carlos. I am the one who hired Carlos and put him in charge of the guards. I am the one Mr. Li trusted."

"Then you must call your friends in the police department." Her hand dropped to her swollen belly. "You must ask them for a job. You must walk away now — before it is too late."

If only it were that easy.

"I cannot betray Shen Li. With just one word, he can keep me from ever finding work as a police officer again. He can destroy our lives."

He stared out at the darkened hallway toward the rooms where his children slept.

"I must find these thieves, Zahra. It is the only way."

26

São Paulo, Brazil

SHEN WATCHED THE sommelier open a bottle of Pinot Noir and offer the first taste of the expensive import to Alonso Quinto — the man who had ordered it.

The lawyer's chubby hand clutched the wine glass, and he swirled its plum-red contents beneath his nose before he took a noisy sip. Only when he nodded to the sommelier did the wine flow into Shen's own glass. And only when the young man in his crisp white shirt disappeared between the tables did Alonso speak.

"I have heard rumours that a miner was killed during a break-in at the Novoteras mine." Alonso leaned in, his voice low despite the empty nearby tables.

It explained the lawyer's frantic phone call just hours ago, requesting an urgent meeting. Shen had tried to put the man off, but Alonso had insisted. But since they had been seated in the back corner of this São Paulo steak house, the lawyer had barely mentioned Tabitha Metals.

"An unfortunate incident." Shen lifted his wine glass. "The man was inside the mine fence after midnight, and he was spotted by one of our snipers."

"No. No, I heard that the man was *in* the mine and that he was shot when he tried to *escape* through an air shaft." Alonso's jowls wagged with each jerk of his head. "I also heard that he was not alone. Is that why you search for Mosi Ongeti?"

He knows.

Alonso had been told only that there was a break-in. Even when Shen had involved the lawyer in the search for Mosi Ongeti, he had shared no details. That Alonso knew this much meant someone at the mine served two masters.

Alonso filled the silence between them. "Why do you not leave this search for Mosi Ongeti to the police? What did he steal that can hurt us?"

An odd question from a man who knew nothing about the tanzanite buried deep in the mine. But only the geologist and engineer knew the truth, and neither of them would betray Chairman Wei by talking to Quinto.

He bluffs. But why would this lawyer who had grown rich as the frontman of Tabitha Metals start asking questions now?

Shen reached into his pocket and fingered the cold steel lighter buried there. "You are right about the man who died, and Ongeti. Both were in the tunnels of the Novoteras mine but they stole only a handful of gemstones. Police would be uninterested in such a minor theft."

He made no mention of the waiting driver or the woman. If Quinto knew these facts, he would soon blurt them out. But the lawyer sat quiet, his hands wrapped tightly around his wine glass.

"Until I talk to Ongeti, I can't know if there are more miners involved or if these thefts are ongoing." Shen folded his hands on the table. "It is a simple matter of internal security. It is nothing for you to worry about."

"A man is dead, and you tell me not to worry?" Alonso shook his head. "My name is on thousands of documents, Shen. Every government document, every financial statement, every export manifest — everything that comes out of Tabitha Metals. On paper, I am responsible for Tabitha Metals, every mine, including Novoteras."

"Yes, and for that you are well paid."

Shen's money had catapulted the struggling lawyer from a shabby one-room office to a twenty-three-lawyer firm occupying an entire floor in one of the most prestigious São Paulo business towers, almost overnight.

He didn't like the man, never had, but he understood him. The banker who had introduced them had also quietly shared Alonso Quinto's imminent bankruptcy, stressing the English-speaking lawyer's urgent need for a benefactor. It had taken little for Shen to discover Alonso's penchant for the finer things in life, a desire that his petty clients could not deliver. And in the contracts Alonso had prepared and the cases he argued in court, Shen also saw a cleverness and a desire to win at all costs. Alonso pushed and pulled the ethical line, navigating from legal to illegal like a meandering river. And like the mighty Yangtze, Alonso rushed forward, prepared to submerge and destroy, when he could not bend around obstacles.

"Not enough." Alonso shook his head. "Not enough for this. Police will investigate this death. They will come to me with questions." His hands refused to lie still. "They will want to know why our guard shot a man dead."

As always, Alonso was quick to protect himself — as quick as he was to pocket the rich retainer Shen paid him each month.

"There will be few questions ... I have seen to that already. But if police do come, *you*, the man responsible for Tabitha Metals, will be the only one they talk to."

Shen watched the colour drain from Alonso's face. Like a cornered rat, the lawyer had realized too late that he stood alone, with no way out.

"There will be no mention of Mosi Ongeti. You will say only that Benjamin Costa, a miner employed by Novoteras, was caught inside the mine fence. Any investigation is to be shut down quickly." Shen leaned forward. "Is that clear?"

Alonso fidgeted with the edge of his linen napkin. "It will take money." He locked eyes with Shen. "And I will need to be paid ... I want triple the usual fee transferred to my offshore account."

A surprising answer. Since their first meeting nine years ago,

Alonso had focused only on the money that flowed from Tabitha Metals, questioning nothing. Until now.

Blackmail? If this were Alonso's game, the man would soon learn the cost of such a dangerous game.

"It is bold to ask for money when you have failed so miserably. Mosi Ongeti was in your grasp."

"We do not yet know if the man seen at the airport was Ongeti," Alonso countered. "My investigator picked the man out of the crowd based on little more than instinct." He shifted in his seat. "If you had provided a photo—"

"You dare to blame me." Shen glowered at the man. "You had Ongeti's name, and yet you failed to stop him."

"It came too late. We—"

"Excuses!"

At Shen's outburst, heads turned from a table across the room. A reminder that he and Alonso were not alone.

Shen lowered his voice. "You should have had enough men at the airport to keep Ongeti from getting on that plane. You…" He let the word sink in. "You let him escape."

Alonso jerked back against his seat, as though Shen's words had slammed against his chest.

Shen didn't wait for him to recover. "Now *you* will keep Tabitha Metals out of the fire."

27

São Paulo, Brazil

SHEN STEPPED INTO the penthouse he had left eighteen hours ago. But his day was not yet over.

He swept through the living room, past his favourite chair near the window, the side table stacked with unread financial newspapers. They would have to wait.

He slid into his leather chair and pushed aside the stack of mail left on the desk by his housekeeper. His fingerprint brought the laptop screen to life, and he scanned the dozens of emails that had arrived in the few hours since he'd left the restaurant. He clicked through the messages, searching for anything from Chairman Wei but finding none. Almost as telling was the lack of email from any of the men who occupied the highest ranks of Long Bridge Merchant Group, the inner circle.

By now they all knew of his situation, and none would initiate conversation. They gave him a gift that allowed him to save face, to present his success rather than his failure in their next conversation. But if that success was not quickly achieved, this silence would grow like a cancer, and Shen would be cut out of the inner circle.

All because of Mosi Ongeti.

Ongeti had foolishly used his real passport, arrogantly assuming success at the mine and a quick exit from Brazil. If Alonso Quinto's investigator had in fact spotted Ongeti at the São Paulo airport, this arrogance would be his undoing.

Shen reopened the email from Jorge that had arrived too late to stop their thief. He studied the unsmiling face in the Tanzanian passport photo, the face of Mosi Ongeti. The man's dark skin, brown eyes and close-cropped black hair loudly announced his African heritage but did nothing to inform about the intelligence or cunning of this thief.

He searched the scanned pages of the forty-two-year-old's passport with its Brazilian visa dated six weeks earlier and a handful of entry stamps for Kenya and South Africa. The man seldom travelled far beyond his home country of Tanzania, which made this trip to Brazil specific — purposeful.

He opened the passport of the Canadian woman, the only person to leave the *pousada* the same day as Ongeti. Alex Graham had entered Brazil just days after Ongeti, using a passport that carried the stamps of at least twenty countries. The timing was suspicious, but it was the thirty-one-year-old's frequent visits to Tanzania that convinced him of her connection to Ongeti.

The green-eyed woman was pretty, but in a country filled with black-haired beauties, Alex Graham was unremarkable and would easily be ignored. Together, though, this white woman and her African travelling companion were a couple that would not soon be forgotten.

And yet. This pair had escaped the country despite the thousands of dollars he'd poured into the greedy hands of police, lawyers and countless others.

The police chief who'd helped him gain access to the car rental records had boldly requested an apartment for his seventeen-year-old mistress. The detective who now dissected the lives of Ongeti and Graham had demanded funds deposited into an offshore account. These costs Shen could calculate, but the unspoken favours yet to come were another matter.

It hadn't escaped him that Ongeti was born and raised in Tanzania, the only known source of the gem Shen worked so hard to conceal. The man could work for the Tanzanian government or

TanzaniteOne Mining Ltd., the largest of the mining companies in the Merelani region.

Scarcity drove up the price, and without it the blue gem would be just another coloured stone. No longer would its limited supply, expected to run out in less than twenty years, make it the "gemstone of a generation." Demand would drop as the mystique of the gem faded and jewellers turned to sapphires as their blue gem of choice. Alongside the Tanzanian government, TanzaniteOne profited most from tanzanite, and those profits would plunge if the rarity of tanzanite were disproved.

Only when these thieves were caught would he know who had sent them to the Novoteras mine. For now, he could only follow the thin trail they did not know they had left behind.

For two days after the break-in, they'd stayed in Brazil, two days that had almost cost them their freedom. He had thought at first that the man's injuries had necessitated the delay, but not a single medical clinic reported seeing him. And if he wasn't injured, why didn't they board a flight in Belo Horizonte instead of abandoning their truck at the airport?

They were waiting for something.

Or someone.

Before morning, the South African flight Mosi Ongeti boarded would be identified. They would know too whether Alex Graham travelled with him, but other accomplices would be harder to find. The flight manifest would be searched for John Michaels, the man asking questions at their Colombian mine, but the name was probably false. And if the man travelled separately, he would be difficult to track.

Even Ongeti and Graham could have boarded separate flights, but Shen thought it unlikely after they'd stayed together for two days. The woman cared for this man's injury when she could have fled.

They travel together. But where?

South African Airway's Johannesburg hub gave access to the Middle East, Europe and Asia, which meant that in less than twenty-four hours these thieves could be almost anywhere. He couldn't afford to wait for information to trickle in, and he couldn't cover all possibilities. He had to decide.

Shen dialled the Chairman's private line. "I need access to resources in Africa," he said when Jianyu Wei's quiet voice came on the line.

"You fear your problem is headed there?"

Your problem. Sweat beaded his forehead. With two simple words, Chairman Wei had made the stakes clear.

"Yes. Kenya, South Africa and Tanzania are all possible." Shen wasn't about to commit to any one country on the African continent — not yet. "I will obtain his flight details shortly. He will be captured when he lands."

"I will have someone call you in a few minutes. He will give you all the assistance you need."

The voice was replaced by a dial tone.

Africa.

A gamble. If he were wrong, his thieves would slip through his fingers. He would be left waiting for news of his tanzanite mine to erupt, like a warrior waiting for an enemy's first bullets in the fiery dawn.

28

Nairobi, Kenya

ALEX SQUEEZED THROUGH the crowd lined up at one of the gates in the Nairobi airport with Mosi close behind her. She glanced back, time and again, making sure he didn't fall more than a few steps behind.

Tracey had worked her magic and booked a fifteen-hour flight, with the shortest of stops in Johannesburg. But Mosi's fever returned even before they'd crossed the Atlantic, and so too did his pain. He had struggled more with each passing hour, while she sat helpless beside him.

"Here. This way." She pointed toward an even more crowded hall in the noisy airport, one she was sure led to the exit.

In the narrow hall, incoming travellers fought the sea of anxious people headed for the departure gates. A pair of robed Saudi men stared at her with open hostility, offended by her cargo pants and clingy T-shirt. Normally, she'd stare back defiantly, but today she dropped her eyes.

She pressed forward, rewarded a few minutes later by the sight of the arrival hall, a space as crowded and noisy as the gated area she'd just left. Planeloads of passengers now huddled near the baggage carousels, most buzzing about their visit to Kenya in a United Nations of languages.

"We need to find a chair for you." She ducked her head, searching the slivers of space between legs and backpacks. "It's been a while since I was here. I can't remember—"

"I can stand." Mosi pointed to the wall. "I will wait for you there."
Before she could argue, he turned away from her and pushed through the crowd.

Alex heard the ping of an incoming message. *Tracey.*

Brian ran into trouble at the airport. He's driving to Ecuador to try again. He said you'd understand. BTW I've booked you into the usual hotel. Two rooms under your name.

She stared at the message, hardly believing it. The Bogotá airport should have been safe. Even if their searchers had believed they'd taken a flight out of Belo Horizonte, they wouldn't have assumed Colombia was their destination.

Unless her dad's questions, and not the Novoteras mine break-in, had triggered the surveillance. If that were true, he wouldn't be safe until he reached a country where Tabitha Metals didn't operate.

Ecuador.

It at least explained his destination.

A quick click brought up her email, and she scanned the long list of unread messages for his name. Nothing.

She typed out a text and left a voicemail, knowing her dad was probably out of cell range again. For now, she could only wait.

She felt her anger rise once more at his decision to leave his satellite phone and laptop behind. While she understood the need for extreme secrecy, this lack of easy contact had made these past six weeks damn frustrating.

Her dad wasn't one for good communication, even at the best of times. He'd write a flurry of emails and then go silent for days if not weeks. She reminded herself that he'd started field geology in the days when once-daily radio contact was the norm and every conversation could be heard by anyone on the same frequency. She herself had sat in camp listening to clipped conversations — the miner who had to be bailed out of jail, the geologist in urgent need of a doctor for an unmentionable ailment — and she understood why her dad avoided the radio.

But times had changed. Satellite phones made private calls possible, and so did email and text messages. Her dad had no excuse for going silent, especially not during a project like this one.

If he stayed true to form, she could expect a call from him only after he crossed into Ecuador. He would put as much distance as possible between him and the Bogotá airport and whatever threat lay in wait there before he risked a phone call. It meant at least another day before she heard from him, longer still before he hit the African continent.

I'm on my own.

She darted over to the rental counter, relieved to be the first one there. Keys in hand just minutes later, she rounded up their luggage and then found Mosi.

He flashed a quick smile as he pushed off from the wall to join her, but his smile disappeared within a few stilted steps. By the time they reached the parking lot, he pressed his hand tight against his thigh and grimaced with every move.

It's worse.

"As soon as we get to the hotel, I'll give you more pain medication. Twenty minutes." She helped him into the back seat of the vehicle. "It's not bleeding again, is it?"

"No." He clutched his leg and swung it onto the seat. "It feels like it did before. The infection, it has returned."

"I'll clean it out again. And I can call Eric."

But she knew they would need something more. Mosi had been on antibiotics for twenty-four hours, long enough to start controlling any infection. It wasn't the right antibiotic.

"If it's not better by morning, we'll have to find a clinic. We can decide then whether to cross the border or take our chances here."

"When does Brian arrive?"

She shook her head. "He didn't make his flight. Something happened at the Bogotá airport ... maybe they were watching that airport too. Or maybe my dad got spooked. Either way, he's driving to Quito, which means he won't be here for at least two days."

A lifetime.

She turned the key in the ignition just as her phone pinged. Another message from Tracey, one that stole her breath away.

Eric arrives Nairobi, 9:45 p.m.

29

Nairobi, Kenya

FIVE HOURS LATER, Alex was back at the Nairobi airport. She scanned the crowd of deplaning passengers for Eric. Her excitement at seeing him was mingled with fear. He shouldn't be here.

She had yet to talk to Tracey. The decision to send Eric to Nairobi without first talking to Alex, a betrayal of her confidence, hit hard. Yet she understood that worry had pushed Tracey into that decision, and Alex needed Eric's help.

"Alex!"

She heard the voice she knew so well. Stock-still, she watched Eric weave through the khaki-clad tourists, not trusting her eyes until he stood in front of her. He reached strong arms toward her, and she pressed herself against his chest. They embraced as though alone in the airport, his breath hot on her neck.

"I can't believe you're really here," she said when she finally pulled away.

"I wouldn't be … not without Tracey. I still don't know how she pulled off those flights." Eric grinned. "Of course, she had me racing out the door so fast that I hardly know what I packed." His smile disappeared. "How's Mosi?"

"Not well. I was going to take him to a hospital when we landed, but then I heard you were coming…"

She didn't say any more, not wanting their first minutes together in months to be tarnished by argument.

"I loaded up on medical supplies. With luck, I can take care of Mosi myself. That's my bag now…" he said as he lunged forward.

They wasted little time exiting the airport, hurrying past safari guides and newly-arrived visitors destined for the Serengeti. With Eric's suitcase loaded into the 4x4, Alex was quick to hit the start button and pull out of the parking lot.

"Twenty minutes to the hotel, give or take. Depends on traffic…" She glanced into the rear-view mirror. "At least we got out ahead of that crowd."

"Why didn't you tell me you were flying to Nairobi, Alex?" Eric asked.

She'd known the question was coming, but her shoulders tensed all the same.

"This … it's dangerous, Eric. It was enough that you helped Mosi." She sighed. "As much as I'm happy to see you, I wish Tracey hadn't dragged you into this mess."

"So why didn't you come home? I planned to meet you in Vancouver … I could have helped Mosi there," he argued. "It would have been so easy."

"It was just too risky to try to get Mosi into Canada — no visa, a bullet in his leg." She counted off the points. "Mosi would have been lucky to make it out of the airport. I needed to get him home. We were trying to get to Tanzania, but Nairobi was as close as Tracey could get us."

"Okay, but why didn't you tell me? You let me believe you were coming home."

"I know … I'm sorry." She sighed. "I was afraid that you'd try to help, and I didn't want to involve you more than I already had." She cocked her head. "Can't say that it worked."

"Nairobi." He shook his head. "I still can't believe I'm here. But just the thought of you trying to find a doctor, dealing with police—" His voice softened. "I don't know what I would have done if you hadn't made it home. You scared me, Alex."

His quiet admission spoke volumes. They'd grown close over

the past ten months, but only now did she realize the depth of his feelings — feelings that mirrored her own.

"I never wanted that, Eric. I just wanted to get Mosi home, and my dad was supposed to meet us here. I just assumed I'd be back in Vancouver in a few days."

"Brian is here too?"

She shook her head. "No, he's been delayed … another couple of days at least." She reached her hand out to him. "I'd be doing this alone if you hadn't come."

They drove in silence, the modern airport buildings slipping behind them. In her headlights, red-dirt shoulders were lined with parked cars and trucks, and in the distance was the glow of central Nairobi.

"It looks different in the dark," Eric softly said.

She glanced over at him. "You've been here before?"

"Back when I was fresh out of medical school." He kept his eyes straight ahead, focused on the pavement. "I spent three months with Médecins Sans Frontières … Doctors Without Borders. Most of the time I was in Tanzania, but I did some work at an AIDS clinic here in Nairobi."

It shocked her that he'd never mentioned it before, not once in the months they'd been together, even when their conversations turned to Tanzania.

"I thought you worked at a Toronto hospital before you moved west."

"I did." He sighed. "It's a long story best left for another time."

She wanted to ask more, but something in his tone warned her off. Instead she rested her hand on his leg. "Do you still know a doctor here? Or maybe a clinic we can go to?"

"I'll reach out to a few docs I know who are still with MSF, if it comes to that. But I'm going to try to take that bullet out, Alex. It's the best way to make it safe for Mosi to get help."

"That's not a good idea, Eric." Her grip tightened on the steering wheel. "I don't know what the penalties are for a doctor treating an unreported bullet wound, and I don't want to find out."

"As soon as an ER doctor sees that bullet, he's going to call police, Alex. I need to at least try."

"This is Africa, Eric. There are a thousand ways a man can get shot here. We'll come up with a story to tell police. You can't put yourself at risk. Not for this."

"I didn't fly halfway around the world without knowing the risks, Alex. The best thing for both of you is to stay out of the hospital. I can make that happen."

She knew he was right. Eric's help was the best way to bring Mosi home. *But the risk!* His medical licence, his reputation, his freedom. She wasn't sure she could live with herself if he lost any of it.

"Eric—"

"I want to do this, Alex."

"Then we take precautions. At the hotel, we go in separately, I'll meet you at the elevator and take you up to Mosi's room. I don't want anyone connecting you to us."

"I can live with that."

"And at the first sign that you can't deal with this, I take Mosi to a clinic. *Alone.*"

30

Nairobi, Kenya

ERIC'S QUIET KNOCK was quickly answered. Alex gave him the briefest smile before she pressed her back against the wall and held the door open just enough for him to pass.

He swept past her to enter a luxurious room that mirrored his own, one filled with hand-carved furniture and the deep reds and browns of Africa. And at the centre of it was a king-size bed on which Mosi lay propped against a stack of white linen pillows.

Eric saw the sweat that clung to Mosi's smooth forehead, his tight grip on the quilt, and his clenched jaw — the warning signs of pain in a patient.

My patient. A man Eric had travelled halfway around the world to treat.

"How long has the pain been this bad?" he asked as he rolled his suitcase over to the desk.

"Six, maybe seven hours."

"Alex, when was the last dose of ibuprofen?"

She glanced at her watch. "An hour ago."

Recently enough for Eric to know that the ibuprofen wasn't doing anything for Mosi's pain. Not any more.

"Let's take a look at that wound and see what we're dealing with."

Eric pulled the quilt aside to reveal Mosi's angry, swollen thigh. He didn't need to touch the taut skin to know it was raging hot. The gauze Alex had tried to pack into the wound must have fallen out, and a new scab had formed, trapping a pool of bacteria.

This man deserved better than a doctor in a hotel room. *What on earth am I doing?* But one look at Mosi's desperate eyes forced the question back.

"The abscess has reformed, so I'll drain it again and then remove the bullet." Eric rested his hand on Mosi's arm. "Sounds worse than it is. And I promise you'll feel better soon." He turned to Alex. "He's been on a steady dose of Clavulin?"

"Yes … five hundred milligrams of Clavulin every twelve hours. He's had three doses." Still standing near the door, she shuffled from one bare foot to the other. "He's due for another pill in two hours."

Almost thirty-six hours. Long enough for a steady level of antibiotics in Mosi's bloodstream, but whether the right medication coursed through his system remained to be seen.

"Alex, can you clear off the table beside the bed and wash it down, please? We'll use that for our sterile field."

She jumped into action, crossing quickly to the marble-walled bathroom. A moment later the sound of rushing water broke the quiet.

Eric dropped down on one knee and unzipped his suitcase. Inside lay a jumble of crumpled T-shirts and jeans hastily thrown into the bag in his race to the airport. How he'd managed to make the flight out of Castlegar to Vancouver, one that boarded less than three hours after Tracey had called with an astronomically priced reservation, remained a blur. So too did the many sleepless hours spent traversing the globe from Canada to Amsterdam before he boarded his final flight to Nairobi. *Eighteen hours of hell.*

From his suitcase he dug out two zippered bags that bulged with medical supplies, one provided by Dr. Lillian Sayer. He'd gone to her for a prescription for morphine, relieved when she did this without question, surprised when she also handed over her own medical kit stocked for a recent mountain hiking trip. Still, he added more: sterile water, litre bags of 0.9% IV saline solution, vials of Tazocin and lidocaine and a plastics kit.

He'd considered and rejected carrying the items onboard, knowing that the morphine alone would raise too many questions. Instead he'd packed everything into his checked bag, relieved when the suitcase safely arrived — unopened.

But now, as he surveyed these meagre supplies, he feared it wasn't enough. Eric tried to imagine his own reaction to a desperate plea from a fellow doctor for morphine, antibiotics, and IV bags. He quickly pushed away the thought, knowing that he'd say no.

With a wet cloth in hand, Alex stepped past him and headed for the side table. He dropped the IV solution and the sterile water bottles onto the bed, and headed for the bathroom.

Hands under the streaming water, he studied his reflection. Other than the shadow of stubble, his face betrayed none of the fatigue that bit into every muscle. He'd tried to sleep on the plane, but it proved impossible in a cramped economy seat that barely allowed his knees to clear the seat back in front of him. Instead, he'd watched endless hours of movies, a blurred backdrop to his worried thoughts.

He scrubbed his hands and reached below the sink for a snow-white towel, soft and heavy. On a rack above a soaker tub, more towels lay ready, and plush robes hung next to a spotless shower door. With Mosi's infection so entrenched, a sterile environment mattered less. Still, the gleaming surfaces and abundance of clean linens reassured him.

"Your turn, Alex." He stood at the bathroom door, drying his hands. "Lots of soap and hot water."

He glanced at her wrist as she approached, knowing he would find the watch her dad had given her when she graduated from geology nine years ago.

"Can you take off your watch, too?" Her fingers reached for the band as though to protect it. "You'll need to scrub your wrists."

She nodded and then slipped past him into the bathroom without comment.

Hands buried in the cotton towel, he stood at the foot of the bed. "Mosi, do you have any medical conditions?"

"No. I broke my arm once..." Mosi lifted his right arm and pointed to a spot near the elbow. "Here. But it was a long time ago."

"What about allergies?" When Mosi shook his head, Eric continued, "That's good. It's all good."

Whether he said the words to comfort his patient or himself, he wasn't sure.

He grabbed a handful of sterile packages and dropped them onto the bed before he spread a blue sterile cloth out on the nightstand. A quick pull opened an intravenous needle package that he set on the cloth before sticking pieces of tape to the table's edge. Everything at the ready, he donned a mask and then slipped his hands into latex gloves.

For the first time he felt the familiar calm, the single-minded focus on his patient.

"Some antiseptic wash on your hand first." He swiped an alcohol-soaked gauze over Mosi's hand. "And now I'll insert the intravenous needle."

Gently, he eased the sterile threader into the largest vein that bulged from the back of Mosi's hand.

"Done." He strapped the needle into place with tape yanked from the nightstand's edge. "Not too bad, was it?"

He pulled the tab from the intravenous bag and attached the tubing, adjusting the flow. Satisfied with the steady drip of saline solution, he reached for a small metal-capped vial and a sterile syringe.

"Now for the pain meds." Eric filled a syringe with liquid morphine and then replaced the needle with a cannula, carefully setting the sharp aside.

"You're going to feel this right away." He pushed the cannula into the IV port and with the gentle pressure of his thumb sent the narcotic into Mosi's vein.

With a practised hand, he ripped open more sterile packages and placed them on the blue cloth. Eric jabbed a saline-loaded syringe into the swabbed top of a vial of Tazocin and swirled the mixture until the powdered antibiotic was dissolved.

"This is a different antibiotic than the one you've been on. It's going to burn, but it won't last." He slowly pushed a bolus injection of two grams of the broad spectrum antibiotic into the IV port. A big dose, one Eric hoped would start to control this infection, but there was no way to know — not without a bacterial culture.

"I'm going to numb the area with lidocaine before I start to work." He reached for another sterile package, another vial. "This will burn a little, too." Eric made several injections into the tissue surrounding the wound.

"Done. We'll give that a few minutes to work." Eric turned to find Alex nervously checking the hotel door.

"Alex, I'll need your help here. I want you to open the sterile packages for me as we go. You know how to do that, right?"

She clutched her hands together and gave a quick nod.

"First the tweezers, please." He watched her peel the package apart with both hands.

"That's perfect, Alex." He reached his gloved hand toward the open package she presented and extracted the tweezers. "And some gauze too. Unwrap lots of it and pile it in the sterile area, close enough for me to grab."

The tweezer tips caught the raised edge of the scab, and he yanked a piece free. He swiped the tweezers against a gauze pad before he dug into scab again, pulling the last of it free. The wound oozed creamy pus.

"Alex, can you give me the hemostat? It looks like a long-handled pair of scissors." He felt the tremble of her hand when he freed the instrument from the package she held out to him. "You're doing fine, Alex."

He pressed his fingers against the sides of the swollen mound. The purulent pus that erupted from the incision was enough to force him to breathe through his mouth. "This is probably the worst part, Mosi … I'll try to be quick."

"The pain is much less than when Alex did this."

The comment brought a smile to his face, unseen beneath his

mask. "Years of training helped by the miracle of lidocaine, my friend." With the blunt tip of the instrument, Eric eased the wound open.

"Now, tell me about yourself. Are you a geologist, too?" He knew enough to distract his patient from the painful process of forcing pus to the surface. And if he were honest, he would admit to his curiosity.

"No. I am a miner, not a geologist."

Mosi added nothing more, a signal that he didn't intend to share his story.

"Alex, I want you to fill those large syringes with sterile water and refill each one when I hand it back to you."

He took his time, flushing the wound clear of pus until he could see only raw tissue beneath the skin.

Now what?

Mosi had put weight on the leg, which meant the bullet probably hadn't gone as deep as the bone. But how deep? *And how close to the artery?*

His thumb and ring finger in the steel loops, he slipped the hemostat into the wound. He slowly sent the instrument deeper, focused on every sensation, waiting for the gentle vibration that would tell him he'd hit metal.

He changed his angle when he felt only the resistance of fatty tissue, aware of how dangerously close he was to the femoral artery. A sigh escaped his lips when he finally felt the slightest tremor.

"I've got it." He clamped the hemostat around the bullet and yanked it free. Black crud, a fibre remnant that had been carried into the wound, clung to the metal. "It looks like the bullet drove a piece of your pants into the wound. Or it ricocheted and picked something up along the way." He dropped the slug on the blue paper. "Either way, it accounts for the infection."

He glanced over at Alex to find her standing stock-still, rigid, her pale forehead lined with beads of sweat.

"Take slow, deep breaths, Alex. Sit down if you have to."

When her chest expanded once, then twice, he said, "Good. Nice and slow. And when you're ready, pick up the Iodoform … it's in an amber-coloured jar."

Eric flushed the wound with more sterile water until Alex finally held the jar out to him. Her hands still shook, but she looked less likely to drop to the floor.

"We're just about done, Alex."

Eric pulled the end of the narrow Iodoform-impregnated gauze until a long length of the woven cotton strip lay near Mosi's leg. With forceps, he packed the wound with gauze until he could add no more. He clipped the strip, leaving a gauze tail to grab when it came time to repack the wound — something that would happen a dozen times before this injury healed.

With a large gauze pad taped over the wound, he finally stepped back and ripped off his gloves.

"Now we wait."

31

Nairobi, Kenya

ALEX SAT CROSS-LEGGED on the bed in their hotel room, watching Eric at the window. He'd said little since they'd left Mosi sleeping in the room next door, choosing instead to stare silently out at the Nairobi skyline.

He finally turned to face her, arms folded across his chest. "Now, I want to know what's going on." He dropped into a leather chair beneath the window. "All of it."

His question was expected, and she knew it was time. She would hold back nothing more from him.

She left the bed and eased into a matching chair across from him. "How much do you know about Tanzanite?"

"Tanzanite?" He shook his head. "I don't even know what that is."

"Not surprising … it's a gemstone that's not very well known. It can be blue, like sapphire, or more purple, like amethyst, but the unique thing about it is that it reflects *both* colours as you move it."

She pictured the rough stone that Mosi had taken from the mine. Not until it was heated to one thousand degrees Fahrenheit would the brownish rock lose its third colour, yellow. Only then would the coveted blue-purple colours that made tanzanite so unique be intensified.

"It's also incredibly rare. It's found in exactly one place and only one place: the hills of Merelani in Northern Tanzania. For the past fifty years people have searched for more tanzanite deposits, but nothing has been found…" She breathed deep, hardly believing her own next words. "Until now."

She plunged into the details of the past weeks, starting with their surveillance of the mine and ending with the night of the break-in.

"You broke into a mine?"

"Only to take the smallest sliver of gemstone … just enough for testing." Her fingernails bit into her thigh. "I was supposed to go into the mine, not Mosi. But the miners who helped us wouldn't go into the mine with a woman."

"God, Alex." He ran his hand through his hair. "If you had been shot—"

The sadness in his blue eyes nearly brought her to tears.

"None of it was supposed to happen this way," she quietly said. "We knew where the security guards were. We were well away from the entrance. No one should have seen us."

"But something went wrong."

She dropped her eyes. "One of the miners who helped us is dead."

The hiss of the air conditioner filled the room for a long minute before Eric spoke. "What about the other miner? Is he hurt too?"

"No." She glanced up at him. "Paulo is the one who got Mosi out to safety. I had to leave…" She clutched her legs to her chest. "Security guards showed up at the highway, and I had to leave."

He stood and walked over the window.

She watched his back, not knowing what else to say.

"You're lucky any of you got out alive." He swivelled to face her. "Why didn't you just call someone, ask them to investigate? I mean, there has to be someone in government in charge of the mines."

"That's just it … this mine is operating out in the open with government approval, as far as I can see. So either the government officials know what's going on and they've been bought off, or they've been duped. The only way to start an outside investigation is with evidence."

"But why you?" He tucked his hands into the front pockets of his jeans.

"I couldn't walk away. None of us could." She shook her head. "If there really is tanzanite in that Brazilian mine, then it's the biggest find in a century. But no one's talking about it. And that means it's tied to something illegal — drugs, guns or terrorism."

"I don't understand the connection, Alex." He dropped into his chair.

"You've heard of conflict diamonds ... diamonds that fund war-lords and corrupt governments in places like Sierra Leone." When he nodded, she continued, "Sometimes they smuggle out a few stones, but in other cases they take over entire mines. Think about it — a few carats of diamonds will give you ten, maybe twenty thousand dollars. Now imagine if you had a whole mine at your disposal."

He let out a low whistle.

"But it's not just diamonds. Any gemstone of value can be traded like cash or sold to a jeweller who asks few questions, and it's untrace-able. This underground money supply came up during the 9/11 inves-tigation, and they suspect that al Qaeda used rubies and tanzanite, as well as diamonds, to fund their attacks. Same can probably be said for ISIL and scores of other extremists."

"You think this Novoteras mine is linked to terrorists? God, Alex. If they find out..." He didn't finish his sentence. "Why didn't you just report it?"

"To whom, exactly? And what do I say? I *think* a mine in Brazil is up to no good. No proof, mind you." She emphasized her point with a careless wave. "Our client couldn't even get police to pay attention when four people were murdered."

"Murdered? What—"

"A diamond courier, a woman, was killed in Amsterdam, and so were her parents and fiancé. She left a piece of tanzanite and a note mentioning Tabitha Metals — the police did nothing, which was when the client came to us."

Eric stood and walked over to the window. She watched him, quiet, waiting for his words.

Please let him understand.

They'd built a solid relationship over the past ten months, despite living seven hundred kilometres apart. They drove four hundred miles through the mountains that separated Vancouver and Nelson as often as possible, but it still left weeks of time between visits. It didn't help when she left the country for extended periods as she had these last six weeks.

"Now what?" He turned from the window to face her.

"That's the million-dollar question." She leaned forward on her elbows. "My dad was supposed to fly out about the same time we did, but something happened at the Bogotá airport. I don't know what … he doesn't have a sat phone, and I haven't been able to reach him. He told Tracey that he was going to cross into Ecuador and try the Quito airport. That means he's still at least two days out."

"Can't you just take the rock to this client on your own?"

"I wish it were that easy, Eric." She studied her hands. "I don't know who the client is, and neither does Mosi. Until I hear from my dad, we're stuck."

"So we wait."

We. A reminder that Eric was in this now too. That he'd probably broken more than one law when he removed that bullet from Mosi's leg.

32

Nairobi, Kenya

MOSI WINCED AS gloved hands pressed the swollen lump on his thigh. He turned to the morning sunlight that streamed through the windows near the bed, trying to ignore the pain that seared with Eric's touch.

He had felt the pain grow stronger with each passing hour overnight, despite the morphine that Eric administered. And he had seen the worried look on the doctor's face. It had been enough to keep him from calling Kanoni to tell her that he was here in Nairobi, just nine hours from home. Only when he could promise his safe arrival without fear of bringing attention from police to his family would he share this news with his wife.

"The infected tissue must be deeper than I thought." Eric reached for a vial of lidocaine and a syringe. "I'm going to open it up a little more and drain it like I did yesterday."

Mosi caught the hint of doubt in the doctor's voice. *This infection is more serious than Eric has said.*

"Alex tells me that you used to take care of her when she visited the gold mines." Eric spoke without looking up, his thumb tight against the syringe plunger. "How old was she when you met her?"

In this moment, the first the two men had shared alone, it did not surprise Mosi that Eric asked about Alex. It brought joy to his heart to see her with this doctor, a man who protected Alex without thought of himself.

"Maybe six—" Mosi winced at the first prick of the needle. "Young enough that she still clung to her mother's hand."

"You knew her mother?" Eric's blue eyes peered over the mask.

He nodded. "Alex has her mother's eyes, her hair ... her smile." Even now, thirteen years after Amanda's death, Mosi could picture the woman who laughed so easily and treated him like treasured family. He still felt her absence. "Amanda was taken by God too soon."

"It must have been hard for Alex to lose her mom at such a young age ... especially when her dad spends so much time away from home."

"Alex was seventeen when her mama died, old enough to be on her own." He didn't miss the puzzled look in Eric's eyes. "Most women here have a husband by that age. My Kanoni was eighteen when she became the mama to my children. She —"

The scalpel that sliced into his skin stole his attention. He expected pain but felt only the pressure of Eric's hand and his blade. And then the first whiff of foul pus that oozed from the wound — a smell so vile, he took his next breaths by mouth.

"How many children do you have?" Eric asked when he set down the scalpel.

"Four girls, and one son ... Abasi. He will soon turn thirteen." His face beamed with pride as he told Eric how well his oldest child did in school. "One day, maybe my son will be a doctor. He—"

A click of the door. He breathed only when he saw Alex slip into the room.

"I talked to Paulo." She set a grocery bag onto the desk as she spoke. "He's been questioned twice now, but so has everyone else on his crew. He doesn't think he's in any danger but ... he said they asked him about a black man. A foreigner who wanted to know about the mine."

Eric's eyes met his. "So they know who you are. How?"

"There were miners I talked to that we hoped would help us," Mosi said. "One of them has told police about my questions." He read the concern in Eric's eyes. "They can know only about me. Alex never talked to any of the miners except Paulo and Benjamin. Even if police have found the truck, they will search only for me."

I did my best to protect her. The bullet in his leg had changed everything.

Alex eased into a chair near the window — a spot he had seen her in each time he had woken during the night. He had tried to send her back to her own hotel room, telling her that she needed sleep too, but she had refused.

"It's not police doing the questioning," Alex shook her head. "Paulo said that the mine manager is the only person he's talked to. They're keeping this tight. It explains why the woman I saw at the São Paulo airport didn't look like police. She must have been a private investigator of some sort."

"Then we are right about this mine," Mosi said. "They do not want to call police."

"Maybe. For all I know, the Brazilian police don't get involved in this kind of thing. There have to be hundreds of mine thefts a year. Maybe unless a significant amount is stolen, they just leave it to mine security. Still…" Alex shifted in her chair. "That woman searching the airport for us sends chills up my spine."

"And Brian?" Mosi asked.

"Nothing since his last text. Tracey hasn't heard anything from him, but he *has* to be in Ecuador by now. It can't be more than a twenty-hour drive from Bogotá to Quito."

If he makes it. The reach of Tabitha Metals remained unclear. Men could lie in wait for Brian at the border crossing and the Quito airport.

"You don't think he'd be crazy enough to try crossing illegally?" she asked.

"If Brian believes it is the only choice, that is what he will do."

"So he's on the back roads. He's in the middle of nowhere, in Colombia of all places. Driving through cartel territory and who knows what else." Her arm swept wide. "And he doesn't have a damn sat phone!"

"I think we should call Nate Taylor," Eric said.

At the mention of the man's name, Mosi saw Alex touch her forearms. He had seen the scars from her burns, and he knew she felt their heat as though it were yesterday. Whoever this Nate Taylor was, he was connected to the events in British Columbia's Slocan Valley that Alex tried to forget.

"I don't know, Eric. The RCMP operate the Canadian arm of Interpol, so Nate can probably reach out to them, but—" She jumped up from the chair. "He's a cop, a damn good one. He's going to ask questions." Alex prowled the room like a lion searching for escape. "If my dad crossed in Ecuador illegally, then Nate's questions could get him arrested the minute he sets foot in the airport."

"This police officer," Mosi interjected. "Do you trust him, Alex?"

"I don't know." Alex sighed. "I met him in Nelson last year … he's with the Royal Canadian Mounted Police. He seems like the sort of cop who knows how to run a decent investigation, but Eric knows him better than I do."

"And I can tell you that Nate will handle this quietly … I know he will," Eric argued. "He'll be able to find out if Brian's been in an accident or if he's sitting in a jail cell, at least. And we can ask him to look into Tabitha Metals. Strictly off the record. He'll do that for me, Alex."

"I don't think he'll get any further than I did with Tabitha Metals. I tracked the owners as far as I could, and I found nothing but international holding companies. It's going to take big guns to unravel this."

"Don't sell Nate short," Eric countered. "There were CSIS and Homeland Security agents on that integrated task force he was part of, so he has contacts. And he's RCMP … that has to get him something."

Alex went quiet and walked over to the window to stare out at the morning sky. Mosi could feel her struggle. As much as she needed help in finding her father, she questioned whether this police officer was the man to ask.

Mosi could offer her little counsel. If Brian were missing anywhere in Africa, there were men he could go to for help, but not in South America. Even Brian's contacts on that continent were few.

The rip of paper brought his attention back to Eric. He had felt little of what the doctor had done to his leg since Alex had arrived. Now it was over, and Eric covered the wound in soft, white gauze and taped it in place without a word. Whether this man's silence was due to the care he delivered or worry, he did not know.

"When can we leave?" It was time to go home to his family, to Kanoni and his sweet children.

"Anytime." Eric pulled the mask from his face. "There's nothing I would do here that I can't do in Tanzania."

"We can't … not yet." Alex swung around to face him. "I'm sorry, Mosi. If that rock we have really is tanzanite, we can't take it into Tanzania. We have to be able to prove that it came from outside the country."

"I have also worried about how we will explain this rock," Mosi said. "Unless they believe that this rock we have came from Brazil, they will believe it stolen."

Eric sighed. "You guys don't make this simple, do you?" He slipped his hands free of the gloves.

"Nothing about this project has been simple." She sat on the edge of Mosi's bed. "There's a gem dealer in Dubai, Marouk Faasad. I trust him, and he's not going to ask any questions. If he confirms that what we have is tanzanite, I can leave the gemstone in Dubai … it will be safe there until my dad arrives."

"Can't you go to a dealer here?" Eric asked. "Taking Mosi home today is one thing, but flying to Dubai—"

"I'll go alone, Eric. It's better that way … I'll fly out in the morning, see Faasad, and be back by dinner." She turned to Mosi. "It's just one more day. You can stay here and rest."

"I don't like this plan, Alex. No." Eric shook his head. "If I need more antibiotics, a hospital … I'll need you *here*. There must be a dealer here you can go to."

Mosi understood Eric's need to keep Alex close. But for Alex to meet a dealer in Nairobi carried more risk than the doctor understood.

"It is safer for Alex to take the tanzanite to Dubai," Mosi said. "There are many smuggled gems here in Nairobi, and a dealer will ask too many questions or call police. My wife's family is here in Kenya. I will call them if we need help." He turned to Alex. "But you must call this police officer. Brian has been out of touch for too long."

He could do no more to keep Alex safe.

33

Vancouver, Canada

NATE TAYLOR HAD EXPECTED Eric, from the caller ID that flashed on his cell phone. Instead he heard Alex Graham's voice and a plea for help in locating her father, Brian.

"When did you last hear from him?" He searched for a pen on a desk crowded with reports that demanded his attention.

"Thirty-five hours ago. Tracey Caminski—"

"Who's that?"

"Our office manager. My dad texted her from Bogotá to say that he was headed to the airport in Ecuador. But he hasn't returned his rental ... at least nothing is showing up on his credit cards yet. No hotels either. And that's what has me worried. He has to stop at some point, Nate."

"I hate to say it ... but an accident is a strong possibility, Alex. Have you tried the hospitals?"

"Tracey is calling hospitals in Colombia and Ecuador ... anything along the route we think he took, but so far nothing."

"I can reach out to local law enforcement down there," he said. "At minimum, I should be able to confirm whether Brian's passport showed up in the system—"

"It might not, Nate. I'm not sure he crossed the border legally."

He shook his head. As if chasing down a geologist somewhere in South America wasn't bad enough, Brian Graham wasn't playing by the rules.

Colombia. Ecuador. Both countries would have to be alerted unless Brian's passport showed up.

"What the hell is going on, Alex?"

"Not what you think. He was asking questions — too many questions. His last message said that he ran into trouble at the Bogotá airport and he was headed to Ecuador to try again ... that's all we know for sure."

Nate stared out the glass wall that separated him from the rest of the RCMP detachment. She wasn't making this easy.

"One more thing. My dad was asking questions about Tabitha Metals, and from what we've found, there may be a terrorist connection."

Shit! This just turned into something above his pay grade.

"How solid is your information?"

"Not good enough — not without my dad." She paused. "I need help, Nate."

She's scared.

Alex rattled off Brian Graham's passport number and flight details, as well as Tracey Caminski's contact information and her own. She extracted his promise of an update tomorrow, whether he had news or not, and then she was gone.

He fired off an email to the RCMP-run Ottawa Interpol office, asking for assistance from local law enforcement in Colombia and Ecuador and a check on Brian Graham's passport.

As for the rest, Nate wasn't sure what to believe. *A crazy story.* Before he kicked this up the ladder, he'd need something more than Alex's accusation against Tabitha Metals.

Alex Graham.

He half expected to run into the petite geologist on the crowded streets of downtown Vancouver, given that her office wasn't far from his own. But he'd seen only Eric in the months since the move, and not often. They'd managed a Canucks hockey game one weekend and a quick beer another, but the friendly ER doc's time in Vancouver belonged to Alex.

Vancouver. After eight months, this west coast Canadian city still didn't feel like home. He and Jess had never thought they'd leave Nelson and the picturesque Slocan Valley, where they'd both grown up and then spent twenty years of marriage. With Olivia moving to Vancouver for her first year at the University of British Columbia, they'd been preparing for life without their only daughter. Instead, the entire family had picked up and left.

He'd been offered his choice of plum assignments after his successful stint with the Integrated Security Task Force, including this promotion to the Major Crimes Unit, based in Vancouver. It was an easy decision for him and Jess. They'd be close enough to Olivia to keep an eye on her and just far enough away from Nelson to keep the dark memories at bay.

But the move had been a big adjustment. Jess had been lucky enough to arrange a transfer to a nearby bank branch, but neither of them was prepared for the daily commute along with thousands of others. Expensive housing had forced them well outside downtown Vancouver, and even then the sale of their spacious home had provided only for the purchase of a modest two-bedroom condo. Skis, hockey gear, winter clothes — so much of their life in Nelson was now crammed into a storage locker no bigger than a closet. Still, they never once regretted the decision.

Liv is safe. He glanced over at Olivia's high school graduation photo. His daughter's days were filled with classes and new friends — and she was happy. In a backhand way, Alex had helped make that possible, and somewhere deep down, he felt he owed her.

Nate's stubby fingers stabbed at the keyboard, typing "Tabitha Metals" into the search box of the security database maintained by the Canadian Security Intelligence Service. Since 9/11, CSIS, together with practically every other security agency worldwide, had ramped up its threat investigations. Everything of value turned up in this database shared with RCMP and others.

Nothing. If Alex was right and Tabitha Metals had ties to al Qaeda or ISIL, no one knew about it. *Not yet.*

An internet search delivered a dozen links, all of them announcing one mine or another in South America. He checked each one, hunting for a name, anything that might point to the owners, but only a lawyer was ever mentioned — a company spokesman of sorts, a name that led nowhere.

He plucked the baseball from its perch and leaned his bulky frame back, his chair squeaking in protest. His eyes on the ball, he lined his fingers up with the red leather stitching.

Nate glanced up as Danica McNulty passed by his desk, her eyes on her cell phone with each tight step. The dark-haired woman had joined their unit only a month back, and he liked her well enough. But whether it was her age or her designer clothes, he felt they shared little in common. She was a good cop, though, and she was tech-savvy.

"Danica ... you got a minute?"

She swivelled his way and shot him a smile. "Sure. What's up?"

"I'm looking for info on a company named Tabitha Metals. Nothing in the security database. I tried the web, but that didn't give me anything other than a few press releases and newspaper articles. Anything else I can try?"

"How important?" She bit her brightly painted lips.

"Hard to say." He tossed the ball from hand to hand, considering how much to tell her. "Could be a terrorist connection, but I've got nothing more than a rumour right now."

"But enough to have you worried." She cradled her cellphone in both hands. "Any names show up in those articles?"

"Just one. A lawyer named—" He twisted his head to the screen. "Alonso Quinto. I can't find much on him either."

With both thumbs hitting the tiny keyboard on her phone, Danica looked up at him. "How do you spell the last name?"

He rattled off the spelling. "Do you think you can find him?"

"Maybe." She flashed a smile. "If we get lucky, he's on Facebook or Twitter." Already on the move, she twisted back. "And if we're really lucky, he's mentioned a friend or two in his postings."

Like old-fashioned police work, but not quite. He still liked to look a person in the eye when he talked to them. Even the phone wasn't as good — you could hear uncertainty, emotion, but it felt like you were working with half a deck and the best cards were missing.

His call from Alex was like that. She seemed nervous, her words carefully chosen and too few details delivered. If she were standing in front of him, it wouldn't take him long to get to the bottom of this. Maybe Eric could convince her to come into the office. Although he likely had his hands full trying to keep her from hopping the next flight to Colombia.

She's in South America!

The thought hit like a freight train. Alex would never sit here with her dad missing. Not for three days.

And Eric is with her.

He slammed the ball against the desk and grabbed the mouse. He scrolled through his list of contacts, pausing at a dozen names, rejecting them in turn. Until he neared the bottom of the list.

Mark Brody. The Dallas-born federal agent had gone to work in Washington after three tours of duty in the Special Forces. Although Nate had only met the thirty-nine-year-old a few times during the Nelson bombings, he knew the man was well-connected. And he knew him well enough to ask a favour.

Nate snatched up the phone, but he couldn't bring himself to dial. He jerked to a stand and grabbed his jacket.

This was one call best made elsewhere.

34

São Paulo, Brazil

SHEN LOOKED UP to find Meilin Yang in the doorway with a silver bucket, awaiting permission to enter his office. With his nod, she glided across the room as though floating just above its surface. As she neared the desk, she gave him the smallest smile.

This woman, meek and obedient, made herself useful — she even hinted at her willingness to meet his most intimate needs. But although her slender body and perfect features tempted him, he resisted.

Her connections within the Communist Party ran deep, and although her loyalty to Chairman Wei was unquestionable, her loyalty to the party trumped all. He questioned Wei's decision to allow her this close to their Brazilian operation, where she might learn about the tanzanite. The only answer was the Chairman's desire to satisfy a powerful ally's demand that this intelligent, well-educated Beijing transplant be given an important position.

He watched her drop ice into a whisky glass before she poured Scotch over the two perfect cubes. She left the drink on the polished buffet and turned for the door, as though unaware that he watched her. At a single word from him, she would sit in one of the leather chairs across from him, awaiting his command — ready to do whatever he asked without question.

But he remained silent and only swivelled to pick up the prepared drink when she had closed the door behind her.

A strategic marriage to Meilin would strengthen his own connection to the party, and even Mother would counsel such a move — as would Chairman Wei. But he felt no affinity to the Communist Party, no desire to ingratiate himself with the Chinese political power brokers like Wei did, not after what happened to his parents.

His hand brushed the surface of the Ming Vase, the porcelain as cold as the ice-filled glass. Both of his parents had been forced into the countryside during the Cultural Revolution simply because they were educated. A neighbour's lie told to overzealous Communist leaders had then jailed Mother for three years, a sentence that almost killed her. Father's health faltered during those years as he struggled to care for himself and two young boys with rations meant for one. Although Father survived to see his beloved wife freed, he died just one year later and Mother never fully recovered.

Years spent overseas had shielded Shen from the Communist Party's pull, and he refused now to acquiesce. Instead, he followed Uncle's advice and carefully cultivated his own network of powerful men and women — people so fearful of the secrets he held, so indebted to him, that they refused him nothing. But if he did not find the thieves and recover any stolen tanzanite, they could not protect him from Chairman Wei. No one could.

Shen turned back to the detective's report that had arrived just an hour ago, a report that contained enough material on Alex Graham and Mosi Ongeti to worry him.

A geologist and a miner.

Little doubt remained that this pair came for the tanzanite.

The Canadian geologist could work for anyone, especially given a passport crowded with entry stamps from almost every corner of the globe. Canadian mining companies vigorously competed for choice mineral rights throughout Brazil, but they were not alone. The United States, Australia, Russia — their mining industry giants were behind many of the most lucrative deals.

The smallest hint of the true nature of the Novoteras mine would entice all of them to Minas Gerais, each frantically searching for a similar tanzanite deposit. He'd heard no rumours, seen no evidence of such activity, but this breach might warn of an impending rush.

But it was her connection to a Vancouver consulting company owned by her father that interested him most. The detective had been quick to discover Graham and Company but had not yet located photos of Brian Graham and the other geologists who worked with him.

Shen was convinced that one of those geologists had been in the Colombian mine, but the motive escaped him. These geologists would have no reason to investigate Tabitha Metals on their own. Someone had directed them.

Long Bridge Merchant Group had many dealings in Canada. A diamond mine in the Northwest Territories, lead-zinc in the Yukon, along with part interest in several oil company drilling projects. All were part of the legal arm of the Chairman's business, and none could tie to Tabitha Metals or the Novoteras mine.

And it did nothing to explain Mosi Ongeti. The man's connection to Tanzania could not be dismissed, but if Graham and Company had been hired by the Tanzanian government or TanzaniteOne Mining Ltd. had initiated an investigation, they would have sent a geologist, not a lowly miner.

Like a match flared in a dark room, he saw only what was in front of him. The edges, the big picture lay beyond his grasp.

What am I missing?

35

Dubai, United Arab Emirates

ALEX LEANED FORWARD as her taxi sped from the Dubai airport. It was early yet, but the roads were already jammed with black SUVs and luxury cars.

Oil. It had changed everything in this tiny Middle Eastern kingdom. Dubai had risen like a phoenix from the desert sand to become the crown jewel of the United Arab Emirates. The sail-shaped Burj Khalifa tower on the edge of the Red Sea, the Atlantis resort on the man-made Palm Island, the Dubai Mall with its ski hill — all of it a flashy display of the immense oil profits in the hands of the ruling royal family.

She felt eyes on her and found her driver watching her in the rear-view mirror. He looked like one of the many immigrants from Russia and the Eastern European countries who flocked to Dubai with dreams of a better life. For most, long hours of menial work for little money and a desperate yearning for home became their reality.

She dropped her eyes to her phone and tapped out yet another text to her dad. Both before she left Nairobi and after she landed in Dubai, she'd tried calling him without success. By now he must have listened to at least one of her messages, yet he remained as silent as the rocks that preoccupied so much of his time. She clutched her phone. What she wanted more than anything was to see her dad's face in the waiting crowd when she flew back in Nairobi.

When she finally stepped out of the air-conditioned taxi, the heat seared like fire against her skin. By the time she walked through the wooden portico of the Deira Gold Souk, her shirt clung to her and sweat dripped down her face. She welcomed the shade of the storefront-lined corridor but not the crush of shoppers in this jewellery market.

Women and men alike gawked at gold-filled windows before they bravely entered shops to barter for their desired necklace, ring or bracelet. Alex caught fragments of Italian, German and Spanish as she wove through the noisy crowd of tourists drawn here to shop for gold and gems. As always, it surprised her that many of the women flouted the modest dress rules of Dubai, wearing shorts and sleeveless tees in a country that expected arms and legs to be covered.

Even in a white cotton shirt and pants Alex felt uneasy. Dubai might be liberal, but neighbouring Saudi Arabia was anything but. Visiting Saudi men in white *thobes*, with their *niqab*-covered women in tow, were quick to condemn the casual dress of Western and European women. Like most of her women friends in the oil industry, here she wore loose, ankle-skimming skirts and long-sleeved shirts to avoid derisive stares. But this trip she'd been lucky to find even this outfit in a suitcase of hiking boots, khaki pants and fleece.

At an unmarked steel door, a sliver between two shops, she left the noise of the Souk behind. Each of her steps on the stone floor echoed loudly in the narrow hallway that led to a second door — the true entrance to the business she sought.

She faced the camera mounted high above the door and rang the bell. Almost immediately, the electronic lock on the door released, and Alex entered Marouk Faasad's outer office.

A slender woman dressed in a flowing navy dress and matching headscarf appeared with Alex's first step through the doorway.

"Please, sit." Her hand waved Alex toward a leather sofa. "You must be warm."

Alex gratefully took a cool washcloth the woman offered from a silver tray and pressed it against her face.

The woman held a silver Arabian teapot high, pouring a stream of mint tea into a small glass cup that she set in front of Alex. "Mr. Faasad will be ready for you shortly."

Alex raised the cup to her lips, breathing in the rich scent. She eyed the plate of figs, deciding that food wasn't a good idea, not when her stomach churned with nerves. Instead, she settled for the piping hot tea, a Middle Eastern tradition that seemed at odds with the desert heat.

She glanced around a room she had last visited with her dad. He was the one who had the connections with gem and gold dealers in this part of the world, not her. If Faasad couldn't help her, she'd be left scrambling for another option.

The woman returned, and Alex was quick to follow her into Marouk Faasad's office. Tea had already been laid out on one corner of an elaborate desk behind which sat the man she'd come to see.

He stood as she entered, his fingers buttoning his suit jacket closed. "Miss Graham. I hope you are well."

As always, he didn't reach out a hand to her, and Alex did not offer her own. She'd learned long ago that a handshake was an unwelcome gesture in a region of the world that often found offence in a man touching an unrelated woman.

"I have no complaints." She smiled and slipped into a chair across from him, setting her backpack on the floor beside her. "I hope you can say the same, and that…" She tried to remember his wife's name and the number of children he had but failed. "Your family is well."

Faasad beamed. "I am a grandfather again. My son is blessed with another boy." The Calcutta-born man sat, his black suit outlined against dazzling blue tile that filled the wall behind him. "And your father? I had thought he might be with you."

"My dad is busy as ever at the Tanzanian gold mine." She picked up a glass of fragrant tea as she delivered her practised lines. "I'm on my way to see him."

"Please, give him my best." He picked up his own teacup. "Now, to what do I owe this most pleasant visit?"

"A gemstone I purchased in Thailand."

Under his watchful gaze, she reached into her backpack for the plastic sample bag that held her prize. She slipped the gemstone free and set it on a white velvet pad on the desk.

Faasad leaned in to pick it up, and she caught the spicy scent of his cologne, an alluring concoction that forced a deep inhale — her first real breath since she'd sat down.

He picked up the gemstone and held it under a high-powered spotlight for a moment. "Tanzanite." He set it back on the pad. "Why bring it to me? You should take it to Jaipur and have it cut. It will make a fine piece of jewellery once it is finished."

"I want to make sure it's authentic."

"You bought it from a reputable Thai jeweller?"

Damn. He was asking more questions than she expected.

"No." She gave a weak smile. "It was an impulse purchase from a market in Bangkok."

"It is unusual to be offered a rough stone, especially one as large as this. It was likely stolen from a mine and smuggled out of the country. Gemstones above five carats are expected to be cut and polished in Tanzania, and every legitimate tanzanite miner in the Merelani Hills follows this practice."

It complicated matters. She'd known that Tanzania restricted the export of tanzanite, but she didn't know the country had taken over the cutting process too. Unless she could prove that the tanzanite in her possession came from Brazil, she'd likely be accused of buying a stolen gemstone. Or worse — she might be accused of stealing it herself.

"It surprised me too … which is why I wonder if it's a fake."

"Your father. Has he seen the stone? He could easily tell you if it is real."

Damn. Damn. Damn.

"No. Not yet. How would I explain to him that his geologist daughter, who should know better, purchased a fake stone?" She flashed a smile.

He laughed. "It is easy to be fooled, even if you are a geologist.

Synthetic forsterite, Tanavyte, Coranite … they are difficult to tell from true tanzanite." He set the gemstone down and adjusted a narrow spotlight on it. "Let us see what you have."

He selected a brass pick and ran the sharp point against the side of the rock. With a jeweller's loupe, he examined the site for signs of a scratch. "Hardness of six and a half, maybe seven … same as forsterite, but not as hard as Tanavyte or Coranite" He held an aquamarine Hanneman filter in front of the rock. "Pinkish-orange."

She didn't know if that was good or bad, and he must have read the confusion in her face.

"Forsterite appears bright green when viewed through this filter." He smiled. "You have nothing to fear from your father. This is pure tanzanite." He set it on a scale. "Total rough weight of 13.8 carats. It will produce a good-quality polished gem of substantial size … eight carats, maybe ten if it's cut by the right person."

It's real! Until this very moment, she didn't truly believe it possible.

She forced a smile, knowing that one would be expected. "Thank you."

He picked the stone up again, turning it from side to side in the light. "Most tourists would not see the hidden beauty in this rock and could not imagine the brilliant blue that will emerge once it has been heated." His eyes met hers. "This is an exceptional stone … one that will command top dollar after it is cut and polished."

He scribbled a name on the back of his business card and handed it to her. "Here is the name of the best gem cutter in Jaipur … I have used him many times. He will do a very good job for you."

"I'll plan a stop in India on my way home, then." She tucked the card and the gemstone into her pack. "Thank you for your help."

As though summoned, Faasad's assistant entered the room, and minutes later Alex found herself back in the crowded passageway. She slipped one strap of her backpack over her shoulder and clutched the bag protectively under her arm as she headed for the exit.

One more stop.

36

Novoteras Mine

JORGE STARED ACROSS his desk at the reddened face of the mine's production manager, Tim Wong. Gone was the affable smile of the forty-three-year-old, in its place a clenched jaw and grim-set mouth. Jorge had seen such anger only a few times in the seven years he had worked with the engineer, and it had never before been directed toward him.

Tim sat perched against the chair edge as though he might leap across the desk at any moment and clutch his hands around Jorge's throat.

"It is your fault that we cannot meet our production quota." The black-haired engineer stabbed his thumb into the air. "You shut down operations for a full day. You drag the miners in here hour after hour for questions. You refuse to assign a replacement for the dead man."

Three fingers now taunted him, each punctuating a fact for which Jorge had no argument.

Their eyes met. Tim had been the one to order air shaft seven sunk during the mine cave-in five years ago, a futile attempt that would have seen the trapped men dead before their escape route materialized. Tim had also been the one who convinced Shen Li to widen and deepen the shaft so it would be ready if disaster struck again. Now the engineer carried the blame of allowing a back door into the mine.

One I should have guarded. Neither of them could afford further failure.

"Mr. Li has ordered that I find the men responsible for this break-in, and I will do whatever is necessary, even if it means I must shut down production." Jorge fingered the pen that sat in the crease of the open personnel folder on his desk. "Besides, only Tunnel Five has been affected … a small crew. Add more men to the other tunnels. Have them work more hours."

"Tunnel Five—" Tim pressed his lips together. "Mr. Li will not look favourably on your investigation when he hears my report. You…" he pointed his finger at Jorge. "And only you, will be blamed for not meeting our deadline. I will not protect you." He shoved back his chair and stormed from the office.

There had been delays before, work stoppages due to flooding and cave-ins, and Tim had never complained. On the contrary, the engineer worked tirelessly alongside the miners, digging rock out of a collapsed tunnel or clearing water as deep as the men's waists, without regard for their production schedule. Today, though, he seemed a different man.

I do not really know him.

Jorge would be the first to say that he had not tried hard enough to befriend the mainland China-born engineer. Schooled in the United States, Tim Wong seemed more American than Chinese, going so far as to adopt an Anglicized version of his true name, Wong Tingzhe. It mattered little, because they had found no common ground in their few awkward lunches together. Tim preferred the company of the Chinese geologist, another man who, although friendly, kept his distance from Jorge.

The ringing phone startled him, and he snatched it up before it rang a second time. He was quick to recognize the voice of Eduardo Rossi, one of the few officers he had kept in touch with after leaving the Policía Civil. He had not seen the man in more than three years, not since Rossi had taken a promotion and relocated to São Paulo. Everything from Eduardo's tone to his lack of small talk, though, warned that this was not a social call.

"I had a strange visitor this morning. An American asking about your mine."

Jorge's hand tightened on the phone. "What did he want?"

"Every detail we have on Tabitha Metals. Every name, every investigation … everything."

Jorge heard the sharp inhale of a cigarette. The last time he had seen Eduardo, the detective had given up smoking at the insistence of his pregnant wife. Like the dozen or more attempts Eduardo had made while the two of them worked together, it clearly had not lasted.

"I told him what I know. That Tabitha Metals owns your mine and fourteen others in South America. That there have never been any problems at any of the mines, not even an environmental protest." Another long draw on his cigarette. "But he did not seem satisfied…"

"What is he looking for?"

"I hoped you could tell me. He seemed especially interested in the Novoteras mine. Asked about it specifically."

"There is nothing about our operation that would be of interest to an American."

Unless.

"You say this man showed up this morning?"

"Bright and early. And Jorge … the commissioner himself called to ask me to cooperate with him."

Jorge swallowed hard. He should have insisted that they involve police, especially when they started to track Mosi Ongeti and Alex Graham. *Foreigners.*

"So this is an official investigation?"

"No. The commissioner made it sound like a favour."

"A favour?"

"I have seen this man before … he is hard to forget, with his cowboy boots and jeans. If I had to guess, I would say that he helped us in one of our drug cartel investigations, and so the commissioner is offering assistance—" Eduardo coughed. "Damn cigarettes. I really should give them up."

"You think this man is with the American DEA?"

"Maybe, but he could also be CIA. The only thing I know for

sure is that he is definitely interested in your mine. He would not have called in a favour unless it was something serious."

Shen Li might not want the police involved, but Jorge could not hold back the truth. Not from a fellow police officer he had once depended on for his life. Not with an American asking questions.

"We had a break-in a few nights back, and there is a possibility that a foreigner was involved. Maybe this American is looking for the same man I am."

"If that were the case, he would have mentioned the break-in. This seemed to be more about the owners of the mine or maybe the mine itself." The crinkle of cellophane and the hiss of a lighter's flare filled a pause. "Jorge, whatever this man is looking for, he is heading your way. I would almost guarantee it."

Jorge picked up his pen. "What is his name?"

"Mark Brody."

37

Mwanza, Tanzania

THE MIDDAY HEAT of Mwanza settled into the prop-engine aircraft now quiet on the runway. Alex felt for an elastic in one of her pockets and yanked her hair into a ponytail, her eyes on the backs of the deplaning passengers.

"Ready?" she asked.

She didn't miss Mosi's white-knuckle grip on the headrest as he lifted himself from the narrow seat.

They'd changed their plans, opting for this three-hour flight instead of a nine-hour drive that would easily take them twelve. Mosi's fever had dropped, but not enough, and Eric had drained Mosi's abscess twice more while she'd been in Dubai.

She climbed out of the window seat and lifted her backpack from the overhead bin, following Mosi slowly from the plane. By the time they finally reached the bottom stair, the other passengers were already inside the terminal, and Eric stood alone on the tarmac with their bags at his feet.

"We're almost there." She wrapped her hands protectively around Mosi's arm. "Lean on me if you have to."

She picked up a duffel and let Eric take the other two bags so she could keep one hand on Mosi's arm. Once through the door of the small, regional airport, they faced a crowd of people, but nothing as bad as the Nairobi airport they had just left. Only visitors heading to the Western Corridor of the Serengeti landed here, with Arusha a

more common starting point for tourists — except during the annual
wildebeest migration.

No matter how often Alex saw this spectacle of nature she, like so
many other visitors to Tanzania, felt compelled to follow the herds.
The annual drought drove millions of wildebeest and zebra north to
Kenya in search of green grass and fresh water. With lions, hyenas
and vultures in their midst, many of the scruffy wildebeest and their
stripped companions never made it to the Kenya border. Those that
did, faced the deadly crocodiles that lay in wait in the dark waters
of the Grumeti River.

Like the guards at the mine. She still wondered if the guards had
known that Mosi, Paulo and Benjamin were below in the mine tunnels and had aimed their rifles at that air shaft, waiting for the men
to surface. It almost seemed more believable than a chance sighting
from a sniper tower more than a mile away and a single deadly shot.

"What is it, Alex?" Mosi's gentle voice.

"Nothing." She squeezed his arm. "We're safe ... you're home.
And—"

"Mosi! Mosi!"

Zawadi.

Even to a stranger, the resemblance between the two brothers, just
nine years apart, was obvious. Zawadi stood just two inches taller and
carried twenty pounds less than Mosi, but he had the same build, the
same gentle brown eyes and round face as his older brother.

The two men held each other tight, talking in hushed Swahili.
They were close enough for her to hear Zawadi ask more than once
if Mosi really was okay.

When they finally pulled apart, Zawadi clutched her tightly.

"It's so good to see you." She hugged him to her, this soft-spoken
giant she hadn't seen in more than a year.

"Thank you for saving my brother," he whispered before he
slipped out from her embrace. He wrapped his arm around Mosi's
shoulder as though he needed to touch him to be sure he was really
here.

"Zawadi, this is Dr. Eric Keenan. He is Alex's friend," Mosi said. "He has taken care of me very well."

"Then you are family, Dr. Keenan. Welcome." Zawadi grabbed Eric's hand and clapped him on the back. "You must meet my wife and children."

"I'd like that." Eric smiled, his hand still firmly in Zawadi's grasp. "And my family call me Eric."

Zawadi flashed an impish grin at Alex. "I like this man you bring with you to Tanzania. He will make a good husband."

"You never change, do you, Zawadi?" She laughed. "Go. Take Mosi home so he can see his family. We'll catch up with you as soon as we're done at the mining camp."

It took no further convincing, and she watched Mosi walk stiffly out the doors, Zawadi's arm protectively wrapped around his waist.

"Younger brothers." She shook her head. "Mosi has six of them, and they're all trouble."

"Six! Big family."

"You don't know the half of it. Two mothers, six brothers and three sisters, most of whom have at least three or four children. Can you imagine what that family get-together is like?"

"Noisy!" Eric laughed. "It's bad enough when my cousin brings his two children over to my parents' house for the holidays. One look at the presents under the tree is all it takes for those kids to start squealing. Even my mother takes cover in the kitchen at that point."

She listened to Eric talk about the last time he and his younger brother Matt had been in Toronto for Christmas, and their parents had invited a house full of guests. It sounded chaotic, but she sensed that Eric wouldn't have wanted it any other way. Between Matt's law practice and Eric's ER shifts, it would be difficult enough for Eric to see his thirty-four-year-old brother, but they also lived on opposite sides of the country. It meant that the two brothers saw little of each other and even less of their parents.

Family. Her dad was all she had left other than an aunt, her mother's sister who married an American and now lived in San Francisco.

Tracey had become her family in Vancouver, and Mosi — he was as close to a brother as she'd known.

She turned to Eric. "You're sure Mosi is okay?"

"His fever hasn't gotten any worse, so I think the antibiotics are working." He ran a hand through his hair. "But we have to stay on top of that abscess."

She heard the uncertainty in his voice.

"But he's going to be okay, right? Please tell me, he's going to be okay."

"With the right antibiotic, he should improve over the next few days. If not—"

"We'll need a doctor," she finished.

"I emailed a couple of doctors I met through MSF … I should hear back soon." He pulled his phone from his pocket and tapped the mail icon. "With luck, one of them is working in East Africa or they can put us in touch with a doctor here. I should hear back soon"

"Zawadi may know someone … and there has to be a clinic here we can go to."

"If I can leverage a connection, it would be better. There will be fewer questions and I'd like a culture of that wound right away in case we have to switch antibiotics." He scrolled through his messages. "Even if I have the right antibiotic, I'm going to need more of it. And I'm hoping that one of the doctors can at least recommend a nurse skilled in wound care."

"A nurse? Can't you take care of the wound? I mean, you've drained this abscess a few times now."

"I can, but a good nurse will be better at it." He looked up from his phone. "This is a serious infection, Alex. We need help."

38

Gold Mine near Mwanza, Tanzania

ALEX TAPPED HER FOOT on the brake, slowing behind a truck that crawled through a rutted section of road, the worst since they'd left the Mwanza airport an hour ago. By now Mosi would be at home, but they still had a half hour or more to go before they reached her dad's mining camp.

She glanced at the long line of traffic behind her through a back windshield coated with red dust.

Red. The colour of Tanzania.

She hadn't been here in more than a year. Her dad had asked her to come ten months ago, while she recovered from her burns, and she had been tempted but refused. Now, as she saw the familiar red earth, she wished she had decided differently.

I miss it. I miss him.

"Look at that, Alex." Eric pointed to a crowd of people standing in front of a ramshackle food stall on the side of the highway. "That Maasai warrior standing next to those boys in their jeans and running shoes. What a mix!"

She saw more than the Maasai in his red *suka*: a woman in a colourful batik dress, struggling with a heavy basket; a girl in a white shirt and green skirt, loaded down with school books; men in jeans and work shirts, looking down at their cell phones.

"It must be a bus stop. There's probably a school nearby, and…" She watched the side of the road. "I think those small wooden buildings with the corrugated tin roofs are stores of some sort. I see a Coke sign on one, and it looks like they sell building materials in the one next to it."

Alex tried to keep the 4x4 on even ground, but her wheels were forced into the gouged tracks, pitching the vehicle — and them — mercilessly. She yanked the steering wheel over hard, only to slam Eric into the side of the door.

"I'd forgotten just how bad the roads are here." He clung to the door handle as though it would keep him upright.

"Sorry. The road is pretty chewed up here." She glanced at him. "Are you okay?"

"Sure." He rubbed his shoulder. "Just took me by surprise."

"The roads are going to get much worse near the gold mines. But we should be in the mining camp in another thirty minutes."

"Does your dad stay at the camp all the time?"

"Mostly. For the past three years he's been developing a gold mine here for a client, so it makes sense for him to be on-site. But he doesn't need to be there all the time. I think this year alone he's been in Russia, China and the Middle East handling work for other clients."

"And I thought *you* travelled a lot."

She laughed. "It does sometimes feel like I spend more time on the road than in Vancouver. I bought my condo four years ago, and other than a few framed photos, the walls are pretty bare. I'm just not home enough to hit the galleries to find something."

"Maybe we can do that when I come to Vancouver next time. I could use something more on my walls than the calendar in the kitchen."

"What a pair we are! You're not home much either ... you practically live at the hospital." She smiled. "Hell, they encourage you to stay over, with nice cozy beds in those on-call rooms."

"Hey, they're not the most comfortable beds. And I do go home." She raised an eyebrow, and he laughed. "Well, sometimes."

Eric turned away to glance out the side window. "This looks familiar, somehow. How close are we to Lake Tanganyika?"

"A long way. It has to be at least three hundred miles southwest of here, between Burundi and the Congo. We flew into Mwanza, which is on the southern tip of Lake Victoria — Uganda and Kenya are north of us, Burundi and the Congo are to the west."

"Maybe I drove through here once … on my way to the Nyaru- gusu camp. It was near the Tanzania-Congo border, close to Lake Tanganyika. We flew into some airport like the one we just left and drove for hours to get to the refugee camp."

For the first time, a single detail about his time in Tanzania. She wasn't about to let the opportunity slip past.

She turned to him. "Why didn't you ever tell me you were here, Eric? It's not like Tanzania didn't come up in conversation more than a few times, but you never said a word."

"I try not to remember the months I spent in Africa. I've never seen such despair, such cruelty." He turned his head and stared out the window. His voice barely above a whisper, he said, "There was a young woman, a girl really, whose face I can still picture. She'd been raped, tortured. How she made it from the Congo to the refugee camp is a miracle."

Alex had seen the orphanages filled to capacity by the unforgiv- ing AIDS virus that took mothers and fathers from their children and left a lucky few in the care of grandmothers, many of them sick with AIDS themselves. She'd assumed that those were the cases he worked on. Not this.

"I treated her the best I could, but the Nyarugusu camp was difficult, often brutal, and I didn't think she would survive. When I left the camp, she begged me to take her with me, but I had to turn my back on her." His voice was little more than a whisper. "There was nowhere for me to take her … nowhere for her to go."

"I can't imagine…" She swallowed hard. "I'm so sorry, Eric."

"It was pretty clear that I wasn't cut out for this kind of thing. I left MSF after three months and went back to my job in Toronto. But that didn't feel right either." He stretched his legs out in front of him. "Maybe it was the big city, or maybe I just needed a change … I'm not sure."

He went silent, as though even after eight years he still struggled to find an answer.

"Anyway, I started applying to small-town hospitals — figured I'd give that a try. The Kootenay Hospital in Nelson seemed like the best choice, and…" he shrugged. "There I stayed."

He put his hand on her leg and smiled. "Lucky thing I did, because I wouldn't have met you otherwise. And maybe it's good that you forced me back to Tanzania. It's time for me to put those ghosts to rest."

He went quiet again and turned his head toward the window.

She wished she could have brought him to Tanzania under different circumstances. She wanted to share with him the country she knew and loved.

Maybe I still can.

By the time she turned the truck off the highway onto the dirt road that led to the mining camp, she had come up with a list of a places to take Eric. As soon as this was over, they'd leave for the Serengeti. She'd call her friend Derek Borman and arrange a stay at the Grumeti River lodge he managed and then head south to Lake Manyara and the Ngorongoro Crater.

"What's that?"

Eric's question jolted her back to reality. She didn't need to look far to know what he saw — a deep gash in the earth dominated the landscape.

"An open-pit gold mine. We're in the heart of the Lake Victoria Gold Belt, and there's everything here from a guy with a pick to these huge open-pit mines. That's what my dad is developing too — an open-pit mine. He thinks he's on top of a pretty good-sized gold deposit. If he's right, the mine will be at least as big as the one you're looking at … could be five years before they produce much, though."

"Five years?"

"At least. Dad said that they've only just reached the depth at which he expects to find gold, so he'll be tied up with this project for a while yet."

Ten minutes later, Alex eased the 4x4 into a spot near a cluster of tents and small wooden shacks topped with corrugated steel.

This was as close to a home as her dad had right now. Whatever he knew about Tabitha Metals would be here.

I need answers.

39

São Paulo, Brazil

QUICK STRIDES TOOK SHEN past richly decorated suites occupied at this early hour by only the most dedicated staff of Tabitha Metals. An analyst glanced up as he passed, and Shen rewarded him with a brief smile. Every one of the men and women who worked here sought advantage in attaining the next promotion, the next rung up, this young analyst among them. They coveted a corner office with commanding views of the São Paulo skyline — and proximity to Shen and his power.

He closed the door to his office and eased into his chair. Although he hadn't seen her, Meilin had been here, as evidenced by the coffee and pastries set out on his credenza.

Already his email inbox held more than a dozen urgent messages, but it was the one that contained the current Novoteras mine production numbers that he opened. A quick scan was all it took to see the dismal truth. The shutdown of Tunnel Five had slowed them, putting them days away from mining enough tanzanite to satisfy the Chairman.

He typed out a message to Tim Wong ordering him to ramp up production. The stink of blame would cling to all of them if the tanzanite was not in China on time. Chairman Wei would lose more than money. His reputation would be tarnished, and this loss of face he would never forgive.

Shen's cell phone flashed with a number he'd seen only once before. *Keambiroro.*

"We have found the people you seek," the deep voice announced.

Shen tightened his grip on the phone at the first good news he'd heard in five days. "Where?"

"Mwanza, Tanzania. They were seen at Nairobi airport this morning too late to stop them, but a small bribe revealed their flight information. We were most fortunate that the plane stopped briefly at the Kilimanjaro airport, and one of my men boarded the flight there."

His hand clenched the phone. "So you have them?"

"No. Ongeti and the woman separated when they arrived in Mwanza. Ongeti was met by someone, a local, and they left too quickly for my man to follow. Instead, he followed the woman. She is not alone ... she travels with a white man."

"Do you know who he is?"

"No, but my man thinks he is a doctor, from part of a conversation he overheard."

A doctor.

It explained why Ongeti had no need of a clinic or hospital in Brazil. Unless the title of doctor meant something else, and this was the man who had visited the Colombian mine.

"Do you have a photo of this doctor?"

"No ... my man did not think to do it. But we will find a way to get the names of everyone on the flight."

He closed his eyes. These men he trusted with such an important task seemed unlikely to deliver. He expected more from Keambiroro, given his connection to the Chairman.

"I will get the flight manifest myself. What is the airline and flight number?" He scribbled the details Keambiroro reported onto the corner of his newspaper. "I am sending you a photo ... show it to your man. Find out if this is the doctor he saw."

Shen held little hope that the photo pulled from security footage would trigger recognition, but it was all he had.

"Where is Alex Graham now?"

"She stays at a mining camp about three hours drive from Mwanza.

There is only a single road that leads into the camp and no way out. My man believes she cannot leave the camp without passing him."

"You have just one man there?"

"For now. The rest of my men must fly from Arusha and Dar es Salaam ... it will be ten, maybe twelve hours before they arrive."

Too long. He pressed his fingertips into his deeply furrowed brow. "Get more men there now. Charter a plane, hire new men — do whatever you have to."

"It will cost—"

"Pay whatever you have to. And if Alex Graham leaves that mine, I want her followed — discreetly. Do you trust your man with this simple task?"

If Keambiroro heard the barely disguised contempt in Shen's voice, he ignored it. "My man has warned that there is little traffic near the mine. He waits at the highway, where he can more easily follow the woman without being noticed. But I cannot guarantee this."

As much as Shen wanted the geologist, he wanted Ongeti too. He could not risk having her learn that she had been followed ... not yet. But he couldn't afford to lose her either.

"Tell him to follow the woman. In the meantime, I want to know everything about that mining camp — everything. Which companies are involved, how many people live and work there. Before tomorrow, I want to know how we can gain entry."

"I do not—"

"If you cannot do it, then find someone who can!"

He dropped the phone into its cradle.

Keambiroro. The man had already proven himself inept, but to replace him would be difficult. Shen had spent years cultivating a powerful network in South America, but he knew almost no one on the African continent.

China was well entrenched in Tanzania, as it was in many other parts of the world. Chinese money had paid for hospitals, schools and stadiums, and their engineers had built the railway between Dar es Salaam and Kapiri Mposhi, a vital link between the Tanzanian port and Zambia. Companies like Long Bridge Merchant Group stepped in to provide supplies and equipment, making huge profits and collecting a treasured network of contacts.

But those contacts belonged to the Chairman, not Shen. And Chairman Wei would not share his most valued contacts or call in a costly favour without exacting future payment from Shen.

He must resist the urge to overreact, a lesson Uncle had taught him well. He would do nothing until he understood the connection between Keambiroro and the Chairman. Only if he discovered that Keambiroro was a lowly, insignificant contact would Shen dare ask the Chairman for another name. To do otherwise showed weakness and disloyalty.

For a brief moment, Shen thought about sending Jorge Silva to Africa to head up the miserable investigation there. But the ex-cop was more valuable to him in Brazil, and he might yet discover the miner connected to Graham and Ongeti.

The man who betrayed me.

40

Novoteras Mine

JORGE SNAPPED ANOTHER personnel folder closed. Another dead end.

Hours ago, when Shen Li informed him that a doctor had been spotted with Graham and Ongeti in Africa, Jorge had tackled the lead with renewed energy.

He scoured the South African Airways flight manifest that landed on his desk in record time. How Li had managed to obtain such a document, he did not ask. Nor did he ask how Li knew about this doctor in Africa.

Jorge found five men on the Nairobi-bound flight who identified themselves as doctors. None carried a surname that matched any of the men who worked at the Novoteras mine. Carlos now rechecked every hotel and car rental list in search of these names, while others determined the maiden names of each married miner's wife and put Benjamin Costa's family under a microscope.

Jorge had saved for himself the job of investigating the background of each mine worker for military and university connections. If one of the employees had befriended a doctor, these were the most likely avenues.

But as he pored over the military records of every man employed at Novoteras, he found only the mandatory twelve months of service required of them at age eighteen. It surprised him to find that fewer than a quarter of the miners had served at all. Like so many others, he believed that only the upper class found ways to avoid conscription

— to find that so few men from this poor state of Minas Gerais had served proved otherwise.

What had not surprised him was that every man had served within Brazilian borders, just as he had when he was eighteen. Only soldiers assigned to peacekeeping missions in places like Haiti and Congo would have worked with a foreign-trained doctor. And so, reluctantly, he had given up on a military connection.

The university angle had also proved a dead end. Only two of the engineers had trained in large enough Brazilian universities to have encountered many foreigners. While both men had been added to his suspect list, his every instinct told him that these men, among the highest paid at the mine, were not his culprits. But he could not yet rule them out.

This was no simple break-in. Not if Shen Li had tracked the thieves in Africa. And not when the dead miner had taken nothing from the mine.

He pushed back his chair and grabbed his jacket. He strode past Carlos's desk and yanked the door open. Swift strides delivered him to the mine building and through the empty change room, where he pulled coveralls over his clothes and stepped into rubber boots he took from one of the visitor lockers. It had been more than a year since a visitor had been in the mines, but they kept equipment at the ready. He reached for a helmet and checked the light, reassured by the strong yellow beam that the batteries were sufficient for a trip into the mine.

If the guard who stood at the entrance to the X-ray machine thought anything of Jorge's unannounced appearance at the mine tunnel entrance, his curt nod gave no hint of it.

Jorge hated being underground. His pulse quickened with each step he took away from the entrance, down the sloped rock ramp into the main gallery. Even here in this vast cavern, he felt the rock walls closing in on him. He resisted the urge to turn around, to run back to the entrance and its promise of freedom.

Nothing had prepared him for the suffocating darkness, for the rock walls and ceiling that wrapped too tightly, like a cocoon, when he descended the elevator the first time. In the days after the ceiling collapse in Tunnel Two, when he had been forced to climb ladders down into the mine, it was worse still. In the deadly dust-filled silence, he could almost hear the screams of the four men crushed beneath massive boulders that had thundered down on them. And he had refused to return to the tunnels again.

Until now.

He forced his eyes on the bare bulbs strung along the ceiling and followed their light through the gallery to a junction of four side-tunnels, all part of the maze of Tunnel One. He had never before been in the mine unguided, but he knew that only largest of these tunnels led to the levels below, and so he pushed on, straight ahead.

Three levels — four hundred metres, thirteen hundred feet beneath the surface. Tunnel Two, which had never fully been reopened, and Tunnel Three, one of the oldest in the mine, shared the next level down. Below that lay Tunnel Four, a multiheaded snake that went on for miles following a thick seam of tourmaline. Most of the miners worked there, except for the few assigned to the deepest level — Tunnel Five.

His boots sloshed through puddles of water, the noise echoing off the rock walls. Alone, he carefully stepped over uneven rock, one hand braced against the wall.

There should be men here. Although he could not be sure. He knew only of the assignments to each level, to each tunnel, not exactly where any of the men worked. *Still.*

He twisted back, staring at the emptiness behind him. The drip of water and his own breath were the only sounds. There should be more — the clank of a hammer against rock, men's voices. Instead, he stood entombed in silence.

He pushed forward, his steps quick, slowing only when he heard the whine of an elevator, unmistakable and clear, and the outline of a man.

Jorge offered no conversation to this lone worker stationed at the elevator except to say that he wanted to go to Tunnel Five.

He stepped into the cage and felt the shudder of metal as the worker bolted the wire door shut. And with the push of a button, he began his slow descent.

Rock surrounded him, too near his face. He pressed his back against the cage wall and forced his thoughts to the surface. To the open fields where he watched his son play football.

At each mine level he saw a face or heard voices, reminders that he was not alone.

The air grew stale and warm as he descended deeper. He dragged the back of his hand across his brow, wondering how the men could work down here. How the thieves could have climbed the ladders up from this depth. *They have to be miners.*

The cage jolted to a stop. He clung to the wire mesh of the cage until the door opened. But even then his fingers held their death grip on the wire.

"Sir, are you okay?"

He tried to force words out of his mouth but could manage only a nod. He forced his hand free of the metal and stepped out of the cage into the dimly lit tunnel.

One hand on the rock wall, he followed the sound of hammers and high-pressure water hoses. Men covered in the day's grime — mud, dirt and sweat — eyed him curiously as he passed by cubbies cut into the rock. Three men, sometimes more, crouched crab-like into these spaces barely big enough for a child to stand. There they dug their picks and fingers into the soft rock, pulling the gemstone they sought from the wall.

Normally there would be but a small crew here … six men, maybe eight, but he had already seen double that number.

Tim Wong.

Jorge bristled at the realization that the production engineer had added workers to Tunnel Five without so much as a mention. As determined as Tim was to meet the quota of tourmaline Li demanded, he had no right to jeopardize Jorge's investigation.

Until this very moment, he had not considered that Tim himself might be here and that Jorge would be forced to explain his own presence in the mine. But the engineer was nowhere to be seen.

An unsmiling Sabion Lacerda slipped his hammer into his tool belt. The men in his crew stood silent, unmoving. Jorge recognized these men who had sat across from him more than once over the past two days. Men whose families, finances — every detail — had come under his scrutiny.

Fear. He felt it emanate from them, saw it in their eyes.

Do they see my fear too?

He straightened. "Is this where you have been digging?"

Sabion nodded.

"And how far from here to the air shaft?"

Sabion turned to face the tunnel that stretched out to his right. "Five hundred, maybe eight hundred metres — about one half mile. I can take you there."

It reminded Jorge that he had not seen the crime scene himself — Carlos and the men under his command had collected evidence from the air shaft ladder. He would never have investigated from afar when he was with the police. *What have I missed?*

"Later." Although even as he spoke the word, he was not sure how long he would last down here. "First, I wish to see the rock seam you follow."

The men shuffled to the side so that Jorge could step closer to the wall.

"You have all mined rock from other tunnels," Jorge said. "Is the rock here the same?"

Sabion shook his head. "This grey rock, here." He ran his hand over a gritty-looking rock that made up much of the wall. "It is very much like the rest of the mine. Here too, this pink rock, it is also found elsewhere. It is what we mine from the other tunnels."

Jorge eased forward and touched the glossy, tapered point that protruded like a spike from the rock wall. He had seen this stone and thousands like it in the production room.

"Tourmaline."

"Yes." Sabion nodded. "But this rock here, this brownish rock." He pointed to a thick band of rock that wove through the grey wall. "It is found only in this tunnel. This is what we fill our buckets with."

Jorge eyed the buckets beside the men's feet, metal pails filled with the same brownish rock. He reached down and picked up a single rock, holding the marble-sized stone close to his face.

"And this too is tourmaline? It looks different."

Sabion shrugged. "All of our rock looks different. Sometimes it is pink, blue or green — here, at this level, we find mostly this rock." He pointed to the rock in Jorge's hand. "If you look closely, you can see blue or purple in it, but it is not as beautiful as the other tourmaline we mine."

This is what they came for.

Jorge closed his hand around the rock. Without another word, he turned toward to the dark tunnel that had delivered him here.

41

Gold Mine near Mwanza, Tanzania

"NOTHING!" Alex clapped the notebook closed and threw it on the pile of folders strewn over her father's desk. "Gold. The only things my dad writes about have to do with gold." She swung around to face Eric, who sat cross-legged on the cot.

"We've only just started looking, Alex."

"Four hours…" Her anger melted under Eric's steady gaze. "You're right. It could take days to get through everything he has in this tent."

From an open folder in his lap, Eric picked up a sheet of yellow foolscap crowded with blue ink. "He uses his own shorthand — abbreviations I'll never understand." He smiled. "And his handwriting is worse than a doctor's."

She lifted a stack of files out of the way so that she could sit down next to him on the cot.

"Nothing about this makes any sense, Eric. Something this important would have a file folder of its own … maybe more than one. There has to be research, maps, notes. My dad decided on five *specific* mines that Tabitha Metals owns." She snapped her fingers. "You don't just magically pull that kind of thing out of thin air."

The hammer of picks and sputter of machine engines intruded into their conversation. The canvas walls did nothing to muffle the back-breaking efforts of the men who swung picks against hard red dirt and bulldozed their way through ancient sandstone and clay less than one hundred yards away.

She couldn't blame her father for preferring a canvas tent over the ramshackle wooden sheds many of the workers retreated to each night. Both were like furnaces during the day, but filtered light bled through the eight-foot canvas walls, and the high, peaked ceiling made the tent feel less claustrophobic and more comfortable.

Her dad had made the effort to lay a plywood floor and set up separate living and working areas in this tent that was as big as some downtown Vancouver condos. It was what she would have done too — or maybe it was just what she'd learned from him.

In the back corner of the tent, a coffee maker sat atop a crowded table; her dad's favourite dark roast was no doubt stored in one of the brightly coloured canisters, with his beloved Walkers shortbread cookies in another. If she looked hard enough, she'd find chocolate, too, one of the treats he always kept on hand for her.

With electricity so expensive, the site had but a single refrigerator housed in the kitchen tent, serviced by the only full-time generator. Otherwise, this tent with its private shower and washroom was more like a small apartment than a temporary home in the field.

And it had been his home for more than three years now. Dad gave up his house in Calgary for the nomadic life not long after her mom died. He'd given Alex everything she'd asked for from possessions collected over a lifetime and then sold the rest. Since then, he'd lived in tents like this one in more places than she could remember.

"This tent is my dad's home ... his office. I can't find any notes on the company's central computer." She swept her hand in an arc. "He must have notebooks here somewhere."

Eric covered her hand with his. "Maybe he did things differently this time ... put everything onto his laptop so only he could access it."

"You don't understand." She ran her finger along the edge of a folder. "I use notebooks to draw maps, record details about the geology of an area, specifics about every rock sample I throw into my backpack — and so does my dad. Hell, he never let me forget the importance of a notebook."

The fire. The value of her notebooks hit home that night in the Selkirk Mountains near Nelson, B.C. She could have salvaged most of the data stored on her laptop and handheld GPS if that equipment had been lost in the fire, but it wouldn't have been enough. Her handwritten notes held critical details that made the electronic data more meaningful. It would have taken her days to retrace her steps and collect those details again — a delay that would have cost her the Donnovan silver claims.

"Mosi has my dad's laptop at his house, and I'll go through it with a fine-tooth comb. But my dad would never store every scrap of data on his laptop. There has to be *something* here." She stood and paced the floor. "I mean, what gives? We work on confidential projects all the time, and he's never gone this far before. He could have called me and told me what was going on, but instead he sends Mosi to Brazil but doesn't even tell *him* everything. I have no idea who this mysterious client is, and neither does Tracey. Hell, she knows *nothing* about this project ... that has to be a first."

"She wasn't very happy about it."

She swung around to face him. "She told you that?"

He nodded. "She thought Brian was acting strange too. I suspect it's why she told me where you were."

Alex turned to face the screened window, wishing they were anywhere but here. From behind her came the creak of the wooden platform bed and then the touch of Eric's hand on her arm. She leaned back against him as he folded her into his arms, his chin heavy on her shoulder.

"Did you have any luck finding a nurse?" she asked, changing the subject.

"I did. One of the doctors I emailed, Trevor Reid, is still here in Tanzania, and he set it up. He's a nice guy — a New Yorker with one of those really distinctive accents, the kind you hear in Mafia movies. Always makes me think of a tough guy, but all it takes is one look at Trevor to think musician: beard, long hair, slender fingers. Anyway, he has a great sense of humour — I think you'd like him."

She smiled. "Hey, he found us a nurse, so I like him already. But are you sure about this? The nurse will know this is a bullet wound."

He squeezed her hand. "It's okay. Trevor told this nurse that he treated Mosi and that I'm following up his care here. Nobody's going to question him … he's in charge of a private wing of a hospital in Dar es Salaam that treats mostly diplomats and expats. Nothing like what we used to do." He dropped his eyes to his lap. "Anyway, he's pretty well-respected, and after eight years here I'd say he's well-connected. It'll be fine."

"How much did you tell him?"

"Only that I needed a favour." He looked up at her. "I trust him, Alex."

She hated the idea of involving yet another person, but she didn't see a choice. But to have to ask this doctor to break the law — something Eric had already done, too — chilled her to the core.

Let this be over soon.

42

São Paulo, Brazil

SHEN TUNED OUT the drone of the dour accountant at the front of the darkened meeting room. He flicked his lighter, aiming its yellow flame against the tip of the cigarette held loosely between dry lips. Then, through the haze of smoke, he stared at the tight columns of numbers on the slide, one of a dozen reports that the accountant would detail over the next hour.

Every gem shipment, every expense reported by the Beijing-born accountant, pointed to the success — or failure — of their South American operation. Their operation had exceeded expectations for the past year, but not enough to cover the Chairman's needs. Not without the tanzanite.

Against his hip, he felt the first tremble of his phone. He stubbed out his cigarette and without apology jumped from his seat, even as he struggled to free the phone from his pocket. Only when he was in the hallway with the door firmly closed behind him did he answer the call.

"We have found Mosi Ongeti. The woman led us to him."

Keambiroro. At least this time the man called with welcome news. "You're sure it's him?"

"Yes. Not only did my man see Ongeti himself, he was able to talk to a nurse who had been inside the house — a woman hired to care for an infected wound that could come only from a bullet."

Shen jerked his head toward the sound of a door, but no one

appeared in the dozen doorways. Still, he kept his voice low and hurried into his office.

"Who hired her?"

"An American doctor named Trevor Reid."

"An American? You're sure?" he asked as he closed the door behind him.

"Yes. The nurse has worked with him for many years. She says that this doctor treats only the rich and privileged in a private hospital in Dar es Salaam. Ongeti must be someone important."

And a threat. Shen no longer doubted that the thieves had descended to Tunnel Five, that they knew about the tanzanite mined there. Ongeti and Graham were a problem — one that must be eliminated.

The stolen gemstone posed no real threat. A single piece of tanzanite would be assumed to have come from a Tanzanian mine, stolen by a worker. No, it was Graham and Ongeti's visit to the Brazilian mine that jeopardized their operation. He had no idea just how much they had seen, how much they knew. Worse, the pair seemed to be one step ahead of the men who tracked them.

There was no way for them to get out through a Tanzanian airport, not with their pictures widely distributed and a rich reward promised. But in truth, there were many small landing strips in the Serengeti from which they could escape in a small bush plane and thousands of ways for them to cross the border by vehicle. If they managed to get into Kenya or Uganda, they might slip through his fingers.

I cannot let them leave Tanzania.

"What about the doctor who flew to Mwanza with Graham and Ongeti — is he the man in the photo I sent you?"

"No. And I have the names of nineteen men on that flight. John Michaels does not appear, and there are no doctors that we can identify."

He slipped behind his desk searching his email for a message from Jorge, and finding none. Jorge had reached a dead end, one only Keambiroro could punch through.

"Talk to this nurse again. Ask her to find out everything she can about Dr. Reid. Where he went to school, where he worked before … every place he has lived. Show her the list of those nineteen men. And send me those names."

If the doctor had been in Brazil, Jorge Silva might find a match within his lists of hotel rooms and car rentals, or the South African Airways flight manifest.

"What about the mining camp where the woman stays?"

"It is owned by an American company named Dallas Resources. But it is not the owner who is important to you — it is the geologist that runs the camp. Brian Graham."

Brian Graham!

His pulse quickened. "Is he there?"

"No. We were told he has been gone for almost two months."

Long enough to ask too many questions about Tabitha Metals and find a way into the Novoteras mine.

Or the Colombian mine.

But for the first time, Shen smiled. Sooner or later, all of his thieves would show up at this mining camp. "Find a way into that camp. And put a man on Ongeti. I want to know every person he sees, everywhere he goes. Search the house. Take anything that might explain who Ongeti is or what he was doing in Brazil."

"What you ask—" Keambiroro sucked in a deep breath. "This is a small village, maybe fifty houses. It will be difficult to get close to Ongeti, or to enter his house unnoticed. I do not—"

"You will find a way or I will report your failure to cooperate to Chairman Jianyu Wei."

In the silence, Shen felt the man's fear of Chairman Wei. *Good.*

"You said that this nurse had been inside the house. Does Ongeti have family?"

"A wife and two children."

Leverage.

In the hours since their last conversation, Shen had quietly investigated the African who searched for his thieves. He suspected

Keambiroro's loyalty to Chairman Wei lay in weapons supplied to his Hutu tribe during the bloody Rwandan conflict and the Chairman's silent protection in the years since. Keambiroro was a vicious warrior who would not hesitate to press a knife against a child's throat.

"Be ready to take them."

43

Gold Mine near Mwanza, Tanzania

ALEX COULD HEAR Eric's soft, even breathing, a rhythm that should have lulled her to sleep. Instead, she lay wide awake, as she'd done for hours since the haunting cry of a hyena had ripped into her dreams.

She ached to climb into Eric's cot but instead tucked herself deeper beneath the wool blanket on her own bed. Jet lag and too many sleepless nights had taken its toll on him. He had fallen into a deep sleep not long after the generator had cut out for the night, and she was loathe to disturb him.

In the lantern light, she watched the rise and fall of his chest. The topic of his work at the refugee camp had not come up again. Yesterday they had read her dad's notes and talked only about her life here in Tanzania. He'd been curious, of course, about her history with Mosi — shocked to learn that Mosi had been given the responsibility for her safety in mining camps like this one while her dad worked underground.

She happily told him how she and Mosi would scramble up hills and race across the grasslands. He'd been the one to teach her Swahili and the customs of Tanzania. They'd watched cheetah kittens grow to hunt dik-dik on their own and lions take down zebra. Her dad had fostered her love of geology, but it was Mosi who made her love Tanzania.

Thank god he's okay.

They'd gone to Mosi's home for dinner and stayed until well after the nurse had left. Alex had sat with Kanoni and the children while Eric and the nurse took Mosi aside. She overheard enough of their conversation to know that the wound looked no worse and that it would be days yet before the antibiotic would clear the infection. Still, Mosi was home.

I couldn't have left him.

She turned away from Eric to reread Tracey's last text message. Eleven hours and half a world away, her friend was nearing the end of her workday in Vancouver. Another day without word from her dad.

Tracey had talked to every geologist who worked at Graham and Associates, but none could offer up even a hint about the client who had brought the tanzanite to her dad. Every project, every client any of them knew about, was also known to Tracey. But it was Paulo that she and Tracey texted about now, not her dad.

"I have a top lawyer lined up … do you want me to send him to Paulo? Or put them in touch?" Tracey's text asked.

Alex had finally told Tracey about Paulo Alvarez — at least enough for Tracey to understand why the Brazilian miner might need a lawyer. But Alex had been purposely vague about her own role in the break-in. Right now, Tracey could truthfully say that she didn't know anything about the crime, and Alex intended to keep it that way.

"No. They might be watching him or checking his phone records."

"What else can I do?"

"Nothing. Paulo will call me if he's arrested. We have to just be ready."

Alex dropped her phone on the bed. She'd heard nothing from Paulo, and as much as she wanted to know what was happening at the Novoteras mine, she couldn't risk calling him. But each day that passed made her more confident that Paulo was in the clear.

She leaned her head back on the pillow — her dad's pillow. The cot Eric slept in was her usual bed when she visited, not this wooden platform with its thick mattress. The camp foreman had been quick to offer a vacant shack, one where she and Eric could have pulled two bunks together. But she couldn't bring herself to leave her dad's tent.

I still can't believe he isn't here.

Above her in the tent ceiling, an awkward strip of canvas had been crudely sewn in place — a patch over what had to be a large tear. She smiled at the thought of her dad, who had never fixed anything in their Calgary home himself, taking the time to repair this tent — taking the time to *sew* a patch. She would have just glued a patch over the tear and hoped that it held. But she'd never called the same tent home for as long as he had.

Nor did she have to deal with monkeys. The sharp claws of those nimble creatures dug into the canvas as they scampered over the top of the tent. And if you didn't secure the tent zipper with a lock, they were quick to rip it open and help themselves to whatever they could find.

But for a tear as large as this, a larger animal had to be involved. She couldn't imagine what exactly could have ripped an almost eight-inch tear through the canvas under the watchful eyes of guards who patrolled the grounds.

Maybe nothing did.

She stood on the bed, her bare feet wobbly on the mattress, as she reached for the patched ceiling. Her dad had a good nine inches on her — still, even for him this would have been a stretch.

She dug her finger beneath the edge of the patch.

A fold of paper brushed against her skin.

She dropped to her knees and reached down next to the bed for her backpack. A minute later, she had her pocket knife and she was back on her feet. Knife snapped open, she stood on the mattress, reaching for the ceiling.

She slid the tip of the knife under one edge of the canvas patch. One thread, then another gave way beneath the razor-sharp blade, and as the patch lifted away, she saw it.

An envelope! One big enough to hold a notebook.

She didn't waste any time. She ran her blade along a second edge of the patch, just enough to let her yank the brown envelope free.

Her head swivelled to Eric. She wanted to shout, to tell him about this discovery. But one look at his sleeping face stopped her.

She dropped to sit on the bed cross-legged, the unmarked envelope in her lap. Her hands trembled as she lifted the unsealed tab and reached in to retrieve not a notebook but several folded sheets of paper.

She'd read thousands of pages of notes made by her dad, but she'd never seen anything quite like this. Lines of impossibly small words were crammed onto tissue-thin paper, some of them so poorly written that they looked like the scribbled words of a child. Worse, smudges of blue ink smeared many of the lines, as though in his haste he had dragged his hand over the wet ink.

Under the light of the lantern, she skimmed the writing, her excitement growing with each page. She clutched the papers to her chest. *Finally.*

44

São Paulo, Brazil

SHEN TURNED OFF the Chelsea football match that had carried him through a late-night dinner, a welcome diversion from emails that delivered little good news. He had caught only the end of the match, but enough to know that Uncle would be pleased at the performance of his favourite player. It was something the two men would discuss during their next call.

He'd avoided a call to Uncle during these difficult days, knowing that he could not hide his worry from the man who knew him best. *Three days.* In three days, when the tanzanite left port, he would call.

He dropped his white napkin on the table beside a plate of seafood that had gone mostly uneaten. As always, Meilin had made careful selections from one of his favourite restaurants, but he had no appetite for it.

She had delivered the meal to his penthouse herself, lingering until he'd turned on the TV. Although she'd come to his home many times before, he grew suspicious at such a choice now, during this critical time. She knew nothing of the significance of the Novoteras mine break-in, but Meilin's cleverness could not be underestimated. He already feared that his urgent calls, the early mornings and even later nights, had revealed too much.

He retrieved his cell phone from the kitchen counter and eased into a leather chair in the corner of the living room. He ran his hand along the edge of the phone, his focus on the lights of São Paulo stretched out below him.

He could wait until morning to make this call, giving himself time to learn more. But it had been almost five days since he updated the Chairman.

I can delay no longer.

Four rings later, after the barest greeting, Chairman Wei asked, "Your problem has been resolved?"

The nuanced wording all but shouted out Shen's sole responsibility for this theft. He sucked in a deep breath and delivered a carefully prepared answer. "No. But we have located two thieves in Tanzania."

"Yes." Wei hissed. "I heard about the most unfortunate mistake in Nairobi."

The Chairman had received reports from another. Someone eager to tell him about the failed capture of Ongeti and Graham, how the pair had slipped through the Nairobi airport to board a flight to Tanzania.

"Your Nairobi contact failed us in what should have been a simple task." In their careful game of words, Shen's subtle suggestion that Chairman Wei shared the blame would not be lost.

"Yet you continue to use him, Director Li."

Shen didn't miss the use of his official title. It hammered home the Chairman's displeasure and his distancing from Shen.

"Only because time prevents me from finding a more suitable assistant with better resources," Shen countered. "Even now, we wait for more men to arrive in Mwanza so that both Ongeti and Graham can be kept under surveillance. We also must watch a third man we have only just learned of, but your contact can provide only one man."

Quiet followed his retort, a sign of Chairman Wei's displeasure. Shen sucked in a deep breath and then plunged ahead. "With both Ongeti and Graham in Tanzania, we must consider the possibility that the gemstone is there. They may have brought it there to the person who hired them."

"I don't have to remind you how difficult it will be to control an investigation by the Tanzanian government or TanzaniteOne."

"Any investigation will proceed quietly," Shen reassured him. "To acknowledge the existence of another tanzanite source would drop the price."

"You forget that they have the power to smear our tanzanite, to call it a conflict gem."

Shen rubbed his temples. It would take little to claim the tanzanite coming out of their Brazilian mine was conflict-related. They themselves had all but assured such a label by keeping the tanzanite deposit a secret.

Their only option would be to sell as much of their Brazilian tanzanite as possible and to do it quickly. But too much tanzanite in the market at one time would drop the price, as it had in 2013 when illegal miners had held the Merelani mines by force, extracting and selling as much tanzanite as they could. Their careless actions pushed the price down, losing TanzaniteOne millions of dollars before the rightful owners were able to regain control of their mines.

"Several of the men who sit with you at the executive table have offered to set aside their current projects to help you. What do you wish me to tell them, Director Li?"

Beads of perspiration dotted Shen's forehead. Not one of the Chairman's inner circle would hesitate to use Shen's disgrace to push him aside and take over his coveted role as Wei's closest adviser.

The dragon's fire is hot against my neck.

"Thank them for their kind but unnecessary offer."

He fought back the panic that surged through his body. If he could deliver this next shipment of tanzanite to China, he might yet survive. But only if the polished gems were free of suspicion and could generate the cash the Chairman demanded.

Shen knew nothing of the man who would receive this cash for a cache of military weapons that would funnel through the Chairman to another — he was the banker, not the one who dealt with the careful negotiations between buyer and seller. What Shen did know was that this deal was like no other the Chairman had ever negotiated.

Chairman Wei, a master negotiator, had built a portfolio of international holdings, everything from engineering firms and construction companies, to oil companies, mines and real estate. Even those in the Chinese government who sought to make inroads into new countries came to Jianyu Wei, whether they needed engineers, architects or construction materials.

The inner circle of Long Bridge Merchant Group managed it all, except for the arms deals, which Chairman Wei handled alone.

Shen believed the Chairman took delight in the carefully orchestrated game. Secret meetings with terrorists, warmongers, and countries no legitimate company would sell to, were followed by even more secret bargaining with manufacturers, governments and black market dealers who cared little about where the weapons they sold were destined. All of it operated under the protective shadow of Long Bridge Merchant Group.

The Chairman had started the company when he was barely twenty and had climbed the mountain of success on the backs of a thousand contracts. He'd been feted and honoured many times over the past forty years, and his was the name mentioned most often to young Chinese entrepreneurs who looked beyond the boundaries of China.

But there were those who had begun to question Chairman Wei's wealth, especially in light of the corruption crackdown that had targeted so many of China's elite. So far, through connections or money, the Chairman had made every investigation quietly disappear. But this deal ... it made Shen wonder if Jianyu Wei also felt the dragon's breath on his neck and had chosen this arms deal to be his last.

The Chairman's name seldom surfaced in the web of companies that held his assets — some arrangements were so complex they might never be untangled. Most money earned through these companies was published in financial statements and legally reported, but the rest flowed into the Chairman's arms deals. There had been audits and questions, but their conservative underreporting of profits and inflated losses had staved off suspicion.

The Novoteras mine was different. Only the tourmaline production of the mine was ever reported, while the tanzanite gemstones slipped into the marketplace to generate millions of dollars of untraceable funds. One word of the tanzanite mined in Tunnel Five would bring investigators to their door.

And the break-in had upped the ante.

45

Gold Mine near Mwanza, Tanzania

IT TOOK EVERYTHING Alex had to keep from exploding with her news the minute Eric's eyes blinked open. She handed him a cup of coffee and waited only long enough for him to pull on a pair of jeans before she pounced.

"It's all here! I found my dad's notes." She waved the paper in the air. "They were hidden in the tent ceiling … I still can't believe I found them."

"Hidden in the ceiling?" Eric eased down to sit on the edge of his cot. "I don't understand. Alex, you have to slow down."

"Sorry." She pulled a deep breath into her lungs before she tried again. "I noticed a canvas patch sewn onto the tent ceiling over my dad's bed. It didn't look right somehow, so I cut it open and I found these … not a notebook but eleven pages of handwritten notes. My dad's notes."

She handed Eric the slim packet of paper and took a seat at the desk. Elbows on her knees and hands clutched as if in prayer, she watched him shuffle through the pages.

"I've read them, and there's detailed research on tanzanite — its unique properties, the petrology of the deposit. But he also goes on about synthetics." Despite her best efforts, the words rushed out like a swollen river over a dam. And just one look at Eric's face told her that he didn't understand anything she'd said.

She sucked in a deep breath and started again. "At some point, my dad thought that the tanzanite he'd seen was fake — a synthetic. But something changed. And whatever it is, it's in there..." She pointed to the paper in Eric's hand. "Somewhere in those scribbled notes, I'll find the reason he believed Tabitha Metals was mining tanzanite in Brazil."

"Does he mention South America? Or the client who brought him the tanzanite?"

She shook her head. "No. Nothing but geology in these notes."

"Is your dad prone to depression?"

She stared at him.

"Paranoia sometimes comes into play with those who are depressed, and they start to think everyone's out to get them. It might explain why Brian went to such extremes to hide the notes ... why he didn't tell anyone, not even you, about this project. All of this — a client he won't talk about, the secrecy — it just doesn't add up for me. Maybe there is no client, Alex."

She jumped to her feet and jammed her hands against her hips. "You think he made all of this up? Have you heard of Daniel Pearl?"

"The *Wall Street Journal* reporter who was beheaded? What does he have to do with this?"

"One of the things Daniel Pearl investigated after 9/11 was how al Qaeda terrorist activities are funded. Diamonds, precious gems ... he tracked sympathizers who buy these from miners and middlemen to places like Dubai and Hong Kong, where dealers pay cash for the stones — no questions asked."

She turned to the doorway and the sounds of men talking. Even the men here might steal gold from the mine and sell it to better their lives, not realizing that they might be helping to fund terrorism or war.

"Pearl's investigations put him in the headlines of the *Wall Street Journal*. Arab extremists kidnapped him and filmed his murder — his decapitation — labelling him a spy. It was horrible." She faced Eric. "The minute my dad believed tanzanite was being secretly mined, he knew enough to be scared."

I'm scared. The bullet in Mosi's leg had thrust them into the spotlight of Tabitha Metals. A company she still knew little about.

"Let's say for a minute that you're right. If this is as dangerous as you say, then why would he have sent you to that mine in Brazil? He sent you *into* danger, Alex. Why didn't he go himself?"

She pressed her lips into a thin line, almost afraid to speak the next words. "I think he did. He believed he'd find the tanzanite in Colombia, not Brazil. He sent Mosi and me to the Novoteras mine only because he couldn't completely rule it out. He wouldn't do any less, not under these circumstances."

She eased herself to standing and walked over to the desk. Eric said nothing, neither while she shuffled through the paper and maps nor when she returned to sit next to him and spread a map out over their laps.

"Here's where the tanzanite mines are." She ran her finger along a narrow stretch of land west of Mount Kilimanjaro. "And here..." She traced a jagged north-south line. "This is the Great Rift Valley."

"It looks like it runs right through the middle of the Serengeti."

"Right. In the Rift Valley, tectonic plates push away from each other, and magma is forced up from deep in the earth. Minerals form as the magma cools, but exactly *which* minerals you get depends on pressure, temperature and a slew of other conditions. Gold, diamonds, emeralds, tanzanite ... they're all possible, but only if the conditions are exactly right."

"Like tumours. Cancer can develop in all of us, but it doesn't, and researchers have spent decades pinpointing the conditions that create cancer cells."

"Exactly." She smiled. "We have this really complex geological environment, and in just this one tiny area..." Her finger traced the Merelani Hills mining block. "Only here were the conditions exactly right for tanzanite to form, and there's not much of it. Some experts estimate that there will be no tanzanite left to mine in another twenty years, and others think that will happen much sooner — ten years at most."

The marketing of tanzanite emphasized its scarcity in order to propel sales. She'd been tempted herself to own a piece of tanzanite, something so rare, but she didn't wear jewellery often enough for such an extravagant purchase for herself. Instead, she'd bought Tracey a pair of earrings set with small but perfectly coloured purple-blue tanzanite.

"If I'm reading this map correctly, each of these small squares is a mine."

She nodded. "Sixteen square kilometres of hell. It's the highest density of mining activity I've ever seen. The mines are practically on top of each other. In block D alone, maybe five or six thousand miners work the deep. Add to that the locals who scramble to pick up whatever they can find and you have barely contained chaos."

"So you've been there? Down in the mines?"

"A long time ago, back when I was still a student at the University of British Columbia. I was keen to go underground ... every geologist's dream, you know." She grinned. "Anyway, my dad took me down into one of the mines."

She'd never forget that day. It was the first time her dad had introduced her as a geologist, not just his daughter.

"I had to squeeze myself through some of the shafts, and the air ... I felt like I would suffocate." Her hand instinctively went to her throat. "They pump air into the deepest tunnels, but it's not enough. So it's hard to move, hard to breathe, and it's darker than anything you could imagine."

"Doesn't sound like anything I'd ever want to do. I'm not claustrophobic, but what you describe would probably make me panic."

She laughed. "It's not for everyone, that's for sure. Me, I draw the line at crawling through caves ... I'm just not one of those spelunkers who shimmy and squeeze themselves through narrow caves just for the fun of it."

"Sounds like the same thing to me."

She shook her head. "In a mine, you build a tunnel and follow it. You know what's in front of you and what's behind you. But spelunkers follow underground cavities … fractures in the rock and hollows carved out by water. Even if they have ground-penetrating radar maps, they really don't know what to expect — dead ends, pools of water — almost anything could lie ahead."

"But either way, you can be trapped in a cave-in," he countered. "And I would think that the risk of a mine cave-in is greater, because you've dug out that tunnel you talk about … surely that destabilizes the ground."

"Engineers work very hard to make sure that doesn't happen, but mining is dangerous work. Cave-ins, flooding, fire, lethal gas, lack of oxygen — they've taken many lives."

"So why not do something safer, Alex? Why not go to work in the oil industry or take a job with the government?"

She'd heard this question before, but never from Eric.

"From the first moment my dad showed me a gold-flecked rock, I was hooked. I knew mining geology was a tough path, especially for a woman, but I couldn't ever imagine not following in his footsteps." She slipped her hand into his. "And I have to follow him now."

"You want to go to Colombia? No." Eric shook his head. "I—"

She held up her hand. "Believe me, I'm not going anywhere near South America. No, I want to go to Arusha. Just a quick flight from here." She didn't pause long enough for Eric to argue. "This is about geology. We were working from Brazilian maps, and we could see similarities to the Merelani Hills geology. And when Mosi went into the Novoteras mine, he saw graphite-rich layers in the mine … the same formations he's seen in the tanzanite mines."

"Mosi's been in the tanzanite mines? I thought he was a gold miner."

"He's a miner, period." She nodded. "He spent years working in the tanzanite mines, just like every other young miner around here, including his brother Zawadi." As though sensing Eric's next question, she added, "But Mosi's not a geologist, so no matter how carefully he describes what he's seen, it isn't enough. I need to see this for myself."

"And you can't get it any other way?"

"I could study a thousand maps and it would never be the same. I want to see what tanzanite looks like *in situ*, in place, so I can see which minerals are associated with it. That's the key."

She stood and walked over to the door, glancing out at the deathly quiet grounds.

"I'm missing something here, Eric. My dad's a better geologist than I'll ever be, but I don't understand why he focused on the Colombian mines. The geology looks good, but it's no better than what we saw in Brazil. And even after I told him about the tanzanite we'd found in the Novoteras mine, he stayed in Colombia to meet with someone."

She turned to face Eric. "I want to know why."

46

Near Mwanza, Tanzania

MOSI STOOD AT the front door, watching Kanoni march down the rutted road that led to the bus stop. Even at forty-three she swung her arms like a child; only her broad hips beneath the sleek skirt her waitress job required betrayed her age. He waited for her to wave, knowing that she would, and before she had passed two of the neighbouring houses she proved him right. Only then did he finally close the wooden door.

For the first time since he had come home yesterday, he was alone in his house. Kanoni had been reluctant to leave for her restaurant shift, despite the assurance of his good health by the nurse, Sanura Diallo, who had shown up at their door just after dawn. She had brought with her *maandazi*, sweet donuts, an offering that his children were all too happy to accept before they trotted off to the school bus. He did not miss the coy smile Abasi gave the young nurse with the long black hair, as though it were to him alone that this gift was directed. Kanoni too had caught their son's adoring stare at a woman at least twice his age and given Mosi a knowing glance. Their son, now twelve, was becoming a man.

He eased his injured leg forward, testing it before he put too much weight on it. The pain had lessened, not like it was when Sanura had prodded and poked at it. He had expected a gentler touch from the woman's slender fingers, but she had worked on his wound as though digging a hole in the hard red earth.

With each step toward the bedroom he grew used to the pain. In the corner of the room he found his backpack tucked beneath a rocking chair that had belonged to Kanoni's mother. On its well-worn seat lay his fleece jacket where he had dropped it yesterday. So unlike Kanoni not to have hung his clothes in the tiny closet or to have emptied his bag, a routine she followed almost without thought after each of his absences. Instead, she had all but flown into a panic when he had limped into the house on his brother's arm.

Nothing he said could convince her, and Zawadi's forceful assurance did nothing to calm her. Not even Eric or Alex, a woman she greeted like her own daughter, could convince Kanoni that he would heal.

Kanoni had clung to his side, insistent on seeing the wound for herself when the nurse arrived. Only when she had almost landed on the floor in a dead faint was Alex able to lead her into the next room.

Long after everyone had left and the children were finally asleep, Kanoni had lain beside him, her finger lightly tracing the wound on his thigh, asking if it were true that he would heal. His arm wrapped around her slender shoulders, he had held her close to his chest, whispering that it was over, that he was fine, until she had finally fallen asleep.

But it is not over.

He snatched the cell phone from the dresser top, scanning its scratched surface for messages before his thumb hit the redial button. When he heard Brian's recorded message, he punched the "end call" button. Another voicemail left for the one man who might be able to stop Alex was not the answer.

By now Alex would be in Arusha, digging into things she should steer clear of. There was nothing more she could do here — she needed to go home. When she had called this morning, he had tried to talk her out of a trip to the Merelani Hills, but he could not dissuade her. She was determined to finish what Brian had started. A dangerous path.

He pulled his notebook from the backpack and headed back

through the house to the front door. Outside, he felt the warmth of the Tanzanian sun, something he had sorely missed these past few weeks. He eased into a plastic chair next to the front door, one shaded by an overhang of the corrugated steel roof, and flipped open the book.

He scanned the pages, searching for names in his scribbles, someone mentioned by Brian. Three months back, six months, a year. He found mention of meetings in Dar es Salaam and Nairobi and Brian's trips outside of Africa. The client who contacted Brian *must* have met with him during one of these absences.

The squeal of laughter from children too young for school preceded a trio of girls who ducked between the houses in a game of chase. At this distance he recognized only one of the girls, the daughter of the grocer one block over. He shifted in his chair, scanning the doorways for signs of life, unsure of what he would say to a neighbour who might appear.

He could hear the scrape of pots from the green-painted house next door. From farther out, the low, murmured voices of men mixed with the clank of tools and whine of engines too old to repair. The only person he could see was a young man in jeans and a blue hoodie perched on a motorbike near the end of the street. Parked near a jumble of broken-down bikes and cars, the man probably waited for his turn with the town's resident mechanic, a wiry man who seldom paid attention to anything but an engine.

The man glanced his way and then quickly turned away.

He watches me.

With fingers too large to type on the cramped cell phone, Mosi's short message took time. He hit the "send" button before he could reconsider his actions and stared at the screen, waiting for a reply. He did not wait long.

He hurried back into the house, ignoring the pain. In the bedroom, he slid the computer into the backpack and hefted the bag onto his shoulder. But as he turned, he hesitated — Kanoni would worry if she returned home early and found him and the backpack gone. He dug out only his wallet before he leaned the pack against the wall.

At the kitchen table, he scribbled a note saying only that he would be back soon, before he looked out the front door.

He is still there.

A car kicked up red dust as it barrelled down the road toward him. And when it rumbled to a stop, he climbed into the front seat next to his brother, Zawadi.

47

Arusha, Tanzania

THE LIGHT BLUE TANZANITE stone nestled in the crease between two fingers looked almost amethyst-purple depending on how Alex held it under the spotlight. This polished stone was just one of a row of five gemstones vying for her attention on white velvet, each stone carefully selected by the jewellery salesman who watched her intently.

Every upscale hotel in Tanzania had a small shop stocked with tanzanite tucked away on the main floor, but she'd chosen instead to visit the Cultural Heritage Centre just on the edge of Arusha. The complex, with its four-storey museum and massive store, showcased an impressive collection of African arts and crafts. More importantly to Alex, it also had a reputation for high-quality tanzanite, and a steady stream of tourists offered anonymity.

"It's beautiful. How many carats?"

"Eight. You won't find many stones of such high quality." The salesman clasped his hands behind his back. "Are you from America? Do you work at the embassy, or maybe your husband is a diplomat? Everyone from the American embassy buys their stones from me."

He was practised and smooth — the consummate salesman. Everything from his perfectly pressed white shirt to the expensive watch on his wrist announced success. She didn't doubt that he had convinced many expats and tourists to buy their tanzanite from him.

"Which mine did this particular piece come from?" She dipped one finger just enough to change the angle of the gemstone in the spotlight and catch a flash of purple in the blue stone.

"All of the tanzanite comes from the Merelani mines, and every mine adheres to the Tucson Tanzanite Protocols." He spread his hands wide. "The gems are ethically mined and are cut here in Tanzania. They are gems that can be truly enjoyed."

It didn't escape her notice that he failed to mention that the Tucson Tanzanite Protocols had arisen from allegations that al Qaeda used smuggled tanzanite gemstones to fund their terrorist activities. Although the allegations had been found to be untrue, the industry sought to protect itself by implementing a protocol to protect the legitimate tanzanite trade.

"Is it possible to see the mines?" She reluctantly set the gemstone on the white velvet pad.

"Yes. Of course." He leaned his head to one side, his brown eyes locked on hers as though trying to read her. "But you will not find anything there as beautiful as this gemstone." He held up the blue gem she had admired.

"I'm sure that's true." She smiled. "But I'd like to know more about this gem."

"Underground tours are available in one of the Merelani mines." He turned to the counter behind him, pulled two brochures from a pile, and handed them to her. "Their visitor centre explains how the stones are graded and cut. There are several reputable companies who will take you there."

The Tanzanite Experience. She wanted more than the canned tourist tour.

"And only the one mine is open to visitors?"

"The tanzanite mines are no place for visitors. They are deep and hot, and access is difficult. Those tours…" He pointed to the brochure in her hand. "They will show you how the tanzanite is mined, cut and polished into beautiful gemstones like this one."

She held out her hand, and he set another brilliant blue pear-shaped stone on the ridge between her left ring and middle fingers.

With each gentle roll of her fingers, the gem morphed from sapphire blue to royal purple.

Exotic. Exquisite. Breathtaking. Each axis in the crystal refracted light differently to create a spectrum from sapphire blue to royal purple — pleochroism, the property of only a handful of gemstones. She couldn't take her eyes off it.

"This gem — it belongs on your finger. And the time to buy one is now. Tanzanite is found in just a single location, making it more than a thousand times rarer than diamond, and in your lifetime all of the tanzanite will be mined. You will wear a unique and rare piece of the earth, a privilege not many women will share."

If he only knew that a rich reserve of tanzanite might exist on the other side of the world.

"Here is another, one that is a deeper blue." He set a larger oval stone between her fingers next to the first. "Both stones are large enough to make a beautiful necklace or ring."

Rings didn't make sense, not for her. During her university days, she'd briefly worn a ring given to her by a boyfriend, but despite leather gloves it had cut deep into her finger when she lifted heavy rocks. But a necklace was something she might wear both in the Vancouver office and away.

"How much is this particular stone?" She pointed to the tanzanite gemstone that had captured her attention.

"It is a gem of exceptional colour and grade." He discreetly turned over the velour-padded case that had held the gemstone. "Fifty-eight hundred United States dollars."

She'd expected a smaller price tag than the seven hundred dollars a carat quoted by this salesman.

"It's very beautiful, but I'll have to think about it."

He quickly removed the gems from her hand. This experienced salesman realized he would not close a sale with her, at least not today.

"Come back when you're ready." He gave her a coy smile. "Every beautiful woman should have such a rare piece of the earth."

His attention turned to a middle-aged woman standing next to

Alex. She couldn't blame him; one glance at the rings that adorned the tourist's fingers telegraphed her willingness to spend thousands on jewellery.

Alex wove through the maze of carvings and masks toward the door that led to the courtyard. Across an ornately carved bridge she could see Eric seated in a shaded spot in the creek-side restaurant.

When she slid into the wooden chair across from him, Eric pushed his cold beer across the table to her. She wrapped her hands around the icy bottle, grateful for the cool relief in the hot afternoon sun.

She raised the beer bottle to her lips, watching a man approach. His eyes were hidden behind dark sunglasses, but she knew he stared at her. It wasn't uncommon here for local men to blatantly ogle foreign women, behaviour she hated. Eyes lowered, she secretly watched him settle into the next table, his back toward her. A small mercy.

"No help on the mine front ... just this brochure for the Tanzanite Experience with their splashy visitor centre." She dropped a brochure on the table. "I need to get into a real working mine, not something set up for the tourists. I just don't know anyone who can help me." She sipped her beer. "Mosi might know someone, but it's my dad who has all of the contacts here."

The man at the next table turned his head ever so slightly in their direction.

He's listening to me!

She eased sideways enough to catch a glimpse of him. Dressed in khaki clothing and boots, he could easily be a guide waiting for his charges to finish shopping inside. But outside the restaurant at a picnic table sat men dressed in much the same manner, laughing and enjoying each other's company. So why had this man chosen to sit alone here in the restaurant?

She chided herself. Too many years of keeping secrets had made her as suspicious as her dad. Still, she changed the subject.

"We have a few hours before our flight back to Mwanza." She picked up the brochure and flipped it open. "Should be enough time for the Tanzanite Experience … not what I want, but it's better than nothing."

She took a final swig of the beer and stood. "What do you say?"

"I'm happy for anything that keeps me out of that bush plane a while longer." Eric eased himself free of the chair.

She grinned. "I take it you didn't care for the bird's-eye view of the animals?"

"The animals were fine." He tucked his hands into his front pockets as they strolled toward the parking lot. "It was the too-near-the-ground part that I didn't care for. I prefer to see clouds out the window … makes me feel better knowing there's time for the pilot to do something before we crash land."

"Then I would guess that a hot air balloon ride is out of the question?"

He stopped midstride to face her. "Balloon? There's no way you're getting me up into one of those damn things. Flames. Propane. What could go wrong?"

She barked in laughter and swung around to see if their lone listener had caught the exchange.

He was gone.

48

Salinas, Brazil

JORGE WATCHED ZAHRA touch the gemstone in her palm, just as he himself had done too often since he had left the mine yesterday. He had kept it close, first in the inside pocket of his jacket and then in his bedside table, but still he had felt the need to touch it, to see it. Only then did his actions seem real.

With their children headed for the school bus, he had finally found the courage to show Zahra the gemstone. Now, chairs tight to the table, they stared at the rock as though hypnotized by the blue that coyly shimmered just beneath the surface.

"You say that this rock—" Zahra held the between her fingertips. "It is the reason someone broke into the mine?"

"Yes." His clutched hands grazed his lips. "The tourmalines we produce are sent to China, mostly to be used for beads and carvings. Nothing that would seem to be worth stealing. But this rock—" He pointed to the gemstone. "Zahra, there is something different about it. It is found only in Tunnel Five ... the part of the mine that I believe the thieves targeted."

"So you took a piece of rock from the mine." She set the rock on the table. "How much trouble will this cause if they find out?"

As the mine manager, he had told himself that he had the authority to take a piece of rock to aid in his investigation — a weak argument at best. But he could come up with no reasonable explanation for removing the gemstone from mine property.

He dropped his eyes. "They cannot find out."

She reached across the table to him. "Can you not just return it? Go to the geologist and get the answers you need?"

"If only it were that easy." He caressed the soft skin of her hand. "The geologist insists that only tourmaline is found in the mine … so does the engineer." His eyes met hers. "These men will report my questions to Mr. Li. It is not safe for me to go to either of them."

"Then we find another way." She squeezed his hand. "We find someone we can trust who can identify this rock. Maybe your father can help us."

Us. He sucked in a deep breath, knowing that Zahra would be by his side.

"I cannot involve my father in this."

She ran her fingers near the corner of her deep brown eyes, a gesture he had seen her make so often. He knew she traced the spray of wrinkles that barely creased her olive skin, wrinkles that were obvious only to her. To him, she had not aged one day since they met almost ten years ago.

"Maybe your brother—"

"No. Zahra, I stole this rock. I cannot involve my father or brother in such a crime. I will ask my brother to defend me if it comes to that, but until then I will not discuss it with him."

"But defendants tell their lawyers about their crimes all the time. This would be no different."

"Mr. Li now tracks our thieves to Africa a world away. He will not rest until every person who was in our mine that night is captured. *Why?*" He spread his hands wide. "Why all of this over an insignificant piece of rock?" He met her eyes. "None of this is what it seems, and anyone I involve is in danger. I hesitated to even tell you about it."

"Jorge, you cannot do this alone." She rested her hands on her bulging belly, comforting the child within. "Call your friends at the police department, at least."

"I have heard from the police … Miguel Rossi called me." He relayed the conversation with his former partner. "If he is right and this man Mark Brody is from the CIA, then there is something wrong at the Novoteras mine."

"Then call him. Let him investigate."

"Zahra, I have no proof. And I cannot call a man I know nothing about and share this theory with him." He shook his head. "This is not like when I was a police officer. Shen Li is my employer, and he expects my loyalty. For all I know, Mark Brody has been hired by a competitor of Tabitha Metals, and he seeks information about the mine."

She rose and crossed the tile floor to stand near the kitchen sink. Her hand reached for a sponge near the dishes left to dry on the rack, and she scrubbed at unseen stains on the counter.

"Zahra. Look at me, please."

She went still but stared at the sponge clutched in her hand rather than at him.

"Please."

Finally, she dropped the sponge in the sink and turned to face him. "I will take the rock. I will find out the truth."

"*What?*" He practically shouted the word. "No." He shook his head. "No. It is too dangerous."

"It is the only way, Jorge. I will take the rock to a jeweller and ask if it is good quality and if it can be made into a necklace or ring. They will not suspect me."

He pressed his hands against the table, his fingers splayed. What she suggested was impossible to accept.

She slid into the chair across from him and rested her hands on his. "Jorge, we cannot trust anyone else." She searched his face, trying to read his thoughts. "I have heard the women at work talk about jewellery they buy in Teófilo Otoni. I can leave now and ask the neighbour to take care of the children." She picked up the rock. "Once we know what this rock is, we can decide what to do next."

He stared at the shimmer of blue in the rock Zahra held. Like everything else since the break-in, this rock was not what it seemed. *Perhaps Zahra is right.* Teófilo Otoni lay more than three hundred kilometres away, and there would be no easy way to connect this rock to the Novoteras mine — his mine. Still, they needed to take precautions.

"Do not give these jewellers your name or tell them where you live." He cradled her hands in his. "I do not know how common it is for someone to have a piece of rock like this. You must tell them that it was a gift, or—"

"I will tell the jewellers that my father-in-law found the rock and gave it to me." She smiled. "They will be more interested in the business than questioning me, Jorge. They will be quick to confirm the value of this rock, if only to decide how expensive a piece of jewellery to suggest."

Her words hung in the silence between them.

With his heart pounding in his ears, he gave a quick nod. Never before had he put Zahra in such danger. But it seemed the only way out of the danger they already faced.

I must know the truth.

49

Gold Mine near Mwanza, Tanzania

ALEX FELT A SURGE of heat as soon as she opened the tent door. She'd lifted the canvas from the screened windows before they left, but the little air that had passed into the tent was no match for the blazing sun. The heat had dogged them all day, from the bush plane to the Merelani mine sites they'd failed to access, and she wished only for the sun to finally set.

"What a long day!" She dropped onto the cot. "And nothing to show for it."

Eric kicked off his shoes before he sat down next to her. "I thought you said that those displays at the Tanzanite Experience museum were helpful … that you learned something about the tanzanite source rock being graphite-bearing gneiss."

She smiled. "I'm impressed. We might turn you into a geologist yet."

"No way. I'm not ready to trade my scalpel for a rock hammer."

"I don't know enough about what's going on, Eric. Shit, I don't even know for sure if that rock *is* tanzanite."

"I thought the guy in Dubai—"

She pulled away and turned to face him. "Faasad only ever confirmed that the gemstone wasn't a fake. It'll take a geochemical analysis to prove that it's really tanzanite, and there's a geology professor at the University of Alberta, Dr. Graham Pearson, who might be the best person to do that."

Since the first moment she'd heard Graham Pearson speak, she'd known that his cutting-edge research into fingerprinting diamonds could change everything, and so did the diamond companies that supported his work.

"Graham has discovered a strontium isotope signature, a chemical fingerprint that seems to be location-dependent. It means that you would know with certainty whether a diamond came from a conflict zone, Russia or Canada. But he thinks he can do more ... this fingerprint might identify the *exact* source mine of a diamond."

"And you think he can do the same for tanzanite?"

"I know his research has been applied to rubies, so it might work with tanzanite too. I'm not sure."

"But you think it's worth a try."

"I do ... there has to be some difference between the tanzanite in that Brazilian mine and the gemstones mined at Merelani." She crossed her arms over her chest. "But unless it's something obvious, we'd be back to square one. A fingerprint is only good if you can compare it to something you know, and I doubt Graham has a chemical fingerprint for the tanzanite gemstones coming out of the Merelani Hills. Still, I'd like to talk—"

She grabbed the cell phone on the first ring. Eyes wide, she whipped around to face Eric.

"Kanoni ... slow down. Why did Mosi go to the hospital?" Eric's face mirrored the alarm that stabbed at her gut.

"I do not know. The nurse must have taken him to the hospital." Kanoni's words spilled out. "Why have they taken him to hospital, Alex? Where is my Mosi? You must tell me. You must—"

Alex's heart broke at the wail that blasted against her eardrum like a siren.

"Kanoni, please listen to me. Mosi can't be in the hospital ... we would know about it. The nurse would have told us." Alex caught Eric's nod. "But Eric will check with the nurse right now just to be sure."

Eric yanked his cell phone from his pocket, fingers rapidly typing out a text.

"Mosi didn't leave a note?" Alex asked.

"Yes. Yes. He said only that he would be back soon … he tries to protect me. He does not want me to worry." Kanoni's voice trembled with tears. "His backpack is gone. He *must* be in hospital."

Alex couldn't imagine Mosi going to hospital without calling her first, not with Eric here.

"Let me try calling him, Kanoni." Alex glanced at her watch. "And I'll try Zawadi … he should be out of the mine by now and headed home. He might have talked to Mosi—"

At the ping of an incoming text, she swung around to Eric.

"The nurse says Mosi's wound looks good," he whispered. "And his temperature was down."

Thank god.

"Kanoni. We just heard from the nurse; she didn't take Mosi to the hospital. When she left the house, Mosi was fine."

The quiet on the phone line gave Alex hope that her words had finally calmed Kanoni.

"Mosi couldn't have walked far." Alex stared down at the floor. "Maybe he's just around the corner … playing *Bao* with a friend. You know how he gets when he's at that board game. He probably just lost track of time."

It was this thought that stayed with Alex after Kanoni hung up.

"Something's not right." Her hand clutched the phone. "Eric, there's no way that Mosi wouldn't be there when Kanoni came home from work. Not when she's been so worried about him."

She hit Mosi's cell phone number, her eyes on Eric as she listened to the incessant ringing.

"Call me. It's urgent," she said when she reached his voicemail.

"Mosi never turns his phone off, but he could be out of cell phone range." Claw-like, her thumbs stabbed out a text. "He'll see a text as soon as he has service."

Her hand trembled and her mouth grew dry. They hadn't come all this way for something to happen to Mosi now.

She dialled Zawadi, but that call also went unanswered. "Zawadi is probably still underground."

Another message, another text — she would have to wait for Zawadi to surface from the depths of the mine for an answer.

She dropped her phone on the bed. "Kanoni said that Mosi took his backpack. He wouldn't take that with him if he was just going out to see friends. I don't think Mosi even unpacked, so that bag still has his laptop, GPS, notebooks, maps…" She ticked each item off with a finger. "It just doesn't make sense."

Where the hell is he?

Arms folded tight against her chest, she walked over to the screened tent door. Outside, men stripped bare to their waists leaned against a dusty bulldozer. At this distance she could just barely make out their dirt-streaked faces — faces turned her way.

She knew some of the men, but most of the more than forty miners who worked the hydraulic excavators, drills and dump trucks were strangers.

As though a bell had rung, one man, then another, headed for the mine pit. They'd work in the searing heat until sunset, shaving layers from the hard, red earth to reveal the precious gold-bearing rock buried below. Most would then take their tired bodies to nearby shacks within sight of the mine pit that both fed their far-off families and tore at their souls.

And when they did, she and Eric would be alone. *Isolated.*

She ran her hand over her arm, quieting the goose bumps that prickled. Enough rumours circulated about the rich gold deposit here to make it a target for thieves. Her dad had hired security guards, but it wouldn't be enough to stop determined thieves — it was never enough. They'd proved that themselves in Brazil.

"Something's wrong." She stared out at the now-empty yard. "I feel it in my gut."

The ping of an incoming text sent her racing for her phone.

"It's from Derek Borman … a friend of mine who manages a safari lodge on the Grumeti River. He's asking me to come to the lodge. Says it's urgent." She glanced at Eric. "How does he even know I'm here?"

She typed out a message and stared down at the screen, waiting for a response. "Mosi! He's heard from Mosi."

"How far to the camp?"

"Two hours." She glanced out at the fading sun. "I don't think we'll make it before dark. It might be better to wait until morning. I'll ask Derek—"

Raised voices rang out. Angry shouts from the men. She searched the yard but saw only the same emptiness as before.

"Sounds like a fight." The hairs on her arms prickled.

She knew enough about the fights that broke out in the mining camps to be wary. They were safe here if they stayed out of it. Still.

"Grab your bag — we're leaving."

She picked up her own duffel and then reached down for her dad's rifle. *One in the chamber.* The rifle would be loaded and the safety on — her dad had taught her always to do the same. And as expected, she found a box of bullets under the bed.

When she turned, Eric stared at the gun in her hand.

"Insurance."

50

Vancouver, Canada

NATE TAYLOR ROLLED the baseball in the palm of his hand while he scanned Danica's email. Although the young cop had prefaced her message with an apology for tracking down so little online information, Danica had sent him a full page of links related to Tabitha Metals, more than he had hoped.

When Nate clicked each press release link Danica provided, he found little more than he already knew — a lawyer named Alonso Quinto was the only person ever quoted. What was more intriguing was the reason Quinto spoke to the press: the Valternas gold in the Atacama Desert.

Pascua-Lama. Everyone from the governments of Chile and Argentina to environmentalists and local citizens had something to say about this gold mine at an unheard-of elevation high in the Andes. Worry over mine waste runoff and glacier damage at that mine had brought intense focus on every operation in the area, including the Valternas mine owned by Tabitha Metals.

Unlike many of the other companies, Tabitha Metals had a spotless record, as Quinto repeated time and again. He emphasized their commitment to environmentally sound mining practices, their excellent safety record and above-average wages and working conditions, highlighting several of their South American mines as examples. But what was missing from every news article was mention of the Novoteras mine.

A quick check of the time and he dropped the baseball into its perch and pulled his leather jacket from its hook. With his cell phone tucked into his pocket, Nate left his office, headed for the elevators.

Long before he reached Danica's desk, he saw that the young woman wasn't there. He wasn't sure how much time she'd spent on this unofficial project of his, but he owed her a word of thanks, maybe lunch.

In his years with the RCMP in Nelson, the men and women he'd worked with were like family — a camaraderie that he'd eventually establish here. In a large department like this one, with more than five times the staff of his Nelson detachment, it took time to get to know his fellow officers. He'd been invited out for a beer by some of the men he regularly worked with, but Danica had never been included — or had chosen not to attend.

Danica had joined the RCMP after the harassment scandals with its long list of women who accused fellow police officers of sexism, assault and bullying. Even after the #MeToo movement flooded the news, some cops only begrudgingly admitted to sexual harassment within their ranks. But the appointment of Brenda Lucki to the head post of RCMP Commissioner pointed to a new direction.

By the time Nate reached the lobby of the building across the street, he'd decided to invite Danica along for coffee with a couple of the other officers. It seemed the best way to help build ties without making her feel uncomfortable — he hoped someone would do the same for his own daughter, Olivia, when she started her first job out of university. Not that Nate knew yet what that would be. Every time he and Jess talked to Liv, their daughter described a different future.

At least she has one. Something he and Jess gave thanks for every day.

Nate eased himself onto a corner of a granite bench that faced a centre fountain. It hadn't taken him long to discover this spot, one that gave him a view of the door and just enough privacy for personal calls.

He'd tried several of the nearby coffee shops, even joining Jess for lunch in a few. The crowds that jostled for too few seats only made them both long for the quiet life of Nelson.

Mark Brody picked up before the second ring, expecting Nate's call. They shared the briefest greeting before Mark switched to work mode.

"There's not much to find on this company, Tabitha Metals. No violations, no complaints."

Mark sounded like a detective on the witness stand instead of the easygoing Texan Nate knew.

"There was a cave-in at the Novoteras mine about five years ago … a bad one," Mark continued in a monotone. "Fourteen men trapped underground for more than a week. Only four men died, which I've been told is almost a miracle."

"But no mention of company owners, just a lawyer named Alonso Quinto, right?"

"You take up mind-reading, Nate?" The Mark Brody everyone knew, the one with a ready smile and sharp wit, broke though.

Nate chuckled. "No. There's a young cop here, Danica McNulty, who did an internet search for me. The only name that ever came up was Alonso Quinto. Danica didn't mention a cave-in … just the usual corporate bullshit."

"Boots on the ground, Nate. Boots on the ground."

Nate groaned at this expression he'd heard too often from Mark. Whether the saying was common to all U.S. Marines or something this Dallas native picked up elsewhere, Nate didn't know.

Just one of the many mysteries he had yet to pry from this quiet Marine who didn't share much about how he ended up in Washington or which agency he worked with. All Nate knew was that Mark had been attached to Homeland Security when they had met in Nelson — not that Mark had told Nate why he was in South America, either.

Has to be CIA.

"This kind of stuff barely makes the local news, never mind the internet," Mark said. "You have to remember that there are cave-ins all the time down here, and most of them don't get much more than local attention."

"I sense a 'but' coming."

"You got it. The cops down here gave me a list of the men who died in the cave-in, and it included a Chinese engineer. Doesn't mean much on its own, but when you add zero coverage of that cave-in and no info on the owners, I'd say Tabitha Metals is connected to—"

"China," Nate finished for him. "And that means the owners will be buried ten deep beneath shell corporations." He ran his hand over his chin. "So there's nothing more to find."

Nate had run into this problem all too recently with a Vancouver real estate investment scam. They'd barely started to untangle the web of corporations that owned the company so many had trusted with their life savings before their only lead fled the country. The woman at the centre of the illegal operation surfaced in Shanghai several weeks later, protesting her innocence from the safety of a country that would never extradite a Chinese national to Canada to face charges.

"Maybe, maybe not."

Nate leaned forward. "Talk to me. What do you have?"

"The mine reported a man shot during a recent break-in ... happens all the time down here, especially at the big emerald mines. There's nothing to investigate, but it's a good excuse for a chat with the mine manager. It won't cost anything except a little time."

His chest tightened. "When was this break-in, exactly?" He forced the words out.

"Seven nights ago."

Alex?

The timing was just too much of a coincidence. With Brian in Colombia, thousands of miles away, it had to be Alex.

Eric would never go along with anything like a break-in. *Never.* Either he didn't know, or he had been told after-the-fact.

What the hell is going on?

He stared at the cascading water in the fountain, as though it could answer the questions that screamed through his mind.

"How long before you can get to the mine, Mark?"

"I'm already at the gate."

51

Grumeti River, Tanzania

ALEX EASED the 4x4 into the Grumeti River, her hands tight on the steering wheel. Security guards on the opposite bank waved her on through the fender-deep water, but the spotlight they shone on the murky flow did little to slow her racing heart.

Eric clung to the dashboard when the vehicle pitched side to side, and she fought to keep the steering wheel steady. She'd driven across this section of the river before and seen the razor-sharp teeth of crocodiles lying in wait for zebra and antelope — this was no place to topple the truck.

She breathed a sigh of relief when the 4x4 finally climbed the bank and smiling guards pointed her in the direction of the tented camp. It wasn't long before she spotted the lights of the main lodge that stood near a row of luxury canvas tents — nothing like the mining camp they had just left.

A guard, alerted by the men at the river, greeted them at the parking lot and led them by flashlight toward the lodge. They followed a path through a wall of vegetation that rose up on either side, the only thing that stood between them and the African predators.

She and Eric had barely stepped into the open-air bar with its leather chairs and sofas before a smiling waiter arrived. Her favourite Scotch and Eric's very dry gin martini appeared just moments later.

"This place is gorgeous." Eric sipped his drink. "So many stars … and it's so quiet."

"One of my favourite places." She breathed deep, feeling her shoulders finally relax after the tense drive.

They'd made the right decision to leave when they did. By the time they'd reached the 4x4, men were running out of the mine pit and angry shouts filled the camp. A full-blown fight — and it happened so fast.

"I can hear splashing, but I can't see anything." Eric stared at the Grumeti River that lay just beyond the lodge.

"Hippos. Hear the grunts, the grumbles?" she asked. "This part of the river is slow-moving and deep ... the perfect hippo pond. Let's hope they stay in the water." She shifted in her seat. "The last time I was here, a young male was constantly being run out of the river by the other males."

Weighing in at more than three tons, these mud-crusted behemoths were dangerous and surprisingly nimble on land.

"Not to worry ... we keep an eye on them. And that male never comes into the bar, although he does like the swimming pool."

They swivelled toward the voice. Alex was on her feet long before the tall, brown-haired man had reached her chair.

"Derek!" Alex hugged him tight. "I've missed you. I can't believe it's been a year."

"Too long, my friend. Too long."

She slipped free of the embrace. "This is my friend, Dr. Eric Keenan." Her hand found Eric's, an unspoken message about the intimate nature of their friendship.

Derek Borman's smile and his two-handed handshake emphasized his pleasure at meeting Eric. Not that she expected anything less from Derek, her friend of fifteen years.

"Susan will be sorry she missed you both." Derek's words betrayed a strong Johannesburg accent, despite his departure from that cosmopolitan city more than twenty years before. "She's in London visiting with friends."

"I'd have more chance of running into Susan in London than here." Alex smiled. "As a matter of fact, I think that's where I saw her last."

Derek's laugh boomed out. "No doubt. She loves it here in Tanzania, but she sorely misses her family and friends back home."

Susan had traded her career as a London gallery owner for a life in Tanzania with Derek when they'd met more than ten years ago. But with three sisters in the UK, all with young children, Susan, the ever energetic favourite auntie, felt pulled between two countries. Alex had long wondered why Susan and Derek hadn't yet started their own family, given Susan's love of children, but it was one subject the two women had never discussed.

They'd barely sat down before a rail-thin staff member approached, but the man backed away at the subtle shake of Derek's head … a discreet signal for privacy.

"We're alone for at least an hour. The lodge guests are at a sundowner about a half mile away, enjoying drinks by the river's edge."

"When did you talk to Mosi?" she asked.

"I didn't." Derek shook his head. "A man showed up here saying that Mosi had sent him. He said it was urgent that you come to the lodge, and he asked me to contact you. Since even I didn't know you were in Tanzania, and he had your private cell phone number and mine, I believed him."

"I don't understand why Mosi didn't just text me himself. It doesn't make sense." She sighed. "And he didn't say why I had to come to the lodge?"

"I'm afraid not." Derek ran a hand over his smooth face. "But if I had to guess, I'd say Mosi is on his way here."

"Then he should be here by now." Her hands tightened into fists. "He knows these roads better than I do … he should be here by now."

"I'm sure he didn't expect you before morning — I didn't."

Alex abruptly changed the subject. "What about my dad? Have you heard from Brian recently?"

Derek shook his head. "He was out here a few months ago, just before we closed the lodge for the season."

"He was here?"

"I know. It's hard to believe, isn't it? The man never seems to take a day off. Usually we meet by chance in Mwanza or Arusha."

"And he was alone?"

"Yes. But you know your father." Derek smiled. "He couldn't have been here more than five minutes before he was deep in conversation with the other guests. There was a Russian couple he seemed to get along well with. They spent most of the evening together."

Her pulse quickened. "Is there any chance he knew the couple?"

"If he did, he didn't mention it."

"Can you tell me who they were? I know there are privacy rules … but it's important."

"What's going on, Alex?" Derek leaned in close. "Tell me."

"My dad was supposed to meet me in Nairobi, but he never showed up. We have police looking for him in Colombia and Ecuador."

She turned her head away to watch the activity in the *boma,* the branch-fenced area with its table and chairs set beneath the African sky. Chefs roasted meat at a wood-fired barbeque and waiters readied tables with linen napkins, silverware and china. Dinner would be served soon, but even the rich, spiced aroma rising from the *boma* wasn't enough to spark her appetite.

Eric's cell phone rang, and he excused himself.

"I know there's more than you're saying," Derek said. "Maybe something you don't want Eric to know?"

She met his gaze, noticing for the first time the wrinkles at the outer corners of his gentle blue eyes. The mark of a man who smiled wide and often, a quality he shared with Mosi — a reminder that Derek, too, was a trusted friend.

"It's not that. Eric…" she smiled. "He's the best thing that's happened to me in a long time."

"Then what?"

"I've seen a piece of tanzanite that appears genuine, but it didn't come from here."

"Impossible." Derek leaned back in his chair. "Tanzania is the only source … it is the pride and joy of the country."

"If I hadn't visited the mine myself, I would be skeptical too."

"Where—"

She interrupted him with a shake of her head and a raised hand. "I can't get into details. I really shouldn't be telling you even this much…" She trailed off at the sight of Eric's grim face. She'd seen the look too often in recent days not to feel her body tense.

"That was the nurse. She's with Kanoni." He dropped into the chair and leaned forward, a move the others mirrored. "Mosi hasn't called or come home. And no one's seen or heard from Zawadi since this morning."

"They're together." Alex hugged her arms to her chest. "A flat tire, engine trouble … an accident. Whatever happened, they don't have cell service, or they would have called. They're out there alone."

"I'll send every Jeep we have out to search the area at dawn," Derek said. "There's nothing we can do until then."

Dawn. Too many hours away.

52

Grumeti River, Tanzania

ALEX RELEASED HER GRIP on the steering wheel just long enough to zip her fleece tight to her chin. The sun had barely inched above the horizon before she and Eric had set out to search the roads near the Grumeti River lodge for any sign of Mosi. As promised, every vehicle Derek could muster did the same, a move that left his high-paying guests stranded in camp.

Their 4x4 bounced hard along the deeply rutted vehicle track that served as a road through the tall grass of the private reserve. For more than two hours, they had been driving this road, listening to the radio chatter between the drivers. No one had yet seen either a truck or evidence of an accident. Her calls and texts to Mosi and Zawadi still went unanswered. The brothers had simply disappeared.

Alex slammed on the brakes when a giraffe stepped out of the trees a hundred yards away. Eric barely waited for her to slip the truck into park before he climbed up onto the passenger seat and poked his head through the open roof.

"Look at that neck — she's incredible. Beautiful." He rested his folded arms against the truck's roof. "I've never seen a giraffe up close like this."

He's as giddy as a boy!

She scrambled up onto the seat to join him. Hand shielding her eyes, she scanned the edge of the road in search of other giraffes.

"Look! Up in the tree about fifty yards to your left." She grabbed the binoculars that hung from her neck. "This is fantastic! Eric, you must be the luckiest man I know. There's a lion sleeping on that low branch."

They watched in silence as the tawny lioness, her head resting on large soft paws, opened an eye. Unconcerned about their presence in this protected spot, the big cat promptly returned to sleep.

"She looks pretty content," he said. "Do you think she's alone?"

Alex shook her head. "There are probably others lying in the tall grass … they're tough to see at this time of year."

The spring rains made the landscape lush and the grasses tall. In another month the scene would be different. Drought would turn the Serengeti into a dry grassland, and animals would be on the move in search of drinking water.

"We can try to get a little closer if you like," she said. "We're in a private reserve, so we can drive off-road."

"This is fine." He rested his chin against his arms. "I can't believe I spent all that time working here and never even got as far as this."

"I don't know how you manage, cooped up in a hospital all the time. I can barely stand to be in the office for—"

She snatched up her phone at the ping of an incoming text. "Derek wants us back at the lodge."

Truck wheels kicking up dust, they bounced down the dirt road toward the lodge, covering the distance in record time.

Derek stood at the bottom of the lobby stairs, waiting for them. One look at his face sent her heart racing.

"There's been a riot at the mining camp. Come!" He took the stairs two at a time with Eric and Alex tight behind him. He made a sharp turn down a hallway to his office.

"You need to see this." Derek's computer screen came alive. "It's video footage from someone that was in the mining camp."

A crush of men, their wooden bats, steel pipe and rocks held high, crowded the jittery image. The footage blurred with branches as the man holding the camera fled. His heavy breath registered above the angry voices, the slam of metal against metal, the crack of wood. And then the image changed.

Bodies swarmed a man who held his hands high in surrender. An empty gesture. He was pushed to the ground, and crude weapons smashed down on him.

"They're killing him!" Eric yelled.

Not just one man. More.

The armed men surged forward, their bloodied weapons swung high before they slammed down on another victim. Frantic shouts, screams and the murmured prayer of the man who held the camera mingled to create the soundtrack of war.

Attackers rushed the heavy equipment and the sheds. A bulldozer wobbled, pushed by a hundred hands until it fell onto its side in a cloud of dust. Corrugated metal, a roof torn away, clanked to the ground.

She would have expected the attackers to drop into the mine pit, where they could steal whatever gold they could find. But this ... these men looked to slaughter the miners and destroy the camp. They operated as a single unit, cutting a path of destruction.

Warriors.

"I've never seen anything like it." Eric had gone pale. "How many dead?"

"We don't know yet, Eric." Derek shook his head. "News reports are giving out different numbers ... twenty dead, fifty. But police have only just started to move into the mining camp. It was too dangerous to go in at night."

"This happened yesterday afternoon?" Alex asked, although she already knew the answer. "Just before we left, it looked like a fight was starting." She stared at the image frozen on the screen. "But I never could have imagined this!"

"In all my time in Tanzania, I can recall only a handful of riots as bad as this," Derek said. "And the man who shot the video said the mob made a beeline for the waste rock piles, the tailings near the rim of the mine pit. They came for the gold."

"There can't be enough gold in those rock piles to draw a mob like that," she said. "The main gold deposit hasn't been reached yet ...

there just isn't enough gold in either the mine pit or the waste rock to get people excited. The mines down the road are more likely targets."

"Exactly." Derek nodded. "I think someone started a rumour to create this riot."

"But why?" Her hand clenched into a fist. "Why start this kind of trouble?"

He breathed deep, as though gathering courage, before he continued. "To come after you."

53

Grumeti River, Tanzania

To come after you.

Derek's words dropped like a death shroud. She clutched her hands to her abdomen, pushing back the bite of fear. Words raced through her mind, but she could form no sentences, make no sound. In the quiet, only the grunt and splashes of the hippos could be heard.

"The man who shot this video is the brother of Rashid, one of my guides," Derek said. "I've talked to him, Alex. He says that men went into Brian's tent ... even before the riot started."

"Then they were searching for valuables his computer, or—"

"Alex, you're missing the big picture." Derek grabbed her wrist. "Why search a tent when there's gold at your feet? They wouldn't do it. That riot was dangerous to every man who was in that camp — even the men who searched Brian's tent. No." Derek shook his head. "I think this has everything to do with you, Alex. Someone knows about the tanzanite."

"No. *No!*" Alex shouted. "You're wrong. This can't be about me." She twisted her head to Eric and knew immediately from his grim look that he believed Derek.

"You need to tell Derek what you told me," Eric said quietly. As though he could read her thoughts, he added, "You can't finish this, Alex. You need help."

He's right. She faced Derek and started the story that began in Brazil and ended in Tanzania, leaving out nothing.

"Only the men who've worked with my dad for years even know I'm here," she said. "None of them could possibly know about my visit to the Brazilian mine. My dad kept this ultra-quiet."

"I have nothing to go on except my instinct, Alex." Derek crossed his arms. "I've been in Tanzania for fifteen years, and I keep a good watch on everything that's happening — I have to, in order to keep my guests safe and protect this lodge. And right now, I'm telling you that something about this riot isn't right. You have to trust me."

Alex turned away from him to stare out at the blue African sky. Derek might have an MBA from Oxford, but he had also served two years in the South African military.

I can't ignore him.

"Where is the tanzanite now?"

"I left it in Dubai." She held her arms tight across her chest, shivering despite the heat in the room. "I didn't think it was a good idea to bring it into the country ... not when I discovered it was real."

"But these men don't know that," Derek argued. "And maybe it doesn't matter. You're a threat to them even without the gemstone."

"Surely they haven't tracked me halfway around the world to this camp in Tanzania." But even as she said the words, an image of the woman at the Brazilian airport flashed through her mind. *They knew about Mosi.*

"Mosi. If they tracked anyone, it was Mosi." She told them about the paper trail Mosi had left behind. "It wouldn't take much to connect him to my dad ... he's probably listed somewhere as Mosi's employer. And that means they could have found the mining camp too. It could explain why my dad's tent was searched."

"It might also explain why Mosi wanted you here," Derek said. "He may have heard rumours about the riot and wanted to get you to safety."

"Oh, god." Her hand flew to her mouth. "What if he was there? What if Mosi was in the camp when the riot started? What if he came to—"

"We would have seen him, Alex," Eric said. "He couldn't have driven up that road to the mining camp without us seeing him."

"But if he drove up later, after we had left. Then—"

Derek held up a hand. "Mosi would *never* have gone into that camp if he saw the men gathered there. You know that, Alex. And he sent you here, where he knew you would be safe. He wouldn't have gone near that camp without calling here first."

Alex turned away from them to stare out the window. She had expected all of this to be over when they arrived in Tanzania, but instead she faced a growing storm of confusion.

"I know this is a lot to take in, Alex." Derek cupped her hands in his. "You *know* me. I would never raise the alarm if I didn't think it necessary. That riot scares me, and it should scare you too. Your life is in danger, Alex."

She closed her eyes. *We're all in danger.*

"What if they have Mosi? What if they found out where he lives?"

"It's possible, but I don't believe it," Derek said. "Not with Zawadi missing too, and Mosi's message to me."

"But it's *possible*," she argued.

"And it's also possible Mosi is in a broken-down truck." Derek shook his head. "The only thing I know for sure is that *you* are in danger. Think about it, Alex … if someone did link Mosi to Brian Graham and that mining camp, then they know about you too."

She leaned against the office wall, afraid that her legs wouldn't hold her. "So what do I do?"

"Leave the country," Derek said.

"If you're right, then these men have already tracked me from South America to Tanzania," she said. "What makes you think I'd be safe anywhere? Until the Novoteras mine is exposed, I'm at risk — so is Mosi, and my dad."

"Your dad never should have involved you in this in the first place." Eric threw up his hands. "*He* shouldn't have gotten involved either. If ever there was a client he should have turned down, this was it."

Eric was as angry as she'd ever heard him.

"You don't know my dad. He didn't purposely put me or Mosi

in danger. He thought he was doing the right thing. He *did* do the right thing."

"Whether Brian was right or wrong is an argument for another time. Right now, I'm worried about you, Alex." Derek put his hand on her shoulder. "You'll be safe here for now. We have good security, and it's difficult for anyone who approaches not to be seen."

"And then what?" she asked. "Even if Eric and I manage to get out of the country, there's Mosi. What happens to him?"

"I know a woman who might help … Hanna Jensen," Derek said. "She's a Danish lawyer who came to Arusha to assist in the investigation of war crimes by the International Criminal Tribunal for Rwanda and stayed to run a non-profit AIDS organization. Absolutely trustworthy and very well-connected."

Derek raised his eyebrows, as though already challenging her rebuttal. She knew too that Eric would be quick to fight any objections she raised. They wanted her to trust Hanna, to invite one more person into this escalating situation, when she still wasn't sure she believed any of it.

That riot wasn't about me. But she couldn't shake the fear that they'd been tracked to Tanzania. They'd never be safe — not until the Novoteras mine was exposed.

"I'll talk to Hanna."

54

São Paulo, Brazil

SHEN BARELY BREATHED. He clutched the phone tight to his ear, listening to Keambiroro's report.

"The riot was very bad. Hundreds of men armed with picks and pipes went into the mining camp. At least two of my men are dead."

Shen couldn't fathom how Keambiroro's men could not have anticipated the riot. How they had missed the mob headed toward them.

"Alex Graham? Do you have her?"

"No. Three of my men managed to get to her tent, but she was not there. If she was in the mine pit when the riot started, she may be dead … the doctor too." Keambiroro said. "But it is possible that she left the camp before the riot started."

"How could you not know where she is? You said that she could not leave the camp without passing your man."

"My men were on foot heading toward the woman's tent when the riot started. It happened quickly … without warning. They could do nothing."

"You say the woman wasn't in her tent … did your men search it?" Shen leaned forward on his elbows.

"No. Clothing and papers were everywhere. They would not risk their lives to take the time to search such a mess. It was very dangerous for them to be in the camp at all … no one was safe."

"Cowards," Shen hissed.

"No. You *must* understand." Keambiroro insisted. "They hid until the worst of the fighting broke off and then went to the tent to find the woman. Lesser men would have run away from the camp as soon as they saw the mob."

Shen ignored the man's pathetic attempt to justify the actions of his men. "Pick up Ongeti. He will give us what we need."

"He is gone. My man tried to follow him when he left his home, but Ongeti must have seen him."

Shen's mouth went dry. Little more than a day ago, he believed this situation was under control. He had Alex Graham cornered in the mining camp and Mosi Ongeti trapped at his home.

Now I have nothing.

"You failed." Shen's words sliced like cold steel.

"I warned you that in such a small village it would be difficult to watch Ongeti."

Arrogant. Impudent. This man must know that Shen sat at the table next to Chairman Wei, and yet he showed no respect.

"And I cannot know if Ongeti was in the mining camp."

Shen's heart skipped a beat. If all of his thieves were dead, it would be impossible for him to reassure Chairman Wei that the tanzanite remained secret.

I need them alive.

"How can you not know if Ongeti was in the camp?" Shen's voice was now brittle and loud. "You said that your men would know if *anyone* came or left the camp."

"The men watching the camp followed Graham and the doctor when they left in the morning, before Ongeti disappeared. They drove to a private landing strip and flew out on a small chartered bush plane." Keambiroro barely paused for breath. "My men waited at the airstrip for the plane to return and then followed Graham back to the mining camp. They believed they had found a safe way to access to the camp and a closer position to watch the woman. They were doing as they were told ... they cannot be faulted for not knowing if Ongeti arrived at the mining camp while they followed Graham."

So Keambiroro sought to bury his mistake about Ongeti within

the other news he reported. They had not just failed to follow Ongeti
— they had lost track of him completely.

"But when Ongeti left, we were able to search his house. I have his
computer, notebooks, and maps." Keambiroro reported. "Everything
that was found in his backpack and a duffel bag."

A glimmer of hope. The stolen tanzanite might yet be recovered,
if Ongeti had foolishly left it behind.

"I want Ongeti's belongings packed up and shipped to London
on the next flight."

To send the items to men Shen trusted in London would mean
another day's delay, something he could ill afford. But he knew nothing
of Keambiroro's history, whether he had ever worked the tanzanite
mines and could recognize the gemstone. And there was no way to
know what the man might discover in the written notes and computer.

"Do you know where Graham went?" Although Shen held out
no real hope that this so-called security expert's team knew such a
critical detail.

"Not yet. Under the circumstances, I thought it best not to question the pilot directly, because it could alert Graham to our surveillance. But I will soon have her flight details for you."

"The first correct decision you've made." Phone cradled against
his shoulder, Shen slipped a cigarette free of its package. "When can
you get into the mining camp?"

"Only now do police go into the camp. It will be hours before we
can enter without fear of slaughter or arrest."

"Find a way." Shen punched the "end call" button.

He ground his thumb into his temple. A simple operation. Find
a way into the camp. Keep Graham and Ongeti under close watch.
Keambiroro and his so-called security experts were incompetent.
It was hard to believe that Chairman Wei would trust this African
with such a delicate problem.

Unless. Had he been set up to fail?

Perhaps Chairman Wei took the advice of others in the inner circle.
Men who sought to take advantage of this theft and would use it to

steal his place at Wei's side. Men who would push the Chairman to sign his death warrant.

Shen lit his cigarette and turned to the darkening skyline. By morning he could be far enough from São Paulo not to be found. He had enough money to live in luxury and make Long Bridge Merchant Group and Tabitha Metals a distant memory.

A foolish thought. Nowhere in the world could he could hide from Jianyu Wei.

Shen had to fight back ... had to convince Chairman Wei that the tanzanite they mined remained secret. And he had to do it with someone other than Keambiroro.

To bypass the African and seek help elsewhere would have to be done carefully — secretly. Even the hint of such a move might offend Chairman Wei or make Shen look weak, unable to control Keambiroro.

Nicotine wafted deep into his lungs. He held it there until his need for air forced an exhale and then watched the rise of grey smoke, strong and pungent.

One man came to mind.

But once down this path, he could not turn back.

Do I dare?

55

Grumeti River, Tanzania

THEY SAT QUIET, alone, in the corner of the lounge. Alex tried to push away the images of the mining camp riot, and she knew Eric did the same.

We were lucky.

Headlines screamed out differing body counts, from thirty-seven to two hundred and eighteen. No one knew the truth. Not yet. Worse, it could be days before the dead were identified, and they would learn if Mosi was among them.

She'd known few of the men who worked at the mine, even less about where they lived or how to contact them. Tracey was tracking them down through Dallas Resources, the American company that owned the mine, but she doubted they had a complete record of the men hired by her dad. Still, they had to try. If they could find just one miner who had made it out alive, he might at least know if Mosi had been at the camp.

Derek remained steadfast in his belief that Mosi and Zawadi were stranded somewhere nearby, as did Eric. He had cancelled the safari drives for the twelve other guests at this exclusive lodge, dedicating every resource to the search for Mosi.

Nate's name flashed on the screen with the first ring of the phone.

"Please tell me you have good news about my dad," Alex said when she answered.

"Afraid not. All I know is that his passport hasn't shown up."

Nate waited a breath before he finished. "After this long ... I have to believe he's off the road somewhere, Alex."

Eric tensed, and she shook her head. She stood and walked over to the edge of the lounge as she listened to Nate, barely able to focus on his words.

"Without a sat phone, there's no way your dad can call for help. Lots of roads out there to search, and I can't promise that even if I can get police to start looking, they'll find anything."

One bad decision after another.

Not only had her dad gone to Colombia alone, he did it without even the most basic backup, a satellite phone. If he had been seriously injured in an accident, each hour without medical care lessened his chance of survival. Three days had passed, long enough for water to be an issue too. Unless he carried a good supply of water with him, he'd have to be mobile enough to find more.

He's running out of time. And there wasn't a damn thing she could do.

She stared out at the Grumeti River and the vast emptiness beyond. *Novoteras.* That single word brought her back to the conversation. "I'm sorry, Nate ... did you say Novoteras?"

"Yeah. They had a break-in a few nights ago. One man dead. Pretty straightforward ... police have already close the file. But we used the break-in as an excuse to sit down with the mine manager. The guy's not saying much about—"

"You sent somebody to Brazil?" She spun around to face Eric. "I just assumed you would handle this investigation from home, just talk to a few guys you know."

"I did ... I am. But turns out that Mark—"

"Mark?"

"Mark Brody ... ex-military and one hell of an investigator. He's in South America, working on who knows what, and he offered to do me a favour. Believe me, this guy is like a wolf. He talked to Brazilian police, and Tabitha Metals is squeaky clean. But he followed up with a visit to the Novoteras mine." He paused. "This might be a good time to tell me what's going on. Mark is still in Brazil, and he can help you and Eric get home."

He knows!

"No judgment, Alex. Tell me what's going on … I just want you two safe."

She hesitated, unsure of how much to say about Eric's involvement. But it had to be done. Nate couldn't help them, if he didn't know it all.

She started with the mine break-in and ended with Mosi's disappearance. Only when she finished did Alex finally breathe. For better or worse, everything was out in the open.

"Tanzania." Nate practically spat out the word. "I was sure you were in Colombia or Brazil, and even that I couldn't understand. But *Tanzania?*"

"There's more, Nate … there was a riot at the mining camp where we were staying. We only just managed to get out." She rattled off what they knew about the riot. "My friend Derek believes that the riot was about me. Scares the *hell* out of me."

"Shit! Alex, you guys need to come home now. *Get out of there!*" Nate roared.

"We're trying." Her grip on the phone tightened. "We're safe for now. We're at the lodge that Derek runs, and he has good security in place. He's arranged for a lawyer to meet with us later today … but it's not enough, Nate."

"No, it's not. My gut tells me that the Chinese are behind Tabitha Metals, and that means money and power. You're in over your heads … go to the Canadian Consulate. If there isn't one, talk to the Americans or the British. They'll help you, Alex."

"They'll put us on a plane home, but they won't do anything else. They're not going to help find Mosi, and they're not going to believe a word about a secret Brazilian tanzanite mine. Right now, we don't even have the rock … I left it in Dubai."

"Let me talk to Mark Brody. Maybe he can pull a string or two in the Middle East and get you a meeting with somebody who'll pay attention."

"I thought you said he was working in South America? Who is this guy, Nate?"

"Ex-Marine, Special Forces … he was with Homeland Security when I met him in Nelson. If I had to guess — and I do have to guess, because he's pretty vague on the subject — I'd say he either still is, or he's part of one of the alphabet agencies. DEA, CIA, or whatever else the Americans have dreamed up. Doesn't matter, Alex. He's connected, and that's exactly what you need right now. Do you—"

She dropped the phone from her ear and twisted left to the sound of a thump too close for comfort. Eyes glistened above the rough grey snout of a hippo, its massive body barely supported on stout legs. Despite its lumbering three-ton bulk, it had managed to get within a few feet of where Alex stood, silent as a slender cheetah.

A bartender motioned Alex back behind a pillar, a trick designed to hide her from the eyesight-poor hippo. She swallowed hard, unable to draw her gaze from the beast that stared her way.

"Alex? Are you still there?"

The sound of Nate's voice broke through her trance.

We're not safe here.

"Call Brody." Alex's hand tightened on the phone. "If this lawyer can't help us, then we need another option. And we need it fast."

56

São Paulo, Brazil

SEATED ON A LEATHER chair in the furthest corner of the room, Shen glanced up at the heavy wooden doors of the São Paulo airport executive lounge. A steady stream of travellers had passed through the doors during the past hour, but none he recognized. Except one.

Shen dropped his eyes to his most private contact list. Once or twice, while he slowly examined the names, hope surfaced, only to be pushed aside just as quickly. Although every man on this list would offer unquestioning help either in repayment of debt or out of fear, none had the needed resources.

It is time.

He searched the room for familiar faces one last time before he swallowed the last of his Scotch and stood. He slid the paper with his handwritten notes into the inside pocket of his jacket and tapped the cigarette package stored there.

He crossed the room, focused on an empty leather chair near the window. In the seat next to it waited a man he'd known for almost twenty years.

The years had not been kind to his college classmate, Park Fàn. Deep lines etched his face, and the tight pull of his white shirt magnified too many extra pounds. In their years at Cambridge, the two men had spent their off-hours rowing, and both had maintained sleek, athletic bodies. Now restaurants, alcohol and too many hours behind a desk shaped them.

Park didn't stand or motion Shen to sit. To the casual observer, the two men might be strangers, travellers bound only by their need for solace between flights. To those who might recognize them, their airline tickets provided an excuse for this meeting beyond security. Their missed flights would be described only as a fortunate circumstance that allowed time with an old friend, if anyone asked. An unlikely question, but he and Park were not men to take chances.

When they had graduated from Cambridge, Uncle had quietly introduced Shen to powerful men in China, and Park had been recruited by a top London law firm, but their bond remained strong, and they met often. But when Shen took a seat at the executive table of Long Bridge Merchant Group and Park became in-house counsel to a direct competitor, they grew wary. Even though both now lived in Brazil, they were acutely aware of the damage an accusation of collusion or disloyalty would inflict. And this meeting was especially dangerous.

"Park. You look the same as you did the last time we met."

"No, no. I look old compared to you. The Brazilian sun must agree with you."

Small talk. Lies. The game of business they had played countless times over the past fifteen years.

"Your bid for the Canadian oil company." Shen reached into his pocket for the cigarette package. "How does it progress?"

"We still have much work to do."

Shen slid the unsealed package across the small table between them, his fingertips gently resting on it. "I understand that Long Bridge Merchant Group is a strong contender."

Park smiled. "It is always the same. We both seek to acquire profitable corporations to expand our diverse holdings."

"Perhaps this time you will be successful."

Shen eased his hand away from the package. The bid details stored on the memory stick hidden among the cigarettes would allow Park to outbid Long Bridge Merchant Group. The loss of the oil company would make but a small dent in Chairman Wei's financial empire. A small price to pay for the continued cash flow from the Brazilian mine.

"It's unusual for a man in your position to wish a rival success." Park tapped a finger against the cigarette pack, acknowledging the gift but refusing to accept it — yet.

"The winds of change affect us all."

Park's eyes narrowed. "I find it hard to imagine a change so profound that you would betray your employer."

Shen expected more from this friend who had travelled dark paths alongside him. Even among mere associates, *xin yong*, the ties binding business partners, demanded discretion and eschewed confrontation. *So be it.*

"There's a woman I need found." Shen mirrored Park's bluntness.

"A woman? You do all of this for a woman?" Park shook his head.

Here lay the risk. Park could easily capture Alex and question her himself.

"This is family business," Shen said. "The woman, a Caucasian, is connected to Jianyu Wei's son, and she must be found."

"I've seen the photos of Kuen's antics in the *Shanghai Daily* ... even some of the international newspapers have mentioned him." Park clicked his tongue against his teeth, an irritating habit Shen had long detested. "Too many women to count. And drugs. It's shameful for a first-born son expected to take the helm of his father's business." Park's finger traced the rim of his wine glass. "But surely you have your own resources."

"Of course. But this matter must be resolved quickly." Shen pressed his fingertips together. "Before the woman's pregnancy is obvious."

From the smile that crept to his companion's lips as he nodded his assent, Shen knew this salacious gossip would be spread everywhere in a few hours. It was of little importance. Chairman Wei tolerated his son's many affairs and riotous nights out with women, for it hid Kuen's homosexuality. No ... Wei wouldn't mind a rumour of his son impregnating a foreigner. And the story provided just enough reason for Park to understand Shen's need to help the Chairman save face.

"Then why not come to me and ask for my help directly? Instead of this." Park jerked his head at the untouched cigarette package on the table between them.

"I am in a difficult situation. This woman slipped through my fingers."

"So…" Park intertwined his fingers slowly, his eyes locked on Shen. "This gift serves a dual purpose. If the woman isn't found, you wish to join us."

Shen hid his surprise behind a neutral mask, one perfected long ago, and stayed silent. Park had surmised his true intention faster than Shen could have imagined, and he would not give any more ammunition to this lawyer so adept at staying ahead of his adversary.

"We can't promise to keep you alive," Park continued, assuming Shen's silence was confirmation enough. "If Wei discovers your betrayal, he will kill you."

Shen said nothing. His failure to find Alex Graham and Mosi Ongeti might deliver the same fate. So too might the shame of imprisonment for the crimes of Tabitha Metals.

Park stared out at the tarmac, undoubtedly weighing the risks of involvement in this dangerous betrayal against his loyalty to Shen.

Shen could remind the lawyer of their secrets, their lies and their desperate acts. But his friend knew these only too well, and such a reminder could be interpreted as a threat, a dangerous escalation.

"I will find this woman," Park finally said. He reached for the cigarette package and slipped it into his suit pocket. "But it is best for all of us if you remain a trusted adviser to Chairman Wei."

Shen drew in a sharp breath. Loyalty had triumphed, but the cost was high. Park expected him to remain on the inside and betray the Chairman repeatedly.

Park stood and buttoned his Italian-made suit jacket, a signal that this meeting had ended.

"I will call you in the morning," Park said before he vanished through the heavy doors.

Park would be on his phone before he hit the busy concourse. His company's bid would be revised before morning, and by the 5:00 p.m. deadline tomorrow it would sit beside the losing bid of Long Bridge Merchant Group. Shen would be committed.

At best, it left Shen twelve hours to find Alex Graham. Only then could he advise the Chairman to increase their own bid for the oil company before the deadline and quietly back out of this deal with Park. The Chairman would not ask why — he would assume insider information and be quick to react. Even if they lost the oil company in the end, the Chairman would not forget Shen's loyalty.

I will be stronger than ever.

57

Grumeti River, Tanzania

ALEX SMILED AT the man who set their drinks and a cheese plate on the table, but Eric seemed not to notice. He seemed lost in thought, as he had been for most of the past few hours.

They had restarted their search after lunch, this time with Tumi, one of Derek's senior guides, at the wheel. Only when Derek had radioed that Hanna Jensen was on her way did they reluctantly return.

"Are you okay?" she asked.

"Just tired." He rubbed the back of his neck. "I feel like I've just come off a night shift ... the kind with patients stacked in the hallways. I'm—" He glanced sideways. "Looks like Hanna is here."

She turned to see Derek headed toward them with the lawyer in tow. He stopped at the table only long enough to introduce them and serve Hanna a glass of wine before he slipped away.

Hanna Jensen wasn't at all what Alex expected. Casually dressed in a rock concert T-shirt, khaki shorts and sandals, the lawyer could easily be mistaken for a tour guide. Alex thought the slender blonde looked no more than forty — hardly old enough to have served on the International Criminal Tribunal for Rwanda. But when Hanna smiled, at least five decades were reflected in the deep creases that framed the corners of her mouth.

The things she's seen. Alex still found it hard to read about the one hundred days of slaughter, rape and terror of the Tutsi people of Rwanda at the hands of Hutu extremists in 1994. *Genocide.*

"Derek told me you have a serious problem. One that needs a quick solution." Hanna's voice still betrayed her Copenhagen upbringing, despite her years in Africa.

Hanna watched her with an intensity that made Alex want to look away, yet she found herself compelled to hold the Dane's gaze. She wouldn't want to be on the witness stand under this lawyer's interrogation.

"I'm not sure where to start. So much has happened I—"

"Walk me through all of it, Alex."

Hanna sat quietly, her wine glass sat untouched as she listened. Only when Alex leaned back, spent from telling her story, did Hanna finally move.

"Here's the problem." Hanna rested her chin on clasped hands, flashing short fingernails painted red. "You didn't go into the mine, right? This man Mosi Ongeti is the one that retrieved the stone. You said he flew to Brazil directly from Tanzania. How do you know he didn't give you a piece of tanzanite taken from Tanzania?"

Alex jerked back, as though punched by the accusation. "He wouldn't do anything like that! I've known Mosi almost my entire life. He'd *never* do that."

"But do you understand my point? Even if Mosi testified, a judge might not believe him."

Alex stifled the urge to flee the lounge, to put distance between herself and this woman.

"We'll need the testimony of the miners who went into the mine with Mosi, to corroborate his story," Hanna continued. "Can you reach them?"

Them. A stark reminder that two Brazilians, young men with families, had led Mosi into the mine, but only one made it out alive.

"Benjamin was shot and killed during the break-in." Alex let out a sigh. "And if Paulo testifies, he'd be arrested ... or worse. I'm not sure I can ask him to take any more risks than he already has."

"There has to be another way," Eric argued. "Alex's testimony must be worth something."

"I'm afraid not. Only someone who was there when the tanzanite was pulled from the mine wall can testify to—"

"Unless the gem itself proves it didn't come from Tanzania," Alex argued.

"I don't understand." Hanna dropped her hands into her lap.

"There *has* to be a difference between the Brazilian and Tanzanian gemstones." She curled her hand into a fist. "Something that would show up in a detailed geochemical analysis."

She turned to the river, fearing her frustration would turn to tears. *Breathe, Alex. Just breathe.*

Hanna's voice brought her back to the conversation. "What about this Novoteras mine? What do you know about it?"

"I couldn't find much on Tabitha Metals, the owner of the mine. So Eric called in a favour from a friend, Nate Taylor, a police officer with the RCMP."

"The Mounties." Hanna smiled. "I've always loved their scarlet-red uniforms. Did he find anything?"

"Nate didn't get much further than I did with the owners. But he does think there may be a Chinese connection."

"Why?"

"Gut instinct more than anything. A Chinese engineer died in a cave-in at the mine a few years back, and Nate thinks that's suspicious. But as I told him, it's not unusual for mines to hire international consultants." Alex said. "A colleague of Nate's is down in Brazil, and he's talked to police … he even visited the mine. He couldn't dig up anything specific on the owners."

"Alex, you said you watched the mine operations over several weeks — were they typical? Is this a large mine, a small one? Examine it like a geologist."

She pictured the sprawling grounds fenced and protected by cameras and snipers. "It's a fairly small mine but about average for this part of Brazil. Five tunnels spread over three levels, a few out-buildings for administration and staff and a large production facility where they crush and separate rock for shipping. I'm not up on development costs here, but in the U.S. a mine like that could cost as much as two hundred million to build and equip. Depending on the tonnage of tourmaline they produce, they could bring in as much as thirty or forty million a year, but it could be a lot less. There must be a hundred men who work there, including geologists, engineers and other specialists, and that's consistent with a profitable mine."

"With that many people involved, how do you keep a mine like this secret?"

"The mine is listed as a tourmaline producer, and you'd need to know your gems to know that what was coming out of the mine wasn't tourmaline."

"But they have geologists on staff, so they're being paid to cover up the operation. There must be red tape, government officials who visit the mine. They would have to be paid off too."

"Right. Which is why I think it's a big player like al Qaeda or ISIL. I know Nate believes there's a Chinese connection, but terrorists make more sense to me."

Hanna shook her head. "People think these terrorist groups operate with big budgets, but in fact their resources are quite limited, and for the most part they don't operate as a single entity. Instead, many of their adherents are lone wolves who decide for themselves how best to serve the cause. But the Chinese?" She raised an eyebrow. "Now you're talking about an arms dealer or drug cartel — powerful, organized crime. They're far more able to invest millions to start up this mine and then successfully run it."

Hanna reached into a tote bag and pulled out a small coil-bound book and pen. It was only then that Alex realized the lawyer had not yet taken a single note. Every detailed question she'd asked thus far had been drawn from her memory of Alex's report of the events of the past week.

"Where is the rock now? The one taken from the mine?" Hanna clicked her pen and pressed the point onto a clean page.

"It's in a hotel safety deposit box in Dubai."

"I'd like to send someone I trust to pick it up." As though sensing

Alex's discomfort, she quickly added. "This way, I can testify to how the rock came into Tanzania. It will be safe here, I promise."

"It's the best solution, Alex," Eric softly said.

"And then what?" Alex asked. "We still have the same problem."

"Maybe … but it's a place to start, Alex. There are experts here who can examine that gemstone." Hanna handed Alex her notepad and pen. "If you provide your full legal name, I will prepare a limited power of attorney document for you to sign. It will authorize the man I send to Dubai to open the box at the hotel on your behalf. It should be enough … if not, then we will have to wait until it is safe for you to go to Dubai yourself."

Alex pressed the pen tip against the paper but formed no letters. She'd only just met this woman who wanted her to hand over their only piece of evidence. But deep down, Alex knew she had to trust this confident Dane who offered help. *I'm out of options.*

She carefully wrote out her full name, Alexandra Graham, before she handed the notepad back to Hanna.

"One more thing…" Hanna held Alex's gaze for a single heartbeat before she continued. "Derek is absolutely right about the riot. They came for you, Alex."

Alex started to protest, but Hanna held up a hand to stop her. "No one that saw that video would question your disappearance … or your death." She turned to Eric. "You believe that too, don't you?"

"Yes." Eric nodded. "They went into Brian Graham's tent before the riot started. It's just too much of a coincidence." He turned to Alex. "This is about you … and it scares me to death."

Alex felt as though a hand choked her throat. They'd all known the investigation into the Tabitha Metals mines was dangerous, but none of them could have imagined it would follow them here.

"You said your dad is missing. If he's been taken, Tabitha Metals might know that you went into the Novoteras mine, and they would know about the mining camp."

Taken. Her mind recoiled from the word. Although Alex had considered a kidnapping, only now did it seem a real possibility.

"No way." She shook her head. "My dad was downright paranoid about all of this. He doesn't have his sat phone, his computer, GPS." She counted the points off with her fingers. "Nothing that would tie him to me or Graham and Associates. Even our texts and calls have only been through prepaid phones."

"Such men, Alex … they have ways of getting information." *Torture.*

"My dad would die before he said—" Alex balled her hand into a fist. "You think that's what's happened!"

"It would explain how they found you and why Mosi is missing."

"No. *No!*" Alex shook her head. "It has to be something else. There were people looking for Mosi at the São Paulo airport. He was the one who rented the truck, and Paulo said the mine manager asked about a black man. They know about Mosi … somehow they've tracked him here."

"Then they followed us from his house," Eric said. "The night we met the nurse there."

"Maybe. There was a man in Arusha … I thought he was listening to us. He may have been following us."

"*Arusha?*" Eric blurted. "You didn't say anything to me."

Alex twisted to face him, saw the worry in his eyes and something more. Anger. "I'm sorry, Eric. I convinced myself it was nothing, that I was getting to be as paranoid as my dad. Now I'm not so sure." She turned back to Hanna. "But it would mean that they tracked Mosi from Brazil … that's how they found me."

"They're going to come for you again, Alex." Hanna pulled a phone from her tote. "We have to assume that they followed you here. You're safe for now — Derek runs tight security here, and his people can protect you. But we need to get you and Eric out of Tanzania."

"Not until I find Mosi. If I was followed, then so was he. I won't leave until I know he and Zawadi are safe."

Hanna shook her head. "You may not have a choice, Alex."

58

Grumeti River, Tanzania

ALEX DIDN'T NEED Eric to say a word. Everything from the way he perched on the edge of the bed to his unsmiling face said it all: he wanted them out of Tanzania.

Alex shifted in her chair. It would be so easy to run, to fly home to the safety of Canada.

I can't.

"One more day ... we give it one more day. I *have* to know that Mosi and Zawadi are okay. Try to understand," she pleaded. "Think of what you'd do if it was your brother Matt out there. I can't do anything to help find my dad right now. But this is something I *can* do ... something I *have* to do."

"You heard Hanna — she's going to call in a few favours and get more people out looking for them. Derek has already alerted the nearby lodges, and every safari driver is keeping an eye out for Zawadi's truck, for *any* vehicle in trouble. They cover a lot of ground, Alex ... more than you and I could ever do alone."

"We're safe here for now, and I'm waiting for Kanoni to call me back." She folded her arms across her chest. "She said that she was going to talk to Mosi's brothers ... she's sure they know some of the men who worked at the mining camp."

"You can do all of that from Vancouver, Alex."

"It'll be two days before we're home. I need to know that Mosi wasn't at the camp when that riot started, Eric. And Nate is calling

Mark to see if he had a contact here. If Mark can get us a meeting with someone in the Tanzanian government who can help us expose that mine, then it's worth one more day."

"It's not a good idea. You—"

His admonishment was cut short by the shrill ring of her phone. *Tracey.* Her heart skipped a beat.

"Do you have news about my dad?" she asked after Tracey's first words.

"Only about an expense on Brian's credit card." Tracey's report was delivered matter-of-factly, without preamble. "I went back over everything from the past year, and I found a charge six months back from what looks like a duty-free store in the Dubai airport. There's no way that Brian's shopping duty-free unless he's in transit, so he booked a flight out of Tanzania with a layover in Dubai. Damned if I know which one, though … no time stamp on that credit charge. I've asked for the actual receipt, but without knowing how long Brian was in Dubai, we could be faced with hundreds of possible flights."

Six months ago. It could easily be the trip he took to meet with the client who started all of this. But from Dubai, he could have flown anywhere.

"I've never seen Brian book his own international airline ticket … not once in all the years I've worked at Graham and Associates," Tracey continued. "And even if he did, he wouldn't pay cash, so I'd see the charge. It makes me think that someone else is making the arrangements — and picking up the tab. Maybe it's the client you're looking for."

Alex paced the floor. "What about hotels? Or restaurants? Do you see anything in Europe or the Middle East?"

"Sure, lots of them … he was on the move a fair bit this past year. But everything connects up with one of his projects, and there's nothing around the date of that Dubai purchase."

"Which projects did he start before that trip, Tracey? It's a long shot, but maybe the client is connected to one of those."

All I need is one name.

"What kind of assistant would I be if I didn't already have that list for you?" Her smile was evident in the lightness of her words. "If you have a pen, I can give you the client names and contact info."

Alex recognized just two of the clients, although she knew about most of the projects. What surprised her most as she jotted down the list was just how many projects there were. Her dad had mentioned trips outside of Tanzania, but it was only now that she realized how much time he'd spent away from the Mwanza mining camp.

"I've also gone over the list of Grumeti lodge guests you sent me. If Brian knows any of these people, damned if I can find it. I ran every name variation I could think of against our contact list, but nothing turns up that's even close."

"I was so sure ... especially when Derek said that my dad spent most of the evening talking to them."

"I wish it were that easy, but we're going to have to dig deeper. I'm just about to start on Brian's expense accounts. If he met with someone for dinner or drinks, there should be a name on the receipt."

She had to smile. Paperwork had never been her dad's strong suit, but Tracey didn't let him get away with much.

Her dad spent all of his time in the field, a hammer in one hand, compass in the other. The only thing that mattered to him was what he found in the ground beneath his feet. That was why he put her in charge of managing the administrative side of their consulting company and why he left all the paperwork to her and Tracey. And left them to nag him about it.

"Thanks, Tracey."

"Nothing on Mosi?"

"Nothing yet." She gave Tracey the briefest update she could get away with. "I promise I'll call you as soon as I hear anything."

"As soon as you hear, Alex. I don't care if it's the middle of the night ... you call me," Tracey commanded before she clicked off.

"Dead end." She dropped onto the bed next to Eric. "It was a long shot anyway, and this client probably knows less about Tabitha Metals and those mines than we do."

"Mark Brody is going to turn up something, Alex. It's just going to take some time."

"I wonder if Mark could find some pretext to get into the Novoteras mine. I know a geologist I trust in Brazil — Scott Miller. He'd be able to get us the evidence we need." She reached for her phone. "He should still be in Minas Gerais, but even if he's back in Buenos Aires, he can be at the mine in a day."

"You talked to him when you were in Brazil?"

She nodded. "I hoped he might be able to get me into the Novoteras mine. He doesn't know anything about the tanzanite. I gave him a story about a client—" She stopped short. "What if my dad's story about a client is a lie? You said it yourself. All of this secrecy … it doesn't add up."

Three quick steps took her behind the bed to the desk with her dad's notes — the only item she'd stuffed into her backpack before their hasty exit from the mining camp.

"Maybe the story about the dead courier is just that … a story. What if someone who had actually been in the mine came to my dad, and he's trying to protect them?" She dropped back onto the bed with the notes in her hand. "A consulting geologist or contract miner … someone who works in both Brazil and Tanzania."

And Colombia.

"Or an engineer! Dad mentioned that he had finally arranged a meeting with an engineer who had worked with Tabitha Metals." Her words tumbled out. "For all we know *he's* the one that started this … but I do know that he might be the last person who saw my dad."

She riffled through pages of tight script, searching for names. It didn't take long, though, before she dropped the pages on the bed.

"Shit! If it's in here, I'll never find it. Dad uses initials, if he mentions names at all." She picked up the phone. "I'll call Tracey … she needs to be looking for an engineer or a geologist, not just a client."

As she waited for Tracey to answer, her thoughts turned sombre.

Even if they learned who this engineer was, Alex might be no closer to finding her dad.

He wouldn't go this long without contacting her, not with so much at stake.

He's in trouble.

59

Salinas, Brazil

JORGE EASED HIMSELF onto the edge of his son's narrow bed. Alberto, tucked beneath a heavy quilt, stared up at him with dark brown eyes and a soft smile.

The innocence of a child.

For the first time in more than a week, Jorge had been home early enough to eat dinner with his family and then tuck his children into bed. A simple joy to listen to Ana chatter on about school, ignoring her older brother's teasing comments. At just six, Ana had already proved herself a fast learner with a natural instinct for math and science, like her mother. Zahra beamed with pride at the thought her daughter might someday become a doctor or an engineer. Their son's future was far less clear. Like his sister, Alberto did well in school, but his energetic curiosity about everything from bugs to computers made it difficult for him to focus on a single endeavour.

"*Pai*, will you come to watch me play football tomorrow?"

The question drove a spike through his heart. It was not something that Alberto had to ask, not before the break-in that had taken so much time away from his family. Even now, Jorge could not promise his son a few hours of his time.

Jorge swept a lock of dark hair across his son's forehead. "I will try."

He switched off the bedside light, and after a whispered good night, he crossed the room. At the doorway, his hand wrapped around the knob, he took one last look at his son before he closed the door.

Back in the kitchen, he found Zahra sitting at the kitchen table, her hands wrapped around a mug of tea. Smiling up at him, she poured tea from an earthen pot into a second cup as he approached. In the soft light of the kitchen, Zahra, with her hair tied back in a ponytail, still looked like the eighteen-year-old beauty who had stolen so many hearts. Why she had chosen him would forever remain a mystery.

"It is good that you had this time with the children today, Jorge," she said when he slipped into a chair across from her. "They miss their father."

He sighed. "It will be over soon." Although in his heart he remained unconvinced.

He clasped his hands together, fingertips white against his knuckles. "Tell me, what did you find out?" He had wanted to ask the question the minute he walked into the house but knew from Zahra's warning glance that she would not discuss it until the children were in their beds.

"This rock you mine is tanzanite, not tourmaline." Even now with the children behind closed doors, Zahra whispered the words.

"Tanzanite?" He leaned forward, speaking in the same hushed tone. "I have never heard of any such a rock."

"It is very rare, Jorge. It is found only in Tanzania, Africa." She pulled her sweater tight.

"Africa? I do not understand. It must be a mistake. I took that rock from a bucket in the mine — a bucket just filled by the miners." His hand tightened into a fist. "I *saw* more of the same rock in the mine wall."

She raised a finger to her lips to quiet him. "I took the rock to two jewellers, and each man told me the same thing. It is tanzanite, Jorge. I do not understand how it can be, but it is the truth."

He slumped back against the wooden chair, his mind swirling with questions, yet he could think of only one. "How valuable is this rock?"

"Not as valuable as emerald, but still very expensive." She wrapped her sweater tight, folding her arms across her chest. "That one piece of rock is worth more than one thousand United States dollars."

In his mind, he pictured the miles of tunnels that snaked beneath the surface, the truckloads of rock chipped from the mine walls. Even if Tunnel Five were the only source of tanzanite—

He pressed his palms against the table. "There could be millions of dollars of tanzanite in the mine, and they seek to hide the truth. It explains why Mr. Li is taking such pains to track our thieves."

I have been such a fool. There were thousands of men more qualified to manage this mine — a fact his father had been quick to point out when the job was offered. Jorge had argued that his impressive rise in the police force had been the reason he had been hired, but now he saw the truth, saw how he had been used.

"Shen Li hired me because I would not know what questions to ask." He dropped his gaze, unable to meet her eyes. "I would not look closely at the mining operation." He could not bring himself to admit that he had been used for his reputation too. Tabitha Metals had sought to hide behind a respected police officer to bring an air of legitimacy to what was clearly an illegal operation.

He heard her soft footsteps and felt her hands on his shoulders. "Jorge, you could not have known. It has been a good job ... it fed our family, bought this house, put money in the bank. And it kept you safe."

"But—"

"No, Jorge. We must think only about what to do now."

He still had friends in the police force, men like Miguel Rossi who knew him, who would not believe him part of this cover-up. Or would they? Many men fell victim to greed, and he had turned his back on his career seven years ago — long enough for his fellow officers to feel they no longer knew him. None could offer strong enough protection, not for this.

Mark Brody. An outsider already asking questions about the mine. A man who was not what he seemed.

"The man I told you about, Mark Brody. He came to see me today asking questions about the owners of the mine. He must know what is going on, or he would not be interested in the mine. I will take the rock to him."

Her fingers dug into his shoulders. He turned and took her hands in his, guiding her into the chair next to him. Knees almost touching, he held her hands, waiting for her to look at him, but her eyes remained downcast.

He could almost hear her beating heart. "Zahra, what is it?"

She studied her hands before she finally said, "The rock is gone. I sold it to one of the jewellers."

He thought his heart would stop. "You sold something that does not belong to us. And now—" He wanted to lecture her but could not. He was responsible. He was the one who had stolen the rock from the mine.

She waited a long minute before she met his gaze. "If Mr. Li had discovered you had it, our lives would be ruined. You said this yourself. But it is more than that, Jorge." She ran a hand over her belly. "What will happen to us, to your *family*, when you show that rock to someone? You have run that mine for *seven* years, Jorge. No one will believe you did not know the truth ... you will be arrested."

"That is what I am trying to prevent, Zahra. I must give Mark Brody a piece of rock from the mine, he—"

"No, Jorge. We must run."

60

São Paulo, Brazil

SHEN LEANED BACK in his chair, the cell phone still held tight in his hand.

No women.

He focused on this small fact, the only positive in Keambiroro's report of sixty-three dead in the mining camp riot. But it left him no closer to finding Alex Graham.

For three days, Ongeti and Graham had been in their grasp, within striking range, yet somehow the thieves had slipped free. It was impossible to believe that Keambiroro and the men beneath him could be so incompetent. He feared the African's loyalty lay with another, someone determined to see Shen fail.

Failure was not tolerated in the Chairman's most trusted advisers. Men who disappointed the Chairman disappeared, driven into hiding or found dead, and their names were never spoken again. Instead, those at the executive table brokered their connections and power to snare the vacant seat or expand their value.

Shen had seen it happen only twice in the eight years since he was welcomed into the inner circle. The first time, not long after his own promotion, had occurred with such swiftness that Shen had barely seen the ripples of discontent. It was an early lesson, one that built on Uncle's advice to stay close enough to his adversaries that they breathed as one. The next time he caught the first hint of weakness, the faint imprint of failure, he stood ready — as others did now.

The latest message from Chairman Wei laid bare Shen's precarious situation in a single line that demanded updates on the Novoteras mine shipment and the theft investigation. He could almost hear the Chairman's steely voice in every word, words that warned of failure and disgrace, announced to seven of the top executives of Long Bridge Merchant Group.

Like bait dropped onto swirling waters, Wei had fed him to men anxious to fight over his coveted role. Whether any of them could control Keambiroro for their own gain, he was unsure.

I will not fail.

Two days remained until the deadline. A lifetime.

He dialled Tim Wong, but when the Novoteras mine's engineer finally answered, it was on a line crowded with machine noise and static. He heard just enough to understand the engineer would call him back in a few minutes.

A gentle knock at his door warned that Meilin had not yet left for the day. And when he failed to respond, he heard her quiet footsteps down the hall.

Once news of his weakness reached her, the lovely Meilin would be quick to spread word, both here and in China. Her feigned feelings for him would disappear, replaced with the hard shell of self-preservation. She'd be among the first to search the hidden shadows for anything that could be used against Shen to advance herself.

She would not be alone. Even the lowliest employee would scramble for advantage, searching his past memos, reports, and emails for any detail that could be used to gain favour with the most powerful among the Chairman's inner circle.

Guanxi. Reciprocity — a concept so few outside of China truly understood. Outside the company walls, it rode the thin line between power and corruption. A favour offered to secure a contract or negotiate better terms, too easily turned into bribery and blackmail. Inside the company, though, *guanxi* flowed like a social network, signalling alliances that were used like currency by the ambitious.

His fist clenched. He could trust no one.

Wong's number flashed on the phone's caller ID. *Finally.*

"What is our production at now?" Shen asked without preamble.

"We are nearing eighty percent of the quota."

Shen calculated the tanzanite value, even though he'd been through the numbers a dozen times since the break-in.

Eighty percent, ninety percent — none of it would be enough. They would barely meet Chairman Wei's exorbitant monetary demand with one hundred percent of their quota, given the current price of tanzanite.

"Not enough." He pressed his fingertips against his forehead, tracing its deep crease. "Can you put more men in Tunnel Five?" He'd never been in the mine, had no idea how many men could work the shaft at one time. "Or add another shift?"

"I did both two days ago. We are now at twice the production, and the men are working twelve-hour shifts."

"How long before we reach the quota?"

"Forty-eight hours."

Too tight. A single incident — a broken machine, an ill worker — and he would miss his deadline.

"Make it thirty." He gambled that Wong had built-in a cushion, exaggerated the time, to protect himself from failure.

"But—"

He cut the man short. "Thirty hours, Mr. Wong."

A pause. No doubt the engineer weighed his position. To promise something he could not deliver would ruin him, but to refuse made him an easy scapegoat.

"To do that, I must work the men sixteen, maybe eighteen-hour shifts." Wong let out a deep sigh that signalled his reluctance. "It means trucks loading in the dark and men too tired to work safely. Even then…"

Shen waited, knowing that Wong wanted him to take responsibility for the added danger, knowing also that the engineer would comply even without it.

"Thirty hours." The engineer sighed. "I will find a way."

Shen greeted the answer with the faintest smile, gone by the time he ended the call. It would take more than meeting the production quota deadline to satisfy the Chairman.

Graham and Ongeti.

Alonso Quinto's detectives had confirmed that Brian Graham entered Colombia seven weeks ago, but they had yet to locate him or determine who had hired him.

Save for the appearance of Mark Brody at the Novoteras mine, there'd been no apparent outside interest in that mine or the others owned by Tabitha Metals. What worried him most was that not one of the Colombian mine managers reported a phone call or visit from Brody.

Novoteras is the target.

The police chief who had vouched for Brody could tell Jorge Silva only that a call from a federal police commander had preceded the man, a call that provided little information and demanded cooperation. Silva had offered to contact the commander, a decorated officer of more than twenty years, but such an enquiry might trigger unwanted attention to the mine. Instead, Shen had asked Quinto to quietly investigate the commander, searching for anything that might reveal his out-of-country connections — and his vulnerabilities.

Blackmail. The police commander would reveal his connection to Brody, given time. And Shen would follow the chain, its winding links, until his adversary revealed himself. His hand clenched into a fist.

I will crush him.

61

Grumeti River, Tanzania

A DISTANT ENGINE ROAR warned that the first of the guests were returning from their early morning safari treks. Staff heard the engines too, and suddenly the lounge where Alex and Eric had quietly eaten breakfast bustled with energy.

They'd lingered in their tent, reluctant to leave the warmth of their bed at dawn. And Eric's soft touch against the swell of her breast and his warm lips against her neck, stirred in her a reason to stay.

Their lovemaking had been urgent, fierce, a need driven by too many weeks apart. Only when Eric later joined her in the shower, did they savour each touch. And only when the sun was well above the horizon, did they finally venture out to this breakfast table by the river.

"Finally." Alex swept crumbs from her khaki pants before she stood. "Now we can take a truck out and join the search."

Eric dropped his white linen napkin on the low table. "Right behind you. Let me grab the camera Derek lent me … I'd like to go home with at least one photo of a lion."

She smiled. "I guess that's fair. I did promise you a safari, after all … I just didn't expect it to be like this."

"You'll get no complaints from me. I've seen more of the Serengeti than I did in all the months I was working here." He slipped his arm around her waist. "And I've gotten to do it with you."

She hugged him then whispered into his ear, "I'm so glad you're here." Although she still could barely believe he had flown halfway around the world on a moment's notice — for her.

Voices filtered through the lodge, and she dropped her arms. "I'll find Derek and get us a 4x4. Can you grab my backpack and whatever you need from the tent and meet me in the parking lot?"

She started out to find Derek, but he was already headed her way. She marvelled at how he remained discreetly distant yet appeared at the exact right moment. *The perfect host.* And right now, their best ally.

"Three of the guides are going back out to search for Mosi." Derek handed her a sack heavy with water bottles and food. "There's a fourth vehicle that you and Eric can take. Talk to Rashid about which direction might be best … just stay in radio contact."

She slipped through the lodge, just far enough away from the guests heading back to their tents to be out of eyesight. By the time she reached the vehicles, Eric arrived loaded down with two backpacks.

They stood with the three guides, poring over a map balanced against the hood of a vehicle. Plans in place, Alex and Eric loaded their gear into the back of the 4x4 and drove southwest toward the road to Mwanza.

She bounced against the seat, hands tight on the steering wheel for mile after mile across the savannah, stopping time and again to sweep the tall grass for signs of a vehicle. All the while, they listened to the chatter of Swahili over the radio, hoping for news about Mosi.

When they passed through a stand of trees into a serene clearing, she parked beneath the shade of a lone tree. With the engine turned off, silence surrounded them, broken only by the occasional call of a lonely bird.

"We're probably safe enough here. I don't see any elephants, but…" She raised her binoculars. "In this grass, it's easy for the big cats to hide."

Eric climbed up onto his seat, and elbows against the open roof, he scanned the grassland. "I don't see a thing."

"All the same, we'll stay right next to the truck."

Her binoculars dangling from her neck, she stepped out of the

4x4. Both hands against her hips, she stretched backward, grateful to be out of the driver's seat after more than two hours of driving.

She lifted the hatch and climbed into the back of the vehicle. Outfitted for long safari drives, it held a stocked cooler, folding table and chairs, blankets and other comforts for long days in the Serengeti. She unloaded a couple of chairs and set them out between the truck and the tree, before making a return trip for water and sandwiches.

Not ready yet to sit again, she walked toward the smooth-barked tree, eyes on the branches high above. Reassured that the foliage didn't conceal a sleeping leopard or lion, she turned back to the truck. She smiled at Eric, hanging out of the roof of the truck, binoculars tight to his face. He might yet spot a zebra or eland, but the lions he so desperately wanted to see were probably deep in the grass, lazing in the afternoon sun.

"Tse-tse flies," she yelled out at the first sound of their heavy buzz. She quickly rolled down her sleeves and tightened the cuffs against her wrists. Without the artificial wind created by the moving vehicle, they were at the mercy of these fierce insects. "Even if you have bug dope on, it won't help."

Eric swatted at the back of his neck. "Shit! They bite hard!"

"It helps to wrap a bandana around your neck. There has to be at least one in the truck." She stuffed her pant legs into her socks and trotted back to the vehicle. Leaning into the cargo area, she riffled through the supplies. "Everything but—"

"*Shit!*" Eric practically fell into his seat. "There's a guy out there with a rifle. Alex, we have to get out of here."

Alex squeezed through the space between the seats and swung her leg over the console. Pain flashed when the gearshift stabbed into her thigh. Her hands clutching the steering wheel, she pulled herself into the seat, eyes darting from the side to the front window.

"Where? Where is he?"

Eric pointed to his left. "Just beyond the tree. At least he was … I can't see him any more."

She saw the glint of a rifle straight ahead.

"Eric, get down!"

She ducked her head just before a bullet punched the tire. To their left, the trees they'd sought out for shade now trapped them. They could do nothing but drive straight ahead.

Toward the shooter.

The man rushed forward, his rifle raised.

Her boot punched the gas pedal, and the truck roared in reply. She steered toward a narrow gap in the trees. But the man blocked their escape.

Another bullet. From a hunter poised to fire again.

She gripped the steering wheel, and ducked low, her foot heavy on the gas.

The unmistakable sound of metal hitting flesh. A man's scream.

Only then did she stomp on the brakes. And Eric flung the door open.

"Eric!" But it was too late.

Eric disappeared behind the front of the truck. One hand on the door handle, she jerked her head around at the sound of a distant engine.

She swung the door open and jumped to the ground, ignoring the jab of pain in her knees. Quick steps brought Eric into view — and the crumpled body of the man on a bloodied mat of grass.

"Eric. Eric. We have to go." She stepped around Eric to scoop up the rifle that lay too near the man's slender hand. "There's a truck coming. We have to go."

Eric pressed his fingers against the man's scrawny neck. "I have to help him, I—"

"We'll send someone back. We have to get out of here. There's someone coming!"

This time he didn't argue. Eric ran for the truck. The doors slammed shut. She slid their attacker's rifle between them and jerked the truck into gear.

"Bullets…" She could barely catch her breath. "I don't know if there are bullets in the gun. How many shots did you hear?"

In front of them, a cloud of dust, the glint of metal — closer than she'd like.

Damn. Damn. Damn.

She slammed on the brakes. Her shaking hand clutched the radio. "Mayday. Mayday. Mayday."

Even as she repeated the only words that might bring help, she heard the screech of brakes.

She grabbed the rifle and stared at the dusty truck now parked not fifty yards away.

And the door that swung open.

62

Grumeti River, Tanzania

ERIC KEPT LOW in his seat, watching the man who stood at the door of the truck — and the rifle in his hand.

Voices crowded the radio. Excited voices chattering in a language he didn't understand.

He hears those voices too. He knows help is coming.

The man did not call out a greeting when he finally took a step toward them.

Instead, Eric heard the sound of Alex winding down the window and saw her ease the rifle through the opening.

Only then did the man stop and shout Alex's name.

"It's Tumi." Alex relaxed her grip on the rifle. "It's okay … it's Tumi."

Tumi. Where he'd come from, Eric didn't know. Right now, he didn't care.

"Go … I'll find a first aid kit and be right there." Alex picked up the transceiver. "I need to answer the radio."

Eric scrambled out of the truck and ran back to the injured man. He dropped to his knees and pressed three fingers against the man's neck, feeling for the carotid artery. Eyes on the second hand of his watch, he counted the strong heartbeats that pulsed beneath his fingers.

"Alex!" The hairs on his neck prickled in the silence. "Alex!"

He caught movement behind him and turned to find Tumi, not Alex.

"Where's Alex?"

"I'm here." Alex's voice, breathless. "There are other guides coming. They're close … no more than five minutes out. And I found a first aid kit."

"Good. Check it out, Alex. I need to know what's in it. And Tumi … get me a blanket, or a fleece."

The guide jerked as though Eric had hit him. Tumi spun around and ran back to the truck, leaving them alone.

"His breathing is okay." Eric slipped his hands beneath the man's neck and ran his fingers along the bony spinal protrusions, checking for step-offs, misalignments that warned of broken vertebrae. "And I don't think his neck is broken."

"Thank god." He heard the rustle of paper as Alex riffled through the bag. "This kit doesn't have anything more than the basics. Eric, we have to get him back to the lodge."

Tumi rounded the truck fender with a rough wool blanket in his outstretched hand.

"Bring that blanket over here," Eric commanded. "We need to stabilize his neck."

Tumi's knee hit the ground beside him. Eric eased both hands under the man's head and lifted it mere inches from the ground. "Slide the blanket under his neck."

He bunched the blanket around the man's neck, stabilizing it. "I need a flashlight."

Tumi pulled a slim-barrelled flashlight from the breast pocket of his shirt and handed it over.

In the tight beam of the flashlight, Eric pushed open the man's eyelid and watched the pupil constrict. He repeated the process on the other eye, to the same response. *Good.*

He unzipped the man's vest and ripped open his cotton shirt. Purple bruises lined the middle of the man's muscular chest. Hands cupped against the man's rib cage, he checked the man's ribs.

"He's got two broken ribs, maybe three. His abdomen isn't swollen, but internal bleeding is likely."

A moan escaped the man's lips when Eric pressed his palms against the pelvic bones. Pain. Worse yet, a crunch, sand-like, beneath his hands. Even in the best ER, this man probably wouldn't survive, but Eric wasn't about to give up without a fight — if only for Alex's sake.

He could still hardly believe that she'd driven straight into the man. She'd saved their lives, but it came at a cost. She'd be haunted by this man's death for the rest of her life, unless Eric could pull off a miracle.

"He's got a fractured pelvis." Eric twisted back to Alex and Tumi. "I need something solid. And it has to be long. Like a backboard. Or stretcher."

"We carry no such equipment." Tumi shook his head. "We will have to go back to the lodge and get help."

"If I leave him here, he'll die." Eric ripped off his shirt and eased it under the man's thighs. "We'll try a sling."

A cuff in each hand, Eric pulled this makeshift sling up until it lay beneath the man's buttocks, centred over his pelvis. The man moaned when Eric tightened the sleeves into a knot, and then he fell back into unconsciousness.

Blood pressure's dropping. Internal bleeding. He could only hope that the sling would slow the bleeding and keep the man's heart pumping.

"He's out. We should be able to load him into the back of the truck … slide him onto the floor." He crouched near the man's head. "You'll have to support his thighs."

Eric waited, watching the tentative movements of his makeshift medical assistants. Tumi squatted and ran his hands beneath the man's slender legs, and Alex followed suit.

"We want to try to do this together. To keep the man as steady as possible … like he was on a board. On my count…"

He slipped his hands beneath the man's skull, cradling its weight in his palms. "One, two, lift."

A primal scream rang out. The man's eyes fluttered open, and he mumbled something incomprehensible.

Eric felt the man's body tilt toward Tumi. Alex tried to match the guide's actions, only to lower the man farther.

"Don't! We can't put him down." He saw the fear in their eyes. "He's going to feel some pain, but we have to get him to the truck. You're doing fine. We just have to go slow, and we have to keep him level."

Eric spotted a kick of dust against the blue sky and a moment later caught the distant whine of an engine.

"You said there's help coming, right?"

"Yes. Three drivers at least."

The hairs on the back of his neck prickled. Something didn't feel right. "You're sure."

"I talked to them myself." As though she read his fear, she added, "But let me get the rifle. Can we set him down?"

He nodded, unable to keep from staring in the direction of the engine noise that grew louder each second.

Alex had only just hiked her foot into the cargo area when an olive drab truck roared into view.

Only when Eric saw Derek's lodge logo on the side of the vehicle did he breathe. Only when he recognized Rashid did he move.

We're safe.

Five pairs of hands now eased the man into place.

"Let's get him into the truck, feet first." He forced himself to walk slowly, the man's head resting in his hands.

Every second delivered them closer to the rear of the truck, but the unmistakable odour of urine warned they were running out of time.

"Slide his legs in … slowly." He inched forward with them while his mind screamed out to hurry. "You'll have to climb into the truck now and lift him again."

Strong arms complied, and Eric felt himself tight against the fender as the men guided the body into the truck.

"Let's get something under his head." Eric flexed his stiff fingers.

"A jacket, a blanket…anything. And we need to find something warm to cover him with."

His request triggered a chatter of Swahili and a rush of activity. Eric pressed his fingers against the man's neck. *Weak.* He was losing this battle.

A jacket was handed to him, and Eric lifted the man's head just enough to slip the soft fleece beneath his skull. He turned to take a woollen blanket from the shaky hands of a second guide, his eyes wide at the sight of the unconscious man. He could offer the scared young man no reassurance other than a tight smile.

He'd barely climbed into the back of the truck before doors slammed, and the engine roared to life under Tumi's expert hand.

Alex sat in the passenger seat, the rifle once again in her hands. She twisted back to lock eyes with him. "Ready?"

Eric wasted no time. He draped a blanket over his patient and dropped to the floor, cross-legged. "Go."

The truck jerked into gear, and his shoulder slammed against the wheel well. Tumi was quick to get the truck into the narrow, rutted road, driving fast — too fast — but speed was this man's only hope.

Eric reached his arms across the man's chest, steadying him against the jarring bounce of the truck. And then, lips close to the man's ear, he whispered a mantra repeated too many times in the ER.

"Stay with me. Just stay with me."

63

Novoteras Mine

JORGE SILVA WATCHED a routine that broke every safety rule, every basic human right. Most of the men working Tunnel Five had not seen daylight in two days. None of them were used to such long hours of pounding hammers into rock walls in the hot, oxygen-poor shafts so deep in the mine. Already, three men had collapsed from dehydration.

But Jorge could do nothing.

Tim Wong had all but taken over the mine operation, and Shen Li's terse email on the subject made it clear that Jorge was to follow the engineer's orders.

The one thing it gave him was time.

Jorge clicked open the security footage folder and found the file from three days ago. He had every right to view this video file, yet his heart pounded when he hit play.

He fast-forwarded through the footage, searching for the precise moment that he had entered the mine shaft and then slowed the replay until he saw his return to the locker room. He froze the scene and zoomed in to search the grainy image for any sign of a slight bulge in his pocket — evidence of the rock he had pocketed so impulsively.

Jorge could delete the footage, eliminate the record of his descent into the mine that day. But the men in the mine had seen him there and had seen him take a piece of rock.

The miners were a closed-mouthed group, intent on protecting one of their own. *Will they do the same for me?* Unlikely. Unless he found the miner who had helped the thieves and used that for leverage.

Blackmail.

The word hit him like he had been kicked in the stomach. He had sworn to uphold the law, dedicated his life to root out criminals. How had he found himself here?

Maybe Zahra was right. They should run. Leave this place far behind them.

He jerked his head up at the rap on the door frame to find Carlos staring at him. How long had his head of security stood there watching him?

"Mark Brody has returned. He would like to talk to you."

He could barely breathe. *Not now,* he wanted to scream. Like every guilty man, he feared that his face would reveal the truth to Brody. But to turn the American down would bring suspicion.

His jerky nod sent Carlos trotting off down the hallway. He stared at the empty door frame, listening for the sound of footsteps, waiting for the American to appear.

When Brody finally did walk in, he reached out a hand, forcing Jorge to his feet. The agent gripped Jorge's slender hand, his blue eyes trained on Jorge's face. And the man remained standing long after he had dropped his hand, his six-foot-two bulk towering over Jorge.

Jorge refused to give in to this attempt at intimidation. He slipped into his chair and pulled himself tight to his desk. He shifted a file folder from the middle of his desk to the crowded stack, all but ignoring the visitor standing in front of him. Only when Brody finally eased himself into the chair did Jorge look up.

"Thanks for seeing me again." Brody smiled just enough to be polite. "I have a few more questions, and it seemed easiest to ask them in person."

"You have not yet said why you are investigating this mine."

"Your company's name came up in another investigation." Brody shrugged. "I'm sure you know how it is."

Jorge did. Too many times, he had been sent to track down people and companies because of a casual reference made during an interrogation. He knew, too, that Brody lied to him.

"There must be more for you to come here a second time." Jorge leaned forward on his elbows, his hands clasped. "As manager, I am responsible for protecting this mine and the company that owns it. I must understand why you are here if you wish further information from me."

Brody's smile vanished, and Jorge felt as though he was finally seeing the true man behind the sun-weathered face — a soldier determined to succeed, whatever the cost.

The two men locked eyes. Jorge could almost feel the heat of the American's intense gaze against his face. He forced himself to remain impassive, unreadable, like he had done so many times as a cop facing a suspect in the interrogation room.

Brody finally broke the deadlocked silence. "You had a break-in here a few nights ago. A man was killed." He crossed his leg over his thigh and clutched his ankle. "That's all I need to ask questions."

The man's body language alone spoke of his arrogance. "Under what authority?" Jorge challenged.

"The local police chief." Brody flashed an insincere smile. "You're welcome to call him."

Jorge called the man's bluff and picked up the phone. He watched for signs of nervousness while he asked Carlos to call the local precinct but saw none. Either the man had told the truth or he did not care whether his story checked out.

"Why would a break-in at a small mine like ours be of concern to you?" Jorge asked.

Brody ran his palm over a clean-shaven cheek. "I know you're searching for two foreigners, Alex Graham and Mosi Ongeti. That makes it my concern."

His mouth went dry. This American knew the names of their thieves, something unknown even to the local police. He picked up his pen, rolling it between slender fingers, his eyes on Brody. He had assumed Ongeti and Graham had worked alone, but for all he knew, this man had sent the pair into the mine. *But why?*

Carlos appeared in the doorway and gave Jorge a quick nod.

So Brody had the backing of the police chief. How and why the two of them were connected, though, had yet to be answered. The only thing he knew for certain was that this conversation with Brody required careful handling.

"What is it that you want to know?" Jorge asked after Carlos had eased the door shut.

"I'm trying to understand why these two people would risk breaking into your mine for tourmaline … frankly, it's just not worth that much."

"I am struggling to understand this as well." He touched his fingertips to the desk. "Their actions make no sense."

Brody leaned back like a man who had just finished a good meal. "Unless you're not mining tourmaline."

He knows! This was his moment to tell the truth. But his stomach churned with biting fear, warning him off. Jorge knew nothing of this brash American, only his name.

"Who do you work for, exactly?" His words were more of a whisper than he intended.

The question went unanswered. Instead, the American turned to the window, squinting in the late afternoon sun.

"You can put these rumours to rest," Brody said before he turned. "I can have a geologist here by tomorrow, and once he's been down in the mine we'll know the truth."

Jorge straightened in his chair. He was not about to play this game, not under Brody's rulebook. If this American wanted to go underground, he would have to go through Shen Li.

"I am afraid, Mr. Brody, that there is nothing more I can offer. Tabitha Metals is a highly regarded company, and if you need further information or wish a tour, you should contact the head office. As for the break-in, I will continue my investigation, and if the motives of Alex Graham and Mosi Ongeti become clear, I will share them with you." His chair scraped against the floor. "Now, if you will excuse me, I have work to do." He stared down at the American, who had yet to move.

Brody shook his head before he stood. He reached into his pocket and pulled out a business card that he dropped onto the desk. "In case you lost the first one."

Jorge made no move for the card. Instead, he clasped his hands behind his back.

"Call the number when you're ready for some help, Mr. Silva." Brody zipped up his leather jacket. "This is bigger than you could imagine."

Only when the American's broad back had slipped through the doorway did Jorge reach for the business card. He fingered the crisp white card with just a name and phone number in raised black letters.

The man must work for the CIA or some other agency practised at walking the line between official and unofficial investigations.

And the Novoteras mine stood in his crosshairs.

I must learn the truth.

64

Grumeti River, Tanzania

ALEX HUGGED HER ARMS to her chest, shivering despite the stifling heat. Beyond the wooden walls muffled laughter mixed with the clank of cutlery against stainless steel bowls. The lodge staff who enjoyed their midday meal next door did not know of the dead man lying here.

Within minutes of their frantic race back to the lodge, Eric had sworn in anger and pounded his fist against the man's chest. Alex had scrambled into the back to kneel beside him, threading her own hands beneath his, to take over CPR when he tired. Together they'd fought to keep this man alive, mile after mile.

She had felt his heart beat beneath her hands and heard a moan escape his lips. She'd been sure that Eric could save this man, if only they could get back to the lodge. But long before they carried the man's limp body into the drivers' quarters behind the main lodge, she knew it was over.

Eric covered the dead man with a blanket pulled from a bunk. "Even if we'd been in an ER, he probably wouldn't have lived. His pelvis was fractured, and he was bleeding internally—"

"Shit! We're never going to know why he came after us. But I had no choice… he would have killed us. I had to do something."

Hot tears traced a path down her cheek, but she made no attempt to wipe them away. She'd slammed almost two tons of metal into the slim-built man. *He never stood a chance.*

Eric reached out to her. "Alex—"

She practically jumped at the creak of a rusty hinge. Derek flung the door open wide, sending a rush of wind into the dimly lit room. Wordless, he stood with his back pressed against the wooden door to allow a man to enter.

"This is a private security consultant who works for me," Derek said of the stranger, who stood a foot taller than him. "I felt it best not to involve the police."

Police. The last thing any of them needed.

With barely a glance at her and Eric, the newcomer crossed the floor, his boots, red from dust, the only sound. He crouched next to the bed, leaving them to stare at his back while he lifted the blanket from the face of the dead man.

Private security in a country like Tanzania could mean just about anything, from mercenaries to hired guards watching over embassy staff or corporate executives. Her dad hired such private security when their projects took geologists into territory best explored under guard. Often ex-military, these men and women were notoriously tight-lipped — and expensive.

With the security consultant's hand still clutching the blanket, he twisted back to address Derek when he finally spoke. She recognized the first words of Swahili as they rolled off his tongue. His Swahili was good, but he wasn't a native speaker. There was a tinge of accent that didn't sound quite right. *American? Or maybe European?*

He turned to face her, switching to almost flawless English. "This man is part of an al Qaeda cell. He's on the watch list."

"Al Qaeda?" Alex shifted her weight from one foot to the other, her eyes on the blanket-covered corpse. "Are you sure?"

The consultant ignored her question, instead asking his own. "You saw just this one man? No others?"

"I never saw anyone but him." Alex turned to Eric. "Did you?"

"No." Eric shook his head. "He came of out nowhere. I wouldn't have seen him at all if I hadn't been standing on the seat."

"How far away was he?"

"Maybe twenty feet … he just kept coming." Eric stared down at the dead man. "He fired two or three shots before we could even react."

Alex hugged her arms to her chest. The shooter had come up on them fast. If she'd seen him sooner, she could have done something.

"Did he have his weapon raised? Like this?" The consultant pointed an imaginary rifle at them.

"Yes," Eric said. "I wouldn't have seen it at all if the sun hadn't hit the metal."

The security consultant turned to Derek, switching back to Swahili, spoken barely above a whisper.

Alex bristled at being shut out. "I want to know what's going on!"

"I'm convinced this was a kidnapping attempt," Derek said.

"You're wrong! He tried to shoot—"

Derek held up his hand. "From that distance, that man could easily have fired a shot through the windshield. He had his rifle aimed at you, but he shot out your front tires. He was trying to keep you from escaping, and I guarantee he wasn't alone."

"How could they even have known where I'd be?" Her hands swept wide. "Hell, *we* didn't know where we'd be."

"He tracked you through the radio chatter between the guides." Derek's eyes met hers. "He knew you were here at the lodge."

She spun toward Eric. One look at his stony face confirmed that he believed Derek's words.

"Nate said there was a Chinese connection, and Hanna doesn't believe al Qaeda is behind that mine." She turned to the body on the bed. "Maybe he was just trying to rob us. We were easy pickings … two tourists alone in the Serengeti. They know people like us carry cash, and lots of it."

Cash, especially U.S. dollars, dominated the Tanzanian tourist industry. Many hoteliers didn't take anything but, and waiters and shopkeepers alike expected the green bills from foreigners.

"This attack coming so soon after the mining camp riot is too much of a coincidence, Alex," Derek said. "And none of us know enough about Tabitha Metals to understand where the threat might come from."

She started to protest, but Eric cut her short. "It doesn't matter who it is, Alex. Someone *knows* you have that damn rock." His voice betrayed his anger. "They want it back ... they want *you*."

She saw the tightness in Eric's jaw, the deep lines etched into his forehead. There was no mistaking his worry for her. But his life was at risk now too. She'd put him in the middle of something far more dangerous than she could have imagined.

He never should have come.

"They're going to try again." Derek's voice softened. "You're not safe here any longer, Alex. Neither of you is."

Derek didn't need to add that an armed attack would put every person at this lodge at risk.

"So where do we go? If they've found me here, they can find me anywhere." She shivered at the thought of being hunted. "I have to expose that mine. It's the only way to stop them."

"You're right," Derek said. "But it's safer for you to do that from Canada. Go home, Alex. Let Hanna do her job. She'll get that piece of rock into the right hands, and then all of this will be over."

Will it? She dropped her eyes to the dusty plank floor. She'd been naive to think that they could slip into that mine without consequence.

"And Mosi?" Alex asked. "If you're right about this guy, then Mosi's in danger too."

"I've heard from him." Derek reached out to touch Alex's arm. "Mosi is on his way here. I tried to call you on the radio, to tell you to come back, but you didn't answer. That's why the guides were looking for you."

"We're lucky Tumi showed up when he did."

"Tumi? I sent Rashid to find you." Derek turned to the security consultant. "Tumi was searching another quadrant ... he shouldn't have been anywhere near her. Find him."

65

São Paulo, Brazil

SHEN STUDIED the five passport photos crowded on his computer screen. Five doctors who had boarded the same South African Airways flight as his thieves, men found by Jorge Silva. Each of them had been carefully investigated in the past twenty-four hours. None of them were the doctor he sought.

The nurse had discovered little about Dr. Trevor Reid, except that the forty-three-year-old Harvard-educated specialist had worked with Doctors Without Borders for four years before arriving at the private hospital in Dar es Salaam. The American consulted with many foreign doctors, and the nurse could provide only a handful of names, none of which matched the South African Airways flight manifest.

He waited now for word that Ongeti's wife and his children had been taken. Ongeti's wife would know the name of the doctor, something she would not withhold to protect her children from Keambiroro's vicious threats. And it might bring Ongeti to him.

But when?

Less than twenty-four hours remained before his deadline. Even if he could deliver the tanzanite on time, he could do little to reassure the Chairman that the Novoteras mine had not been compromised — not with an American asking questions of Jorge Silva.

Alonso Quinto must be pushed to learn more.

"What have you learned about an investigation into Tabitha Metals?" he asked when Quinto answered the phone.

"I can find nothing," Alonso said. "The police, the mining officials … Tabitha Metals is not a name mentioned by either. If an investigation is underway, it did not originate here in Brazil."

"What about Graham and Associates? What have you learned about them?"

"It is a private company, and there is almost nothing to find. Their clients, their employees … none of this information is out in the open. I will have to send a detective to Vancouver to learn more. Even then, I cannot promise more information. But it may not be necessary."

There was something about Quinto's smug tone that made Shen cringe.

"I have learned from Colombian police that Brian Graham has been reported missing."

"He is *here*? He is still in South America?"

"Yes. They believe Graham drove off the road somewhere between Bogotá and Quito. I will be told the minute he is found."

"Can you add men to the search?"

"It is already done … but I cannot express too much interest without revealing a problem. We must be cautious." Those were Quinto's last words before he hung up.

Shen barely dared to hope that Brian Graham might soon be in his grasp. But with the Chairman's deadline looming, the geologist's capture might come too late.

He snatched up the phone, demanding Meilin send the production manager to him immediately. Hurried footsteps in the carpeted hallway heralded the man's race to comply.

The fifty-three-year-old who arrived planted himself in the doorway, afraid to enter, even though summoned. Only when Shen nodded did the skinny man sweep into the room, closing the door behind him.

Hands clasped tight against his chest as though praying, the engineer stood near the desk, awaiting instructions.

"How much can we push production at our mines?"

"Ten percent is easily achievable." He pressed a finger against the bridge of his glasses. "Except at two of the emerald mines where we have faced equipment failures."

"You allow the mines to sit idle due to *failure*?" Shen let the word hang in the air.

"No, Manager Li." The man clutched his hands together and bowed his head. "The mines operate at capacity. It is only increased production at those mines that I cannot promise until our replacement equipment arrives next week."

Swaying, the engineer stood silent, waiting for Shen's next words. Expecting the worst.

Shen's lips curled into a tight smile. For this man to cower so in his presence confirmed that word of Shen's disgrace had not yet spread beyond the executive suite.

Mianzi. Face. Once lost, it could not easily be recovered. His employees would distance themselves from him, and his carefully tended network would wither. Even those who owed him — Park among them — would simply shrug and walk away.

"I need more. What about the Valternas mine? It is underproducing … how much more gold can you pull from it?"

"Fifteen percent is possible. Twenty percent perhaps … but such a move carries more risk."

Mine operations high in the Andes were under constant scrutiny, and their Valternas mine was not exempt. Environmentalists and government watchdogs were determined to prevent mercury, cyanide and sulphuric acid, all used to extract gold, copper and silver, from contaminating the Huasco River Valley. Increased production at this Argentina mine would not go unnoticed for long.

"Do it. And do the same for *every* mine. Buy new equipment, hire more men … whatever is necessary. Do you understand?"

"Yes, Manager Li." Eyes bulging, the engineer bobbed his head as though overtaken by spasm.

"Prepare a report. I want to see your projected production at every mine by the end of the day. Do not disappoint me." Shen swatted the man away.

The man had barely scurried from the room before Meilin appeared in the open doorway.

"Is there anything else you need, Manager Li?"

He toyed with the idea that she had listened at the closed door. But if she had heard anything, she would be quick to assume it linked to Alonso Quinto's investigation into the Novoteras breach.

"More coffee, and—"

The ring of his cell phone cut short his request.

"Shut the door," he commanded when he saw the caller ID.

Only when Meilin complied did he answer.

"I have found the woman," Park Fàn simply said.

Shen dug the finger deep into his temple. Here was the solution he sought, but it came at a high cost.

I expected more time.

"Where?" With a single word, he committed himself to Park.

"She stays at a lodge in a private reserve near the Grumeti River with a doctor."

He held his breath. Fate had turned his way.

"But there are others watching her," Park continued.

Keambiroro? The African had said that he knew nothing of Graham's whereabouts, that his men remained stationed at the mining camp and Ongeti's home.

"Who?" he asked.

"It is difficult to know for certain."

Shen pressed his lips into a tight line. He'd known Park too long to believe the vague answer.

"But you must have some idea?" he pressed.

"Is it possible that others know of this woman, and they would…" Park chose his next words with care. "Exploit her condition?"

Whether Park knew that Chairman Wei had bought his son out of trouble once before was unclear. The woman, a model for a New York agency, had been quietly paid off and now lived in Europe under careful surveillance, a situation Shen believed was known only to those closest to the Chairman. What was certain was that Park had just raised the stakes.

"I know of no such situation. But Jianyu Wei would be grateful to learn the identity of these men," he added.

"It will take time."

Shen's hand tightened around the pen. He'd been certain that Park already knew the identities of the men who watched Graham and their motive. He could not wait.

"Can you get to her?"

"Yes. If that is what you want, then I will deliver her to you."

Father and daughter.

I will have both of them soon.

66

Grumeti River, Tanzania

ALEX CHECKED HER WATCH — again. For more than two hours, she, Eric and Hanna had been holed up in the back corner of the lounge, waiting for Mosi. She tried to focus on the splash of hippos and the mercifully cool breeze that brushed her skin, but the face of the dead man intruded.

And Tumi.

She'd felt safe here, protected. The gun pointed at her and Eric proved otherwise. She didn't want to believe that Tumi had tried to kidnap her, but Derek's arguments were persuasive. Only when they found the guide would they know the truth.

And then she finally spotted him. *Mosi!*

She scrambled to her feet and raced toward him.

In his tight embrace, she whispered, "I've been so worried. I thought you might be…" *Dead.* Even now, she couldn't say the word aloud.

"*Nafisa.*" Mosi smoothed her hair. "I could not come before now. I had to take my family to Kenya, where they are safe."

"Safe?" She pulled away from him. "What happened?"

Derek interrupted. "The road is empty — you were not followed. Men I trust are stationed at all entry points. Every one of them is armed, and they will radio in if they see anyone. I will be monitoring the radios … no one will get close to this lodge without my knowledge."

She'd never seen Derek like this, his face drawn tight with fear, his eyes like dark pools. And his words to Mosi — it was like the two men prepared for war.

"What's going on? One of you tell me."

"Come." Mosi pressed his hand against her back. "Eric must hear this too."

"There is more I must do." Derek turned away from them, even as he spoke.

Mosi's strong hand guided her across the floor toward the others at a pace that left no question of the urgency. But in his hurried steps she felt his weakness too, the injury that hampered his every move.

Eric rose as they neared, but his smile quickly disappeared at the sight of her fear. Hanna too saw the warning of bad news in their faces, for she sat deathly still, her fists tightly balled.

"Your leg is worse." Eric reached his hand out. "I'm going to need to repack the wound … give you some IV antibiotics—"

Mosi shook his head. "First we must talk."

Alex saw Mosi glance at Hanna. "This is Hanna, a friend of Derek's. I've told her everything, Mosi … she's trying to help us."

"Good. Thank you," Mosi said to Hanna as he eased into a chair, his leg held stiff. "I do not know how, but men search for us here in Tanzania."

"How do—"

Mosi held up his hand. "Two days ago a man on a motorbike followed me and Zawadi when I left my home. This man did not know the roads well, so it was not difficult to escape him." His eyes met hers. "When I tried to return later, there was another stranger paying too much attention to my home."

"How?" She clutched Eric's hand. "Even if they know your name, they couldn't know where you live."

Hanna leaned forward. "If you were seen at the Mwanza airport, then they followed both of you. It explains how they knew you were at the mining camp, Alex."

"They knew?" Mosi's eyes went wide. "I did not come to the camp, because I was afraid they would follow me. Instead, I asked

Derek to call you here. When I heard about the mining camp riot, I went to find you ... I could not get close enough. But one of the workers who ran from the mine said that you left before it started."

"Why didn't you at least text me? You must have known how worried I was ... how worried Kanoni was. You and Zawadi disappeared without a word to anyone!"

"We threw away our phones. We could not risk leading anyone to our families ... or to you if we were caught." He shook his head. "Only when darkness came was it safe for me to go to my brothers. They watched over Kanoni and my children until we could take them to safety."

Suddenly she understood why she'd not heard anything more from Kanoni.

"Alex, men waited at the school my children attend and the place where my wife works. They hunted us all." He looked out at the river. "My family is safe now in the Kenya, in the village where Kanoni's parents live ... no one can reach them there."

A shiver rippled down her spine. They had gone after Mosi's family, his sweet children, his wife.

"You don't think they followed you?" Hanna asked.

"No. My brothers and I made sure of it."

Alex didn't ask what they'd done, because she could see it in his eyes. The hunters had become prey to a man determined to protect his family. Their bodies would never be found.

She turned to Hanna. "It would take someone with a lot of power — and money — to track us halfway around the world. You said that groups like al Qaeda and ISIL don't have much money, but that dead man is al Qaeda."

"What dead man?" Mosi asked.

"We were attacked this morning when we were out searching for you. I ran into the man who shot at us."

"How could they know you were here?"

"One of the guides here at the lodge has vanished, and we believe he told someone that Alex was here. We just don't understand why."

Hanna folded her hands in her lap. "Until we know exactly who is behind that Brazilian mine, we won't understand what's going on. Even then—"

"Only my dad can fill in the blanks," Alex finished.

"You have not yet heard from Brian?" Mosi asked.

Alex shook her head. "Nothing. Police are searching the roads, but there's too much ground to cover. And honestly, I don't think it's a priority for them. They probably figure this is just another kidnapping."

"Is that a possibility, Alex?" Hanna asked.

"Always ... especially if someone finds out my dad is a geologist. These kidnappers know that petroleum and mining companies have deep pockets — and insurance. Even we carry kidnapping insurance." She shook her head. "In fact, I'd expect my dad to tell them he's a geologist if he's captured. It would keep him alive."

Her dad's words of advice flashed through her mind: *Any advantage, Alex. Take any advantage that buys you time.*

"But by now I'd expect a ransom demand." Alex faced Mosi. "Dad's even more paranoid than you are. He won't risk linking us to him through a number on his cell phone."

"His computer ... Alex, it was stored at my house. Kanoni said that my bag was missing, so men came into my home. They have my computer, and they probably have Brian's computer too."

His words hit like a punch. Nothing about the Novoteras mine had been committed to paper or email. *Nothing.* But the computer held every last one of both men's personal contacts.

"Where—"

Derek burst into the lounge, stopping Alex cold. "You're leaving. *Now!*"

67

São Paulo, Brazil

THROUGH THE PENTHOUSE windows, Shen watched the orange flare of sunset descend, etching black towers against an indigo sky. The darkness spread, blurring the rigid edges, extinguishing the light, until the sun disappeared beneath the horizon.

He turned from the window at the first chirp of his phone.

"This woman you seek … she is well-protected." The smallest sigh escaped Park Fàn's lips. "And you have lied to me about the true reason you search for her."

Shen's chest tightened at such a direct accusation.

"It did not take me long to discover that al Qaeda watches this woman, and so does a man named Keambiroro, who is paid by you."

Al Qaeda? A dangerous player had just stepped out of the shadows, one that Keambiroro had failed to mention.

"This morning, al Qaeda attacked Alex Graham," Park continued. "Whether they sought to kill her or kidnap her, I do not know. What I do know is that they would not take such risk unless there was great reward. It makes me believe that I should question this woman myself."

"So you have her?"

"No. She was warned of our approach and escaped. We will find her."

"When you do, go ahead and question her." Shen's hand tightened on the phone. "But be warned that I will tell Jianyu Wei of your involvement. How I came to you but you lost this woman. How you interrogated her and tried to use what you learned for your own advantage."

"You threaten me? You forget that you handed your loyalty to me when you gave me those bid details. You will not survive if the Chairman learns of your betrayal."

"Then we are at an impasse."

Two powerful men, each held back by secrets that could destroy them.

"I know nothing about al Qaeda or why they might be interested in Alex Graham," Shen said. "Only the man, Keambiroro works for me … you could not be arrogant enough to believe that you were the only one I trusted with this task."

Silence greeted his words. Shen knew that Park weighed his explanation, deciding whether to believe it, and whether to risk further help.

"I need that woman found," Shen pushed.

"She is gone … outside the country, by now. I cannot help you."

The phone line went dead. The next call from Park would involve a demand for insider information, secrets Shen had promised to deliver for a lifetime.

I'm on my own.

Shen glanced at the time on the glassy surface of his phone. Each minute that passed brought him closer to the deadline and left him with fewer options.

There is only one answer.

He punched in Tim Wong's number and blurted out a single question without preamble.

A sharp intake of breath, and then silence. Long seconds passed before Wong finally spoke.

"Can you repeat? Our connection … it is very poor."

Shen ignored the gift Wong offered — an opportunity to change his words without losing face. "You heard me the first time, Engineer Wong," he challenged. "Now, can it be done?"

"To seal off Tunnel Five using explosives, yes it is possible Mr. Li. But no matter how carefully I proceed, the upper levels of the mine will likely be affected by an explosion. I cannot guarantee that the entire mine might not collapse."

Miles of underground tunnels lined with rock might crack and shatter under the force of an explosion. It would be years before they could regain access to the tanzanite seams if that happened. As with a single card at the baccarat table, everything could be lost in this one move.

"And the air shaft? Can we block access to it from Tunnel Five?"

He could almost hear Wong's thoughts, the calculated questions that ran through the sharp mind of this Chongqing-born engineer. Whether Wong dared voice those questions remained to be seen.

"I will set explosives at both the entrance of Tunnel Five and near the only air shaft that drops that deep," Wong finally said. "There will be no way in or out."

Shen's lips curled into a smile. *Good.* "How long before you can be ready?"

"Four, maybe five hours to set the explosives and the remote detonator. For safety, we should schedule the blast for two hours after that, to be sure all miners are out of the mine." Wong methodically outlined a plan. "There could be thirty, maybe forty men working in the mine right now. I will have to check with—"

"We will not be evacuating the mine."

The exact nature of his request had become clear. Now came the test of Wong's loyalty. He didn't wait long for an answer.

"It adds to the difficulty. The men ... they will see the dynamite."

"Then you must be ready with an explanation, Engineer Wong." He punched the "end call" button.

Forty men. Fewer than half of them worked the upper levels, tunnels that might escape cave-in. The miners in Tunnel Five, though, the men who had been pushed to work double-shifts to meet the tanzanite production quota — a quota reached just two hours ago — would slowly suffocate.

Tunnel Five could be dug out again and mining operations restarted when the questions stopped and eyes turned elsewhere. The tanzanite and the untraceable wealth it provided would be salvaged. Chairman Wei would feel the sting of loss from the sudden stoppage in the mine, but Shen would find a way to make up for the lost cash.

Jorge Silva.

The former cop had a pivotal role to play in controlling the investigation.

Silva would eventually prove an intentionally set explosion. Blame would then be cast on their recent intruders — Alex Graham and Mosi Ongeti. If a connection between them and al Qaeda became clear during the investigation, even better.

They would deny such an accusation, but Graham and Ongeti could not claim the tanzanite in their possession came from the Novoteras mine without admitting they had been in Tunnel Five.

Cornered.

68

Tanzania

ALEX KNEW ONLY that they were west of the Grumeti River, nothing more. Under a sliver of moonlight, they'd avoided the roads and instead crossed the Serengeti grasslands, listening to the radio chatter, waiting for news. Derek had rushed them from the lodge after perimeter guards had spotted suspicious vehicles approaching from the southeast, but they'd heard nothing more. And with each mile the radio signal faded, until it finally went silent two hours ago.

The slight woman who opened the door when Hanna knocked only nodded before she stepped aside to let them pass.

They came through the four-room house to the back, where mismatched chairs were crowded around a table. The woman, her hair tucked into a tight bun, poured water into glasses, the beads of her brightly coloured bracelet jangling with her every move. Then, without a word, she disappeared out the back door into the darkness.

Hanna held out a hand to steady Mosi as he clumsily lowered himself into a chair, his injured leg held straight.

"Let me give you something more for the pain. And if there's time—" Eric glanced at Hanna, waiting for her nod. "I want to take a look at that wound. If the abscess has reformed, then you're going to be in pain until I drain it again."

"No." Mosi waved his hand. "I will be fine."

"Take the care while you can." Hanna crossed her arms. "We need you ready to move. Quickly."

Alex held her breath, sure that Mosi would continue to argue. Instead, he pressed his hands against the table and eased himself to stand.

"The bedroom is through the second doorway," Hanna pointed the way. "We'll be here for at least an hour, so there's time for you to do whatever is needed, Eric."

She's been here before.

Eric grabbed his bag. "If we can manage some boiled water and clean towels, it would help."

Hanna pushed the back door open and asked a quiet question. Her Swahili was good, but Alex expected no less.

"There are clean towels in a small dresser in the bedroom. My friend will put a kettle of water over the fire outside ... shouldn't be too long."

Alex felt Eric's hand, warm against her shoulder, as he passed. She smiled as she watched him follow Mosi from the room.

Hers was a profession of risk-takers, but she'd never met a man quite like Eric. He'd give his life to save her, or Mosi — she knew that as certainly as she breathed. But it was something more. She was convinced that he wouldn't hesitate to run into a bloody battlefield if he thought he could save just one man. She'd seen it in his reluctance to leave their attacker in the Serengeti grasslands.

"Is there any way to reach Derek?" Alex folded her hands on the table, her eyes on Hanna.

Hanna shook her head. "Not from here. We'll have to wait until we get to the airstrip." She clutched her hands together. "Derek knows to send a plane there, and he will get a message to us through the pilot, if nothing else."

"How long?"

"Two hours, maybe more. The pilot will fly you to Uganda. They won't be looking for you there, and from Uganda people I trust will get you on a flight to Canada." She smiled. "You and Eric should be home in two, maybe three days."

Home. Vancouver seemed a lifetime away.

"And Mosi?" She dug her thumb into the palm of her hand. "What about him? He's in as much danger as I am … maybe more."

"He'll be safe in Kenya with his wife's family. We'll keep an eye on him, but in a small village strangers are easy to spot. Mosi's family and friends will help protect him."

"At least he'll be with family. And once we've analyzed the rock—"

"The rock is gone, Alex." Hanna sighed. "Staff at the hotel in Dubai say that a woman closed out the hotel safe. She produced a legal document purportedly signed by you, authorizing her actions."

"Impossible!" Alex stared at Hanna, waiting for her to say more, something that would convince her. But Hanna sat silent.

"How long have you known?" Alex asked in a voice too loud. "Why didn't you tell me back at the lodge?"

"To be honest?" Hanna spread her fingers against the tabletop. "I thought that Mosi might be involved … his disappearance was just a little too convenient. Twice while he was gone, men came for you."

"*What the hell?*" Alex's face flushed with anger. "I don't know how for one minute—"

Hanna held up a hand. "I had to consider everything, especially after this morning's attack." Her voice softened. "Many good men have turned to the fanatical teachings of al Qaeda or ISIL — Mosi could have been one of them. It was only when he was there at the lodge tonight and another attempt was made that I knew I was wrong about him."

"So wrong." Alex shook her head. "If you had just come to me…" Beneath the table, she clenched her hands. "Mosi didn't even know which hotel I left the rock at. No one—"

In that instant Alex knew.

"Marouk Faasad." She sighed. "I took the tanzanite to him in Dubai. He either had me followed or he guessed at the hotel — he's met with both me and my dad there before. I should have kept the tanzanite with me. I should have known better than to have left it at that hotel."

More than once, she'd been with her dad in that hotel, listening to Faasad negotiate a price for whatever packet of gemstones on offer. Brian had always gone to Faasad first, and never had she heard him say that the gem dealer couldn't be trusted.

"For Faasad to risk his reputation to steal a single piece of tanzanite doesn't make sense." Alex shook her head. "He works with millions of dollars of diamonds, emeralds and gold every day. A rumour — even a hint of dishonesty on his part — and his business would grind to a halt."

"If I had to guess, he didn't want you to show it to anyone else. He didn't want the competition. That Brazilian mine is like a buried bank vault ... men would do anything for that much wealth."

"But Faasad? He's known us for years. I would never — shit!" Her hand clenched into a fist. "I told him that I was on my way here to see my dad. He knows exactly where the gold mining camp is — he knew where to find me."

"It explains a few things." Hanna reached into her bag for a notepad and pen. "I'll get Faasad's name into the right hands. In the meantime, I have a plan to steer interest away from you and Mosi." She tapped her pen against the page. "I'm just not sure how you'll feel about it."

"Tell me…" Alex leaned forward. "At this point, I'd do anything."

"I want to seed a story in the press, one that says that you reported a new tanzanite mine, but that it has been proved false. We'll state that you were on someone else's claim, and you've been charged with trespassing."

"Hanna, what you're asking…" Alex blew out a breath. "It could cost me my reputation."

"A small price to pay for your life."

"But is it even going to work?"

"It takes away the prize, Alex. Marouk Faasad's followers will lose interest when they learn that they can't steal a tanzanite mine from you. And it makes anything you say about the Novoteras mine suspect ... something the Tabitha Metals owners will understand. I believe it will take the pressure off both you and Mosi."

Hanna's plan offered the only exit in a fire that burned in every direction — a leap through the flames that could destroy Alex.

I have no choice.

"And the Novoteras mine? You've already said that Mosi won't be believed, and now no one will believe anything I have to say either."

"Mark Brody believes you, and he'll find a way into the mine with your geologist. Even if they can't take a piece of tanzanite, their testimony alone should be enough to start an investigation. I can't think of one agency that won't be eager to shut down a source of terrorist funds."

"And if they can't get into the mine?"

"They *must* find a way, Alex."

69

Novoteras Mine

PAULO OPENED HIS EYES to see darkness so thick, it threatened to suffocate him. He breathed in grit-filled air, heavy and foul. Each quick breath, hot against his lips, registered no sound. Neither did the scream for help that rattled his vocal chords.

He shook his head, trying to clear his ears, forced to stop by the shriek of pain that pierced his skull. Wetness, sticky and thick, met the hand he reached to the side of his head. Blood.

Rubble weighed heavy against his legs and jabbed into his back muscles. Whether he lay on the mine floor or was pinned against its wall, he didn't know. He remembered only a percussive blast that had hurled him into the unforgiving rock of Tunnel Five.

Hands stretched out in front of him, he felt for the boulders that pinned his legs. Grunting, he heaved a rock aside, then another, until the pressure eased. Muscles tense, he yanked his left leg free, but his right remained trapped.

He wiped the sweat from his brow before he felt for the edges of the boulder that held his right knee fast. His hands traced the jagged surface of the rock until he found a cleaved edge he could grip.

He buried his hands deep beneath the edge and pushed. Jaw clenched, he ignored the scream of his vibrating muscles. He pulled his leg and twisted his knee with each push, rewarded finally with freedom.

His hands ran the length of one leg, then the other, feeling the wetness there. His bones, though, seemed intact. He pulled his feet toward him, his boots scraping against rock and gravel. Only when his knees were tight to his chest did he breathe.

I can walk. I can escape.

He swept the tunnel floor with his hand, searching for his helmet, his only light. He stretched his fingertips until his shoulders ached, tracing the sharp-edged rock that surrounded him. Nothing.

He slumped forward, head pressed against his folded arms. Without light, he could do nothing but wait for others to find him.

His mind flashed to the men who had been standing closest to him. Many of them, men who had been assigned to Tunnel Five only in the last few days, he barely knew. But among them was also the familiar face of his supervisor, Sabion Lacerda.

He must be near.

Paulo screamed out again, hearing the faintest muffle of his own voice. Relief flooded him — his hearing would soon return. But the endless minutes of silence that followed drowned out hope.

Sweat trickled down his back. He pressed his hand against the back of his neck and felt its heat and slick wetness.

It was getting warmer.

Generators supplied air to these lower levels — generators that may have been damaged. Even if the machinery were intact, the pipes that delivered sweet, cool air from the surface may have broken.

Men trapped in Tunnel Two had been dug out alive after three days. The narrow shaft sunk by dozens of hands operating equipment around the clock had reached them first. While bulldozers and drills cut through rock that trapped the men, the shaft delivered vital oxygen, food and water. And now, that same air shaft, the one he had descended with Mosi Ongeti and Benjamin Costa a week ago, might save him.

I am alive. There is still hope.

A hand gripped his arm. His eyes wide, he jerked his head up to the dust-streaked face that peered at him.

Light! This miner has light. Almost giddy, Paulo grabbed the man's arms.

"Are you injured?" came a muffled question from Sabion Lacerda. Paulo shook his head. "I can walk."

With Sabion's help, Paulo stood for the first time since the ordeal began. He shifted his weight from one leg to the other before he stepped tentatively over the rocky ground, guided by the dim beam of light.

"What happened? Do you know?"

"The ceiling collapsed…" Sabion pointed to his left. "Just six feet from here, the gallery is blocked by rock. We cannot get out."

Paulo's chest tightened at the jagged outline of boulders. A few more feet and he would have been buried beneath that rock wall. Dead.

"The other men?"

"Seven of the men are here, some are badly injured." Sabion dropped his gaze. "Three men are dead. The rest…"

Crushed beneath tons of rock. An entire shift of miners had been ordered into Tunnel Five to try to meet their quota deadline. Thirty men.

"There has to be another way out." Paulo turned his back on the rock wall that entombed them. "We can climb the air shaft."

Sabion shook his head. "We cannot reach it. We are surrounded by rock."

The supervisor gripped his elbow, guiding Paulo away from the rock wall. Ahead, pinpoints of light. As they grew closer, Paulo saw men seated on the rock floor who watched their approach.

He lowered himself onto a boulder next to a miner who held his arm tight across his chest. When the man turned to him, eyes wide, he recognized a boy hired just two months ago, one who never should have been assigned to this tunnel. Tim Wong had pulled workers from all parts of the mine to meet the quota deadline — a mistake.

"Is it broken?"

A tight nod. "My arm was trapped beneath a rock." The boy looked down at his hand, held claw-like. "I cannot feel my fingers."

Above them was a fully equipped medical clinic, but here they had nothing to help the boy. Paulo slumped back against the wall. They lacked even the most basic of supplies — food, water — except what the men carried. And soon they would run out of the oxygen.

How long?

It took but a glance at the men to know they all asked the same question.

"They will find us. They will come." Sabion looked from face to face. "Every man outside this mine is working to free us."

Paulo had been among those who had worked round-the-clock to save the men trapped below five years ago. Men had come from the surrounding mines, bringing equipment and strong backs, to dig the life-saving air shaft and haul tons of rock from the mine. Women had comforted the wives of men trapped below and cared for their children. Now his wife would be among the ones who waited for news.

One by one, the men doused their helmet lamps. Paulo pressed his back against the rock wall and forced breath into his lungs. Stale, dust-filled air.

"They will find us," Paulo whispered. He clutched his knees tight to his chest. "They will come."

He switched off his helmet light.

The black shroud of darkness descended.

70

São Paulo, Brazil

SHEN PACED THE living room, watching the live news feed coming from the Novoteras mine, unable to keep still. Cameras and microphones were thrust toward anxious wives, their children clutched tight. Helicopters hovered overhead and cameramen dangled from their open doors, anxious to capture the moment a survivor emerged from the mine.

Alonso Quinto would be at the mine soon. The lawyer had successfully deflected the press from looking too closely at Tabitha Metals after their last cave-in, and Shen expected him to do so again. But this time Quinto needed to also steer the press toward the break-in as the reason these miners suffocated below.

For now, Quinto would merely mention a suspected connection between the breach and this cave-in — a warning to Graham and Ongeti. Only if it became necessary would Quinto thrust the thieves into the spotlight.

Shen snatched up the phone on the first ring, his eyes still on the television screen.

"Mr. Li, we have lost access to all but the shallowest level of the mine — Tunnel One." Tim Wong spoke without emotion. "I believe all three of the deeper tunnels have collapsed."

Shen dug his fingers into his temple. The tanzanite now lay buried beneath a mountain of rock.

"Thirty-two men remain unaccounted for," Wong droned on.

"We are drilling ventilation shafts into the lower levels, into sections where we believe the men may have been working. Until we lower sound equipment into the shafts, we will not know if anyone survived. We can—"

Shen heard a shout, and then Wong's muffled voice. He drummed his fingers against the lamp table, waiting for the engineer to continue.

"Men have just arrived from another mine, and I have assigned them to help drill ventilation shafts." Wong paused. "Until I determine if it is safe to send heavy equipment into the mine to clear the rock fall, I will keep every worker at the surface."

In the face of growing attention, Wong had chosen wisely. The world would see an aggressive rescue effort, one stalled by unfortunate circumstances. More help would arrive from throughout Brazil and nearby countries, but Wong knew what had to be done to delay rescue until it was too late.

For at least a few hours, with attention urgently focused on the men buried beneath the rock, few questions about mine operations would be raised. But if just one of the families crowded by reporters spoke of the long hours the miners had worked, a fact proved by the late-night shift that had trapped so many men, things would change.

"Where is Jorge Silva?" Shen asked. "I have tried calling him several times."

Silva must be the one who stood alongside Alonso Quinto when the lawyer talked to reporters, not Wong. The ex-cop would become the face of this tragedy, and Tabitha Metals would hide deep in his shadow.

"I do not know." Wong sucked air through his teeth. "I have not personally seen him since this morning, Mr. Li."

Shen turned back to the grainy video coming from the mine. Camera lights punched through the darkness, revealing only what lay in their immediate circle. Every person, hunched and huddled at the mine entrance, stared straight ahead, as though expecting the miners to walk through the gaping maw.

Why isn't Silva there?

"Right now, Silva is not a priority."

The impudence! He clenched his fist. "Find Jorge Silva. *Now!* In the meantime, steer clear of reporters. Give them any excuse." The last thing he needed was a Chinese face flashed across every television screen. "And I want updates every half hour."

Shen punched in Silva's phone number, again without success. He hung up without leaving a message and tried the man's home number, only to give up after five unanswered rings.

Could Silva be in the mine?

There were few reasons that explained why Jorge himself would descend into the depths of the mine. New evidence, something that he didn't trust another to collect, or couldn't collect, might explain such a move. Otherwise, he would have sent an underling into the mine.

Shen lit a cigarette and breathed in its smoke to tame his fear. *Speculation. Conjecture.* Until the security tapes were reviewed, he must not assume the worst.

He practically jumped at the ring of the phone. One glance at the caller ID and he ground his cigarette into the half-full ashtray. Heart pounding, he forced air into his lungs with each ring, until he felt ready to confront the Chairman.

"This cave-in, it is most …" Wei's smooth voice dropped to a whisper. "Damaging."

The word, so carefully chosen, hit like a sledgehammer against his chest. It left Shen the narrowest sliver in which to negotiate.

"I believe the foreigners, Ongeti and Graham, again broke in, this time to destroy the mine. They will be made to pay for this crime. We are most fortunate that the shipment of gems destined for overseas had already left." He held his breath, waiting for understanding to take hold.

"Most fortunate, yes," the Chairman hissed. "However, we are now left with a worthless mine, at a most inopportune time."

"Money will continue to flow." Shen dug his thumb into his temple. "I have already ordered increased production at every mine. The Valternas gold mine alone will deliver the cash we need."

"It is but one necessary measure. We meet shortly to decide how best to solve your problem."

They meet without me.

"The problem *is* resolved. A report will be ready shortly, and I am sure you will be pleased with the income projected from our South American mines. Increased production will allow us to recover much of the losses suffered in the Novoteras mine shutdown."

He held his breath, waiting to see if it was enough. Shen had successfully funnelled billions of dollars into the Chairman's illegal activities — Wei must know that Shen could deliver now.

"Your assistant has already sent the report to the executive boardroom. We will review it there."

Meilin Yang. She had played the game well, had found a way to save herself from the disgrace that engulfed him like a raging fire.

"Goodbye, Shen."

He heard a tinge of regret in these two words that ended the call. It gave him hope that he might yet convince the Chairman to keep him at the executive table.

Shen heard the click of the front door. Soft steps across the marble foyer.

Her jasmine perfume reached him first. And then Meilin, dressed in a simple black dress, appeared in the doorway.

"You are bold to come here. I have spoken with Chairman Wei."

She stepped into the room. Only then did he see the gun in her hand.

"I, too, have spoken with Jianyu Wei."

In that instant he knew that the Chairman had turned his back on him. It was over.

He could overpower her, take the gun from her hand, but others would follow. He would be forced into hiding, and news of his failure would spread like wildfire. Uncle would bear his shame.

I cannot.

He turned away from her to stare out at the fiery sun that broke the horizon.

One last sunrise.
Before a bullet pierced his heart.

71

Kampala, Uganda

ALEX TOOK THE COFFEE cup Eric offered, her fourth since they'd arrived in Kampala, Uganda. She managed a quick smile, one that he didn't return.

"You okay?" Alex asked as he slid into the seat next to her.

"Just tired." He sighed. "We've been going now for what — ten, twelve hours?"

Well before dawn, they had waited for a small plane to arrive at an airstrip that was nothing more than compacted dirt tracks in the grass. As Hanna predicted, the pilot delivered a message from Derek, but only to say that he was safe.

"I've lost track. Hell, I'm not even sure what day it is any more." Alex eased the lid off her plastic cup, staring up at the distant television screen that spewed an endless repeating cycle of news. "How long have we been at this airport anyway? I swear I know every news story by heart."

"Maybe we should have stayed the night." He stretched out his legs. "We could be sound asleep in some cushy hotel bed right now."

"It'll have to wait." She stared out at the fiery midday sun. "We'll be in London by evening, but I'm sure Hanna has us booked on something out before midnight."

She snatched up her phone on the first ring. "Hanna," she said before she answered.

"Any word from Derek?" She flashed a smile at Eric, but it

disappeared just as quickly. "You're sure?" She didn't speak again until she said goodbye.

"What's going on?" Eric asked.

"Tumi fired on police when they tried to arrest him ... he's dead." She slumped back in the chair. "He was the only lead we had, Eric. Without him, there's no way to really know who was behind that attack."

"Damn. Damn!" Eric scrambled to his feet. Arms tight across his chest, he stared out the wall of glass to the tarmac. "What the hell do we do now?"

"That story Hanna is feeding the press *has* to work. And we have to count on Mark Brody—"

The image that flashed across the television screen stole her attention.

"No!"

"What—"

Eric's question went unanswered. She was already on the move.

Eyes locked on the television, she wove down the aisle of the airport waiting area, past suitcases and people sprawled at back-breaking angles.

She jolted to a stop beneath a television screen. Bold letters announced a live report from the Novoteras mine disaster, but she could hear nothing of the details. The ticker of headlines repeated only news she'd seen too many times already. She was at the mercy of the closed-caption text that echoed the newscast, one painful word at a time.

Come on! Come on!

"What's going on, Alex?"

She swung around to face Eric. "The mine ... the Novoteras mine. There's been a cave-in, and it looks bad." She reached into her back pocket for her cell phone. "There has to be something on the internet."

Her phone's screen filled with headlines almost before she'd finished typing in the mine name. "Oh my god!" She scrolled through a BBC News report. "At least thirty men are trapped ... it happened sometime last night, I think. They're drilling shafts to try to communicate with the miners and get air to the deeper levels."

Paulo!

72

Araçuaí, Brazil

JORGE HEARD THE FEAR in the single sentence Zahra spoke. He bolted from the chair and started for the door even as he ended the call, but Mark Brody stopped him.

"I must go! There has been a cave-in at the mine, I *must* leave! That is why Mr. Li has been calling me."

"No, Jorge. Sit down."

He took a step toward the door, unwilling to comply. For four hours he had sat with Brody in this house near Araçuaí. He could stay no longer, not with men trapped in the Novoteras mine.

My men.

"Jorge, you must listen to me. This is your only chance to escape."

Only then did Jorge sit down.

"You must tell your wife that she is to go to the mine and wait with the others. She is to tell everyone that you are *inside* the mine."

In this disaster, Brody saw opportunity.

"You want me to disappear. To run." Jorge shook his head. "I will not leave without my wife and children."

"It will only be temporary. Your family will follow you in a few weeks … when you have been presumed dead."

Dead. When Jorge had called Brody, he had never expected this. Neither man had. Worse, it could have been true.

Jorge had almost gone back into the mine to get another piece of rock from Tunnel Five to bring to Brody. Only the thought of the tunnel crowded with miners breaking rock to meet the looming deadline had kept him from doing so. He had reasoned that it could wait until after he talked to Brody — especially since he was not yet sure how much he trusted the American.

This one small decision had saved his life.

Mark Brody listened to everything Jorge had to say about the mine, Tabitha Metals, and Mr. Shen Li. The American had yet to reveal exactly what he knew or who he worked for, but Jorge felt that the decision to call Brody had been the right one.

Unless Shen Li discovers my betrayal.

"No one will believe it. There is no reason for me to go into the mine — it will not be believed. And as soon as the security tapes are reviewed, they will know that I am not there."

"But you said you were in the mine. That means that there is security footage that shows you entering and leaving. I can make that footage work … I can make people believe this, Jorge."

Who is this man?

"The first step is to make all calls to you impossible." He pointed to Jorge's cell phone. "We can't have your location traced, and we need all calls to go directly to voicemail. I want to pull the battery from your phone."

Jorge stared down at the phone in his hand, knowing that this was the only way. "I must call Zahra first."

"We will do that from my phone … the number will not show up. Keep the call short and tell your wife to go to the mine. Arrange a time in the morning when you can call her again. But for now, she is to go to the mine and stay there."

Jorge took the phone Brody offered and set his own phone down on the table.

He made the call to Zahra, wishing that Brody would leave the room. But the man sat watching him across the table, listening to his rushed Portuguese, as though he understood the words.

I know nothing about this man. Yet he must trust him with his life — and the lives of his family.

"It is done." Jorge slid the phone across the table. "Zahra understands what she must do."

"Good. Now, this quota you mentioned — the rock you were expected to ship," Mark said. "You say it's been reached."

"I believe so. The deadline was important, and I heard many times that the rock must be shipped out by tomorrow. Even now—" He dropped his head. "They will ship whatever rock they have, even if it is not all that Mr. Li demanded."

"Where will they take that shipment of rock from Tunnel Five, Jorge?"

Of course. Jorge had been ashamed to admit what Zahra had done with the gemstone he had taken from the mine, but an entire shipment of gemstones lay within their grasp.

"I do not know. Once the trucks are loaded at the mine, I do not have any further involvement. But I have been told by Mr. Li that the rock goes to China, so it must be loaded onto a ship at one of the ports. Maybe the biggest one, Porto de Santos, near São Paulo … but Tabitha Metals may have built their own private port, as other mining companies have done."

"I'll talk to Alex Graham. She may know something about how they're transporting the rock."

"You have talked to her?" Jorge felt his chest tighten. This American he had just confided in may well have been responsible for the break-in.

"Yes." Mark nodded. "Graham's running scared, and she reached out to a cop I know in Canada. What she had to say was enough to get my attention." His eyes narrowed. "She thinks the mine is funding terrorism."

"Terrorism?" Jorge shook his head. "This operation is too cleverly run for that. It is more likely a skimming operation, theft that is lining someone's pockets. But if you met Shen Li, you would not believe even that much."

Or is it what I want to believe? To have worked Major Crimes and be duped into running a mine with deep criminal ties seemed almost too much to contemplate.

"We need to intercept that shipment." Mark reached for his phone. "And I'll get an update on the mine," he added as he left the room.

Jorge wished for a television or computer so he could see for himself what was happening at the mine, but this house held the barest of furnishings. He was sure if he opened the cupboards and fridge, he would find little food. A can of coffee, sugar, and perhaps soup or crackers would be all that was needed for a safe house — and Jorge was under no illusion that this house was anything but.

"Everything in the mine below Tunnel One is completely cut off by rock," Mark said as he entered the room. He leaned against the kitchen counter, his arms folded. "They think there could be forty men down there."

Forty men. Jorge closed his eyes. Almost half of the men who worked for the mine were trapped below.

"A couple of men at the surface say that they think they heard an explosion just before the cave-in."

"Blasting." Jorge spread his fingers against the table. "There are many sections of tunnel that require dynamite to dislodge large boulders. We have done it many times but never…" He swallowed hard. "Never has it caused a cave-in."

"I hope you're right, Jorge. The timing just doesn't feel right to me, and I learned a long time ago to trust my gut."

Mark slid into his chair and leaned his elbows on the table before he spoke again.

"This kind of operation — there has to be someone on the inside."

An insider. For more than a week, Jorge had been seeking just such a man among the miners. Someone with foreign contacts, a too-large bank account or massive debt. Not one of the men he investigated seemed likely to partner in the break-in. Brody, though, was asking about a different kind of partner. Only one name came to mind.

"Tim Wong. The mine's chief engineer." Jorge shook his head. "I should have seen it for myself. Two men, both from China — the engineer and geologist — were assigned to the mine by Mr. Li directly. Almost every other employee was hired by me in the first months the mine was operational."

"Why the engineer? Why not the geologist?"

Jorge was not sure himself. For eight years he had worked along-side the engineer, and never had Tim Wong given him any reason to believe him dishonest. Abrupt, even unfriendly, yes, but the man had never lied to Jorge. Nothing in his personnel file, scrutinized over the past week, suggested anything but a professional, competent engineer. Jorge had seen it in the way Tim worked out a plan to free the men trapped in the mine five years ago. And he could picture him now, heading up the efforts to dig out the collapsed rock.

A thought cracked like lightning against the dark sky.

"The explosion … the one that was heard before the cave-in. All blasting in the mine is planned and overseen by the engineer."

"Tell me about Tim Wong."

73

Kampala, Uganda

ALEX LISTENED TO one ring after another then disconnected and tried Paulo's home number instead.

No answer.

She stared at the television. Behind the reporter with his perfect hair, a crush of weary people, families waiting for news. Every worker from the nearby mines would be there too, each of them painfully aware that they could be trapped like these men.

"How long can the men survive down there?" Eric asked.

"It depends on whether the ventilation system is intact. If it's not, then those men could have just a small pocket of air, or a mile of it … there's no way to know." She shifted her weight from one leg to another.

The image on the television switched to men operating drilling equipment. She searched the background for a landmark, something she would recognize from the weeks spent scrutinizing the grounds before their bold entry.

"I'm not sure where they are…" Her hand tightened around the cell phone. "Oh, god."

"Alex? What?"

"The air shaft to Tunnel Five. They're drilling at the shaft that Paulo—" She couldn't finish, couldn't bear the thought of their young friend suffocating almost a quarter mile underground.

"You don't know he's down there, Alex." He stared at the television screen, arms folded across his chest. "And if there's already a shaft there, it means less drilling to get to the men, right?"

"They shouldn't have to drill out that air shaft at all…" Eyes fixed on the screen, she shook her head. "It must be blocked by rock."

Surviving miners would gather near the known shafts if they could, so there was a chance. But time was running out. Even a high-speed drill working twenty-four hours a day might not reach Tunnel Five, the deepest level, in time.

"What the hell?" Frozen in place, she read each word as it formed on the screen. "Investigation into last week's break-in and its connection to the mine's collapse continues." She spun to face Eric. "They think *we* did this!"

"It's speculation, Alex. You see it all the time when there's been a workplace accident." He shook his head. "Company managers point fingers in every direction rather than take the blame themselves. That's all this is."

How she wanted to believe him. But a thought, so dark she could barely breathe, pushed back.

What if I am responsible? Had the owners ramped up production to get one last shipment out before investigators descended on the mine? A single explosive incorrectly set by an overtired miner would be enough to cause a collapse. Whether true or not, hundreds of feet of rock now stood between them and the tanzanite.

"There's no going into the mine now. Mark Brody—" She caught the flash announcement of an incoming call. "This is Mark now."

"We caught a break, Alex," Mark said when she answered. "The Novoteras mine manager, Jorge Silva is cooperating and he's with me now."

Thank god.

"I just saw the news about the cave-in. Paulo Alvarez … can you ask this manager if Paulo was in the mine?"

"Silva won't know, but I'll try to find out."

"What about the collapse? All they're saying is that it's deep." She paced a tight circle. "Can you find out which tunnel is blocked?"

"It'll have to wait. Right now, I need to get a handle on a shipment that left the mine today. It could be tanzanite, Alex."

A lifeline.

"What do you need?"

"The port. The ship. Anything you know."

She came to an abrupt halt. "Shit! We never thought to look at how they were moving the tanzanite. We were too damned focused on the mine and the owners." She stared down at the floor. "I'd try São Paulo ... that's where most of the other mining companies ship out from. Scott might know if there's a closer port, maybe something privately held."

"I'll talk to him. If we can't stop the ship at this end, we'll try Hong Kong."

"Gem cutters ... that rough tanzanite has to be going to a cutting room. I know a few people in Hong Kong who might be able to help you find the cutters. I'll send you their names."

"I'll take anything you can give me, Alex. Where are you now?"

"Entebbe airport, we're heading for home. Our flight leaves in an hour ... I can delay if you need me."

"No, I want you in Vancouver, where Nate can keep an eye on you. It's over, Alex. We've got them. But I'm about to rip into a hornet's nest, and things could get nasty."

74

Kampala, Uganda

ALEX TURNED AWAY from the TV screens that repeated nothing new. On the tarmac, a dozen jets readied for takeoff, their flight to London not far behind. For twelve hours they would be out of touch.

Paulo. Those forty men in the mine. She closed her eyes. If the rescuers could at least get oxygen into the tunnels and deliver food and water, the men might yet be saved. But time was against them.

"I have to call Tracey … I want her on top of the news coming out of that mine while we're in the air." She dropped into the seat next to Eric. "She'll—"

A crackled voice over the speaker system announced their flight. Around her, people gathered their belongings to slowly trudge toward the gate.

"Shit! I need more time. Mosi—"

"He's safe, Alex." Eric spoke softly, his gaze steady. "It's over … that's what Mark said. Mosi is safe."

"Mosi doesn't know what's happened. He needs to be ready, to be protected when Mark exposes the mine. I have to call him."

"Tracey can track Hanna down and give her an update. Hanna will pass it along to Mosi." He smiled. "I almost feel sorry for Hanna — Tracey will hound her until she's absolutely sure that Mosi is safe. You know that, right?"

"I know." She sighed. "I have to let Tracey take care of this … Hanna too. It just doesn't come easy."

She hit Tracey's number. But Tracey blurted out news of her own before Alex could say a word.

"You're sure?" Alex spun to face Eric, her smile wide. "They found my dad! He's hurt but he's okay." She handed him the phone. "Tracey wants to talk to you."

She paced the floor while she listened to talk of air ambulances and hospitals, stopping only when Eric went silent.

"Brian is being airlifted to hospital in Quito." He handed her the phone. "We'll know more about his injuries then."

"Then we have to stay here. I can't get on that flight. Not—"

"It could be hours before we know anything, Alex." Eric reached for his own phone. "I'll call Lillian Sayer, a doctor I work with in Nelson … she can monitor things while we're in the air. By the time we get to London, we'll have a better idea of what's happening."

"You trust Lillian to do this?" She searched his face. "This is my dad, Eric."

"There isn't any doctor I trust more. She'll coordinate with Tracey to arrange an air ambulance." He scrolled through his contacts as he spoke. "As soon as Brian is stable, he'll be transferred to Vancouver General. That's where we need to be, Alex. Not here."

She simply nodded before she left Eric to his conversation and crossed over to the windows.

He's coming home.

More than once this past week, she'd believed her dad gone forever. But as much as she rejoiced at finding him alive, she also fought down anger.

The Novoteras mine break-in had been her decision, hers and Mosi's, and she had to live with that. But she might have decided differently if her dad had shared everything with her from the start. His decision to withhold crucial information, a selfish decision, had risked too many lives — including his own.

I won't do the same. Not again.

She saw Eric's reflection in the window before she felt his arm around her waist.

"Lillian is going to take care of everything. She promises an update on his condition by the time we land in London."

She hugged him tight. "Thank you. First Mosi, now my dad ... thank you."

"It's what I do, Alex. Although I'd be the first to say that when I boarded that flight a week ago, I never thought I'd be performing medical procedures in a hotel room or trying to save a man in the Serengeti."

"Has it really only been a week?" She leaned back, releasing her hold.

He nodded. "And I don't want another one like it any time soon."

"I never did ask ... when are you expected back in Nelson? How long can you stay?"

"For as long as you need me, Alex. I'll take a leave if I have to..." He smiled. "Callaway can't do anything worse than fire me."

And then you can stay. But she kept this thought to herself.

"But..." His face turned serious. "I won't do this again, Alex. I won't be kept in the dark."

"Believe me, it's something I already decided," she smiled. "I even have Nate on speed-dial."

A number she never wanted to call again, knowing too that Mark had pushed her into the cop's care, until the men behind Tabitha Metals were in handcuffs.

It's not over.

São Paulo, Brazil

New Owner for Tabitha Metals

D. WALLACE
THE ASSOCIATED PRESS

Tabitha Metals confirmed today that their fifteen South American mining properties have been sold to an undisclosed buyer. The privately held company was hit hard two months ago when thirty-seven men were killed in the Novoteras mine disaster and owner Shen Li was shot dead in his São Paulo penthouse. Allegations of Mr. Li's involvement in organized crime have led many to believe the billionaire was killed by one of his own; however, police will confirm only that the murder investigation is ongoing.

No charges have yet been laid against Timothy Wong (Wong Tingzhe), the production engineer at Novoteras mine, despite reports that an explosion preceded the mine's collapse. "We were saddened to learn that police

> suspect improperly detonated explosives were
> the cause of the cave-in that killed so many
> men, including mine manager Mr. Jorge Silva,"
> said company spokesman Alonso Quinto. "We
> continue to assert that every mine employee
> at Tabitha Metals, including Mr. Tim Wong, is
> fully qualified and properly trained in mine
> operational safety, and that this cave-in
> was an unfortunate accident."

Park Fàn admired his ring with its perfectly cut ten-carat tanzanite. *Shen was such a fool.*

It had taken only a few careful questions for Park to uncover the true reason behind Shen's desperate hunt for Alex Graham. And only a few phone calls to recover the stolen tanzanite the woman had carelessly left in a Dubai safe deposit box. Park had known then that the woman was as valuable to him as she was to Shen, and he held her in his sights.

He'd thought the endeavour lost when the woman slipped through his fingers at the safari lodge. But the Novoteras mine collapse provided the answers he sought and made the woman irrelevant.

There was nothing he could have done to save Shen Li from the wrath of Chairman Jianyu Wei — made worse when Wei learned of Park's involvement.

But only Park could deliver his tanzanite shipment.

He had intercepted the shipment as it left the Novoteras mine, diverting it to his own European-bound container ship. A bold theft of Wei's precious cargo and a steep price for its return: Tabitha Metals.

In time, eyes would turn away from the Novoteras mine, and the unsubstantiated rumours of tanzanite would disappear. Tunnel Five would be cleared only when the Merelani Hills tanzanite supply dwindled to nothing, something Shen had failed to consider in his rush to the top.

Patience. It would deliver everything.

Author's Note

ALTHOUGH THIS BOOK IS A WORK OF FICTION, it is based on scientific and historical fact. It also reflects current concerns in the gem trade regarding smuggling, a crime that often puts funds in the hands of those financing conflicts and terrorism.

The city names are accurate, as are the rivers and other geographical features. The Tanzanian safari lodge is based on similar lodges in the region, and it is not intended to represent a specific facility.

For ease of reading, the Chinese names are presented in the North American style of first-last name, rather than following the Chinese standard of last-first name. The exception is Tim Wong, whose given Chinese name Wong Tingzhe is correctly shown.

Tanzanite

At the heart of this story is tanzanite, a remarkable pleochroic gemstone prized for its simultaneous blue and violet colours and considered to be a thousand times rarer than diamonds. To date, this blue vanadium-bearing variety of zoisite has been found only within an estimated 8 km by 2 km region within the Merelani Hills of Northeastern Tanzania in the Pan-African Mozambique Belt. Within this region of the African Rift Valley, other rare gems such as tsavorite and kyanite are found together with garnet, ruby and sapphire deposits. The geology in the Rift Valley is unique, and tanzanite may never be found elsewhere in the world; however, several countries, including Brazil, exhibit similar mineral-rich geological regions.

The story of tanzanite's discovery by a Maasai tribesman after a lightning-sparked fire is widely believed. Only after heating to 500–600°C for an extended period of time do the blue-violet colours become prominent. Most tanzanite found in the marketplace has been heat-treated, but naturally blue, untreated tanzanite is sometimes found, and its price is reflective of its rare occurrence.

The gem was introduced to the marketplace as Tanzanite by Tiffany and Company in the late 1960s. Estimates vary, but most geologists believe the supply of tanzanite in the Merelani Hills will be depleted in less than twenty-five years. The price per carat is sensitive to supply, and generally it has been rising as the tanzanite deposit diminishes; however, the opposite is equally true: when illegal miners dumped large quantities of the gem into the market in 2012–13, the price dropped dramatically.

The popularity of tanzanite has given rise to imitations. The detection methods for synthetic Fosterite, Coranite® and Tanavyte® as mentioned in this novel are accurate but incomplete. Nanosital®, a glass-ceramic, and blue-coloured glass have also been presented to unsuspecting buyers as tanzanite, but they are easily identified by professional jewellers and gemologists.

Tanzanite Tucson Protocols

The 2003 Tanzanite Tucson Protocols (TTP) arose from published reports that suggested a link between tanzanite smuggling and terrorism, one of them written by Daniel Pearl (see below). That link was never proven, but the suggestion pushed the tanzanite industry to implement a set of principles that ensure ethical mining practices and a legitimate route to market.

TanzaniteOne Mining Ltd. is one of the largest stakeholders in the Merelani Hills mining block, and it is committed to the TTP. It and other mining companies support the Tanzanite Foundation, a non-profit organization with a mandate that includes adherence to the TTP and improvement of lives in the community.

Both the TanzaniteOne Mining Ltd. and the Tanzanite Foundation websites provide a good starting point for accurate information on tanzanite mining in Tanzania. For readers who visit Tanzania, the Tanzanite Experience offers a unique opportunity to walk the route of tanzanite from mine to market.

The Tanzanian government banned the export of gemstones weighing above one gram (five carats) in 2010 and is committed to local processing of tanzanite, a source of employment for the people. Despite these efforts, over 80 per cent of rough tanzanite was exported in 2016, partly due to the lack of internal skill in processing gems.

To counter the problem, the Tanzania Gemological Centre in Arusha opened in 2015 to provide gemology training in gem cutting and polishing, jewellery design, and manufacturing technology in collaboration with the Tanzania Mineral Dealers Association (TAMIDA). Through the fundraising efforts of Arusha Gem Fair (AGF) Committee, forty-seven women had graduated from the seven-month program, and another eighteen were enrolled as of May 2017.

The GIA

The Gemological Institute of America (GIA) has operated since 1931 and is considered a world authority in gems. It informs and educates through research, and its standards in gemstone, pearl and diamond grading serve to protect buyers.

Gemstone Fingerprint

The promising gemstone fingerprint research of Dr. D.G. (Graham)

Pearson, Canada Excellence Research Chair in Arctic Resources at the University of Alberta and his colleagues, began with diamonds and has now extended to rubies. The "fingerprint" is a measure of a gemstone's isotope and trace element levels, which differ depending on the geological environment in which the gem formed. This research lays the foundation for accurate provenance of diamonds and coloured gemstones, an important factor in the ethical gem trade. Dr. Pearson has not yet investigated tanzanite, but he believes that this research would also apply to that gemstone.

Daniel Pearl

The kidnapping and murder of *Wall Street Journal* reporter Daniel Pearl by Pakistani al Qaeda terrorists in 2002 shocked the world. His investigation into al Qaeda's use of smuggled tanzanite gems to finance terrorism included testimony heard after the U.S. embassy bombings in Tanzania and Kenya. The Daniel Pearl Foundation, established shortly after his death, strives to continue his work and provides access to his articles.

Brazilian Paraíba Tourmaline Smuggling Operation

The premise of the illegal Novoteras mine openly operating is drawn from the headlines. While diamonds, sapphires, tanzanite and other valuable gems are often stolen from mines and sold abroad, bolder operations actually run mines. A Paraíba tourmaline smuggling operation in Brazil did just that, with the help of a state deputy who licensed the mine but never reported its production. The tourmaline gems, cut and polished in Brazil under false documents, were shipped to Bangkok, Hong Kong, Houston and Las Vegas for sale to unsuspecting dealers. Only after a six-year investigation into the mine were the complex web of offshore accounts and owners unravelled, resulting in arrest warrants in 2015 for eight men and seized assets valued at $15 million USD.

Chilean Mine Disaster

The Novoteras air shaft used to rescue their miners is based on the events of the 2010 Chilean mine disaster. The collapse of the San Jose copper-mine near Copiapó in Chile's Atacama desert held the world's attention in 2010, when thirty-three men were trapped seven hundred metres (2,300 feet) underground for sixty-nine days. More than two thousand media employees are believed to have provided nonstop coverage of the rescue, which mobilized equipment and experts to drill three holes into the mine shaft: a five-inch diameter hole to deliver food and water and communicate with the men, and two wider holes that would allow the men to be winched to the surface. Miraculously, all thirty-three men survived, a first for a mining accident that saw workers trapped for so long.

Pascua-Lama Mining Project (Chile-Argentina)

The Novoteras mine, the Valternas mine and other aspects of the Tabitha Metals company business are fictional, but the nature of the mines is not. References to other mines, including the Cruzeiro mine and the Pascua-Lama gold mines, are accurate.

The Pascua-Lama mining project straddles the Chile-Argentina border in the Atacama region of the Andes Mountains, one of the richest mineral belts in the world. But at an elevation of 5,200 metres (17,060 feet), it is also one of the driest and most fragile environments. It is dense with glaciers that supply the rivers of Huasco Valley, which support the Diaguita indigenous community.

In this sensitive region, owner Barrick Gold, a Canadian mining company, originally proposed an open-pit mine to extract gold, copper and silver. Fear of mercury, cyanide and sulphuric acid in the mine's wastewater runoff required Barrick to build a water management system to divert runoff through a system of canals. Barrick's unfortunate decision to start mine construction in 2013 before that water system was completed resulted in the collapse of a canal that triggered a mudslide and caused the diversion of runoff into a protected area. That mistake levelled a $16 million USD fine and twenty-five charges against Barrick and led to a court-ordered re-evaluation of the project.

Barrick was swift to clean up the affected area and proposed changes that would further reduce environmental impact; however, the project remained contentious. In 2017, Barrick sold a 50 per cent share in Pascua-Lama to Shandong Gold, a state-owned Chinese gold mining company. As of January 2018, the Chilean government had ordered the closure of the operation, which Barrick plans to appeal.

It is important to note that Argentina remains supportive of the Pascua-Lama project, but approximately 75 per cent of the gold deposit lies on the Chilean side. As a result of this project, all mining activities in the Atacama Desert region are now subject to intense scrutiny.

Acknowledgements

Blue Fire was an ambitious project that would never have succeeded without the help of many experts who gave generously of their time.

I am grateful to Dr. D.G. (Graham) Pearson, the Canada Excellence Research Chair in Arctic Resources at the University of Alberta, for sharing his gem fingerprint research with me. From the first moment I heard him speak about this cutting-edge research, I knew it had to be part of this novel. I wish to thank him for providing me with specific relevant research and discussing whether his techniques could be used to fingerprint tanzanite.

Dr. Laura Lee Copeland has generously worked with me on both Alex Graham novels, advising on medical procedures, terminology and the life of an ER doctor. I value her patient instruction, willingness to read and reread draft medical scenes, and her creativity when challenged by this story's timeline! She makes my detailed medical scenes possible, but more importantly, she breathes life into Dr. Eric Keenan. All errors introduced during the final edit of the medical scenes are my own.

I wish to thank G.B. Henderson, who was instrumental in providing insight into the character of Shen Li. Over several weeks, he collaborated with colleagues from China to answer my questions about Shen. Together they contributed to Shen's background, mannerisms and ideals, and provided key information for Shen's interaction with Park Fàn and others.

My early readers, long-time friends Kelly Pearson and Don Reid, provide valuable feedback that I couldn't do without. They have both worked with me since my debut novel, and I trust their instincts for good storytelling and compelling characters.

Kelly encouraged the relationship between Eric and Alex, and she is the reason Eric returned in this novel. She inspires me to create interesting characters and to explore their lives, and for that, I am deeply grateful.

Don's scientific perspective and geology expertise are critical to the stories I write, and he is responsible for the inclusion of maps in my books. He pushes me to tighten my storylines, and I thank him for setting a high bar.

Special thanks to Karen Copeland and Madalena Patacho, who jumped in with ideas when a dinner party turned into an impromptu brainstorming session. For me it was a fortuitous turn, because Karen salvaged a difficult scene that had kept me up too many nights. And Madalena, the ceiling fan is for you!

Many thanks to Allister Thompson, a talented editor who stepped in to provide help with the final draft. His thoughtful comments contributed to a better story, and the manuscript benefited from his meticulous copy edit. I also wish to thank editor Britanie Wilson for giving the manuscript its final polish.

My thanks also to Margaret Kernaghan, who created the maps of Brazil and Tanzania. A true professional, she makes the process effortless. Her maps are works of art, and I look forward to continuing to include them in the Alex Graham thrillers.

The Alex Graham series exists because of my editor, Kit Schindell. Her expert guidance turns my drafts into finished manuscripts, but just as importantly, her unwavering support gives me the confidence to push forward. Thank you for taking this path with me!

I also wish to thank Robin Harlick for her mentorship, and I am grateful for her continued support.

My journey into the world of thriller writing began twelve years ago, and throughout it all my husband Bill has offered encouragement and support. Each novel I write is my gift to him.

About the Author

Katherine Prairie brings her own experience as an international geologist to the Alex Graham thriller series. *Thirst*, the first book in the series, was nominated for the 2017 Whistler Independent Book Awards.

She is an award-winning presenter, and the author of *The Essential PROC SQL Handbook for SAS Users*, published by SAS Press in 2005.

To learn more about her, please visit www.katherineprairie.com

Praise for *Thirst*

"*Thirst* leads the reader down a literary mineshaft where oxygen is running low and time short. Flavoured with insider expertise and a natural storyteller's flair, *Thirst* is a gripping and fun ride."

- Daniel Kalla, bestselling author of *Nightfall Over Shanghai*

"With compelling characters and an extraordinary setting, *Thirst* is a fast-paced thriller that will keep you on the edge of your seat until the very last word."

- R.J. Harlick, author of the popular Meg Harris mystery series

"*Thirst* not only goes where other detective/thrillers fall short; it provides a rivetingly absorbing story line that's hard to put down."

- D. Donovan, Senior Reviewer, *Midwest Book Review*